*Mission Lisbon*

*The V-1 Double Cross*

*By*

*Toby Oliver*

*Cover Design: Spiffing Covers*

*First published Aug 2014*

*Republished Mar 2017*

*Copyright 2014 Toby Oliver*

*This is a work of fiction. Names, characters, places and incidents are either the products of the author's imagination or are used fictitiously, and any resemblances to actual persons, business establishments, events or locales are entirely coincidental.*

*With thanks to David Morris, Jill Langley and Heather Osborne for all their kind patience and support.*

*Success is not final, failure is not fatal: it is the courage to continue that counts.*

*Winston Churchill*

## Chapter 1

Chief Inspector Luke Garvan parked up outside King's Cross Station, and turned off the engine of his car. He checked his watch, and was relieved to find he was in time for his meeting with Major Spencer Hall. It was now some two years since his secondment from Scotland Yard in 1941 to the shadowy ranks of MI5, and the inner sanctum of the Double Cross section, whose remit was to feed disinformation to Nazi Germany through turned German agents.

Garvan lit a cigarette, and picked up the latest issue of *Picture Post* off the passenger seat. There was a picture of a pretty brunette splashed on the front cover. The subheading read, *'A girl sets out to be a star.'* Beneath her smiling face, was an article titled, "25 Years of the USSR." He puffed out his cheeks, and began idly flicking through the magazine. He liked the *Post*'s photojournalism and the hard-hitting political editorials.

His boss, Colonel Tommy Argyll Robertson, or Tar, as he was known on account of his initials, had ordered him to King's Cross Station to meet Major Hall. Tar hadn't explained why, but, then again, he didn't have to, an order was an order. Garvan suddenly became aware of a cabbie, parked on the other side of the road, shouting at him. He couldn't hear what he was saying, and so wound down the window.

'You're parked in a taxi rank, mate,' the cabbie shouted, and indicated in a short, sharp, stabbing motion toward the parking bay.

Garvan fumbled for his wallet, and flashed his warrant card through the open window. 'Scotland Yard,' he yelled back across the road. 'I'm on business.'

The cabbie raised his hand in apology. 'I'm sorry, mate.'

Garvan was almost on the point of checking his watch again, when he caught sight of Spencer Hall crossing the road, carrying a battered manila envelope. On approaching the car, Spencer leaned down and peered through the window.

'Will you grab hold of this,' he said, passing him the envelope. 'I'll be with you in just a minute.'

'Aren't you getting in?'

'No,' he said sharply. 'Not yet.'

Hall promptly turned tail, and retraced his steps back into the Station, leaving Garvan holding the battered envelope. It was ripped down one side, but, with a little bit of persuasion, the contents fell into his lap. There were five passports in varying nationalities. He went through them methodically, one by one. The names meant nothing to him. Gorski, Tyler, Chevalier, Roux, Norton. Roux and Chevalier looked suspiciously like the same person.

When Spencer eventually emerged from the Station, Garvan hurriedly shoved the passports back inside the envelope. It was only then, he noticed Spencer was accompanied by a man of stocky build. Garvan guessed, he was probably in his mid to late forties. He possessed a somewhat lived-in face, with a large hooked nose, piercing blue eyes, and a shot of blond hair. His complexion was florid. *A drinker, perhaps?*

They got into the car and sat themselves down in the back seat. Garvan instinctively checked the rear-view mirror, and recognised the man's face from one of the passports. He had to be Aleksander Gorski. There was no mistaking that nose.

'Where to?' he asked, starting up the engine.

'Tar's new office,' Spencer said.

'Victoria?' Garvan queried, glancing over his shoulder.

Hall nodded.

They drove off in silence. Garvan hadn't seen Spencer for at least three months. He knew better than to ask why Spencer had suddenly disappeared from their office in St.

James's. Garvan again checked his rear-view mirror. Gorski was staring resolutely out of the passenger window, his body half-turned away from Hall.

'We've missed you,' Garvan said trying to make conversation.

Spencer smirked. 'Yeah, like a hole in the head.' He lit a cigarette, snapped the lighter shut, and glanced briefly toward Gorski.

'No, really. It's not been the same around the office. We've missed.'

'Missed, what, my ready wit?'

Garvan laughed. 'No, *that's something I didn't miss*.'

'The one thing I can guarantee is, you'll be wishing me to hell by the end of the week.'

Garvan instinctively looked in the rear-view mirror, and saw Spencer pulling a face at him. The bastard was up to something, but he always was.

As they headed toward Victoria, Luke recalled their first meeting in the Assistant Commissioner's office at Scotland Yard. There'd been a murder one Sarah Davis, Hall's lover and Double Cross colleague. It turned out Sarah's killer was one of their own German agents. In effect, they had become a triple agent. Fearful of being exposed they'd taken Sarah's life before she had the chance to reveal their identity.

On the surface, Hall appeared to be over Sarah's death, but Garvan had long since suspected he was still struggling to cope with her loss. Garvan recalled discovering her body during the height of a bombing raid in a terraced house in South London; even in death, it was obvious Sarah had been stunningly beautiful. He firmly believed she would probably always cast a long shadow over his life.

Garvan drew up outside a rather unprepossessing red-bricked building situated close to Victoria Railway Station. Spencer peered through the passenger window. The walls of the former Edwardian house were banked high with sandbags, and the windows were plastered in a diamond pattern of sticky tape for protection against bomb blast.

'Is this it?' Spencer asked, none too impressed.

'I forgot you haven't been here before,' Garvan said, picking up the tattered manila envelope.

'Why did he want to move out of St. James's?'

'Lord knows. I think it's only temporary.'

Holding up the envelope, he asked, 'Do you want this back?'

Hall reached forward, and took it out of his hand. 'Thank you.'

By the time Garvan had climbed out of the car, Hall was already halfway up the shallow steps to the entrance, when he suddenly stopped dead in his tracks. He looked back toward Garvan and pointed to a brass plaque beside the black painted front door; it read "Tarlair."

'Is this some kind of bloody joke, or what?'

'The boss thinks so.'

Spencer shook his head in disbelief, and pushed the door open, finding himself in a rather small, dingy hallway illuminated by a single bare light bulb. He couldn't help wondering what on earth had possessed Robertson to take the place on in the first place, but no doubt Tar had his reasons for wanting a bolt hole away from MI5's HQ in St. James's. He turned to face Garvan.

'Where's the old man's office?'

'Upstairs,' Garvan said, gesturing toward a narrow flight of stairs to the right of the hallway. 'It's on the first floor.'

'Are you okay?' Spencer asked, turning to Gorski.

The man nodded, and silently followed him across the hallway.

Garvan led the way upstairs to the end of a dark, narrow corridor, which opened onto a cramped office. Sitting opposite the door was a young girl, who looked scarcely old enough to have left school, let alone be working for MI5. She smiled nervously at them, as they entered the office.

'Chief Inspector,' she nodded in recognition.

'This is Major Spencer Hall, and...' he looked questioningly at Hall.

'Aleksander Gorski,' he supplied.

She instinctively checked the printed list on the desk, and traced her finger down the foolscap page, looking up hesitantly.

'I'm sorry, Chief Inspector. They're not booked in.'

The door to Colonel Robertson's office opened. It was Lil or "Fag Ash Lil" as she was known to the Twenty Committee, on account of her trademark cigarette, which rarely, if ever, appeared to part from her lips. She swiftly took in the situation, and closed the office door. Lil was a no-nonsense cockney, through and through. Volatile by nature, she took no prisoners, and had a reputation for erupting at the slightest provocation, effing and blinding in equal measure at senior officers and politicians alike. Grey-haired and of middling height, she was formidable, and more importantly, Robertson increasingly found himself relying on her; plucked from the typing pool, she'd now become his unofficial gatekeeper.

Lil smiled warmly at her young colleague. 'Put that away, luv,' she said, gesturing toward the list. 'I can vouch for this ruddy lot.'

'Hello, Lil,' Spencer grinned extending his arms in welcome.

Her expression softened, she smiled. 'Where the hell have you been to this time? I've missed yer, yer bugger,' she said throwing her arms out in response. They embraced.

'I've been on a bit of business; you know how it is, Lil. The Colonel likes to keep me busy.'

She inclined her head in greeting toward Garvan, and then folded her arms, as she slowly appraised Aleksander from head to foot. 'And you must be Mr. Gorski.'

He snapped to attention, and dipped his head. 'Yes, ma'am.'

'We've been expecting you.' She gestured toward Tar's office. 'The Colonel's waiting to see you.'

'Take hold of this,' Spencer said, handing over the manila envelope to Lil.

Tar was standing by the window deftly packing a Meerschaum pipe with tobacco. He was dressed in his customary khaki army jacket and the tartan trousers of the Seaforth Highlander's Regiment. It was often remarked Tar's charm could melt an iceberg, and without it, some said the Double Cross would never have survived and thrived the ruthless in-fighting within the Intelligence community. He'd fought his corner across Whitehall, and had repeatedly outmanoeuvred his rivals. The Double Cross system was now secure, and had a pivotal role in the Government's plans for the future conduct of the War against Nazi Germany.

'Gentlemen, come in, please take a seat,' he said, gesturing toward three green leather Chesterfield armchairs strategically placed in front of his desk. 'Good to see you again, Aleksander.' He warmly shook the man's hand.

'Thank you, sir. I have to say, without Major Hall's help, I doubt very much if I'd have made it to London in one piece,' he responded in his heavily accented English.

Garvan decided Gorski was possibly Polish, or, at an outside guess, even Russian, but more importantly, he found himself at a complete disadvantage. Even "Fag Ash Lil" had heard of him, and knowing Lil, she probably knew his life history inside out.

'How was the Channel crossing?' Tar asked.

Gorski gave him a rueful smile. 'You have to understand, Colonel, even as a child I used to turn a sickly shade of green on the local boating lake.'

Robertson sympathised with him. 'I hope our submariners looked after you well?'

Aleksander shot Spencer a rather embarrassed, half-hearted smile. 'They did indeed, Colonel, but I'm afraid I put them to a great deal of trouble.'

Robertson arched his brows questioningly.

'Unfortunately, I ended up making a fool of myself. In fact, I refused point blank to leave the rowing boat, and climb aboard the submarine.' Gorski briefly closed his eyes. 'It was utterly unforgivable of me. So many brave men had already placed their lives on the line to save my neck. But, I was talked aboard by a rather large Chief Petty Officer,' he said, with a smirk.

The penny finally dropped. 'My dear boy, are you claustrophobic?'

'Yes Colonel, I am.'

'I didn't have the faintest idea.'

'By the time I discovered we were to cross the Channel by submarine, it was rather too late to expect anyone to change their plans; it had all been set in motion by then. I thought I'd be okay, but as the Major can tell you, I sadly panicked at the last moment.'

'I have to admit,' Robertson agreed with him, 'the idea of being confined in a tin can a hundred feet below the sea doesn't exactly appeal to me either.'

Gorski smiled, uncertain if Tar was merely trying to mollify him. Either way, he was grateful all the same.

Robertson cupped the meerschaum in his hand. 'I am terribly sorry we put you through such an ordeal. Had I known there was a problem, we'd have pulled out all the stops to bring you over from France by some other means.'

Gorski raised his hand. 'No, please, Colonel, I quite understand. Besides, your sailors plied me with so much rum during the crossing, I really couldn't have cared less by the time we reached Dover.'

'I can vouch for that.' Spencer grinned.

'So, Alek, do we have the microfilm?' Tar enquired.

Aleksander looked to Spencer, who answered for him. 'Yes, we have. I've handed it over to Professor Jones and his team to evaluate.'

'Good, good,' Tar said, with a tight smile.

'Jean Giscard, do you know if he's safe?' Aleksander asked uneasily.

'The SOE managed to deliver him in one piece to Lisbon.'

'Portugal's neutrality will not stop the Gestapo from trying to kill him; you must have him moved from there as soon as possible.'

'I'm well aware of the risks, Alek.'

'You have to fly Jean to England without delay!'

'Trust me; it's all in hand,' Robertson said reassuringly. 'You've enough on your plate already, without worrying yourself sick about your Jean.'

'I'm sorry, Colonel, I know I shouldn't be trying to tell you how to run things. But, you see, I owe my life to Jean, and more importantly, he holds the key to the information on the microfilm, whereas I'm,' he searched for the right words, 'I'm just the mule, the courier. Jean is a brilliant scientist.'

Tar looked thoughtfully at Gorski. 'That's as may be, but without men of your calibre, and bravery, we wouldn't have the microfilm.'

Aleksander looked rather embarrassed at being praised.

'To be honest, we really can't begin to thank you enough, Alek, for all you've done over these past six to eight weeks. It has been incredible. So many lives have depended upon your actions. And to cap it all, we then stuffed you in a Royal Navy submarine, and very nearly succeeded in killing you off where the Germans had failed; now that really would have been the icing on the cake.'

Gorski gave out a short, throaty chuckle. 'I think you would have made the Gestapo very happy, sir.'

'Please accept my sincere apologies.'

'Accepted, Colonel, but I have a request to make.'

'What's that?'

'No more submarines?'

'You have my word.' Robertson reached forward across his desk, picked up the phone, and pressed the green button. 'Lil,' he said, speaking into the receiver, 'would you pop into the office.'

The door was duly opened, Lil stood in the doorway, arms folded, and her customary cigarette clenched firmly between her lips.

'Is the car waiting for Mr Gorski?' he asked.

'Yes, Colonel.'

Tar stood up from behind his desk, and leant forward to shake Aleksander by the hand. 'I've arranged for you to stay at the Savoy.'

Aleksander's face registered surprise. 'The Savoy,' he repeated incredulously.

'Yes,' Robertson grinned. 'Under the circumstances, it's the very least His Majesty's Government could do. A member of my team, Hugh Dickinson, will contact you later this evening. We'll take things from there. Over the next couple of days, or so, we'll need a full de-brief, and then, we can start discussing your return to France. In the meantime, relax, have a few drinks, and enjoy your stay. We'll meet for lunch tomorrow.'

'Thank you, Colonel.'

'Come on, Alek,' Lil said, gesturing toward him.

Gorski came to his feet, and thanked Robertson profusely; he then turned toward Lil, bowed his head slightly, and formally clicked his heels.

As Lil closed the door on them, Garvan asked, 'Would someone care to tell me what's going on?'

Robertson eased himself back into his chair. 'It's complicated.'

'It's always complicated,' Garvan smirked at him. 'Your Mr. Gorski...is that his real name?'

Robertson struck a match, and lit his pipe. He examined Garvan's expression questioningly. 'Why do you ask?'

'The envelope I handed over to you at King's Cross,' Spencer interrupted. 'I take it you checked out the contents?'

'It was already torn they fell out onto my lap.'

'Pull the other one, Garvie,' Hall chuckled. 'So, you already know there were five passports, then?'

'Yes, I do.'

'All of different nationalities.'

'Two of them were made out to the same man, Roux and Chevalier.'

Spencer winked at him. 'Yes, they were. We weren't entirely sure how to get Gorski safely back to England. We had some routes open to us, but for obvious reasons, we couldn't plan too far in advance. The passports all belong to various colleagues of Gorski,' he explained. 'We needed them as a form of insurance policy, should Gorski not have made it. You see, we had some other agents lined up to help smuggle out the microfilm.'

'Where does Gorski fit into all this, exactly?'

Robertson sucked heavily on his freshly lit pipe. 'Gorski's real identity is entirely immaterial,' he said matter-of-factly; it was a statement, and didn't invite question. 'The upshot is, the Special Operations Executive managed to get him out of Peenemunde in northern Germany, via a small underground network run by Dr. Fernand Schwachtgen. He's a physician by trade, but runs an efficient outfit under the Codename Lean l' Aveugle. To get Gorski back to England, we took advantage of some well-established MI6 escape routes. But all in all, it wasn't plain sailing. At the end of the day, we just struck lucky in getting Alek and the microfilm out in one piece.'

'I've never heard of Peenemunde?'

'There's no reason you should have,' Robertson mused, blowing out a cloud of pipe smoke. 'It's on the Baltic coast of northern Germany. We think the Nazis have an experimental site there, developing advanced military weapons. Last year a Spitfire pilot on a routine reconnaissance flight returned with photographs of the airfield. Initially, there didn't appear to be anything out of the ordinary. There were a couple of circular emplacements, possibly for defensive purposes and a few other signs of construction. The photographic interpreters weren't too worried by the findings until another intelligence report a few months later indicated a rocket had been test-fired from the site.'

'A rocket, what do you mean?' Garvan asked.

'We've managed to intercept a certain amount of intelligence from the German army's weapon development branch, the Heereswaffenamt. The reports mention a winged rocket, or pilotless plane, capable of being launched by a form of catapult device.' Robertson leant back in his leather chair, and thoughtfully placed his hands together. 'It's all way above my head, Chief Inspector. But what I do know with some degree of certainty is, they've not quite perfected the damn thing. Otherwise, they'd have launched it by now.'

'Launch it where?'

'London. They're becoming increasingly desperate to bring the War to a rapid conclusion, and what better way, than by obliterating the capital, and killing thousands of innocent people in the process, in the hope we'll end up capitulating.'

'And the microfilm, how important is it?'

'Hopefully, it'll provide us with conclusive evidence. The technical interpretation is of course, down to Professor Jones and his scientific colleagues at the War Office.'

'And, presumably, our boffins are eager to get their hands on Jean Giscard?'

'Yes, they are. He's been working on the project at Peenemunde for about eight months now. He was drafted in by the Germans from France, not quite as slave labour, of course. You see, he's a very talented scientist, and they needed his expertise in developing the project. Let's just say, Giscard didn't exactly volunteer his services; we know for a fact he was placed under a great deal of pressure. He was fearful. If he didn't comply with their offer, his family would end up being threatened with incarceration, and worse. When he started working there, and realised the kinds of weaponry he was being forced to help develop, he made a very brave decision. Giscard learned all he possibly could about the project, before deciding to escape.' Robertson puffed thoughtfully on his briar. 'To cut a long story short, the SOE eventually managed to extricate him from Peenemunde to Lisbon. But, the bottom line is, we still need to get Giscard out of Portugal, before the Gestapo track him down.'

'And that's where you come into the plan,' Spencer said, with the faintest of smiles.

'Me?' Garvan said uneasily. 'What the hell can I possibly do to help?'

Hall's rich, caramel-toned Welsh lilt had never seemed more annoying. 'If, and when, Professor Jones confirms the intelligence from the microfilm, then, that's it. We're off.'

'Off where exactly?'

'Lisbon.'

'Why?'

'To bring Giscard safely back to England, before the Gestapo get a chance to kill him.'

Since being seconded from Scotland Yard, Garvan hadn't factored in the possibility of being sent abroad on a mission. It sounded at face value to be way out of his league.

'But, why me? I'm a bloody copper, not some gung-ho MI5 or SOE field agent.'

Robertson gently rested his pipe down in the ashtray on his desk, and listened, as Garvan argued his secondment to the Security Services had been on the strict proviso. He was employed as a desk officer and not a field operative; it was a different ball game altogether. There had been an agreement of sorts; he'd taken them at their word, though not without some soul searching. In hindsight, he should have known better than take anything they said at face value.

Robertson clasped his hands behind his head, and swayed slowly from side-to-side in his leather swivel chair, allowing Garvan to vent his protest, until he finally ran out of steam. In fairness, he understood his gut reaction to their proposal. He'd been loosely promised a sedentary life within the Double Cross team, interviewing agents, writing up reports, ploughing methodically through classified material, and helping MI5 desk officers to analyse complex transcripts from the Abwehr to their British-based agents. Over the last eighteen months, he had become both a valued and popular member of Tar's tightly knit team.

Garvan's protest eventually ground to a halt under the steady scrutinising gaze of his colleagues. *God*, he began thinking, *I could have handled that one a bit better. There was no point in his flying off the handle. If nothing else, it was totally unprofessional.*

Robertson allowed a protracted silence to fall between them. *He was good, bloody good.* Garvan mused. In the past, he'd adopted precisely the same tactic during interviews. He was skilfully playing him at his own game, for it had the desired effect of placing the person sitting across the desk firmly on the back foot.

Robertson rested his hands on the desk. 'Do you believe I haven't taken all the options into consideration?'

'I'm sure you have, sir.'

'I have to admit, I probably don't have the right to ask you to do anything over and above your current duties. But, I've come to the conclusion you're the best man for the job. After all, Portugal is a neutral country, Garvan, and it's not as if I'm asking you to place your neck on the line, is it?'

Garvan didn't respond.

'I know the place is something of a hotbed for the Allied and Axis intelligence services, but that's the nature of the beast. It's open season, in a neutral country like Portugal.' Tar was as quietly enigmatic as ever, he smiled thinly. 'Did you know Churchill's dubbed Lisbon the capital of espionage?'

It wasn't what Garvan wanted to hear. 'Let me get this straight. This Jean Giscard has gone to ground in Lisbon.'

Robertson inclined his head in agreement.

'But, the Gestapo wants to kill him?'

'In a nutshell,' Tar mused, 'yes.'

'Am I missing something here?'

Robertson raised his brows questioningly.

'Lisbon might be neutral, as far as we're concerned, but has anyone thought to tell the Gestapo?

Tar smiled enigmatically.

'If the Gestapo wants this scientist of yours dead, it doesn't strike me as being entirely risk-free.'

'Life is never entirely risk-free, Chief Inspector, you of all people must appreciate that. You see,' Tar went on, 'I find myself somewhat between a rock and a hard place, at the moment.' He paused thoughtfully. 'I know what you're thinking, that one way, or another, I've *always* found myself between a rock and a hard place.'

'It crossed my mind.'

'I think I probably owe you an explanation. There are some other agents I could call upon to help rescue Giscard from Lisbon.' Robertson sat back, and ran his fingers through his hair. 'As things stand, some very brave people have already put their necks on the line to save us from potential disaster. Earlier this year, we received smuggled sketches and notes from two Polish slave labourers working at the Peenemunde Camp. They also described some sort of rocket and a launching tower there.' Robertson spoke softly, thoughtfully, and with great intensity. 'Have you any idea, Chief Inspector, of the risks these people are taking by passing this information to us? The facility is guarded by the SS. If our moles were ever to be discovered,' he paused, not only for effect, but to emphasise the gravity of their situation. 'If our moles were ever discovered, they'd be slowly tortured to death, and on a lucky day, they might, just might, be shot on the spot, and mercifully killed outright.'

Robertson reached into his desk drawer, and pulled out a bottle of malt whisky, followed by three tumbler glasses, and poured each of them a generous tot. 'The Lisbon mission requires someone steady, and reliable. More importantly, someone Spencer can trust implicitly.' Robertson took a sip of the whisky, and then slowly swirled the amber liquid in the glass. 'I don't mind admitting to you, your name wasn't exactly top of my list for the Lisbon mission. In fact, come to think of it,' he added, with a wry smile, 'it wasn't on there at all. If it's any consolation, I was initially dead set against the idea of involving you. I thought it was too much to ask.'

'What changed your mind?'

'The mission is Spencer's call, and, in the end, he won me over.' His smile was taut. 'As you know, he can be very persuasive.'

Garvan shot Hall a long hard look. 'Thanks for that, mate!'

'You could still back out, of course,' Tar continued smoothly. 'At the end of the day, Chief Inspector, as you so rightly say, you're only on secondment from Scotland Yard, and not a fully-fledged member of the Security Services.'

The comment, so charmingly executed, was barbed, and guaranteed to raise Garvan's hackles. If he backed down now, there'd be comments amongst the team. He'd lose face, and, more to the point, he'd lose their trust.

'When are we due to fly out?' He found himself saying, as if by rote.

'That all rather depends on Professor Jones, and his report on the microfilm, but all being well, you'll be flying out this Saturday coming,' Robertson said, draining his malt.

## Chapter 2

Garvan was surprised to discover Spencer lived in Dolphin Square. It was an upmarket address, and he assumed it would be way out of his price bracket.

'Robertson must be paying you well,' Garvan observed, surveying the spacious living room.

Spencer closed the front door of the flat. 'If only he was. I moved here in January. My maternal aunt, bless her, left me a tidy sum in her will. She was a lovely old girl, even lovelier when I found out I had enough ready cash to splash out on the odd luxury or two, this place being one of them. Cup of tea?' he asked.

'Yes, thank you.'

Hall disappeared into the kitchen, leaving Garvan to take a look around the living room. He wandered over to the window, and tweaked the net curtains. The evening was drawing in, and the light starting to fade, but he could still get a feel for the neatly laid out private gardens belonging to the residents. The flowerbeds and shrubbery had long since disappeared, and had been replaced by a mini-allotment of vegetables.

As he turned from the window, a wooden framed photograph perched on a small circular table caught his attention. Garvan recognised the face, even at a distance; it was Sarah Davis. He went over to pick it up, and as he did so, his thoughts returned to 1941, and to Monkton Drive, where he'd discovered her lifeless body. The single fatal bullet wound to Sarah's forehead hadn't destroyed her glacial beauty; even in death, it had been quite magnetic, her distinctive light blue eyes frozen in the last terrifying moment of her life.

Spencer re-emerged from the kitchen carrying two cups of tea; he hesitated, seeing him holding Sarah's photograph.

'It's a lovely picture,' Garvan found himself saying.

Spencer set the cups down on a sideboard. 'Yes, it is,' he said stiffly.

'If you don't mind my asking.'

He cut across him. 'I probably will.'

They looked at each other, deadpan for a while.

'You still miss her, don't you?'

Spencer's initial reticence to respond stemmed from a real place of hurt. He found himself groping for the right words, and not quite sure what to say, or how to express his feelings. The intensity of his love for her, was still so powerful, and so raw. But, over time, he had finally come to accept her death. Even so, Spencer knew he'd probably never feel for anyone in quite the same way. Sarah had quite literally been the love of his life.

'The pain and the guilt don't dissolve with time, if that's what you're asking. Besides, someone like Sarah only ever comes along once in a lifetime, and only then, if you're very lucky. The one thing I have learned is, even though you think you're never going to get through it, you do. Grief can be all consuming, but you've got to learn from it, and you've got to move on, otherwise it'll eat you up.'

Garvan felt a frisson of envy at the depth of his friend's feelings. His own marriage had ended, somewhat acrimoniously, when his wife joined the Royal Air Force: he would almost have forgiven her, if she'd fallen in love with some dashing fighter pilot, but no, Joan had fallen in love with a woman, a WAAF Officer. It was all in the past now, but it still rankled with him. The only positive note was their two sons had long since accepted the situation, and were growing up fast. After deciding to have Harry and John evacuated from London at the outbreak of War to stay with friends in Lyme Regis, he'd rarely seen them, but had tried to squeeze in visits whenever work permitted, and kept in touch regularly by telephone and letter.

Garvan took a sip of his tea. 'Is there any news on this microfilm Aleksander Gorski managed to smuggle out of Peenemunde?'

Spencer offered him a cigarette; he accepted. 'By all accounts, the contents appear to confirm the RAF reconnaissance photographs of the site.'

'What does the microfilm show us?'

'That the left tip of the peninsula is clearly some sort of military test centre.'

'You mean, for an experimental aircraft or rocket?'

'Yes, it clearly shows some cigar-shaped projectiles, which Professor Jones believes are pilotless planes. It all seems to tie in nicely with the RAF findings. The trouble is, at best, the information we have now is, at least, a month old.'

'Is that important?'

'Important enough,' Spencer said, flicking open a gold cigarette lighter. 'But at the end of the day, it's Jean Giscard who holds the key to Gorski's microfilm. Having worked on the project for the last eight months, he's been at the very heart of the Kirschkern.'

'The Kirschkern, what's that?'

'It's a codename for the project. It roughly translates to "cherry stone."'

'Why call it "cherry stone"?'

Spencer took a drag on his cigarette. 'In the grand scheme of things, the name isn't particularly important. It's the result we have to focus ourselves on.'

'You mean, to get Giscard safely back to England?'

'Precisely,' he replied, and moved over to an ornate Georgian bureau. He opened the drawer, and retrieved a passport; he swung round, and tossed it across the room to Garvan. He caught it, and eyed Spencer questioningly.

'That's for you,' he said casually.

Luke opened the passport, and found a photograph of himself; the name beneath it read "Steven Howe."

'Steven Howe?' he queried.

'It's your *nom de plume* for the trip.'

'Oh come on. Is this really necessary?'

'Tar Robertson thinks so, and, for what it's worth, so do I. As things stand, there's no way we can have you flying to Lisbon under your own name.'

'Give me a good reason why not.'

'The Abwehr routinely check all the arrivals and departures at the airport, and it really wouldn't take too much effort on their part to match your name and details back to Scotland Yard. Let's face it; over the years, you've been involved in some very high-profile trials at the Old Bailey. Even I can recall seeing your ugly mug splattered over the front pages.'

'Who the hell am I supposed to be?'

'A Foreign Office civil servant. The purpose of your visit is to touch base with your diplomatic colleagues at the British Embassy. They won't bat an eyelid at that; FO civil servants travel out to Portugal on a weekly basis. You'll just be a new face on the scene, so your arrival shouldn't arouse too much interest.'

Garvan glanced down at the passport again. 'You've made me two years older than I am.'

Spencer grinned, and said jokingly. 'Nice touch on my part, don't you think? I've always said you haven't worn too well, Garvie. It's all those late nights spent rooting out criminals in seedy nightclubs. You know, too much booze and fags; it was bound to catch up with you in the end.'

'Well, thank you for that.'

'I'll have the briefing notes ready for you in the morning.'

Garvan closed the passport.

'It'll be the usual sort of stuff, background details about the Foreign Office staff working out there. They'll be more than enough to get you by, if anyone questions the purpose of your visit at Border Control.'

'I take it, then, you won't be travelling under your own name?'

'I rarely do.' Spencer held up another passport, before returning it back to the desk. 'I'm down as David Choules, a Wolfram expert.'

'What the hell's a Wolfram expert?' Garvan asked blankly.

'I'm meant to be a mining engineer,' Spencer explained. 'Tungsten is extracted from the Wolfram ore and is used in the manufacture of armour piercing shells.'

'What's the connection with Portugal?'

'Portugal is rich in the stuff, and has become the biggest supplier in the world.'

'We're talking big money?'

'We certainly are.' Spencer took a drag on his cigarette. 'Of course, the thing is, as a neutral country, they can't afford to show any bias publicly.'

'So, they sell the stuff to the Allies and the Nazis?'

Spencer eased himself into an armchair. 'Yes, they do. So far, our diplomats and businessmen in Lisbon have managed to secure the lion's share of supplies. Despite this, it's still a minefield of negotiation and double dealing.'

'You mean, bribery?'

'They do whatever it takes. For their part, the Portuguese want to play an even hand. They certainly don't want to risk compromising their neutrality status by cutting off supplies to the Nazis. That doesn't mean to say their president, Antonio Salazar, hasn't come under enormous international pressure to do so. The Reichsbank pays for the Wolfram in gold deposited at the Swiss National Bank based in Berne; from there, the bullion is then transferred to the Bank of Portugal's coffers. The bottom line is, the Portuguese have found themselves stuck in the middle of not only a physical war, but also, an economic one as well.'

'Why don't the Nazis pay cash for the Wolfram?'

Spencer inhaled heavily on his cigarette. 'Last year, the Germans were found to be paying for the ore with counterfeit money. So, not unnaturally, the Portuguese asked for all payments to be made in gold. Of course, on the downside, a great deal of it appears to be coming from the central banks of their occupied territories, not to mention the stuff they've stolen from the Jews.'

'Why so much counterfeit money?'

'Most of it originates from Sachsenhausen Concentration Camp; they have some very skilled inmates, who have been forced to forge US and British currency. It's been churned out on an industrial scale to flood the markets, in the hope of undermining our economies. Fortunately, it hasn't worked. However, we still need to keep a constant eye on the situation.' Spencer rested his cigarette on a silver ashtray. 'You have to understand, Garvie, it's a dirty business, and getting even murkier, as the War progresses.' He leant forward, as if to emphasise what he was saying. 'Do you remember how it was for the Double Cross when you came on board from Scotland Yard? At the time, our primary task was to turn German agents, and deceive Berlin about our defences. You know, beef things up a little, and con them into believing they were stronger than they actually were.'

Garvan nodded.

'Over the last six to twelve months, there's been a subtle change in our role. Robertson has started to ratchet things up, and involve us in strategic policy. By feeding Berlin with false information, we can literally determine the fate of tens of thousands of people, from Bomber Command, to helping the merchant convoys crossing the Atlantic dodge U-boats. The technical detail in the transmissions sent by our double agents is far more complex than it ever was.' He picked up the cigarette. 'You must have noticed the changes with the kind of stuff landing on your desk.'

'Of course I did, but Robertson's hardly likely to discuss policy with me, is he? When all's said and done, I'm only on secondment from the Yard; I'm not exactly one of his inner-circle.'

'Maybe not, but he trusts you implicitly. Don't you understand that's why he agreed to your coming with me to Lisbon?' He began to toy thoughtfully with his gold lighter. 'Working for the Double Cross is a little like trying to put the pieces of a giant jigsaw puzzle together, and people like Jean Giscard take us one step closer to the end game of invading Europe and defeating Hitler.' He took a puff of his cigarette. 'But, there are still no guarantees we'll pull it off, and if we don't get Jean Giscard out of Lisbon, or, at least, get our hands on the blueprint, then we might still find ourselves ending up in the shit.'

'I take it we'll be flying out together?'

'Yes, of course.'

'Does this blueprint hold the key to the design of the rockets?'

'Yes. He smuggled it out with him, when he went to ground. From what I understand, it contains most of the technical data about the programme, and, in particular, the cigar-shaped planes we picked up on in the RAF reconnaissance photos. The trouble is our scientists are afraid if we don't manage to get a handle on this, and soon, the Nazis could manage to bomb us out of existence.'

It was a sobering thought, and Garvan wasn't quite sure how best to respond, taking his time. 'Realistically, what do you reckon our chances are of stopping them from deploying them?'

Spencer shrugged. 'Hitler calls them his *Vergeltungswaffen*.'

'Which means?'

'His vengeance weapons. I assume once we know precisely what we're dealing with, the RAF will be ordered to bomb the site at Peenemunde.'

'Will it make any difference?'

'It's believed we might manage to slow production down for a few weeks, but the consensus is, we're probably already too late to inflict any lasting damage. Whatever Bomber Command throws at them, we have to expect, at some stage, they'll deploy them. Let's face it, they've nothing to lose, and everything to gain.' He rested back in the chair; hands behind his head, and absentmindedly began to idly blow out perfectly formed smoke rings. He glanced across the room at Garvan. 'As things eventually start to become more desperate, the Nazis will rapidly start running out of options. Hitler views the weapons as retribution for the Allied bombing of Germany, but he also sees them as a means of bringing us to our knees, by wiping out whole swathes of southern England.' He stubbed out his cigarette, and swiftly changed the subject. 'Lil will have a file on Peenemunde, as well as the briefing notes, ready for you first thing in the morning.'

Garvan consulted his watch; it was nearly a quarter to nine. 'Lord, is that the time already.'

'It's been a long day,' he agreed. 'I just thought it might be better to have a chat, without having constant interruptions at the office.'

'No, you're right we needed to clear the air.' As he eased himself out of the chair, Garvan looked speculatively at Spencer. 'I still really don't understand why you chose me for this lark when you have ex-SOE colleagues, like Hugh Dickinson, on the team.'

Spencer's eyes glistened mischievously, as he let out a smooth, throaty chuckle. 'Hugh wouldn't be quite right for this job.'

'He's one of your best agents. Why not?' Garvan shot back at him.

'A year or so ago, Hugh was in Lisbon, and had a run in with the PVDE. For a start, he'd never get through passport control.'

'Who are the PVDE?' Garvan queried.

'They're the Portuguese State Police; not quite coppers as you or I know them, but their equivalent. Their job is to fight all forms of espionage and subversion against the State.' He smiled faintly. 'Seeing as how Lisbon is the only current European city where the Allies and Axis powers operate out in the open, they've more than got their work cut out.' Spencer let out another chuckle. 'Poor old Hugh got on the wrong side of the PVDE; he took his eye off the ball, and was being a little careless. I won't bore you with the nitty-gritty, but let's just say their chief, Captain Lourenco, curtailed his stay somewhat, and he won't be going back anytime soon.'

'You mean he was thrown out?'

'In a word, yes, he was.'

'So, then, I wasn't exactly your first choice for the Lisbon Mission?'

'Now, Garvie, that's where you've got it all totally wrong. Right from the off your name was the only one in the frame.'

'I'm just surprised I'm in the frame at all.' He smirked at him.

'Even if Hugh hadn't been barred from Portugal, it wouldn't have altered my decision to select you. I can see you don't believe me, but if I thought for one second you'd screw things up, I'd much rather travel on my own. There's simply too much at risk to start gambling on people who might jeopardise the mission.' He paused in the hallway, and turned around to face Garvan. 'I'm not going to lie to you; why the hell would I? Besides, I'm not into playing mind games with friends,' he said gravely.

'No, I realise that.'

'And you know how the boss works.'

'I'm beginning to.'

'Tar always keeps people in mind when they've made a particular impression on him. He stores them up, a bit like mental reference cards. The fact he's agreed for you to accompany me to Lisbon is surely endorsement enough; at least, it is for me, and I hope it is for you as well.'

'I guess so.'

'What's wrong?'

'I was just thinking about Giscard, that's all.'

'Is there a problem?' Spencer smiled. 'On second thoughts, there's always a problem.'

'If he was based in Northern Germany at Peenemunde, then, there's something I don't quite understand.'

'Fire away.'

'Why take him all the way across Spain, to the Portuguese border, and not through France. It doesn't make sense, or, at least, it doesn't to me.'

'It wasn't for the want of trying.'

'What happened?'

'There were a number of reasons why we decided against it.'

'Like what?'

'Even before we managed to cross into France, things had already started to get out of hand. Three of the SOE agents, who had been assigned to escort Giscard, and rendezvous with the Maquis, were arrested by the Gestapo.'

'Had they been betrayed?'

'What do you think? We were rapidly running out of options; we didn't know how much of our escape chain and the French network had been compromised. We couldn't afford to take any chances and risk Giscard falling into the hands of the Nazis, so we turned to a man named Dr. Fernand Schwachtgen. He's always proved to be a safe pair of hands, and runs a slick underground network. He's a Belgian by birth, and, through some of his contacts, had already provided us with valuable information about the testing site. But, more to the point, he was out with the French Resistance. We called on his services to help us smuggle Giscard to the Spanish border. I can't say it was ideal, but we figured travelling through France was going to be fraught with even more danger.'

'Where have you been for the last three months.'

'Do you want a list?'

'Did you help organise his escape?'

'Only in a manner of speaking. I didn't have a hands-on role, if that's what you mean. I've never personally met the man.'

'So, what were you doing?'

'I was in the background,' he said self-effacingly.

'What does that mean?'

He seemed reluctant to say. 'I was in overall charge of coordinating the operation to smuggle him out of Germany.'

'Rather you than me.'

'We certainly had a few close shaves in Spain.'

Garvan looked at him questioningly.

'The Abwehr have an extensive network there with General Franco's.' He searched for the right words.

'You mean, his approval?' Garvan offered.

'Well, let's just say, Franco hasn't thrown them out. He's playing something of a tactical game by claiming neutrality, but, at the same time, offering support to Italy and Germany. He's living on a knife's edge by allowing Spanish soldiers to volunteer to fight with the German Army against the Russians, but at the same time, decreeing the Spanish can't fight in the West against the Allies. To be perfectly honest with you, I was more concerned about the transfer across the Spanish border into Portugal than moving through France.

We've had just one too many escapees being picked off at the last minute.'

'What's been going on?'

'I wish to God I knew.'

'Is there a pattern?'

'There is, of sorts.'

'Have you managed to nail it down?'

'If I had, we wouldn't be having this conversation.'

'I guess not.'

'We've had a few whispers the Abwehr might be onto us.'

'But, how could they?'

'The devil's in the detail; we're not sure.'

'Where is Giscard now?'

'MI6 have him under lock and key, in a safe house.'

'Where is it?'

'Lisbon.'

'If the Abwehr is onto us, it's not going to make our job any easier getting him back to England.'

Spencer broke into a smile. 'Garvie, it was never going to be easy.'

'No, I don't suppose it was,' Garvan said. 'Thank you for the cuppa.'

Spencer showed him to the door. 'I'll see you at the office in the morning.'

*Chapter 3*

As Garvan set off home from Spencer's flat in Dolphin Square, the gut-churning, spine-tingling wail of the air raid sirens blasted out ominously over London. The *Luftwaffe* had continued to attack British cities since the height of the Blitz in mid-May 1941. But, thankfully, the intensity of the raids had steadily declined in ferocity. Sporadic though they were, the so-called comparative "lull" didn't, in any way, lessen the fear and anxiety associated with the terrifying attacks. During the intervening period, the Germans had mainly concentrated on bombing ports, such as Cardiff, and the so-called tip and run attacks were generally conducted at low level on specific industrial or military targets. But, for whatever reason, tonight, the *Luftwaffe* high command had decided to wreak havoc, once again, on the already decimated streets of the capital.

Garvan had almost reached home when he heard the first sinister hum of the enemy bombers. The night sky was already illuminated by the stark, dazzling, finger-like beams of the searchlights; the black silhouetted shape of a plane occasionally strayed into the crisscrossing beams, caught like a fly in a trap, as London's anti-aircraft guns sent up an incessant, deafening barrage.

Garvan couldn't quite decide whether to take cover in the nearby public shelter, or chance his luck, and walk the short distance home. The Blackout was in full force, and he found himself going as much on instinct as anything else. He retrieved a pencil torch from his jacket pocket, and navigated his way through the pitch-black streets. As he neared the shelter, an air raid warden emerged, and lit himself a crafty cigarette. Garvan turned off the torch, but he'd already noticed.

'What you doing, mate?'
'It's only a pencil torch.'

'You know the rules.'

'Do you think the bastards are going to see this ruddy thing? The batteries are almost dead.'

'Rules are rules.'

Once out of the warden's sight, he flicked it back on, and glanced up at the night sky again. It had already taken on a hideous red hue, reflecting the fires burning out of control on either side of the Thames. The overpowering stench of acrid smoke started to catch the back of his throat. He pulled up his collar, and carried on walking the short distance along the embankment to his flat in Millbank, accompanied by the constant metallic tinkling of incendiaries crashing onto nearby rooftops. On impact, they burst into a classically blinding white flash followed by an equally intense bluish glow, as they ignited. Occasionally, the urgent bell of a fire engine cut through the explosions, as a tender hurried past him down the road. *This is madness*, he thought to himself. Perhaps he should have taken cover in the local shelter, after all.

Having finally negotiated his way safely back to his flat in John Islip Street, he glanced through the window at the searchlights crisscrossing the night sky, and the constant flashes and rumbles of the bombs, as they thudded to the ground, like an endless roll of thunder. He was tired, and closed the heavy blackout curtains. The so-called "lull" since the height of the Blitz appeared to be drawing to a deadly end.

The sunshine was hazy, as a mist clung tenaciously to the cold morning air. The surrounding streets were strewn with masonry, rubble, and jagged shards of glass. Severed telephone lines fluttered aimlessly in the breeze from wooden telegraph poles, and a ruptured sewer spewed gallons of contaminated water along the main road. The stench was almost overwhelming, and he started to gag.

Close to Pimlico Underground Station, the overstretched auxiliary services were attempting to take control of the situation, but an electricity sub-station had taken a partial hit, and huge sparks were spluttering across the pavement, like demented sparklers on Bonfire Night.

Outside the tube, a newspaper seller was setting up his pitch. The headlines on his billboard grabbed Garvan's attention, and he stopped dead in his tracks. "Hollywood actor Lesley Howard dies in plane crash." He fumbled in his pocket for the right change and purchased the paper. The leader column was scant on information, but confirmed Howard's plane; BOAC Flight 777 had been shot down somewhere over the Bay of Biscay, having just left Lisbon. The actor had apparently just completed the last stage of his visit to help bolster British interests in neutral Portugal. The plane had crashed, with the loss of four Dutch crew members and thirteen passengers, including Lesley Howard.

As he stepped onto the escalator, still focussed on reading about Howard's tragic death, his upcoming mission to Lisbon was starting to play on his mind. He couldn't help wondering if Howard's plane had been deliberately targeted by the Germans, or if it had simply been a random act by the *Luftwaffe*. There was no way of telling, but it fleetingly crossed his mind Howard might well have been working for British Intelligence.

If there was one thing he'd learnt, since leaving Scotland Yard, you could never take anything at face value. Working for MI5 was akin to peeling an onion; there were always hidden layers. *What was the real truth behind Howard's visit to Lisbon?* He certainly wouldn't have undertaken such a high profile visit without the tacit approval of the British Government.

By the time Garvan entered the Double Cross office in Victoria, it was evident "Fag Ash" Lil, and her young assistant, Sue, had already read the news.

'It's so sad. I loved him in *Gone with the Wind*.'

Lil sniffed dismissively. 'Maybe, but he wasn't a patch on Clarke Gable,' she said, drawing heavily on a cigarette. 'Now, that one could park his slippers under my bed anytime he liked.'

Sue giggled. 'But, did you see him in the *First of the Few* with David Niven?'

Lil suddenly became aware someone had entered the office, and glanced over her shoulder. It was evident Garvan had been listening in on their conversation.

'Have you read the news?' she said, waving a newspaper in the air.

'It's all over the placards. You can't exactly miss it.'

'I guess things like this bring everything home, don't they?'

'I suppose so.'

'Do you want a cup of tea,' she asked.

'Thanks, Lil, I'd love one.'

'The Major hasn't arrived yet. He phoned in to say he was running late, so you better take a look at this before he arrives.' She reached up to one of the pigeon holes in a large oak cabinet behind her desk, and handed him a buff-covered file, with a large red cross printed on the outside. The title was "The Peenemunde Project," with a subtitle "Codename Bodyline."

'Thanks, luv,' he said, and wandered out of the registry along the corridor to his office.

Garvan opened the desk drawer, and pulled out a packet of cigarettes. His first of the day. He wasn't a heavy smoker by any means, but had convinced himself the odd cigarette helped his concentration. He opened the file, and started reading. It was heavy stuff, but then again, it always was.

*December 1942,* it began, and Garvan read on, absorbing all the information to the best of his ability. Intelligence received from a Danish chemical engineer coerced to work on the project, stated there were three prototypes of the so-called V2 rocket launched from

Peenemunde, with varying degrees of success. The first recorded successful launch was conducted on the 3$^{rd}$ October 1942, from a large vertical column estimated to be around at least forty foot in height.

Further confirmation of the experimental programme had been confirmed when British Intelligence successfully bugged a conversation between two German generals in custody near London. Wilhelm von Thoma, Rommel's second- in-command had been captured after the Battle of El Alamein in Egypt, and General Ludwig Crüwell had fallen into British hands by default when his *Luftwaffe* pilot mistook British troops for their Italian allies, as he landed in Libya. Quite what Crüwell thought about his pilot's fatal error of judgement wasn't held on record.

During their conversation, von Thoma had indiscreetly confided to his fellow general there was "no progress whatsoever in this rocket business." Having worked out they were imprisoned somewhere close to London, and as he hadn't yet heard any large explosions since their arrival, Thoma had concluded there must have been a delay in the development of the rocket programme.

"I saw it once with Feldmarschall Brauchitsch," he had explained to Crüwell. "There is a specific area near Kunersdorf. They've got these huge things, which they've always said would go fifteen kilometres into the stratosphere. Just wait until next year, and the fun will really start."

Alarm bells began to ring across Whitehall. The bugged conversation between the two generals came on top of reports, smuggled via a young man from Luxembourg. Leon Henri Roth had been a student, but was expelled from his studies, when he was discovered to have started an underground Resistance cell. For his sins, along with a number of his fellow countrymen, he found himself conscripted to work at Peenemunde. Ever resourceful, Roth managed to smuggle out a series of letters to his father, who was a member of a Belgian Resistance network. Leon described in graphic detail how the missile made a noise like a "squadron flying at low altitude." Further intercepted intelligence, from the Weapons Department in the German High Command, mentioned so-called winged rockets operated by remote control, and launched by a catapult method. On Hitler's express orders, London was destined to be their primary target. In fact, it was through Roth's help Giscard had eventually managed to make contact with the SOE.

Jean Giscard was described in the report as being a brilliant scientist. Although a Frenchman, before the outbreak of War, he had attended Berlin University, and this had inadvertently sealed his fate. By studying alongside many of the scientists now working at Peenemunde, they had remembered him well, and requested he was brought in to work on the top-secret project with them. With his family under increasing threat of arrest, he was reluctantly coerced into joining the development programme. Garvan couldn't help wondering what had finally sparked his decision to take his chances, and flee with the top-secret blueprint to Lisbon, when the threat to his family must surely have remained very real back in France.

Garvan drew heavily on his cigarette. As he was about to close the file, he looked up with a start, suddenly realising Spencer was standing in the doorway.

'Christ, how long have you been there?' he asked.

'Not long. I was just wondering how much you'd managed to get through,' he said gesturing toward the file. 'I didn't bother including all the technical stuff I think it's probably best left to the eggheads. Mind you, I doubt if I'd understand most of it anyway.'

As he approached the desk, Garvan noticed Spencer hadn't bothered to shave. It was unusual; he was normally meticulously turned out.

'You look a bit worse for wear. Did you have a late night, or something?'

'After you left my flat last night, Tar phoned, and asked if I'd meet him at the Savoy.'

'Why was that?'

'He wanted me to meet a friend of his from the Home Office. I very nearly didn't go, but what the hell. We ended up having a good time, probably too good a time. Do you know I think I must be losing my stamina,' he said, patting his jacket pockets. 'Have you got a fag to spare? I must have left mine at home.'

Garvan handed him a pack and his lighter. 'Help yourself.'

'There's nothing like the first one of the morning.' He lit one and drew swiftly in dire need of a quick nicotine fix.

'Have you seen the newspaper headlines?'

Spencer glanced down at the *Daily Sketch* sitting on Garvan's desk; he picked it up and scanned the leader column about Howard's plane being shot down over the Bay of Biscay.

'Yes, I heard about it on the radio. He was a cracking good actor.'

'The report says his plane hadn't long taken off from Lisbon.'

'So I believe,' he replied, with a hard-eyed stare, and placed the newspaper back on the desk.

'Tell me something, Spence, how sodding dangerous is this caper to Portugal going to be?'

Spencer didn't immediately respond, and moved over toward the window, rolling the cigarette thoughtfully between his fingers.

'Howard's plane was shot down by mistake.'

'What do you mean?'

Hall waved his hand in the air, wafting a stream of grey smoke. 'It's complicated.'

'Complicated means you're not going to tell me what happened.'

'It's all conjecture, at this stage of the game,' he said with a shrug. 'If I were you, I wouldn't worry myself too much about trigger happy *Luftwaffe* pilots.'

'What should I be worried about?'

'The Gestapo,' he said bluntly. 'They'll stop at nothing to prevent us from getting Giscard back to England.' He was about to leave the office, when he paused. 'By the way, we're booked to fly out to Lisbon on Saturday morning.' With that, he disappeared back along the corridor.

## Chapter 4

Garvan and Spencer travelled to Whitchurch airport by train from Paddington Station, and a taxi to the nearby airport. Since the outbreak of the War, Whitchurch was the only civil airport to remain fully operational in Britain. In addition to the scheduled flights to Portugal, there were connections to Shannon Airport in Ireland, where passengers could catch flights over to the United States.

Usually, passengers destined for the Lisbon flight were expected to check-in at The Grand Hotel in Bristol the night before departure. In the morning, they were taken by a coach, with blacked out windows to protect the exact location of the airport. Priority was given to agents, Whitehall trade, and diplomatic representatives, the SOE, and, on the return journey, to escapees from occupied Europe. The passenger lists were operated by British Overseas Airways Corporation staff, more commonly known as BOAC. Every application to fly required both a name and background check. But, ultimately, movements were strictly controlled by British Intelligence. In other words, no-one could step on a plane, unless they were officially sanctioned by the Government. The DC3 Dakotas were frequently piloted by Dutch ex-KLM crews, who had managed to escape their homeland after the Reich's invasion in May 1940. Due to the heavy fuel load required to reach Lisbon, there was a maximum capacity of only eighteen passengers on each of the flights.

Garvan had flown only once before in his life, when he was attached to Special Branch. Personally, he hadn't found it to be a particularly enjoyable experience; they'd hit a patch of turbulence over the North Sea, and then, on their approach to the airstrip, the pilot had suddenly aborted the landing. For some unknown reason, they'd then proceeded to circle the airfield twice, before the pilot decided to chance his luck again, and land the ruddy thing, and even then, the plane had thudded and bounced its way along the runway, until eventually grinding to a slithering halt. Garvan had sworn he'd never willingly fly again, and yet, here he was, at Whitchurch, about to take the longest flight of his life. He couldn't duck out; it was way too late, and more importantly, he'd lose face with Spencer.

The passport control staff cursorily glanced at their documentation; it was a rubber stamp job, at this stage. The passengers had already gone through so many checks, and counter checks; they knew precisely who was boarding the plane. There was also a permanent member of MI5 on duty, to ensure no-one managed to slip through the net.

'Are we running late?' Garvan asked Hall.

He checked his watch. 'I guess they've probably started boarding by now.'

The DC3 was virtually full, as they made their way down the aisle to the rear. To Garvan's mind, it seemed to be filled with a rather seedy collection of shadowy Allied industrialists, and a veritable who's who of Britain's leading spying fraternity. By the time they took their seats, Garvan was beginning to feel increasingly anxious. His mouth had dried, and the palms of his hands started to feel sweaty.

'I've only ever flown once before,' he announced.

Spencer looked at him questioningly.

'We hit so much bloody turbulence, the pilot aborted the landing.'

Spencer smiled, or was it a smirk; he wasn't entirely sure which.

'At least he made it the second time around, or we wouldn't be having this conversation, would we?'

Well, that put me back into my box, Garvan thought to himself. Spencer folded his arms and closed his eyes, and, to Garvan's annoyance, started to doze off. He was always so incredibly calm; nothing ever appeared to rattle him, but, then again, he'd always lived his life at full tilt, either in the army, or working undercover with the Special Operations Executive. It required a unique brand of courage to operate behind enemy lines. A type of courage few people were blessed with.

There was one more seat left to fill on the opposite side of the aisle. Garvan nervously checked the time. They were due to take off in ten minutes; whoever it was, they were cutting things pretty fine. The smartly uniformed KLM pilot emerged from the cockpit. He was tall, good looking, and at least, six-foot-three, with cropped fair hair. He stood in the open doorway, and threw his arms out in welcome.

'Darling, how are you?' he called.

Garvan raised his head, and then, he saw her the tall, statuesque figure of Joyce Leader. *Jesus wept, what was going on? Why hadn't Spencer warned him she was on the flight?* She was flirting with the pilot. They'd obviously met before, but, then again, she flirted with everyone. Over the years, Joyce had become one of Colonel Robertson's leading double agents. But, back in 1941, she was a prime suspect in the murder inquiry of Sarah Davis, Spencer's lover and MI5 colleague. Even then, she'd made the odd pass at Garvan, but he'd always assumed it was almost like a reflex action, and had meant nothing to her; it's what she did.

Joyce's recruitment to the Nazi cause had come about almost by default. Neither she, nor her family, were ardent members of Hitler's Nationalist Party. Joyce had been born in London, her mother, Bridget Artois, was French, and her father, Kurt, was of Anglo-Austrian origins. Kurt came from an extremely successful family of engineering manufacturers, and had inherited a large fortune from his late mother's family. He'd never worked a productive day in his life, and had enjoyed a luxurious playboy lifestyle before the war.

Joyce had always claimed her recruitment to the German Intelligence Service had stemmed from nothing more than a desire to protect her family from the Nazi regime.

Whatever the truth, she'd proved herself time again as an increasingly crucial member of the Double Cross network.

Garvan was well aware of Joyce's importance, not only in the eyes of British Intelligence and the SOE, but, the Abwehr, who'd never once doubted her integrity, or the quality of her work. By nature, she was coldly calculating and invariably ruthless. She also enjoyed Colonel Robertson's trust in her abilities as a spy, and that was all that really mattered.

He wanted to know what in God's name Spencer was up to. Why he hadn't bothered telling him she would be on the flight. It wasn't as if he wouldn't have known. As Joyce's desk officer, he controlled every facet of her life.

Garvan watched Joyce sashay down the aisle of the DC3. She possessed a certain cat-like grace. Blonde, blue-eyed and curvaceously sexy, dressed in a tight-fitting tailored jacket, and pencil slim skirt, which emphasised her figure. At five-foot-eight, she was tall for a woman, but with high heeled black leather court shoes, to Garvan's mind, she looked like a modern-day Valkyrie, and just as deadly.

She smiled in recognition before taking her seat.

Garvan sharply elbowed Spencer in the ribs.

He blearily opened his eyes, and grunted. 'What's up?'

Garvan inclined his head toward Joyce, and demanded, 'What's she doing here?'

'She speaks Portuguese.'

'That's not what I asked?'

'Tell me,' Spencer said, raising his index finger toward him in a stabbing motion. 'What would you have said, if I'd mentioned Joyce was coming along for the ride?'

Garvan held his gaze, but didn't respond.

'The look on your face says everything,' Spencer shot back at him. 'You'd have turned me down flat. You know you would! I guess, right now, you're probably wishing me to hell. But, you can't deny she's bloody good at what she does.' Hall paused for a moment, wondering what was running through Garvan's mind, before continuing, 'Trust me, it'll all come right in the end.'

'You're a bastard, Spencer, you really are!'

'That's as may be,' he replied, sanguinely. 'But, bringing Joyce on board wasn't just my idea.'

Luke shook his head in disbelief. 'Don't try passing the buck onto Colonel Robertson. It won't wash with me.'

Hall gave a dismissive shrug.

'Where does she fit into your plan to rescue Giscard?'

'Joyce has been ordered by Tar to try and sniff around the Abwehr about him. Once we know for sure what they do, and don't, know, then, we can start finalising our own plans to spirit him out of the country.' He hesitated, before admitting, 'You're quite right; I should have been upfront with you from the off.'

Garvan glanced around the plane. 'Somehow, I don't suppose we're the only ones here travelling on forged documentation, *are we*?'

'What do you think,' he winked.

'I was just wondering what kind of cover story you dreamed up to get Joyce on board. It's got to be good enough to convince her German controllers she's managed to get official permission to fly out of Britain, without compromising her cover.'

Hall's gaze locked onto him. He casually lit a cigarette. 'I guess there's no easy way of breaking it to you. But, the Abwehr are under the distinct impression you're a notch on her bedpost.'

Garvan grimaced. 'Oh, come on, give me a break. You're *kidding*!'

A slow smile crossed Hall's face. 'I kid you not.'

'For Christ's sake, how long have you been planning this? There's no way, you could have set me up like this over the last week.'

Spencer slipped his gold cigarette lighter back into his pocket. 'Just long enough to convince the Abwehr.'

'What are we talking about weeks, months?' Garvan demanded angrily.

Spencer wasn't about to be drawn into the nitty gritty of the transmissions between London and Berlin. 'Let's just say, when the Colonel received confirmation MI6 were on the point of getting Giscard across the Spanish border into Portugal, we had to move fast. We'd already formulated the bare bones of the plan.' He blew out a cloud of swirling grey smoke. 'We had to implement it, pronto. There was a lot of work to be done, and we needed to draw up the documentation for our false identities. So, we contacted the Foreign Office.'

Garvan looked at him questioningly.

'We needed to keep them in the loop, to keep them on side, so to speak, and explain why we wanted you to pose as a senior FO diplomat. It was they who came up with the name Steven Howe. He'd been on their books before the War. If the Abwehr turned nosy, their spies could quite easily confirm Howe's identity. In the meantime, the Foreign Office kept the British Embassy in Lisbon up-to-date with our plans.' Hall paused. 'Are you following this?'

Garvan looked long, and hard at him. Hall always exuded an air of innate confidence; it was almost bordering on the arrogant. 'So far, yes I'm following it,' Garvan said in a deadpan voice.

'Good,' Spencer said. 'The upshot is, Hamburg believes you've called in a few overdue favours in Whitehall to wangle her a seat on the flight.' He paused for effect, before continuing, 'After all, she wouldn't be the first mistress to get a free holiday in Portugal at the tax payers expense.'

'No, I suppose not. In the brief, you mentioned we're staying at the Metropole Hotel.'

'Yes, that's correct.'

'And the sleeping arrangements?' he demanded testily, unable to disguise his irritation.

It wasn't quite a smirk on Hall's face, but it was as near as damn it. 'You're booked into the family suite. Don't worry; it has adjoining rooms.'

'Won't the German's question it?' he queried.

'No, not at all. The suite is earmarked for visiting British diplomats. Of course,' he winked, 'I'll leave the sleeping arrangements entirely up to you.'

Garvan was already suffering from a sense of humour bypass, and Spencer's smugness wasn't exactly helping. 'Is there anything else I should know about before we land, or is that it?' he said coldly.

'No, I think that's about it.'

He was on the verge of telling Spencer what he could do with himself, when the engines of the DC3 suddenly spluttered into life. The plane began to rattle, and the noise inside the fuselage almost became unbearable.

'Here take this,' Hall said, handing him a hip flask, 'I nabbed some of Tar's whisky before we left the office. I thought you might need it!' He knew Garvan was anxious about the flight, and had felt under the circumstances, it was the least he could do. Over the last couple of years, they'd built up an excellent rapport with one another, but Spencer had a nasty feeling, in the last few minutes, there was a very real possibility he'd probably destroyed their friendship forever.

Garvan silently snatched the flask from his grasp. *Why hadn't Spencer trusted him?* At least trusted him enough, to confide in him about Joyce Leader's involvement in their mission to Lisbon. To a certain extent since his secondment, he'd always felt like an outsider, and only on the periphery of Colonel Robertson's shadowy inner sanctum. But, on a separate level, he'd managed to build up a close working relationship with Spencer. *Or so, it had seemed.* Part of him understood his reticence to share intelligence. But, he had a right to know about Joyce, as soon as he'd agreed to place his life on the line by flying out to help rescue Jean Giscard from the clutches of the Gestapo.

Spencer decided it might be wise to change the subject. 'You really ought to think yourself lucky.'

'Why?' Garvan asked tetchily.

'That you're not sitting in the back of a Lancaster, waiting to launch yourself out onto a DZ in the middle of the night.'

He looked at him completely nonplussed. 'What's a DZ?'

'It's a drop zone in occupied territory.'

*No*, Garvan thought, *he wouldn't have fancied launching himself out of a plane into oblivion.*

Spencer stubbed out his cigarette, and again relaxed back in his seat. On the opposite aisle, Joyce was busily re-applying her bright red lipstick. The plane remained stationary for several minutes, before slowly starting to taxi across the apron.

By the time the pilot finally opened the engines to full throttle, and thundered down the runway, Spencer had already begun to drift off asleep. Garvan, on the other hand, braced himself, as the DC3 slowly started to lift itself into the air. His heart was racing with anxiety; his sweaty palms clung desperately to the armrests, and he seriously began to wish he hadn't taken the window seat. Now seemed like as a good time as any to take a large swig from the hip flask. He glanced fleetingly across the aisle. Joyce Leader was calmly flicking through a magazine. He needed to get a grip; this was madness. No-one else on the plane seemed in the least bit bothered about flying, but most of them were probably seasoned regulars on the shuttle service to Lisbon.

Half an hour out of Whitchurch, Garvan opened his briefcase, and retrieved this morning's issue of the *Daily Sketch*. He had to do something. He couldn't just sit there, becoming increasingly paranoid, listening for changes in the sound of the prop engines. *It was pretty stupid*, he told himself. Just as long as the buggers kept the ruddy thing going, he figured there was no point in worrying.

Two hours into the flight, he'd already finished the hip flask. Joyce decided to stretch her legs, and took a stroll down the length of the plane, occasionally stopping to pass the time of day with a couple of passengers, before returning to her seat.

Garvan gestured to her.

'Hello.' She smiled broadly.

He glanced out of the window; she instinctively followed his gaze. 'Does this thing usually fly this bloody low?' To Garvan's mind, the Dakota seemed dangerously low, as it skimmed over the white-crested waves below.

Joyce leant across Spencer. He was still dead to the world, and peered through the window. 'Yes,' she said reassuringly. 'The crew usually fly between one and three thousand feet, to escape the *Luftwaffe*. I think you'll find the sea looks a lot closer than it actually is.' She straightened herself up, and grabbed hold of the headrest of the seat in front. 'Mind you, if you think this is bad, you ought to try flying with the RAF across the English Channel.'

'I'm not sure I would.'

Joyce smiled. 'It's a white-knuckle ride all the way; they fly even lower. Sometimes as low as fifty feet.'

Garvan inwardly shuddered at the idea. 'No, thanks. This is low enough.'

'One other piece of advice,' she added, before returning to her seat. 'Only use the toilets, if you have to. It's not for the faint-hearted with this kind of turbulence.'

At the start of the war, aircraft flying out of Whitchurch were largely left unmolested by the Axis powers in respect of Portuguese neutrality. However, since 1942, things had begun to change, as the air war heated up over the Bay of Biscay, and off the west coast of France. The BOAC flights found themselves increasingly under attack, most managed to escape with nothing more than shrapnel damage, but there had been umpteen close shaves, even before the death of Lesley Howard.

Joyce wondered whether Spencer had been entirely truthful with Garvan about the potential risks involved in flying to Lisbon. But, under the circumstances, it had probably been an act of kindness not to tell him the whole truth.

*

Spencer slowly started to rouse; he began to stretch wearily in his seat, and opened a bleary eye. 'I needed that,' he said, automatically glancing at his watch. 'We can't be too far off now.'

'God knows,' Luke said, peering out of the window again.

Spencer leaned across him. They were flying over land now, probably at no more than about five hundred feet. 'We're nearly there,' he announced.

The DC3 appeared to nosedive sharply down toward the runway, the sound of the prop engines changed rapidly, as the pilot slowed his air speed. The aircraft began to vibrate as it thudded onto the landing strip. The Dutch pilot slammed on his brakes with a jolt, and momentarily, they found themselves jerked forward in their seats with the force. Garvan blew out his cheeks in relief scarcely able to believe they'd made the journey in one piece. This lark wasn't good for his blood pressure, but he finally started to relax, and almost enjoy himself, as they taxied toward Portela Airport's terminal buildings.

Having a window seat didn't seem such a bad idea now; he became almost transfixed by the sight of the Axis planes ringed around the airfield. There were *Lufthansa* Junkers' tri-motors bedecked with swastikas, parked up uniformly beside BOAC and American planes. Security on the ground appeared to be very tight; each of the aircraft had a heavily armed Portuguese policeman standing guard beside them. To Spencer, such sights were bread and butter stuff, but to Garvan, it was a whole new experience; he was both intrigued and unnerved in equal measure.

The Dakota slowly pulled up in front of the small terminal building. The ground staff opened the aircraft door and a wave of intense heat swept through the length of the fuselage. *God, it was hot*, Garvan thought, much hotter than he'd expected. Once they'd disembarked, he was the first to negotiate his way through the control desk manned by a border guard. He presented him with his passport and false supporting documentation, purporting him to be Steven Howe from the Foreign Office.

Without bothering to look up, the guard barked, 'Purpose of visit?' He'd probably done it a thousand times before, and was simply going through the motions; no-one visiting Lisbon was ever quite what they seemed.

'I'm here to meet the British Ambassador,' he lied.

The official snorted derisively, snapped the passport shut, thrust it back into Garvan's hand, and waved him through impatiently.

'Next,' he grunted, gesturing for Spencer to step forward; he was met by the same set of routine questions, as the guard idly flicked through the passport. 'What is the purpose of your visit?'

'I'm with the British Trade Mission.'

The border guard looked up, narrowing his eyes speculatively. 'What's the name of your employer?

'Sledge & Trust. They're a mining company.'

The Portuguese rolled his eyes and handed the passport back. 'Your firm sends many people here. Go through,' he said bluntly.

As they waited for Joyce to negotiate her way through the control desk, Garvan couldn't quite get over the rather bizarre sight of Allied servicemen dressed in full uniform, mingling seamlessly in the terminal building, alongside their German counterparts in the grey uniform of the *Wehrmacht*. He almost felt as if he wanted to pinch himself; it all seemed strangely surreal.

Joyce breezed up to the control desk. The border guard looked her up and down appreciatively; his expression softened, and he became quite animated. She flashed a smile. *She was good at that*, Garvan thought to himself, as they waited for her. She even started chatting to him in Portuguese.

'*Obrigada*,' Joyce flashed another smile, and thanked him, as he returned her passport.

'So, are you fluent in Portuguese?' Garvan queried, as she joined them.

'I know enough to get by. As a girl, my family spent the odd summer here on the coast at Estoril. My sister and I played on the beach, while my father spent all his time at the Casino.' She placed the passport into her handbag, and asked Spencer, 'Did the Embassy book us a taxi?'

'No, I never bothered asking.'

'Why?' she tutted.

'Because we'd have ended up with some undercover PVDE copper driving us, that's why. Come on,' he said sharply. 'There's usually enough taxis waiting outside.'

With that, he picked up his suitcase, and led the way out of the airport.

## Chapter 5

Garvan opened the French windows leading out onto the balcony of his hotel room overlooking Rossio Square. Their journey from the airport in a dilapidated taxi had been interspersed by Joyce pointing out the local landmarks. He stood on the balcony, watching the world go by, and admiring the view of the Square, with its beautiful monuments and fountains. The Rossio was paved in a wavy mosaic pattern, and in the centre, was a statue of some Portuguese king, or other. He thought Joyce had mentioned his name was Pedro, but he might have got it all wrong. On either side of the Square were two large fountains, which she'd described as being baroque. It hadn't meant anything to him, and at the time, he hadn't liked to ask her what baroque meant, but they were impressive.

The Square was bustling, filled with people relaxing in the late afternoon sunshine. On the drive from Portela Airport, the first thing which struck him was the shops, stocked to the gunnels with produce. He'd probably seen more fruit and vegetables on display in the last hour than he had since the outbreak of the War, and the introduction of rationing in Britain.

Spencer had explained to him Lisbon was caught in a kind of pre-war time warp. In many ways, they were immune to the horrors of the outside world, but they were living in the eye of the storm. Although Portugal had manoeuvred itself into remaining neutral, President Salazar had increasingly found himself forced to walk a political and economic tightrope between the warring factions. With the ever growing need for Wolfram ore, and its integral use in the hardening process of steel, Portugal had become gold rich, bartering between the Nazis and the Allies. Neutrality might have saved the country from a terrible fate, but even Salazar now realised Portugal couldn't entirely escape the ramifications and the political pressures. The British and American governments were hardening their line, and trying to force his hand to cut back on providing the ore to the Nazis.

The war had intruded on Portuguese shores in entirely unexpected ways, for Lisbon had now become an uneasy mix of refugees from the length and breadth of Nazi-occupied Europe. They lived cheek-by-jowl, alongside informers, prostitutes on the take, shady businessmen, and, of course, the continual presence of Axis and Allied spies. By night, its streets became a shadowy world of intrigue, where deals were made down dark alleyways, and informers made a profit trading intelligence for the right price to the highest bidder.

After 1939, the backstreet red light brothels huddled around the docks were run effectively by the Germans, and used as a means of duping Allied seamen into giving details of convoy movements crossing the Atlantic. A seemingly harmless conversation with a prostitute about a sailor's ship, and their next trip would be systematically reported back to the girl's Abwehr pimps; in turn, they would then receive extra cash for the information. For both the girls, and the Abwehr, it had proved to be a somewhat lucrative means of extracting information from unsuspecting Allied seamen.

The British and American intelligence services pooled their resources, and worked together to expose the spy ring controlling the dockside brothels. In due course, the British Ambassador was chosen to present the Portuguese President with a dossier of the Reich's illegal activities, which eventually resulted in the Abwehr's dockside activities being effectively closed down. Officially, Salazar couldn't afford to show bias to either of the warring factions. His decision was viewed by the Allies as an enormous success, as they'd managed to expose the Nazis spy ring, while at the same time, continuing to cover their own tracks and double dealing under the noses of the Portuguese authorities.

Apart from the on-going turf wars between the Allied and Axis intelligence services, the city was awash with refugees from occupied territories. For many of them, Lisbon was their last hope of escaping the Nazis regime. On a daily basis, they gathered pitifully at the Tagus dockside, in the desperate hope of catching a ship to freedom, and to a new life, far away from the ravages of war-torn Europe. The majority were Jewish refugees, fighting for a place on one of the scheduled vessels sailing either to Palestine or the United States.

One way, or another, most of the refugees, whatever their nationality or religion, found themselves trapped in Lisbon for months on end, and in many cases, they spent years there, before an opportunity arose to escape the crowded, fetid Tagus dockside. As they kicked their heels, waiting for a chance of escape, most of them spent their time eking out a meagre existence in the dark cobbled alleyways, and the backstreets surrounding the dockside. They were mainly dependent on the soup kitchens and shelters, provided by various foreign aid charities.

For the wealthiest amongst them, the right price could purchase a seat in a luxurious Pan Am Clipper flying boat, which operated a regular service to New York, flying via the Azores and Bermuda. While others simply chose to batten down the hatches, and stay put for the duration of the War, by either living the good life in Lisbon, or along the coast, in places such as Estoril, with its long sandy beaches, expensive hotels, and casinos.

The more Garvan discovered about the so-called "Capital of Espionage," the more intrigued he became. He remembered reading in Spencer's brief, the Portuguese President had recently decreed spying by foreign nationals was a criminal act, and anyone caught doing so would be dealt with severely by the police and the courts. Spencer had described the decree as being a little like shutting the stable door after the horse had bolted. The situation in Portugal was already way beyond any belated attempts to control the opposing intelligence operations. There was simply too much at stake for either the Allies or the Reich to take any real notice of Salazar. They might well pay lip service to the law, but no more than that. There had been one or two incidents where spies found themselves deported by the authorities, but the President's actions were simply too little, too late; the die had already been cast.

The espionage battle between the warring agencies was keenly fought, but on a bizarre level, it could, at times, be almost intimate, in so far as everyone knew their opposite numbers, and were often on nodding acquaintance with one another in the crowded bars and cafes. While the opposing agents were locked into an endless game of smoke and mirrors, the Portuguese secret police had their work cut out, spying on everyone.

Garvan reluctantly dragged himself away from the balcony and into the elegantly spacious bedroom. British diplomats certainly lived high on the hog; the bathroom, with its hand-made Portuguese tiles, was almost larger than his flat in London. Spencer had arranged to meet him in the hotel's foyer at six o'clock. Since checking in, he'd had time to order a light lunch, have a wash, and change of clothes.

He paused momentarily at the interconnecting door to Joyce Leader's bedroom. Since 1939, the suite had been reserved exclusively for visiting British diplomats and politicians alike. He didn't know if it was locked, and wasn't about to try; he was still smarting from the fact Spencer hadn't bothered telling him she was meant to be his lover. Cover story, or not, the next few days weren't going to be easy. Rescuing Giscard was one thing, but handling Joyce Leader was an entirely different matter altogether.

As Luke stepped out of the lift into the black and white tiled lobby, he caught sight of Joyce heading out of the hotel. Since their arrival, she had changed, and was now wearing a pretty floral dress.

'Where's she off to?' he asked Spencer, who was loitering near the reception desk.

'Jo's arranged to meet one of her contacts.'

She skipped lightly down the steps, and into a waiting Opel saloon parked outside the hotel's main entrance. Stretched out on the back seat was a portly, middle-aged man, with a florid complexion. Garvan couldn't help thinking his pallor had probably more to do with booze, than any overindulgence sunbathing in the hot Portuguese sunshine.

'Who the hell's that?' he asked.

'Baron Ernst von Gruber,' Spencer told him. 'He's the Head of the Abwehr here in Portugal.'

'Where's she going to?'

Spencer didn't seem particularly interested. 'I think they're having dinner together later.'

'Why did you want to meet up?'

'There's a car waiting to take us to the British Embassy.'

'Why are we going there?'

'I've arranged a meeting.'

Garvan looked at him questioningly. 'Who's it with?'

'With George Rowlands. He's a Field Officer working out of the MI6 Station.'

There was always a certain indefinable quietness about Hall, coupled with a tough mental discipline, but, even by his standards, he seemed unusually reticent.

'Listen,' Garvan said to him. 'You've dragged me on a bloody plane all the way here, and I'm still getting the distinct impression you're holding out on me!'

'It's for your own good,' Spencer answered tersely.

'If I'm about to place my sodding neck on the line, then I think I have a right to know exactly where I stand.'

Spencer examined his face shrewdly, before saying, 'Wait until we've seen Rowlands. It might be all or nothing.'

As Garvan followed him out of the lobby into the warm afternoon sunshine, a large Bentley was waiting for them. He was impressed, as it had diplomatic plates; the driver ushered them in the back, and set off for the Embassy.

On arriving, they filled out some paperwork at the main reception desk, before being escorted up to Rowlands' office on the second floor. They found him seated behind a small, unprepossessing desk, surrounded by a bank of brown metallic filing cabinets. He had a cigarette poised lightly between his fingers, and a slight smile of recognition played around his mouth on seeing Spencer.

'Gentlemen,' he said in a clipped manner. 'Good flight?'

'Can't complain,' Spencer said, and introduced Garvan.

Rowlands stood up, and shook his hand. 'Chief Inspector, good to meet you at last. Please take a seat. Tea, anyone?'

They declined.

'How are things?' Spencer asked.

He rolled his eyes. 'A guinea a minute. Hate the ruddy place, but what can you do.'

'How's Frank?'

'Just the same as usual living on his nerves, and worrying about everything.' Rowlands shot Garvan a glance, and felt obliged to explain. 'Frank Lucern is the MI6 Head of Station here in Lisbon.'

'I see.'

As they began to chat, Rowlands kept a cigarette on the go, and occasionally toyed with a sleek silver fountain pen, twisting it deftly like a majorette's baton between his fingers. Garvan guessed he was probably in his early forties. There was a droll, witty flamboyance about him, a certain poise which reeked of the theatre; an actor, perhaps, before the war.

'And Giscard,' he heard Spencer saying, 'what's he like?'

Rowlands gave a rather theatrical shudder. 'An utter little shit!' he said, with considerable feeling. 'He turned up with a wad of money stuffed into a condom, of all places!'

Spencer found it faintly amusing. 'I, actually, think it's quite inspired.'

Rowlands sniffed disapprovingly. 'You would, dear boy. The bugger might be some kind of genius, but, he's an argumentative so and so. I tell you, Spencer, it's just as well you've brought the Chief Inspector with you.'

'Why's that?'

'I guarantee you'll end up trying to throttle the darling boy before the week's out; that's why.'

Hall let out a chuckle. 'Was it that bad, eh?'

'Are you still holding him in Lisbon?' Garvan asked.

'Not at the moment. Things were starting to get a little too close for comfort here. The Gestapo were all over the ruddy place like a rash, so we decided to move him down the coast to Estoril.'

'You mean to a safe house?'

'No, too obvious, dear boy. He's bedded down in a private flat at a casino. It belongs to the manager, who only uses the place, if he can't be bothered to go home.'

'Can you trust the manager?' Spencer queried.

'He's one of our local recruits; he's a reliable sort.' George hesitated, and fixed Spencer with a troubled expression. 'But, we do have a slight problem.'

'Only one?' he shot back sarcastically.

'Giscard's been joined by his fiancée.'

Hall pulled a face. 'What are you talking about?'

'With the help of Dr. Schwachtgen's network, and the SOE, his girlfriend, a certain Claudine Gregorie, was smuggled out of Peenemunde, before the Germans realised Giscard had jumped ship. You really can't blame him for wanting her out of harm's way, can you? Besides, he'd already told her to be prepared to follow him.'

Spencer didn't like surprises, and it showed.

'Claudine was handed over to MI6 at the Spanish border, and we, then, passed her down the line, using one of our usual escape routes over the Pyrenees, with a couple of POW's in tow.'

'Why weren't we told about her?' Spencer demanded.

'She only arrived here on Monday of this week; there simply wasn't time, dear boy.'

He looked at Rowlands suspiciously. 'There's something else, Georgie, isn't there; you might as well just spit it out!'

'She's three months pregnant.'

Hall shook his head slowly. 'We'll never get them out at the same time. She'll just have to follow on at a later date.'

'He's kicking up a fuss and says it's non-negotiable.'

Spencer's expression hardened. 'I'll *bloody* tell him what's non-negotiable!'

George folded his arms and smiled indulgently. 'As I said earlier, it's just as well the Chief Inspector here is along for the ride. Just try and remember, Spence, London wants to get Giscard back safely, in one piece.'

Hall steadily held his gaze, but decided against rising to the jibe.

'You want us to collect him from Estoril?' Garvan asked.

'Yes,' Rowlands replied. 'I'll take you down there myself, and do the necessary introductions.' He toyed with the pen again between his fingers. 'I do hope you don't mind, but

I took the liberty of contacting London about your measurements.'

They both stared at him blankly.

'Estoril, the casino,' he went on airily. 'You'll need dinner jackets. They'll be delivered to your hotel first thing in the morning.'

'I take it,' Garvan pressed him, 'Giscard still has the blueprint?'

'Yes, he has. Won't part with it, of course. He says it's his insurance policy. In his shoes, I'd probably do the same thing.'

'Before we set off from London, you sent a message to the Double Cross team,' Spencer said.

'Yes, I did.'

'Is there any news? Has our friend arrived yet?'

'Dear Otto, yes, it seems he arrived two weeks ago. But, it was only yesterday we were able to confirm he was here, when one of our operatives saw him having lunch with Baron von Gruber.'

'Do you know where he is staying?'

'They booked him into the Avenida Palace Hotel.'

'No surprises there, then.' Spencer said.

The Avenida had a reputation for being pro-German, and had become the favoured meeting place for the German community in Lisbon. It was located in a district called Baixa, a downtown part of the city, and had a convenient rear access leading to the Rossio docks for those not wishing to be seen entering or leaving the hotel.

'Are you two going to let me in on this, or what?' Garvan asked testily; he'd already had enough of being blind-sided.

George apologised. 'I'm so sorry, Chief Inspector. We're talking about a German called Otto Stackler.'

'Who's he?'

'He holds the rank of colonel and has been sent here on *Reichsführer* Himmler's specific orders, to kill Jean Giscard.'

'Why bother sending this man Stackler? I already thought half the local Gestapo were out to kill him, anyway.'

'Our dear Otto is a member of the *Einsatzgruppen*.'

'I've never heard of it.'

George considered his reply carefully. 'The *Einsatzgruppen* could at best be described as a kind of mobile killing unit, an extermination squad, if you like, who follow the regular *Wehrmacht* troops. Their remit is to liquidate the Jews, political opponents, and men, like Giscard, who know too much about the Reich's State secrets.' George paused for effect. 'I think it's fair to say, the *Einsatzgruppen* probably make the Gestapo look like a bunch of kindergarten teachers.'

'And the other spanner in the works,' Spencer said, with characteristic understatement, 'is that I've met him. It was a few years ago, now, but even so, he could well end up blowing my cover.'

*Chapter 6*

They stopped for a coffee and a bite to eat at one of the many cafés surrounding Rossio Square. The medieval St. George's castle stood proudly silhouetted against the darkening sky on an escarpment. Having arrived straight from the Blackout in London, the stark contrast between the two cities could not have been greater. Lisbon was a vibrant, bustling city, and as dusk fell, it was illuminated in a blaze of twinkling lights. Sitting at one of the café tables on the Square, soaking up the atmosphere, Garvan could quite happily have sat out the rest of the War in Lisbon. He began to think it would probably be quite difficult, when the time came to leave, knowing they were returning to rationing, and a country suffering after three years of war, and the ever-constant threat of bombing raids.

'It's been a long day,' Spencer said unnecessarily, as he spooned sugar into his coffee. 'Maybe we ought to start thinking about heading back to the hotel.'

'I think we need to clear a few things up first.'

Spencer looked at him searchingly. 'Do you mean about Otto Stackler?'

'Where exactly did you meet him?'

Hall picked out a couple of cigarettes from his case, and handed one to Garvan, then lit the other. 'It was in Berlin.'

'When was that?'

'In 1939, I'd been working undercover there for about six months.' He tested his coffee, and then, spooned in another sugar. 'I guess you could say, being fluent in German sometimes has its drawbacks.'

'So why were you there?'

'MI6 wanted insider information about the Nazi Party.' He looked reflective, world-weary. 'Believe it, or not, I became a fully paid up member of the Party. I went to meetings, and helped distribute leaflets.' He gave a chuckle,

'And I even attended a rally to celebrate Hitler's fiftieth birthday.'

Garvan was impressed. 'What happened?'

'There was a massive military parade during the day,' he said. 'Organized by Josef Goebbels, followed by a torchlight parade in the evening.' Spencer rolled the cigarette thoughtfully between his fingers, as he explained how he'd watched the celebrations with a mixture of bemusement, and then, a sense of increasing horror at the sheer scale of it all, and the baying crowd whipped into a blind frenzy of adulation for the Führer. He placed the cigarette casually between his lips.

'It was after the rally I met Stackler. We sank a few beers, sang some songs, and then, we parted company.'

'What's he like?' Spencer gave a dismissive shrug. 'Let's just say, at the time he didn't particularly stand out from the crowd. He was just another ardent Nazi having a good time after the rally.' He drew heavily on the cigarette. 'The one thing you have to know about Otto is, since then, he's developed an almost pathological taste for killing people. Quite simply, he seems to enjoy it. After coming to Himmler's notice, he's started to move in exalted circles. Never underestimate him; he's not only unpredictable, but dangerous.' Spencer rested his cigarette down in the ashtray. 'The intelligence reports about him contain evidence he's taken part in numerous atrocities across Occupied Europe. Five months after I met him in Berlin, he was let loose during the invasion of Poland. The *Einsatzgruppen* was tasked with identifying enemies of the State.' He picked up the cigarette again. 'They rounded up priests, politicians, prominent Jews, in fact, anyone Reinhard Heydrich, the Head of the SD, thought was undesirable. There were mass killings on an entirely unprecedented scale. So many, in fact, even some of the army commanders formally complained about the activities of the *Einsatzgruppen.*'

'I bet that went down like a lead balloon.'

'You could say that. Heydrich had a series of meetings with the *Wehrmacht* commanders, but they were never going to stop the killings. Hitler had given his full support to both Heydrich and the *Einsatzgruppen*. He told his generals you can't fight a war using Salvation Army methods. That, in effect, put an end to their protests. They'd tried their best, but failed to bring a stop to the brutality.'

'And Otto Steckler,' Garvan said. 'I presume he commands a certain amount of respect within the Reich?'

'Oh God, yes. He holds the Knight's Cross, with swords, for so-called valour.'

'Why was he awarded it?'

'The citation was for outstanding bravery fighting on the Russian front. The honour is rarely bestowed, so it naturally brought him to the attention of the Nazi elite, but even more so, when he was personally presented the Knight's Cross at a lavish ceremony in Berlin by Adolf Hitler himself. And since he came to the attention of *Reichsführer* Himmler, let's just say, his particular skills have been channelled into somewhat specialist missions. He settles old scores for his boss, assassinations and the like; he tortures suspects. There's no set pattern to his role, other than acting as Himmler's personal henchman. Otto does whatever he's required to do. In Giscard's case, he's working not only for Himmler, but on behalf of the State, so, in other words, on Hitler's direct orders. You can imagine, the Baron is in a bit of a flap about it all. If he and his colleagues don't manage to flush Giscard out into the open, he might well find himself on the first plane back to Berlin.'

'And what about Stackler? How will he fare, if we manage to get Giscard back to London?'

'That's anyone's guess.' He took a drag on his cigarette. 'The Baron's been tasked to track the Frenchman down. At the end of the day, Stackler's the hired assassin, and nothing more; he's not involved in the intelligence side of the assignment.'

'With any luck, he might not remember meeting you,' Garvan suggested.

He pulled a face. 'But, if he does it could jeopardize the entire operation.'

'What do you want to do now?'

'Carry on as usual. Rowlands' agents will keep a close eye on Stackler's movements. If he leaves Lisbon, and heads down the coast to Estoril, I may well have to take a step back.'

'What about Giscard?'

'Then, it'll be down to George Rowlands to help you get him to the airport.'

Garvan puffed out his cheeks in something approaching despair. 'Blimey, Spence, are you seriously expecting me to go it alone?'

'I'm sorry, but we really may not have any choice in the matter.'

'Tell me something.'

Hall blew out a cloud of smoke. 'Go on.'

'I might well be talking out of turn, and you must tell me if I am, it's just George Rowlands doesn't exactly strike me as your average MI6 field officer, at least not the ones I've met before.'

A slow grin crossed Spencer's face. 'There's no need to worry about Rowlands helping you out in a tight corner, if that's what you mean. Don't let appearances fool you. Camp or not, he's bloody good at what he does.'

'What did he do before the war?'

'George was a successful West End theatrical agent. I believe he was a close friend of Lesley Howard. I certainly know they met up for dinner during Howard's last trip to Lisbon, before his plane went down.'

'But, how did he end up working for MI6?'

'Rumour has it his powerful contacts in the Masons secured his recruitment.' He cast Garvan a bemused smile. 'George is known throughout the Service as the Grand Poobah.'

'Do…what?' Garvan said blankly.

'He's the head of his local lodge. Don't you belong to the Masons?'

'Me?'

'I thought all you coppers belonged to the Masons.'

'Well, not this one. I've never really fancied prancing around wearing an apron, or whatever they do.'

A silence fell between them. They were surrounded by the sound of people chatting, laughing, seemingly without a care in the world. Garvan sat motionless, staring out across the Square toward the ornate fountains. They were illuminated now, and lights flickered brightly from the buildings.

'When are we off to Estoril?' he asked breaking the silence.

'That's Frank Lucern's call,' Spencer explained. 'Portugal's his patch, after all. He'll give us the nod, once he thinks it's safe for us to make our move.'

\*

Garvan was about to head downstairs for breakfast, when Joyce Leader opened the interconnecting door between their hotel rooms.

She flashed him a smile. 'Good morning. Where did you and Spencer get to last night?

'I might say the same to you.'

'I had dinner with the Baron, but I was back at the hotel by nine. I was hoping to meet up with you at the bar.'

'We ended up having coffee and a bite to eat at one of the cafés in the Square.'

'How did your meeting go at the Embassy?'

Before he could answer, there was a knock on the door. 'Not interrupting anything?' Spencer winked.

Joyce folded her arms, and cocked her head to one side. 'What do you think?'

'It's none of my business, Jo. What time did you get back last night?'

'I was just saying it was about nine o' clock.'

'How was your friend, the Baron? Was he in good form?'

Joyce suddenly looked like she'd sucked on a bucket of ripe lemons. 'That was below the belt, Spence!'

'I asked a question, that's all.'

'You know how I feel about him.'

'I'm not interested. You don't like the old bugger. What did he have to say for himself?' he said sharply.

'Usual stuff.' She shrugged. 'He wanted to know about the Chief here, I mean Steven Howe, and anything else I might have got wind about the Foreign Office.'

'They're still swallowing the story about you two being lovers, then?'

'So far, yes.'

'Did he have anything to say about the local stuff?'

'Nothing much,' she said, and then, touched her forehead. 'But, there was one thing.'

'What was it?'

'He said something about going out to dinner with some friend or other of Himmler's.'

'Did he mention his name?'

'I'm sorry, no, he didn't.'

'Did you manage to arrange another meeting with him?'

'We're having lunch tomorrow.'

Spencer didn't so much look at her, as through her.

'What do you want me to do?' Joyce asked tentatively.

'I need you to confirm the name of Herr Himmler's friend.'

Joyce knew better than to question him, and, with difficulty, she buttoned her lip.

'Right,' he said rubbing his hands together. 'I'm starving. Are you two ready to come down for breakfast?' He didn't bother waiting for a reply, and left them staring at him, as he disappeared into the corridor.

'What was that all about?' she said, looking up at Garvan.

'You'll find out soon enough. Come on,' he said, propelling Joyce toward the door. 'We'd better join him.'

Until Frank Lucern eventually gave the all clear for them to travel down to Estoril, Garvan found himself with spare time on his hands, and decided to take the opportunity to explore the city. He'd probably never get another opportunity again, so armed with a map from the hotel's reception, he set off to visit the Belem Tower and St. George's Castle, which had so impressed him last night, silhouetted against the darkening sky. Travelling around the bustling city, it was easy to forget the deadly serious nature of their visit to Portugal.

He caught an old tram to negotiate a steep hill, and by the time he navigated his way back to the hotel it was already dark, and the young prostitutes were beginning to gather on the street corners. There wasn't much trade around at this time of night. But, he guessed business would start picking up, when the restaurants and clubs began to empty out.

\*

Over the coming days, Joyce kept herself busy, and was forever flitting off to meet with her Abwehr contacts, or indulging in some serious upmarket shopping in the district of Chiado. Her seemingly endless meetings finally paid off. It seemed Gustav von Bertele, the Baron's Deputy, was in daily contact with Otto Stackler; Berlin was becoming increasingly impatient for Giscard to be tracked down. It was during one of her wine fuelled lunches with the Baron, he had let slip they suspected the British had spirited Giscard out of Lisbon, after he had narrowly escaped falling into German hands.

Spencer still harboured grave concerns about Jean Giscard being holed up at the casino in Estoril. He accepted it was probably the last place the Germans would think of looking for him, but to his mind, he was still in a very vulnerable position. However trustworthy the manager might be, there was always the distinct possibility a member of staff might start sniffing around, get a bit too curious, and blow his cover. At the leading hotels in Lisbon and Estoril, the waiters and concierges were frequently on the payroll of several intelligence services. Spencer was convinced the same applied to the staff working at the casino. For the moment, his hands were tied; that is, until Lucern gave them the green light to head to Estoril, at which point, Spencer would then assume control over the entire mission.

## Chapter 7

Garvan closed his suitcase, and then, double checked the wardrobe and drawers to see if he'd forgotten to pack anything. His wash bag was in the bathroom, and his clothes were already draped over the back of the dressing table chair, ready for an early start in the morning. Frank Lucern had finally given them the green light to travel down to Estoril; for security reasons, it had been decided Spencer should go separately by train from Lisbon's Cais do Sodré Station. It was well known, some members of staff at the Metropole Hotel were on the Abwehr's payroll. Lucern had, therefore, decided to avoid any unnecessary interest in their departure, by having them book out of the hotel at different times. According to Rowlands, the half-hour journey by train followed a picturesque route along the golden beaches of the coastline, and passed through various quaint fishing villages. While Spencer travelled by train, Joyce and Garvan were to be driven down by Rowlands directly to the Plaza Palacio Hotel, where rooms had been pre-booked by MI6 for the three of them.

Garvan needed an early night, and was about to get undressed, when, without warning, Joyce Leader suddenly flung open the interconnecting door between their rooms, with a bottle of champagne clutched in one hand and two flutes in the other. She was dressed in a long black slinky satin nightgown tied at the waist. As she moved across the bedroom toward him, there were flashes of thigh teamed with black suspenders and matching lace underwear.

'I ordered from room service,' she announced, setting the bottle and glasses down on a small occasional table.

*Christ almighty*, Garvan thought to himself, she was on a mission alright, a mission to fulfill their cover story to the letter. He was, after all, meant to be some big wig in the Foreign Office, who'd taken his mistress on a joy ride to Lisbon. Obviously, this wasn't her first drink of the night, he decided. She'd no doubt been propping up the hotel bar, downing cocktails. They were relatively cheap, and Joyce loved her cocktails.

Joyce had always been aware of her powerful attraction to men; right from the beginning of his investigation into the murder of Sarah Davis in 1941, Joyce knew Garvan found her attractive, and had wanted to take her, but he'd been totally professional, and made a point of keeping his distance from her. But, now, it was different; they'd been thrown together by default. Joyce understood his reticence; she was a double agent and tarnished by her past, but tonight, she hoped he might forgive her just enough to forget the confusion and anger he felt toward her as a member of the Abwehr. There was no point going over old ground, trying to explain and to justify how she'd fallen into their hands. How her family had been threatened with arrest by the Gestapo. He'd read her file, and knew all the gory, occasionally embarrassing, details inside out; there was nothing left to hide from him.

Joyce poured the champagne into the flutes, and offered him a glass; he accepted. 'To us,' she said, raising her glass.

He stared at her in an expressionless way, almost giving the impression of disapproval.

'You do realise we'll be damned lucky to smuggle this Frenchman out of Estoril alive,' she said.

Garvan tentatively sipped the champagne. 'I've been around the Service long enough to realise anything Spencer involves me in has more than a degree of risk attached to it.'

Joyce smiled at him. 'In my case, coming here has more than a degree of risk.' She set her glass down, and continued, 'I'm sure you realise my meetings with Baron von Gruber aren't exactly risk-free either.' She looked at him searchingly; he was giving nothing away to her. 'I have to pump the old bugger for information, but it isn't easy, at least not without rousing his suspicions.' She sat down on the edge of the bed, and sipped the champagne. 'Just one slip, one mistake with the Baron or any other of my contacts, and I'll end up signing my own death warrant.' Joyce took a sharp intake of breath. 'Don't you understand? I'm having to pick the lesser of two evil's here!'

His face remained impassive.

'If von Gruber thinks I'm pressing too hard, or starts to believe I'm unreliable, Berlin will close me down.' She drained the glass dry. 'And if they do, the Double Cross team will also close their file on me as well.' She folded her arms, looked at him, waiting for a response.

He knew what it meant for an agent's file to be closed; they were no longer considered active, and as far as British Intelligence was concerned, she was no longer useful to the end game, the invasion of Europe. She'd either spend the rest of the war imprisoned on the Isle of Man, or face a firing squad or the hangman at Wandsworth prison, that was the stark reality.

Garvan recalled reading her security file, and how her family had always moved in the highest echelons of German society, and how her father, Kurt Leader's, well-documented ambivalence to the Third Reich had made him a marked man with the Regime. His daughter's subsequent recruitment to the Abwehr was nothing more than a means to an end to protect her family from the Nazis. Garvan was sympathetic to her plight, and knew her only way to survive had been to conform outwardly, and appear to be a faithful member of the Nazi Party.

Perched on the edge of the bed, she almost looked vulnerable; Garvan felt curious. Joyce didn't normally do vulnerability; it wasn't in her nature. She was usually as hard as nails, and calculating, to boot, nor did spontaneity come quickly to her. Spencer had once told him Joyce could turn on and off the charm like other people turned on and off a tap. He had a point.

Joyce slithered off the bed; she wasn't quite drunk, but she'd had too much to drink. She was in front of him now, and leaned her face close to his. He could feel her breath on his face.

'There's no guarantee either of us will get out of this alive,' she murmured.

He looked into her shrewd, calculating clear eyes; she was certainly on a mission to bed him. A part of him felt deeply flattered by her advances, but the dogged, implacable copper in him wanted to know why she'd turned on the charm now. There'd been plenty of other opportunities, since their arrival in Lisbon, and yet, she'd held back, and had never once come onto him.

'You know, if we're going to convince my German controllers we're lovers, we need to start acting the part, as if we really are.' She smiled gently, and brushed her hand against his face. 'Anyone worth their salt can tell there's a lack of intimacy between us.'

He caught hold of her hands, saying, 'What's this all about, Joyce? Has the Baron, or someone else, said something to you?'

She smiled tightly. 'We're under surveillance, for God's sake; you know that.'

'Of course, I do.'

'Since we arrived at the hotel, every morning, I've made a point of making the bed, just as the maid left it. I didn't want her to start becoming suspicious.' She broke free from his grasp. 'The Baron has made some pointed comments, that we don't exactly appear to be,' she hesitated, 'to be in love.'

Garvan poured her another glass. 'What did you say to him?'

She gave a shrug. 'The usual stuff; *that* you're English.'

'Which means?'

'That your uptight, and keep your feelings under lock and key.'

'How did he take it?'

'What do you think? He laughed a great deal, and made some unflattering comments about the English. The trouble is, I'm not entirely sure if he swallowed it. You're meant to be this Foreign Office high-flyer, who has placed his neck on the line by securing his mistress a seat on the flight to Lisbon. I know what you're going to say; it's been done before so why would he question it.'

'If you were *that* worried about the situation, why didn't you say something before?'

She rolled her eyes. 'What bloody difference would it have made?

Garvan only half bought her story about trying to appease the Baron; he'd been around Scotland Yard long enough to know when someone wasn't telling the whole truth, and as slick and clever as Joyce might think she was, it didn't entirely ring true with him. Although his feelings for her were confused, he needed to retain the upper hand, to keep his distance, and not compromise his position.

'Why not just cut the crap,' he said to her.

Joyce looked offended, and set her glass down on the small table beside the bed. 'I'm sorry. What do you mean?'

'This story about trying to convince von Gruber we're lovers, well, it just doesn't add up, does it?'

Her expression hardened.

He held up his hand. 'Why are you here tonight, why now?' His expression unexpectedly softened, and he smiled at her. 'For Christ's sake, look at you, Jo, dressed to kill in all *that* bloody black satin and lace.'

She suddenly became very self-conscious and instinctively tightened her dressing gown from revealing too much flesh.

'I'm not going to be a notch on your bedpost, darling,' he said to her. 'You're one of my boss' Double Agents.' He lit a cigarette, and took in a lungful of smoke, letting it slowly exhale through his mouth. 'I've gone along with Spencer's plan, and our cover story, and although I'm willing to play the game so far, it's one thing to socialise with criminals or agents, but there's a fine line between that and taking a step too far.' He paused, and took another drag on his cigarette, before saying, 'and sleeping with you, my love, would be more than a step too far.'

Without another word, she drained her glass, and moved back over to the interconnecting door. She briefly glanced back at him, before shutting the door, and returning to her room.

Joyce felt ashamed and embarrassed by his rejection. By her own admission, she'd possibly sunk one too many cocktails at the bar, but even so, until this evening, she'd always been able to exploit men, to bed them, and use them to her own ends.

Right from the start of her recruitment to the Double Cross, Joyce had accepted Spencer was way beyond her reach, and strictly off limits. Not only because of his almost obsessive love for Sarah Davis, but, more importantly, he was utterly ruthless and focussed on his work. Although Garvan gave very little of his real personality away, somewhere along the line, she'd misread his attraction to her, and mistakenly interpreted it as a possible chink in his armour.

Joyce leaned against the interconnecting door, and began to cry. Her thoughts cascaded back to Sarah's murder, and the first time she'd met Garvan when he headed up the investigation into her death. Over the intervening years, Joyce had found herself increasingly attracted to the taciturn Detective. He'd intrigued her, and a part of her had fallen in love with him, but now, she realised there could never be anything between them. The war and circumstance had destroyed her life, and a chance for happiness, and now, Garvan's rejection seemed like the final nail in the coffin.

\*

Garvan overslept, and missed breakfast. By the time he met up with George Rowlands in the foyer of the hotel, Spencer had long since booked out, and caught the train to Estoril. They loaded up the car with their suitcases, and set off along the coastal route toward the Plaza Palacio Hotel. Rowlands turned out to be great company during their drive down to Estoril. Garvan was cramped on the back seat wedged in by Joyce's accumulated extra baggage. George kept them amused with his uncanny impression of Spencer, whose caramel Welsh accent he had down to a tee, which resulted in Joyce doubling up in hysterics. After last night, she seemed a little cool toward him, but it certainly wasn't enough for Rowlands to pick up on.

Despite being cramped for space, Garvan sat back enjoying the view of the picturesque sandy beaches, and the colourful splashes of bougainvillea growing in such abundance along the roadside, they were almost like weeds. The hotel in Estoril was a white-fronted building, which shared a palm-lined park with the nearby casino. The setting was quite outstanding, and Garvan loved it. The hotel rooms, while not overtly opulent, unlike the Metropole, were clean and well-equipped. It was popular with not only displaced members of the aristocracy and European royalty, who were permanent residents at the hotel, but also a tried and trusted haunt of British and Axis spies.

Garvan opened the French windows and stood on the balcony, taking in the immaculately landscaped gardens and the spectacular view of the sea, with its white topped waves rolling remorselessly toward the yellow sandy beach.

Spencer let himself into Garvan's room and stopped dead in his tracks, seeing three large leather trunks scattered across the floor. 'Where the hell did they come from?'

'Where do you think? Joyce spent most of her spare time in Lisbon shopping.'

'I didn't think she had *that* much spare time on her hands. She'll never get permission to get this lot onboard the flight home!'

'She mentioned something about getting it shipped back to England.'

'It'll cost an arm and a leg to shift this bloody lot; that's for sure.'

He joined Garvan on the balcony, and admired the scenery. 'What do you think?' he said.

'It'll do.'

'Where's Jo?'

'In the bathroom, next door; she's been in there ages, so Christ knows what she's up to.'

'We've managed to pull a few strings to get you the adjoining suites. His Majesty's Government doesn't normally cough up for the Plaza Palacio; it's even more expensive than the Metropole.' Spencer rested his arms on the balcony. 'I just thought, after last night, things might be a bit tricky between you two, having to share the same room.'

Garvan turned to face him. 'She told you...told you what happened?'

'Over breakfast,' Hall said quietly. 'You look surprised.'

He examined his face. 'A little,' Garvan admitted.

'Aren't you forgetting I'm her Desk Officer? However opinionated and bloody-minded Jo is at times, she knows better than to keep anything from *me*, especially coming onto you like that.' He reached into his jacket pocket, and produced a pack of cigarettes. 'You have to understand, Jo has always got a bit carried away with herself.' He smiled, drawing heavily on the cigarette. 'I know you've been thrown together, but I guess she probably just misread the situation.'

'But, why come to me last night?'

'I got the impression she was a bit tipsy. To be honest with you, I reckon she just wanted to try her luck to see what happened. If I were you, I really wouldn't read too much into it.' He sat on the ledge of the balcony, with his back against the shoreline. 'Besides, she won't be trying it on again anytime soon. I've had a word with her. If anything, I think she's probably feeling a tad embarrassed today.'

'Well, she's certainly been a bit standoffish with me.'

'She'll get over it,' Hall snorted, wandering back into the room; Garvan followed him. 'The reason I popped in was to let you know George Rowlands has arranged a meeting with Jean Giscard this evening.'

'Is Joyce coming along with us?

Spencer shook his head. 'No, not yet. I need to see how the land lies first, before we start getting her involved. I've arranged for us to meet up with George at the hotel bar at seven-thirty. We'll have a quick drink, and then, take a walk through the gardens to the casino. Is that okay by you?'

'Yes, of course. I'll see you downstairs,' Garvan said, closing the door on him.

## Chapter 8

George Rowlands drained his gin and tonic at the hotel bar, checked his watch, and said, 'Right, gentlemen, are you ready to meet the little darling?'

'Let's just get it over and done with,' Spencer said.

'The trouble is,' George continued seamlessly, 'Giscard has one fatal flaw.'

'What's that?' Garvan queried.

'The little shit thinks he's perfect. I don't mind admitting I'll be glad to see the bloody back of him.'

The evening was still warm, but there was a gentle breeze blowing in from the coast. It was a welcome change from the blistering heat of the day. As they walked through the spacious landscaped gardens, the air echoed with the continuous chirping chorus of crickets. George explained to them the serious gamblers didn't start getting into their stride until later in the evening. Rowlands unlocked a small, unobtrusive door at the rear of the casino, and led the way up a narrow stone staircase to the first floor. Waiting to greet them was the manager, Rafael Delgado. He was in his mid-forties, and cut a rather short, rotund figure, with thinning dark hair. He was immaculately dressed in a black evening suit, white shirt, and bow tie. He'd nipped up from the gaming tables to meet them.

Rowlands made the introductions, using the names they'd adopted for their cover story, Garvan as Steven Howe and Spencer as David Choules. Delgado had been working with British Intelligence long enough to realise they certainly weren't their real names; nothing was ever quite what it seemed.

'How is the boy wonder today?' George asked.

Rafael threw his arms out in a gesture of despair. 'Difficult. He wanted to take himself off for a walk this morning around the gardens. He reckons he'll go mad, if he's cooped up here much longer. I tried explaining it wasn't safe for either of them to risk leaving the flat, as they might be recognised by the Gestapo, but he still was having none of it.'

Rowlands raised his hand in agreement, and said waspishly, 'I know. There's no telling the little prick anything, is there?'

Delgado was in his stride by now, and explained how Claudine and Jean appeared to do nothing but argue all the time. 'I'm sure that's why he's so desperate to get out of the flat.' He pulled a face. 'But, then again, they're both as bad as one another, screaming and shouting all the time. I wouldn't mind, but they're not even married!'

'It doesn't bode well for the future, then, does it?' George sympathised.

'Are you certain they've never left the flat?' Garvan asked Delgado.

'Yes, I am. We keep them firmly under lock and key.'

'Do they prepare their own food?'

'Yes, Mr. Rowlands' people supply everything they need.'

'And none of your staff at the casino know they're living here. *Is that right*?'

'As sure as I can be,' he answered truthfully. 'They don't have access to this corridor. I have one set of keys,' he said, patting his jacket pocket, 'and Mr. Rowlands has the spares. There are only two entrances, an internal one from the casino and the private one at the rear. The door to the flat itself is also kept locked at all times.'

'It's worked out, so far,' Rowlands interrupted. 'As you know, things were getting too close for comfort in Lisbon. Being here has at least allowed us some breathing space. Garvan appeared relatively satisfied with his answer, or so Rowlands believed.

Delgado led the way along the corridor, explaining as he lived in a nearby apartment, overlooking the sea, he'd rarely found a need to make use of the flat. Although, he understood, his predecessor had lived there on an almost permanent basis. In the ordinary run of events, looking after Giscard and his girlfriend wouldn't have posed too many problems, but Jean's continual arrogance and rudeness were slowly wearing him down. He didn't hold back and made it quite clear; he wanted both of them out of the casino, as soon as possible.

Rafael unlocked the door to the flat, which opened directly onto the living room. Inside, Giscard was slouched in an armchair, with his legs slung over the side, and his arms folded tightly. The air was thick with the strong and distinctive aroma of a French cigarette. The Gauloises was perched casually in the corner of his mouth. He had a shot of blond hair and piercing blue eyes. His gaze set upon them, without a trace of either emotion or acknowledgment. Standing in front of the window was his pregnant girlfriend, Claudine. *She was probably not much older than twenty*, Garvan thought. She was slightly built, and constantly played with her hair, nervously twisting and untwisting a single strand around her finger.

Even before he'd opened his mouth, Spencer had decided to take an instant dislike to the Frenchman. Whether it was just his cold dead-eyed stare, or his arrogant indifference toward Delgado, who was not only risking his job but also his life by agreeing to hide him at the casino, it seemed not to matter to him at all.

'These gentlemen,' Rowlands told him, gesturing to Hall and Garvan, 'will be responsible for getting you safely back to London.'

Giscard slowly removed the Gauloises from his mouth. He spoke in his heavily accented but passable English. 'And how, Monsieur Rowlands, do they propose to do that?'

'Why don't you ask them yourself?' Rowlands allowed the merest hint of a smile to cross his face; for the first time since Giscard's arrival in Portugal, he was almost beginning to enjoy himself. Spencer's expression had hardened; as things stood, the signs weren't looking too promising for the Frenchman.

Spencer took a step closer toward Giscard. Garvan had seen that same look on his face once before, the last time being when he'd shot Sarah's murderer dead with a rapid double tap to the chest.

'When, and if, you need to know anything,' he said, in a measured tone, 'you'll be kept informed. In the meantime, all you need to do is stay put, and keep your mouth shut!'

Giscard held his gaze just long enough to know he'd more than met his match. He took a drag on the Gauloises. 'I don't even know your names,' he drawled.

'It's safer you don't!'

'You have to understand, Claudine and I have been trapped in this *place* for over three weeks now!'

'You'll be here for as long as it takes.'

Spencer examined his face, and guessed behind the apparent arrogance and brashness hid a very troubled, complex individual. They'd certainly drawn the short straw on this one; it was difficult enough smuggling individuals out of Portugal, at the best of times, but with someone who was potentially unstable, they were more than going to have their work cut out. He started to wonder if it might not simply be easier just to extricate the Peenemunde blueprint from him, and to hell with the consequences, but then again, he'd have some serious explaining to do back in London.

'A lot of people from the Resistance and the SOE,' he said to him. 'Have put their lives on the line to get you out of Germany, and it hasn't stopped there, has it? Rafael Delgado is taking one hell of a risk allowing you to stay here in his flat.' He looked through him. 'I think you're too full of bloody self-pity to understand and appreciate the risks others have taken to save your neck.'

Giscard looked genuinely affronted.

'British Intelligence want you to be wrapped up in cotton wool, and safely delivered into their hands. But, make no mistake, Monsieur, if you endanger a single member of my team, I'll not hesitate to take you out. At the end of the day, it's the blueprint our scientists need, and not you.' He looked him up and down. 'Let's face it; as far as they're concerned you're just the icing on the cake.'

Giscard continued, self-importantly, 'You do realise, the longer I'm kicking my heels around here, the less likely the Allies will be able to stop the Germans from completing their work at Peenemunde.'

'I think you're missing the point!'

Jean narrowed his eyes questioningly.

'You have to remember the intelligence about the rocket programme comes from several sources. There are other scientists and technicians supplying us with information. What I'm trying to say is, no-one is indispensable, not *even* you Monsieur!'

Giscard looked visibly shaken. Since his escape from Germany, he'd been treated with kid gloves, so why was this British agent, the man supposedly charged with his safe conduct to England, threatening to kill him, if he stepped out of line. There'd been no anger or passion in his delivery, just an overwhelming feeling he wouldn't hesitate to carry out the threat. Giscard had been so wrapped up in his infallibility and importance as a scientist, he never once believed anyone would question his worth. He wondered how many others were feeding information to London, but, however many there were, Giscard started to suspect his position was no longer quite as assured as he'd first imagined. Unusually, he bit his tongue, and held back; there was no point in making a difficult situation even worse than it was.

Rafael Delgado was looking distinctly uncomfortable, and had surreptitiously started to edge his way back toward the door. Spencer informed Giscard he'd return to the casino, once London had given permission for him to be moved to Portela Airport. But, until then, he'd have to remain in the flat. Giscard realised all too well; it wasn't up for discussion.

The meeting was over. Delgado locked the door of the flat, and silently followed them back along the corridor. During his time living and working in Estoril, he'd met many Allied and Axis agents before, but Spencer was a different beast altogether to the others; he frightened the life out of him. So, God knows how Giscard was feeling. Delgado shook hands with them, before making his excuses, and hurrying off downstairs to the casino.

'Well, that put him back in his box, didn't it?' Rowlands said to no-one in particular. It was such a pity his boss, Frank Lucern, hadn't been there to witness Spencer in action. His face would have been a picture of nervous anxiety, fearing his precious cargo was apparently in more danger of being liquidated by Spencer, than the Gestapo.

Outside the casino, Rowlands fell in beside Garvan, as Spencer walked slightly ahead of them through the gardens back toward the Plaza Palacio.

'He was in good form tonight,' he said, nudging Garvan.

Garvan smiled tightly but didn't answer him.

'It was short and sweet, but then again, Spence has never been keen on polite conversation. It's not exactly his metier.'

'I've noticed.'

Back at the hotel bar, the waiter handed out drinks on the moonlit terrace. There was a slight chill in the air, as the surrounding palm trees rustled in the cooling breeze.

Rowlands picked out a couple of cigarettes from his case, and handed them around to Spencer and Garvan before taking another. 'How are you planning to get Giscard to the airport?'

'I need to discuss it with London first,' Spencer said.

'You mean, with Colonel Robertson?'

He nodded.

Rowlands thoughtfully fingered the heavy gold watch on his wrist. 'If you like I'll speak with Frank Lucern tomorrow morning, and get you a secure line.'

Garvan swirled his scotch on the rocks, admiring the heavy cut glass tumbler. 'In the meantime,' he suggested, 'I think one of us should keep in close contact with Giscard.'

Spencer's expression suddenly relaxed. 'That's down to you, then.'

'Why has it got to me?'

'I think George might have had a point.'

'What you do you mean?'

'I think I'll probably end up killing the bugger.'

Rowlands laughed. 'You're no bloody diplomat, that's for sure!'

'If they'd wanted some smooth-talking bastard for this caper, they'd have chosen you, George, and not me.'

'My dear boy, thank you.'

Garvan, resigning himself to the fact he'd drawn the short straw, said, 'I'll need a set of keys to the flat.'

'Don't worry I'll drop a set by in the morning.'

'The trouble is, I can't help thinking.' Garvan said, 'his arrogance is masking the fact, he's not only running scared, but his nerves are shot to pieces. The Gestapo are hard on his heels, and he's pinning all his hopes on us, somehow, getting him and Claudine to Bristol.'

'But, if he doesn't calm down in between times, he'll end up jeopardising the entire mission,' Spencer shot at him.

'I'm well aware of that, but even before we can start thinking about getting him on board the Dakota, I'll need to gain his trust.'

'That'll be a tall order,' Rowlands snorted into his drink.

'I think you forget, George, Garvie here, was, I mean is, a first-rate copper. That's why Tar wanted him in the first place.'

Garvan raised his glass in salute. 'I still can't quite fathom out how we're going to get him to the airport in one piece.'

'I have an idea I want to run past Robertson tomorrow,' Spencer explained.

Rowlands tapped the table with his lighter. 'The problem is, we can't simply plonk them on the backseat of a car, and drive them to Lisbon; it'd be far too risky. The other suggestion was we used the train, but that was vetoed out of hand. It's too public; they'd be spotted a mile off.'

'How did you manage to get him out of Lisbon?' Garvan enquired.

'We chucked him into an ambulance.' Seeing the expression on his face, Rowlands chuckled. 'Simple, isn't it? Who questions an ambulance moving from A to B, no-one, that's the beauty of it.'

'Why not use another one to get him to Portela Airport?'

'We thought about it,' Rowlands said, draining his glass.

'It wouldn't work,' Spencer told him.

'Why wouldn't it work?'

'At some point, he'd have to get out of the ambulance, through passport control, and then, get himself on the plane. Believe me, he'd be long dead, before he even reached the steps.'

'Then, I don't quite see how we're going to do it.' Garvan said.

'The devil's in the detail,' Spencer smiled, finishing his gin and tonic.

Rowlands ordered another round of drinks; it was going to be a long night.

## Chapter 9

Garvan had a sore head. They hadn't finished drinking on the hotel's terrace until the early hours of the morning. His tongue felt like dry leather, and his head was pounding. He shaved, had a wash, and made his way down to breakfast. George Rowlands was already there, bright and breezy, and apparently without suffering any ill effects from the night before. Spencer hadn't yet surfaced.

'My dear boy, you don't look well.'

'That obvious, is it?'

Rowlands poured Garvan a cup of black coffee. 'Take this,' he said, offering him a cup. 'It'll help.'

'Thank you.'

He handed him a set of keys to Giscard's flat at the casino. 'You'll want these.'

Garvan placed them in his jacket pocket.

'Spencer and I have a meeting with Frank Lucern this afternoon,' Rowlands said, tucking into a plate of scrambled eggs.

Garvan looked at him quizzically. 'Is that to arrange a secure line to London?'

Rowlands nodded. 'To be honest with you, I haven't the faintest idea what Spencer's up to,' he confessed. 'I'm not sure he particularly needs a secure line.'

'I'm sorry, why not?'

'I think you'll find he's probably already in direct contact with your London office.'

'But, how can he be?'

'I presume by Morse Code.' He wiped his mouth with a serviette. 'I don't know about you, but I always end up finding myself clinging to his shirt tails and hoping for the best.'

Garvan smiled an enigmatic smile. 'I know what you mean; Spencer talks the talk. Perhaps, in another life, he'd have made a good salesman.'

Rowlands leaned back his chair tickled pink at the idea. 'Could you seriously imagine Spencer as a jobbing salesman; you'd be too ruddy scared not to buy anything from him.'

'True,' he conceded. 'The trouble is, whenever he starts discussing some hair-brained scheme or other, he always makes it sound so plausible, like coming here to Lisbon. It's only later you begin to question what the hell you're doing.' Garvan took a sip of his coffee, before pushing the cup away; it was far too bitter for his liking. 'I still can't see how he's going to get Giscard to the airport.'

Rowlands was on the point of responding, when he noticed Joyce Leader snaking her way through the dining room toward their table. She flashed a smile, and joined them.

'Where's Spence?' she asked.

'We had a late night,' Garvan told her. 'I guess he might still be in bed.'

A flicker of irritation crossed her face. A waiter appeared at the table; she declined breakfast, but ordered a pot of Earl Grey.

'We have a problem,' she announced.

'What kind of problem?' Rowlands queried.

'As I was coming out of the lift guess who I saw standing at the reception desk?'

'Don't tease us, darling, who was it?' Rowlands smiled.

'Baron von Gruber.'

'Is he staying here?' Garvan asked her.

'Yes, but he didn't say for how long.' She paused, as the waiter returned with the Earl Grey. She thanked him. 'But, von Gruber isn't the main problem.'

'Well, my love, that's a matter of opinion,' Rowlands snorted condescendingly.

Joyce stared at him, her gaze penetrating. 'He introduced me to a colleague,' she responded coldly, 'to Otto Stackler.'

She had the satisfaction of seeing the condescension wiped off Rowlands' face.

'Christ almighty!' Garvan cut in. 'Do you think they've got wind Giscard's holed up at the casino?'

She savoured the distinctive aroma of the Earl Grey, before taking a sip. 'I haven't a clue,' she admitted, setting the cup down on its saucer. 'But, someone needs to let Spencer know what's going on.'

'Do you know if Stackler's staying here at the Plaza?'

'I got that distinct impression.'

'It could be all or nothing,' Rowlands surmised. 'A coincidence. Maybe they're just up here for the weekend; it happens all the time.'

Joyce calmly returned his gaze; her nostrils flared, as if reinforcing her derision. 'Spence doesn't believe in coincidences,' she responded witheringly.

'I'm sure he doesn't,' Rowlands replied flatly.

Garvan cut in. 'I take it you both know, he met Stackler in Berlin at a rally for Hitler's fiftieth birthday.'

'Yes, yes, I did know,' Rowlands said thoughtfully.

'You'll have to let Lucern know.'

Rowlands excused himself leaving his breakfast half eaten, as he hurriedly pushed his chair back from the table, he said. 'I take it you'll let Spencer know about Otto?'

Garvan nodded. 'Yes, of course.'

Rowlands left them alone.

Joyce held Garvan's gaze, and waited for a reaction. When none was forthcoming, she suggested, 'I think I should arrange another meeting with von Gruber.'

Somewhat reluctantly, he was forced to agree with her, but was already fully aware she was walking a dangerous tightrope. One slip, or misplaced word, and she'd not only endanger her own life, but the entire mission. Baron von Gruber was a deceptively bluff character, and was almost a caricature of an old-school German aristocrat, but beneath the bluster and the bonhomie, lay a shrewd, brutally efficient Abwehr operator. He was one of their most effective spymasters, and had been personally chosen by the *Führer* to head their pivotal counter-intelligence operation in Lisbon.

Garvan left Joyce by herself to finish the Earl Grey, and made his way back upstairs to Spencer's Hotel room. He knocked on the door.

'Who is it?' Spencer said; he sounded croaky.

'Luke.'

'It's unlocked; let yourself in.'

As he opened the door, Hall padded barefoot across the room in his dressing gown, and slouched down in the chair in front of the dressing table.

'You look awful.'

Spencer smirked. 'What time did we get to bed?'

'God knows.' Garvan perched himself on the edge of the bed. 'I've just seen George Rowlands at breakfast.'

'How is he?'

'He looks a bloody sight better than we do.'

'He gets a lot more practice.' Spencer lit himself a cigarette, and shot Garvan a quizzical look. 'Is there a problem?'

'When Joyce was coming downstairs to breakfast, she bumped into von Gruber and Stackler in the Hotel lobby.'

'Are they staying here?'

'She believes so. Do you think they might have got wind of Giscard's whereabouts?'

'That's anyone's guess,' Spencer said, taking a deep drag on his cigarette. 'But, there's no point jumping to conclusions.' He rummaged on the dressing table, searching for an ashtray; he couldn't find one so used the waste bin instead. 'What does Jo want to do?'

'Arrange another meeting with the Baron.'

'She's right; we haven't anything else to go on, at the moment. For the time being, we just have to sit tight, and carry on as usual.'

'But, she's taking one hell of a risk,' Garvan ventured.

Spencer pulled a face. 'Jo knows the risks. She's got her head screwed on, and knows exactly what she's getting herself into.' He made another half-hearted attempt to look for the ashtray. 'Besides we don't have a choice.'

'What if you bump into Stackler?'

'We'll have to cross that bridge when we come to it.'

\*

Joyce Leader was dressed to kill in a slinky pale blue silk dress, as she strode confidently into the popular Santa Eulália beachside café. It was renowned for its breath-taking views overlooking the sweeping sandy coastline. Gruber and Stackler were already downing the local beer with enthusiasm. Judging by the number of empty glasses stacked up on the table, she guessed they'd probably been there for quite some time.

As she approached their table, Joyce steeled herself, and said with a broad smile, 'Good morning, gentlemen.'

The Baron raised his hand in greeting. 'You look particularly lovely this morning, my dear,' he said appreciatively.

'Thank you.'

'What would you like to drink?' he asked expansively.

'A gin and tonic, if I may,' she said sitting down.

He snapped his fingers at the waiter and ordered a round of drinks in his stilted Portuguese. Stackler was smiling at her. She didn't respond, and coolly averted her eyes. There was something about him, which had started to make her feel distinctly uncomfortable.

After Stackler's arrival in Portugal had been confirmed by MI6, Spencer had decided to pass Joyce a dossier about him, while they were still staying at the Metropole Hotel. Having read the file, Joyce was under few, if any, illusions about what she was up against.

There were the atrocities in Poland, and then, later in 1941, Otto had found himself posted to Prague, and obeying orders from Reinhard Heydrich, the Deputy Reich-Protector, to round up the Jewish population, and any other miscreants the regime decided were undesirable. There were killings aplenty, and by all accounts, Otto appeared entirely immune to the remorseless bestiality of the *Einsatzgruppen*. Even amongst their own hardened ranks, Stackler had stood out for his apparent willingness to play the executioner, and to watch people dig their own graves, before shooting them on the spot. He was always the first to volunteer his services. To Otto's mind, he was merely doing his duty, but the intelligence reports suggest his blind obedience was far more complex than that. During his time in Prague, it was noted, he'd rapidly developed an almost pathological enjoyment for torturing and killing his victims.

The dossier hadn't only contained reports about his apparent lust for killing but had also included details about his frequent visits to brothels, and his overtly sadomasochistic tendencies. She guessed it was all of a piece, really, the atrocities, the torture, and the rapes committed in the name of the *Einsatzgruppen* and the Führer. In any other time or place, he'd almost certainly have been certified as criminally insane.

After Reinhard Heydrich was shot and killed by a British-trained team of Czech and Slovak soldiers, Stackler had found himself unexpectedly recalled to Berlin, being sent later that same year to the Russian Front. He served under General Stahlecker, the commanding officer of *Einsatzgruppen* A, which was deemed to be the most notorious of the four "death squads." It was during this same period Stackler was awarded the Knight's Cross, with Swords, "for prodigious valour on the Russian front." By now, his reputation had reached the ears of Himmler. The *Reichsführer* was apparently deeply impressed by his unstinting loyalty to the Reich, and his ruthless pursuit of the regime's ethnic cleansing. Before Heydrich's assassination, he had written to Berlin, commending Stackler as being worthy of note for future promotion in the *Einsatzgruppen.*

Stackler, who was rising rapidly through the ranks, was now socialising with the Nazi elite, and his contacts were second to none. Watching him enjoying the warm afternoon sunshine, with a straw hat perched jauntily on his head, no-one would have given this cold-blooded mass murderer and torturer a second glance. He seemed just like anyone else, enjoying the beautiful scenery.

Joyce placed a cigarette in her sleek ebony holder, and said casually to von Gruber, 'When we met for dinner, you never mentioned you were coming down to Estoril.'

'No,' he conceded, 'it was a spur of the moment thing. I just happened to mention to Otto how lovely Estoril is at this time of year, and here we are.'

Stackler proffered his lighter to her; she thanked him stiffly, and lit her cigarette. 'I thought I'd like to spend some time away from Lisbon,' Stackler explained. 'It's exquisite here, *Fräulein,* and even more so, since I met you at the hotel.'

Von Gruber smirked at his companion's rather clumsy attempt to compliment her, and knew only too well; it would be a cold day in hell before she found him attractive. The trouble was, the man hadn't managed to pick up on the signals. But, then again, he wasn't renowned for his ability to empathise with anyone, least of all women. The glacial expression in her eyes remained impenetrable. She decided the best course of action was to ignore him. A potential awkward silence between them was avoided, as the waiter arrived at the table with their drinks.

Joyce coolly savoured the taste of her gin and tonic, before saying, 'How long are you planning on staying in Estoril?'

'A week, perhaps,' Stackler said. 'I haven't decided yet.' He raised his glass clinking it against the Baron's. '*Prost*,' he said jovially, toasting his somewhat reluctant colleague. 'We were thinking about going to the casino this evening.'

'Yes, so we were,' von Gruber chirped. 'We thought about having a bite to eat first, maybe at the Cascais Restaurant; they're meant to serve the most exquisite fish dishes there. Have you been?'

'No, I haven't.' Joyce didn't allow her expression to falter; in fact, she carried it off rather well. 'So, hopefully, I might see you at the casino then,' she said casually.

'By the time we've had dinner, we'll probably be there about nine.' Gruber nudged Otto and chuckled. 'Joyce loves the tables, but sadly, her pockets are far deeper than ours are ever likely to be!'

'Like father, like daughter,' Stackler responded coldly.

She cast him an unflinching, penetrating smile. 'Do you know my father?' she asked, drawing slowly on the cigarette holder.

'I know of him.'

Joyce casually retrieved a pair of sunglasses from her handbag.

'Is he still living in Austria?' Stackler pursued.

She slowly pushed the sunglasses onto the bridge of her nose. 'Yes, he is, as well you know.'

It was common knowledge Kurt Leader had never been won over by Hitler and his henchmen's rhetoric, and had initially refused to join the Nazi Party. As a result, of his very public stance, the family had found themselves plagued by increasingly menacing threats, and visits from local party members to test their loyalty to the *Führer*.

When her sister, Elisabeth, married a *Wehrmacht* officer, it had the effect of temporarily helping to ease the pressure, but it wasn't to last. Soon afterward, the threats of arrest and imprisonment continued unabated, until Kurt felt compelled to sign on the dotted line, and join the Nazi Party. But, even then, they didn't entirely go away. As far as Berlin was concerned, his loyalty was still an unknown quantity. The family was still very much out on a limb, and vulnerable to accusations of being enemies of the Third Reich.

It was during this period of upheaval and uncertainty in her life the Abwehr approached Joyce. At the outbreak of war, she had decided to remain in France, in a somewhat futile attempt to distance herself from the problems facing her family back in Austria. Unfortunately, after the Nazi occupation of France, being highly intelligent, attractive, and multi-lingual, she'd found herself a prime target for the German Intelligence Service. After much soul searching, she had accepted their offer, for no other reason than to help save her family from the brutality of Hitler's National Socialist Party. In some sections of the Abwehr, her recruitment had raised eyebrows, and many within the Reich's intelligence community questioned the decision, but as Admiral Canaris, in his role as Chief of the Abwehr had personally endorsed the decision to recruit her, the initial rumblings about her suitability were soon silenced.

Whatever doubts there were initially about her integrity and willingness to serve the Reich, from Berlin's point of view, they had long since been forgotten. Joyce had continually delivered valuable intelligence, and in turn, her personal grudges and antagonism toward the Reich had also contributed to her becoming one of Britain's most valued double agents.

'Your father's loyalty to the Party, *Fräulein*,' Stackler continued, 'has always been the subject of much speculation.'

'Speculation does not equate to proof.'

'I believe he's spirited much of the family wealth abroad, has he not?'

'My father has business interests in many parts of the world.'

'Including America?'

She pursed her lips together, and blew out a cloud of smoke in Stackler's direction. 'Since the outbreak of the war, his assets have been frozen.'

'And Switzerland?'

'What about Switzerland?'

'I understand he has several secret bank accounts stowed away in Zurich and Berne?'

Joyce shot him a wry smile. 'He's certainly not alone, then, is he?

'I'm sorry, what do you mean *Fräulein*?

'Why not try asking some of your Party colleagues where they're siphoning off *their* ill-gotten loot!'

His expression hardened.

'It's an open secret, isn't it?' she said beguilingly.

'I'm sorry, *Fräulein* Leader, you've completely lost me.'

'How many millions do you believe they've stashed away in their numbered Swiss bank accounts?'

'I think you had better be very careful what you say,' he said menacingly.

Von Gruber didn't want things to start getting out of hand between them, and decided to put an end to their bickering. He certainly didn't want Otto to antagonise Joyce any more than he already had. It seemed to him as if Stackler was deliberately spoiling for a fight. Gruber also knew only too well Joyce certainly wouldn't have shied away from locking horns with him

Gruber rested his arms wearily on the table. Hurriedly changing the subject, he said to Joyce, 'I forgot to mention to you the other day; I've heard from Bernard Drescher.'

Joyce flicked her eyes toward him; she hadn't been listening. 'I'm sorry, Ernst,' she apologised. 'What did you say?'

He repeated himself. Drescher was her current German controller in Berlin; she expressed her interest.

'George Rowlands,' he continued, 'is the name he's interested in.'

Joyce took a sip of her gin and tonic and looked at him questioningly. 'Did he say why?'

'I believe he drove you and Steven Howe to Estoril.'

She held the ebony cigarette holder lightly between her fingers. She smiled inwardly to herself; at least, they still seemed to be buying Garvan's cover story. Always the accomplished actress, she held von Gruber's gaze steadily, and asked airily, 'Is Rowlands important?'

'He's the Deputy Head of the MI6 Station in Lisbon.'

'Who runs the show there?'

'A man called Frank Lucern.'

She smiled.

'You've heard of him, of course,'

'You mean Rowlands?'

'Yes.'

'We've met socially, of course, 'she said off handily. 'Steven's work at the Foreign Office brings him into contact with all sorts of interesting people; that's why he's so useful to us.' She shot Stackler a penetrating look; for some reason, he avoided her gaze.

'Has Steven met Rowlands before?' von Gruber pressed her.

'I'm not sure.' Joyce stubbed out her cigarette. 'I guess Lucern might have asked him to show us the sites here in Estoril, but it's only a guess. But, I'll say this for him, Rowlands is rather good company.'

'So I've heard.' von Gruber smirked at her.

She didn't know what he meant, and discarded the cigarette into the ashtray, returning the holder to her handbag.

'Drescher wants you to find out more information about someone else.'

'Who might that be?'

'David Choules,' Gruber continued.

Joyce closed the bag, hoping they didn't suspect anything was amiss. 'What about him?'

'It's just we haven't come across him before now; he's a new face, and name, to Portugal.'

She gave an indifferent shrug. 'I'm not surprised.'

'Why?'

'Well, the last British Wolfram expert, a mining engineer, I believe, he went down on the same plane as that Hollywood actor.'

'Lesley Howard?' Stackler asked.

'Yes,' Joyce said, and finished off her drink. 'But, there's not much more I can add, other than we met Choules on the plane coming over to Lisbon.' She appeared to give the matter some thought. 'I know Steven hadn't met him before the trip. But, since we arrived, they have attended meetings together at the British Embassy.' Joyce paused, before pointing her index figure at the Baron. 'I thought I'd already told you that.'

He threw up his hands in an expansive gesture. 'Maybe you have. I must be getting forgetful in my old age.' Whether he was lying, or not, was difficult to tell. 'But, you've met him since then, haven't you?'

'Yes, we've had dinner several times, and cocktails here and in Lisbon,' she continued glibly. 'But, you know how it is; when they're together, they don't tend to talk shop in front of me.'

It was a loaded question; it was obvious they had been placed under surveillance, but she wouldn't have expected anything else.

'You'll keep us informed of course if you come up with something,' Gruber went on.

'Have I ever let you down?'

'No,' he said. 'No, you haven't.'

Stackler continued to sit in stony silence across the table from her, nursing his drink; he looked a little flushed from one too many beers. The only thing which unnerved Joyce was the completely indescribable dead expression in his eyes. They were unblinking; it simply wasn't normal, and made her skin crawl.

During an appropriate lull in the conservation, she decided to make her excuses, and leave. 'I'll be in touch,' she smiled disarmingly at the Baron.

With an undisguised sigh of relief, Joyce left them sitting at the café. As she glanced back over her shoulder, there was a faint look of amusement on her face. Von Gruber's expression said it all; there was no disguising the fact he hated chaperoning Stackler. There was certainly no love lost between the Abwehr and Himmler's SS. Just as the Reich looked down upon the Jews, she knew the Baron and his boss, Admiral Canaris, viewed the likes of Stackler with equal disdain. In private, they called him *der Bauer* or the peasant. But, in order to survive, Gruber had learned to dance to their tune, and pay lip service to Berlin, and more importantly, to *Reichsführer* Himmler.

She recalled the Baron describing his one and only meeting with Himmler, at Hitler's picturesque retreat at Berchtesgaden in the Bavarian Alps. His description had been quite chilling; the grey-blue eyes behind the glittering Prince-nez glasses were watchful and calculating, and beneath the neatly trimmed moustache lurked an almost mocking smile, which had played on his mouth throughout their conversation. Von Gruber openly confessed it was an experience he had found intimidating, and one, he had no wish to repeat; at least, not again in a hurry.

In the grand scheme of things, she guessed, right now, given the choice of meeting the *Reichsführer* again or babysitting his unhinged protégé, he'd probably have taken his chances with Heinrich Himmler.

*Chapter 10*

Giscard was still in his dressing gown when Garvan let himself into the flat, even though he had washed and shaved. In spite of George Rowlands having pre-warned Giscard of his visit, there was still a flicker of annoyance on the Frenchman's face as he opened the door. His girlfriend, Claudine, was more amenable, and offered to make him a cup of coffee. Garvan accepted. Giscard grumpily stuffed a Gauloises between his lips, snapped open his lighter, and lit it.

Rowlands mentioned the first time he'd met him; Jean had spent the entire meal drinking vodka and chain smoking. There'd been two courses, and Giscard had barely touched his plate throughout. On the other hand, Claudine had struck him as something of a free spirit, who'd possibly found herself trapped in the relationship with her intellectually morose partner.

"You'd never have put them together, would you?" Rowlands had said to him. "They're like chalk and cheese, dear boy, so God only knows what they see in one another. It's a classic case," Rowlands had concluded. "He can't live with her, and can't live without her."

Giscard drew heavily on his Gauloises. 'Is there any news from London?'

'Not yet I'm afraid.'

He could barely constrain his irritation. 'Why bother to come here, then?'

Garvan coolly held his gaze, but didn't respond. Claudine brought in the coffee, and as he sat down beside her at a small circular dining table, he suddenly became aware of a pile of books stacked up behind the door. 'Are they yours?' he asked Giscard.

'Yes, a gift from Monsieur Rowlands,' Giscard said. 'When I first arrived in Lisbon I made a list of the books I wanted to read.'

By now, Giscard had started to pace the room like a caged animal, hands thrust deep into the pockets of his dressing gown. Garvan decided it might be better to focus his attention initially on Claudine for a while. As they chatted, Giscard would occasionally pause and listen in on their conversation.

'This can't have been easy for you,' Garvan said to her.

She breathed deeply and clasped a coffee cup tightly between her hands. 'I'll be honest with you, the last few months have been a complete nightmare for both of us.'

'I can well imagine it has been,' he said gently.

As her eyes started to well up with tears, she briefly placed her hand over Garvan's. 'I know we haven't been here too long,' she sobbed, 'but not being able to get out of the flat isn't easy.' Through her tears, she glanced toward the window. 'Especially when you can see how lovely it is out there. I just want to be able to walk through the gardens and breathe some fresh air.'

Garvan was outwardly sympathetic, and looked toward Giscard, who was four square on listening to what his girlfriend was saying, as she sobbed her heart out to a complete stranger. But, he seemed either unwilling or unable to reach out to her. His face remained devoid of expression. Garvan couldn't quite work out their relationship, but of one thing he was certain. Rowlands had been right all along; they were like chalk and cheese. He knew Claudine had been smuggled out of Peenemunde, before the Germans had realised Giscard had defected with the help of the SOE. They'd passed her down the line using one of their many well-tried escape routes over the Pyrenees. Once she'd safely arrived in Portugal, Rowlands' team had taken over responsibility for her care.

'It must have been very frightening, at times,' Garvan said, stirring his coffee.

Brushing away her tears, Claudine agreed with him. 'Yes, it was, but at least, I knew Jean was already safe.' She looked at Garvan searchingly; he seemed very different from his colleague, the one who'd threatened to kill Jean, if he stepped out of line.

'Have you known each other long?'

'Long enough.' She smiled.

'Did you two meet at university?' he asked.

She threw back her head and giggled. 'Lord no, we met at a café in Paris; I was with some friends at the time. Jean was by himself, and I,' Claudine hesitated and smiled almost sheepishly at her boyfriend. 'I guess, I thought he looked rather lonely sitting all by himself, with his head in a book. To be honest with you, he seemed rather annoyed with us.' She gave a shrug. 'We were probably making too much noise.' She glanced nervously toward Giscard, almost as if for reassurance she hadn't perhaps, spoken out of line. Judging by his expression, he was none too pleased with her, and resumed pacing about the room.

'It doesn't sound like a promising start.' Garvan ventured.

'Not really,' Claudine confessed. It ran through her mind; she rather liked this British Agent.

'What happened?'

'I just sat down beside him, and started talking.' As Claudine recalled their first meeting, Jean's face began to colour in embarrassment at her artless candour.

He was essentially an introverted character, and disliked Claudine's apparent willingness to discuss their relationship in detail with strangers, especially with members of British Intelligence. God only knew what they had in common; she was almost childlike, young and vulnerable, whereas Giscard appeared cold and emotionally stunted in his approach to life.

'Was Jean already working at Peenemunde when you met?'

'I think so,' she answered uncertainly. 'Were you?' she shot at him.

He nodded. 'Yes, I was home visiting my family.'

Garvan took a sip of his coffee. 'I should imagine the security at Peenemunde is very tight.'

'Of course.' Claudine smiled.

'There's something I don't quite understand,' he said, resting his elbows on the table.

She looked at him questioningly.

'Peenemunde is a top secret establishment.'

'Yes, it is.'

'How on Earth did you get permission to join him? It's not a decision the Germans would have made lightly.'

She instinctively looked across the room at Giscard, not quite sure what to say. He stopped pacing the room again. 'You're quite right; it wasn't easy.'

'How did you get permission?'

'It was a favour from an old friend. Let's just say, he managed to pull a few strings with the SS.'

'He must be a pretty important friend,' Garvan suggested.

'Before studying for my doctorate in France,' Giscard explained, 'I attended the Technische Universität in Berlin, where I graduated with a degree in aeronautical engineering. I made some very good friends there, and studied alongside Wernher von Braun.' He paused for effect. 'I take it you may have heard of him?'

There was an edge to Giscard's voice; the inherent arrogance had re-surfaced. Garvan confirmed he'd read about von Braun, and knew him to be one of the leading figures in Germanys rocket development programme. Garvan didn't tell Giscard he'd read von Braun, although an expert on liquid rocket propellant, needed someone of Giscard's calibre to take his theoretical work and turn it into practical aeronautical engineering.

'I'm not saying it didn't raise a few eyebrows. Our boss, Walter Dornberger, took some considerable persuading to agree, and in the end, he only did so with the proviso Claudine had to stay in the local village. At no point was she allowed access to the rocket site itself. So, in that respect, security was never too much of an issue.'

'Were there many other foreign engineers and scientists working on the project?'

His eyes locked onto Garvan's. 'Dornberger always fought against their involvement and was quite adamant; he didn't want outsiders on the programme. He considered it too risky.'

'Why was that?'

Giscard shrugged. 'The usual stuff. Dornberger wanted a closed shop, and demanded only German nationals were to be used on the project. He was concerned, by employing foreigners, it might leave the site open to possible sabotage.'

'What happened?'

Jean stubbed out his Gauloises; it was the first of several. He smoked almost continuously. He lit another, and took in a lungful of smoke. '*Reichsführer* Himmler apparently took a slightly different view.'

'Which was?'

'That sabotage and spying could be reduced to a minimum by employing German overseers and the threat of severe punishment.'

Garvan sat back and folded his arms, thoughtfully sucking in his lower lip. 'But, that doesn't explain how you managed to secure a position at Peenemunde. Even with the backing of von Braun, how did you get past, not only Dornberger, but SS security as well?'

'My mother was born in the Sudetenland.'

'Her family was German?'

'Ethnically, yes. At the end of the day, the Munich Agreement was nothing more than a means of permitting the Nazis to annex portions of Czechoslovakia along its borders. At least, the bits inhabited by German speakers.' Giscard smiled firmly. 'Daladier, the French President, and your Prime Minister, Chamberlain, acted for the greater good supposedly for world peace, but at what price?'

'I'm no politician,' Garvan admitted frankly, 'but my understanding is, there was a groundswell of local support for the annexation amongst the German population.'

'All true,' Giscard accepted, 'and, as a result, Dornberger accepted me into the fold, albeit reluctantly. Look at me, blond, blue-eyed, the perfect Arian German.' Jean suddenly let out a cannonade of laughter. 'But, God knows what he must be thinking now!' He smirked. 'I never had any say in the matter. Once von Braun had put my name into the frame, one way or another, my fate was sealed. I arrived at Peenemunde, and was immediately ordered to join the National Socialist Party. I'm not sure why, but they were the rules, and so I joined, as if doing so would somehow make me a full-blown Nazi. To my mind, it didn't make any sense at all.'

Claudine had been sitting listening patiently, but could no longer contain herself, and asked anxiously, 'When do you think London will give us permission to leave Estoril?'

'London,' Garvan said evenly, 'does not want to take any unnecessary risks. We have to hold on tight until they give us permission to leave, and even then, it'll be up to a colleague of mine to judge the situation here on the ground, to ensure its safe enough to make a move.'

Claudine looked at him speculatively. 'I know things must be quite tricky, but we've made it this far across Europe. How difficult can it be to get us to Portela Airport?'

Giscard perched himself on the arm of the sofa. 'What exactly are we talking about here?' he demanded. 'Why has there been so much of a delay? I would have thought MI6 would have been glad to see the back of us by now!'

Garvan gave him a long hard stare. He could have fobbed Giscard off with some lie; it might have been simpler that way, but he felt, he was owed an explanation, and judged it was probably the right moment not to pull any punches with him.

'There's no easy way of telling you, but Himmler has sent a member of the *Einsatzgruppen* to Portugal to track you down.'

Jean's face instantly drained of colour; he knew they were some kind of SS paramilitary death squad. 'You mean, they're here in Estoril?' he asked uneasily.

'Yes, we know who they are; it's just a matter of trying to keep the situation under control.'

Claudine looked helplessly from one to the other. 'Will someone please tell me what the *Einsatzgruppen* is?' she pleaded.

Jean glanced uneasily toward Garvan, and started to explain. She sat in stunned silence, and tears began to burn her eyes and roll slowly over her cheeks.

'Believe me, there's no hidden agenda,' Garvan assured them. 'We'll get you to the airport and on the flight to Bristol when MI6 think it's safe to move, but not before.'

Giscard cupped his hands over his face in despair. 'Dear God, what have I done?'

'Where are your parents?'

'They were under surveillance by the Gestapo in Paris, but shortly after I arrived in Portugal, the underground network who helped me to escape promised to take care of them, to place them in hiding. Have you heard anything?'

Garvan shook his head. 'If there were a problem, we'd probably have heard by now.'

Jean moved over to the window and leaned against the wall, staring out across the gardens surrounding the casino. He looked reflective, and even more uneasy than he had before. Claudine made to join him, but Garvan gently caught hold of her hand and shook his head.

'Leave him,' he whispered.

She looked unsure before deciding maybe it was for the best.

Giscard's thoughts turned back to the Peenemunde facility, with its menacing SS guards in their black uniforms. If he'd been discovered with the blueprint, or suspected of leaking information to the Allies, he would have been slowly tortured to death.

He vividly remembered the day Himmler had arrived to observe a test launch. Fortunately for everyone involved on the project, the rocket had risen several hundred feet into the air, without a hitch. The scientific team had been on edge; they'd been lucky that day; the previous test flight had ended disastrously, with the rocket exploding in mid-air. The *Reichsführer* had been wrapped up in a fur-lined leather coat against the biting Baltic chill. He'd seemed attentive enough, but distant, and completely unemotional as Dornberger explained their achievements in creating the *Führer's* missile programme, his vengeance weapons.

It had struck Jean, rightly or wrongly, Himmler appeared to be somewhat less enthusiastic about the project than the *Führer*. But, with the fighting on the Russian Front going from bad to worse, and the Allies threatening a future coastal invasion of Europe, suddenly the *Führer's* faith in the *Vergeltungswaffen* had taken on an even greater significance.

By now, von Braun had growing suspicions; Himmler was actively conspiring to take control of the rocket programme himself. As the *Reichsführer*, no-one dare interfere, or question his motives. Over the coming months after his initial visit to the site, the first batch of concentration camp prisoners had arrived at the site to provide the manual labour they increasingly required to help maintain both the launch pads and the construction plant. The prisoners were a ragged set of individuals, Jean recalled, with fear permanently etched on their gaunt faces, as the SS guards kept a constant watch on their activities around the site.

During this period, Jean had found himself increasingly at odds with his work, and also with Hitler's aims to launch his weapons of mass destruction against Britain in a desperate bid to bring the country to its knees, and thereby rendering the threat of an Allied invasion of Europe all but impossible. Giscard could have kept a low profile, of course, and simply have retained the status quo, but his conscience and a keen sense of guilt wouldn't allow it. Giscard knew his only real option had been to escape Peenemunde, and to distance himself from the barbarous cruelty of the Reich and their warped plans for world domination.

Gazing out across the colourful splashes of bougainvillea beyond the confines of the casino's flat, his one regret was, he'd placed Claudine and his unborn baby in so much physical danger. In hindsight, he probably hadn't thought it all through properly and had completely miscalculated the situation and the consequences of his actions. He knew there'd be risks, but hadn't bargained on a member of the *Einsatzgruppen* being dispatched to kill him on Himmler's express orders. He also knew it wouldn't stop there, no, Claudine would have to die as well.

'It will not do,' he announced suddenly, and promptly disappeared into the bedroom.

'What's going on?' Claudine whispered to Garvan. 'I've never seen him like this before. I'm scared.'

'Don't worry. We'll sort everything out,' he said reassuringly. The fact was, he didn't know how the hell they were going to get either of them to the airport in one piece, nor could he fathom what Giscard was up to.

Jean emerged shortly from the bedroom, carrying a large envelope. 'Get me a bag,' he said sharply to Claudine.

'A bag,' she repeated. 'What kind of bag?'

'Any bloody bag,' he snapped irritably, 'what about one of those they bring the groceries' in!'

Claudine scurried off into the kitchen. Giscard handed over the envelope.

'What's this?' Garvan asked.

'It's the blueprint from Peenemunde, the rocket programme.' Giscard explained. 'Your scientists will need it, and God willing, the plans might help them find a way of shortening the war.'

Garvan found himself looking down at the envelope. 'But, didn't you tell George Rowlands you were keeping hold of them as some sort of insurance policy, in case we decided to abandon you at the last minute?'

'I did,' he said thoughtfully, 'but that's all changed now.'

'How has it changed?'

'Himmler has ordered a member of the *Einsatzgruppen* to kill us. There's no point in holding onto the blueprint any longer.'

'You've lost me,' Garvan confessed.

'The blueprint holds the key to it all. If Himmler's hired assassin manages to kill us, then it might well fall back into their hands. I really can't allow that to happen. Do you understand what I'm saying?'

'Yes, I do.'

'Himmler is worried, once the cat's out of the bag, the Allies will bomb Peenemunde. Depending on how successful the raids are, they'll delay the programme, if we're lucky, for a few months.' He gave a shrug. 'But, it's the technical information he doesn't want your scientists to share. Even so, it's still already too late to prevent the weapons from being launched. Peenemunde isn't the only available launch site. The Nazis have set up others in Northern France. You have to understand, their scientists have a march on yours, and in wartime, that's a very dangerous situation to find yourself in. Your best hope is that *your* scientists find a way of counter attacking Hitler's vengeance weapons.' He paused, and drew breath, before adding, 'So, you see, MI6 and London won't abandon us, not now; they'll want the blueprint, yes, but more importantly, they'll want to pick my brains.' A sudden flicker of annoyance crossed Jean's face; he still wasn't entirely convinced Garvan thoroughly understood the enormity of the situation. 'I'm talking about radical designs, Monsieur; in essence, we've created jet-propelled rocket torpedoes capable of killing thousands of people at the press of a button.'

Claudine was hovering in the doorway, waiting until he'd finished talking, before handing Garvan a brown paper grocery bag. 'We are safe here, aren't we?' she asked him nervously.

'As safe as you can be,' he assured her. Garvan glanced round the room. 'Do you have a phone?'

'Yes, over there,' Jean said, pointing toward the windowsill.

Garvan dialled the Plaza Palacio Hotel, and asked for room one-twelve. *For Christ's sake, please let Spencer be there,* he said to himself. After a few rings, the receiver was picked up, Spencer answered.

'Is George with you?' Garvan asked abruptly.

'What's wrong?'

'Just give me a straight yes or no!'

'Yes, he is.'

'I need a car to meet me at the main entrance of the casino right away.'

'Are our two friends okay?' Spencer pressed him. He didn't want to appear too alarmed, in case the hotel's telephonist was listening in on the conversation.

'They're fine.'

'Good, the car will be there in ten.' Spencer slammed the receiver down.

\*

'What the hell's going on?' Rowlands demanded, once Spencer had hung up the phone.

'I've no idea,' he said, heading for the door. 'Got the car keys on you?'

Rowlands patted his trouser pockets. 'Yes, yes, I have.'

'Where did you park up?'

'Just near the front door.'

They drove the short distance from the hotel to the casino to find Garvan sitting outside on a low wall, clutching a brown paper bag. They pulled up. Hall wound down the window.

'What's wrong?' he called out to him.

Garvan climbed in the back, and passed the bag forward to Spencer. 'You'd better take this.'

'What is it?'

'It's Giscard's Peenemunde blueprint.'

The car lurched forward, as Rowlands unexpectedly stalled the engine. 'I'm sorry,' he apologised. 'How the hell did you manage to prise it off him?'

Garvan lit a cigarette; he needed one, and explained how he'd mentioned the *Einsatzgruppen* had been ordered to track him down. He still wasn't entirely convinced whether Giscard hadn't felt a little flattered Himmler had personally ordered his assassination.

'He's certainly arrogant enough,' Spencer said, peering inside the bag.

'If I drop you two off at the hotel,' Rowlands said, 'I'll drive back to Lisbon and pass it over to Frank Lucern; the sooner we get this to London the better.'

'That's okay, George. Lisbon's only twenty miles away. We might as well come with you.'

*Chapter 11*

Garvan and Spencer had just returned from Lisbon, having delivered the blueprint to Frank Lucern, when the hotel's receptionist called out to Spencer, as they crossed the lobby.

'*Senhor* Choules, I have a message for you.' She smiled, waving a folded piece of paper at him. Spencer thanked her, and opened it, as they headed toward the staircase.

'Who is it from?' Garvan asked.

Spencer scrunched the note up tightly in his fist. 'You don't want to know.'

Garvan followed him upstairs to room one-twelve; Spencer placed the key in the lock and let them in. He ripped the note up, and then threw into the waste bin.

'It was from Michelle Rookwood,' he explained.

Michelle was known to the Double Cross team as Agent Camber. She dressed well, and had a particular weakness for unforgiving high heels. Michelle was renowned for changing the colour of her hair on a regular basis, sometimes just so it didn't clash with a particular outfit. She'd once told Garvan having the same colour day in and day out was like eating the same breakfast every day. "You know, kind of boring without ringing the changes." In a different life, Garvan mused, she really ought to have been a hairdresser.

Michelle loved her men and drink in equal measure. On joining Tar Robertson's team, Garvan had been surprised to find Michelle was on their books. Their paths had first crossed before the War in the West End of London. Michelle had flitted aimlessly between various part-time jobs, before drifting into petty crime, nothing too serious, the occasional minor theft and then, there was the illegal gambling den she had helped to run with her then boyfriend, Charlie McClelland, which had resulted in her spending a stretch in

Holloway prison. Charlie was a West End wheeler-dealer, and had become something of a renowned safecracker on major gangland heists across the Capital.

After Michelle's release from Holloway, she ended up joining another ex-boyfriend in Paris, where she worked in a bar. At the time of the German invasion, she found herself on the wrong side of the Channel, and, in effect, trapped, without any viable means of returning home to England. Ever resourceful, she offered her services to the Germans, and was eventually parachuted back to Britain, with the express aim of providing daily reports on the weather and troop movements across southern England. It hadn't taken long before MI5 discovered Michelle's whereabouts, and quickly tracked her down via intercepted decrypted German messages from the code breakers at Bletchley Park.

A decision was made to leave her temporarily in place, and allow her to operate under controlled conditions. Michelle's clandestine wireless communications were strictly monitored, and the delay in picking her up allowed MI5 enough time to check out whether there were any other active agents they could have missed, and who might well try to make contact with the new arrival. Although given enough rope to hang herself, Michelle knew when to quit; she'd no great love of the Nazi regime, and when arrested, promptly offered her services to British Intelligence. Michelle's gut instinct was survival; she was a chancer, and had successfully played the system.

She was run through the usual interrogation process at Latchmere House and appraised for her suitability as a double agent. Michelle subsequently passed muster, and ended up working out of Lisbon, providing the Germans with disinformation fed to her via the Double Cross team back in London.

Over the last year, she had achieved some success in gaining valuable intelligence regarding some underhand deals in the smuggling of Wolfram ore to the Nazis across the Spanish border. Michelle's activities in Portugal hadn't entirely passed without incident; nothing ever seemed to be plain sailing with her; she was feisty, and, at times, confrontational with her Abwehr contacts. At one point, the Germans considered dispensing with her services altogether, only the intervention of her team, by upping the quality of her disinformation, had eventually saved the day. Ostensibly, the Abwehr believed she'd secured a role working in a minor clerical capacity for Britain's Ministry of Economic Warfare set up in Lisbon. They also had an office in the coastal town of Estoril, where she was more often than not based. However minor her supposed role at the Ministry, they believed she had access to classified material, which MI5 played up to by feeding the Abwehr false intelligence.

Spencer was concerned by leaving a message at the hotel, Michelle had risked endangering their covers.

'Must be significant,' Garvan suggested to him. 'I've no particular liking for the woman, but all the reports indicate she's not doing too a bad a job over here, and usually doesn't take unnecessary risks. Where does she want to meet up?'

'At a place called the Alvor Courtyard.'

'Where's that?'

'I'm not sure; I think it's somewhere along the beachfront. I'll check with George in the morning.'

'Do you think she might have something on Giscard, perhaps?'

Spencer shrugged. 'Who knows. We'll just have to wait and see. Would you like a drink? I can offer you gin, whisky, or Bacardi.'

'Whisky, thanks, with a splash of water. How did Joyce get on with her meeting with von Gruber and Otto Stackler, do you know?'

Hall poured a whisky and handed it to him. 'She didn't do too badly.'

'Did she manage to find anything out?'

Spencer beamed at him. 'Apparently, Stackler and the Baron are going to the casino this evening.'

'You're joking!'

'I wish to God, I was,' he said, and took a large gulp of his drink. 'But, at least, the dinner suits George had made for us will have an outing.'

'What time do you want us to be there?'

'We can't take any chances; I've asked George to meet us here about eight thirty.'

'Do we know when their planning on getting to the casino?'

'Joyce reckons about nine, but Rafael Delgado has promised to give us a call if they get there any earlier.'

'Wouldn't it be wiser for you to steer well clear of the place.'

Spencer looked at him questioningly.

'In case Stackler recognises you.'

The penny dropped. 'I see what you mean, no, I've already discussed the whys and wherefores with George and Frank Lucern. On balance, we've come to the conclusion. If anything kicks off, I'd better be your wingman.' Spencer smiled broadly. 'That reminds me,' he said, and wandered over to the wardrobe before returning with a shoebox. 'It's a present from George.'

He opened it, and found an Enfield revolver inside.

'We can't afford to take any chances tonight. All of us will be armed, including Joyce.'

\*

Joyce had insisted on taking a taxi the short distance from the hotel; she didn't fancy walking through the gardens, as she planned on wearing a pair of strappy leather evening sandals, with perilously high heels. Spencer had mentioned she might think about wearing something else, but his suggestion had been met by a wall of resistance. It wasn't significant enough to make an issue out of, and so, he'd left it up to her to decide what she wanted to do.

By nine o'clock, they were waiting in the main lobby of the casino for her to arrive. The local bourgeoisie and wealthy refugees were slowly beginning to turn out in full force.

By the time her cab arrived, Rowlands was already getting impatient at having to wait for her. Joyce stepped out of the taxi, dressed in a stunning midnight blue velvet evening gown, accessorised by a large diamond necklace and matching earrings.

'I bet they're not paste!' Rowlands observed drily.

'I bet they're not.' Garvan smiled.

'She's like a bloody magician,' Rowlands quipped. 'Where does she keep conjuring up all these bloody clothes from?'

'I think it's fair to say she bought up half of Lisbon.'

Joyce turned heads, as she sashayed into the casino; even Spencer grudgingly admitted she looked incredible.

'You look absolutely stunning,' Rowlands announced, throwing his arms out to greet her.

'Thank you.' She smiled flirtatiously. 'Well, gentlemen, are we ready?'

'As ready as we're ever likely to be.' Spencer suddenly glanced down at her tiny silver clutch bag, and said in a low, urgent voice, 'Where the hell's your pistol?'

She winked at him mischievously. 'You really don't want to know, Spence.' She sailed past him, without missing a beat, through the lobby.

This was her world; she adored the atmosphere, the glitz of the casino, with its sparkling crystal chandeliers and ornate art décor interior. Much of her childhood had been spent trailing after her father to a succession of glamorous locations, Monte Carlo one week, Estoril and Paris the next. He was an inveterate gambler, who had spent most of his time playing poker; some said he could have been a professional; they'd also said as much about his daughter. Logical and analytical by nature, she loved the complexity and strategy involved with playing.

The air was already heavy with smoke, and the gaming tables were a heady mix of anxiety, excitement, and, above all, the driving force of greed. Joyce had once tried explaining to Garvan, as a gambler, she lived for the next turn of the card or the wheel, and, of course, the big win. "But, I'm not addicted. I know when to call it a day." She'd said. "When to pull back, and walk away." He hadn't been convinced, at the time, and his opinion still hadn't changed. In his experience as a copper policing the casinos and illicit gambling dens of Mayfair and Knightsbridge, gamblers always readily bragged about the big win to anyone who'd care to listen, but invariably developed a selective memory when it came to the losses, their growing debts, and ultimately, their bankruptcy. For the next turn of the dice could change everything, and reverse their fortunes. Admittedly, few gamblers had deep enough pockets to match Joyce's fabulously wealthy family, but in the end, it was all relative. Although Garvan was forced to concede, she was lucky at the tables. At Estoril, there were more than twenty gaming tables in the establishment, from roulette, blackjack, and baccarat, and, Joyce's favourite poker.

Spencer handed Joyce a glass of champagne; she inclined her head toward a nearby gaming table. He followed her gaze; Gruber was sitting there playing poker, and judging by the expression on his face, he was down on his luck.

'Do you mind if I join in?' she asked.

'No, not at all.' He took a quick glance around the casino. 'Have you managed to spot Stackler yet?'

'No, I haven't. Why don't you try checking out the bars. I think you'll find there's about four or five dotted around the place.'

'We'll do that. In the meantime, you stay here with the Baron, and we'll have a nose round.'

'Shouldn't someone be keeping an eye on the flat?' Joyce quizzed him.

'George brought a colleague back with him from Lisbon this afternoon; he's already upstairs guarding Giscard and the girl.'

She sauntered off to join von Gruber at the gaming table. Several smaller rooms were leading off from the central area which clients could hire out for private functions and gambling matches. Rowlands decided to have a drink with Rafael Delgado. From their vantage point on the first-floor balcony, they had a perfect bird's eye view of the main gaming area, but more importantly, the exit to the entrance lobby. At least Stackler wouldn't be able to leave the casino without their knowing.

Garvan and Spencer circulated separately before meeting up in one of the smaller bar areas, where they finally came across Stackler having a drink in a secluded alcove with some cohort.

Spencer sat himself down on a barstool beside Garvan at the bar. 'Have you checked out the cocktail list?'

'Do you want to take a look?'

'Surprise me.'

'Two Horse's Necks, please,' Garvan ordered.

Spencer instinctively decided to check the cocktail menu to see what the hell he'd ordered. It was a mixture of gin, bourbon, lemon rind, topped with ginger ale. 'That'll do,' he said, placing the menu back down on the bar.

'Who's that sitting with Stackler?' Garvan asked.

'I might well be wrong, but I think I saw him the other day sitting by the pool at our hotel.'

The bartender handed them their cocktails. Garvan glanced up at the mirror, which ran the length of the wall behind the optics, and checked out the reflection of Otto's drinking companion. He was slightly built, pale in complexion, with short greased back hair.

'Gestapo?' he queried.

'I'd bet my life on it. I must ask Delgado if he's seen him at the casino before.'

Stackler and his drinking partner appeared to be sinking a heady mixture of beer and schnapps, like it was going out of fashion.

'I suppose,' Spencer mused, 'if *Reichsführer* Himmler is funding your visit to Portugal, you can afford to run up a large bar bill.'

Garvan laughed. 'Judging by the price of these ruddy cocktails, I can't imagine Tar Robertson's going to be too pleased with us, either!'

'Don't worry; it's all taken care of. I've put all our expenses on George Rowlands' charge sheet.'

'Christ, does he know?'

Spencer lit a cigarette, and exhaled slowly through his lips and nostrils. 'I'm sure he won't mind.'

'So, he doesn't know, then?'

Spencer pulled a face. 'It's what we in the trade call a "technicality." I'll explain everything to him before we leave, of course, but it isn't George we have to worry about. It's his boss, Frank Lucern, who'll kick up the fuss.'

'I'm sure he will.'

'Tar won't care a fig what we do, and Lucern won't have a choice, other than to write it off the MI6 budget.'

'Something tells me you've done this before,' Garvan mused; Spencer didn't deny it. 'You'd have made a bloody good criminal in Civvy Street.' His companion took it as a compliment.

Neither of them had noticed Stackler was weaving his way unsteadily toward the bar; he bumped into a leather stool, before clicking his fingers at the barman, and demanding a packet of cigarettes. He began fumbling in his trouser pockets for some money and threw a pile of coins down in payment. He hadn't a clue if there was enough to pay, and the rather nervous barmen weren't about to argue the point, anyway. As he began to sway drunkenly away from the bar, he suddenly caught sight of Spencer, and did a double take, before sharply tapping him on the shoulder. He looked round at him.

'*Haben wir nicht schon einmal getroffen?*' Stackler slurred at him.

He was asking whether they'd met before, Spencer understood him perfectly, but narrowed his eyes questioningly, feigning ignorance; he didn't quite understand what he was saying. Otto grabbed the pack of cigarettes off the bar, and repeated the same question, only louder this time. Much to Garvan's relief, Spencer kept his cool, and calmly addressed everyone in the bar.

'I'm sorry, does anyone here speak German? I don't understand what our friend here is trying to say.' A young couple sitting at a nearby table studiously avoided his gaze, and suddenly became engrossed in each other's company. He'd overheard them speaking German earlier, but couldn't blame them for not wanting to get involved. Whether they knew Stackler or not wasn't the issue; he wasn't only drunk but on the point of being abusive.

Otto's drinking companion began hammering on the table with a clenched fist in a bid to attract his attention. '*Kommen sie her.*' He kept repeating the same words over and over again, gesturing for Stackler to re-join him in the alcove.

Otto hesitated, and then said in fractured English, 'I've met you before, haven't I? I always remember a face.'

But, without waiting for a response, he drunkenly staggered his way back across the bar.

Once he'd safely sat himself down again in the alcove, Garvan said, 'That was a close shave.'

Spencer didn't seem at all concerned, but then again, he rarely seemed to be ruffled by anything, not even at the prospect of being outed by a member of the *Einsatzgruppen*.

'He's as pissed as a bloody newt. I doubt if he'll remember too much about this evening.' He finished off his cocktail. 'I think I'll have the same again, what about you?' he asked, passing the barman his empty glass.

'Go easy on the ginger ale this time, would you.'

'Yes, sir.'

'Make it two,' Garvan said. 'But, what if he does remember you?'

Spencer shrugged indifferently. 'If he does, then he does. At worse, my cover will be blown, but at the end of the day, London's only remit is to keep Giscard out of harm's way, and get him back to London.'

'What about Claudine Gregorie?'

His eyes locked onto Garvan. 'You've been around the system long enough to know she's not our top priority. If we get her back, then all well and good, but if we don't...' His words hung in the air.

'Then, it doesn't matter. Is that what you're saying?'

Spencer paid for the drinks. 'I guess I am.'

'What do you want to do now?'

'Call it a day.'

'What about Stackler?'

'He's too pissed to cause us any trouble tonight.'

Garvan knew he hadn't said it lightly; it was a fact, and lives were lost. They were expendable; Claudine was expendable. Garvan's world had always revolved around dogged detective work. The Double Cross team had needed his experience, he accepted all that, but he was still trying to get to grips with the wider issues, the politics, and the cut-throat world of espionage in war-torn Europe. By his own admission, he was nothing more than an amateur, whereas Spencer had seen it all before, and was immersed in Britain's deadly spy network pitted against the Third Reich.

They were still propping up the bar when von Gruber appeared in the doorway. The bar had emptied out rapidly when Stackler and his friend began a drunken rendition of *Das Deutschlandlied*, the German National Anthem, leaving only Garvan and Spencer downing their cocktails. With a look of disapproval on his face, Gruber swiftly appraised the situation, before beating a hasty retreat. Shortly afterward, he dispatched one of his Abwehr agents to keep a close eye on Stackler and his companion.

At the gaming tables, Joyce had just finished playing a round of poker, and was chatting animatedly to a croupier, when Garvan gently placed his hand on her shoulder. She swung round and smiled up at him.

'Ah, there you are. I was just wondering where you'd got to,' she said.

'Have you had a good time? How much are you down?'

'I can't complain,' she replied, as Spencer joined them. 'Do you want the good news or the bad news first?'

Spencer didn't appear to be particularly bothered either way. 'Let's start with the good first.'

Joyce excitedly held up a thick roll of banknotes. 'Look! I can't fit it into my handbag!' She giggled.

'Lucky you,' Garvan grinned. She shot him an excited smile.

'And what's the bad news?' Spencer asked resignedly.

'Von Gruber's going back to Lisbon in the morning.'

He screwed up his face doubtfully. 'So *that's* bad news?'

'He's going by himself.'
'What about Stackler?'
'He's staying on here in Estoril.'

It had been a long day. Spencer looked drawn, and the very last thing he wanted to hear right now was Stackler was staying on in Estoril, and not returning to Lisbon with the Baron.

*Chapter 12*

Spencer consulted the local map he'd picked up at the Plaza Hotel's reception desk. Michelle Rookwood had asked them to meet up with her at the Alvor Courtyard.

'I think this must be where it is,' he mused, pointing at the street plan.

'It can't be that difficult to find,' Garvan said, glancing over his shoulder.

'I think we need to turn right out of the hotel and head down toward the beach.' As they set off through the hotel gardens, Spencer orientated the map. 'When we get to the beach road, it should be the second turning on the left.'

'I wonder how Stackler got on last night. By the time we left, he was already three sheets to the wind,' Garvan said.

'I called Delgado first thing this morning to find out what happened.'

'And?'

'He said Stackler and his mate didn't leave the casino until about half two this morning. It's probably just as well the Baron left someone to keep an eye on them. Apparently, the poor sod had to carry the buggers practically out to the car, and even then, Otto kept insisting on finding the nearest brothel. So, God only knows what happened after that.'

'Why do you think he's staying on in Estoril?'

'It's a difficult call,' Spencer said. 'At the moment, there's no reason to believe he's got wind of Giscard's whereabouts, but then again, it doesn't mean to say he hasn't had a tip off.' Spencer examined Garvan's face, and sensed he was holding back about something. He gently nudged his arm. 'Is anything wrong?'

'It's just a gut feeling.'

'So, spit it out, then.'

'From what I've heard about Stackler, I don't think he'd waste his time kicking his heels, if he didn't think Giscard was here.'

'You have a point,' Spencer conceded.

'Otto's a dyed in the wool Nazi, and needs to get results, if he wants to impress Himmler.'

'All true. You don't end up being recruited from the SS to a death squad, like the *Einsatzgruppen,* if you haven't shown a blind belief in the Reich, but more importantly, the ability to kill and commit mass murder without an ounce of mercy.'

'I assume since Himmler marked him out as a man of the future, he's gained a certain amount of power within the ranks of the SS and the *Einsatzgruppen*.' Garvan looked to Spencer to gauge his opinion.

'Go on,' Spencer said to him.

'From Stackler's perspective, I imagine he's become almost untouchable within the regime.'

Spencer agreed with him. 'But, he's only untouchable until the *Reichsführer* says otherwise, and decides to cut him back down to size. You have to understand Stackler's playing with fire. He's with the big boys now, and is completely out of his league. At the end of the day, Stackler's living on borrowed time, and he knows it.'

'Precisely, and that's what makes him so effing dangerous. He'll stop at nothing to retain his position with Himmler.'

'But, more to the point, if he's got wind of Giscard's whereabouts, then we have to question seriously whether Rafael Delgado is our mole.'

Garvan seemed hesitant. 'I think he's too obvious. For a start, Delgado knows the score, and according to George Rowlands, he's an old hand. I don't reckon he's our mole.'

'You may be right.'

'I just figure Rafael has too much to lose; he's already placed his neck on the line by working with British Intelligence. He also has a nice steady income from MI6.'

'It doesn't mean to say he wouldn't like doubling his money by working for the Abwehr as well. It happens all the time.'

Spencer glanced down at the map, and pointed toward a narrow side turning on their left. 'I think the restaurant's down there somewhere.'

The Alvor was nestled within a cool cobbled courtyard surrounded by traditional stone buildings. The yard was filled with wooden tables covered with starched white tablecloths, and lovely flower arrangements in small glass bowls. Garvan checked out the chalkboards displaying the lunch menu. The restaurant appeared to specialise in locally caught sardines from the nearby fishing village of Cascais. Although the Alvor was only a stone's throw from the main coastal road, the tables appeared to be filled with locals, rather than the usual mix of foreigners to be found at the more expensive seafront cafes and restaurants. The Alvor was a small family run business, and two of the three sons waited table; the eldest did most of the cooking, while their mother occasionally helped out when things were getting a bit hectic.

A flicker of recognition crossed Michelle's face, as they threaded their way toward her through the crowded tables. True to form, she was wearing heavy make-up, a pretty cream cotton dress, and an assortment of cheap, locally purchased jewellery.

With a flourish, she removed her sunglasses, and stood up to greet them. Michelle had crossed paths with Spencer before at MI5's HQ in London. He'd struck her as being something of a tough bastard. The smart suits still couldn't quite disguise his uncompromising attitude. Michelle had heard on the grapevine Garvan was working for the Colonel, but hadn't met him since her arrest for helping run an illegal gambling den before the war. He was then a young up-and-coming detective, working out of West End Central. Even then, he'd been something of a high flier, someone who'd earned the respect of London's leading gangsters.

They were a deadly combination, she decided, the slick Met Detective and the hardened MI5 spy. Michelle was seriously hoping Spencer understood she hadn't taken the decision lightly to leave him a message at the Plaza Palacio's reception desk. The last thing she wanted, or needed, was to rock the boat, and endanger not only her own life but that of her Double Cross colleagues. She knew only too well one detrimental word from them would have meant there was a very real risk of Robertson closing her down, and she could end up facing a firing squad at Wandsworth Prison.

As they joined Michelle at the table, Spencer's gaze remained unwavering in its directness. It was obvious he still wasn't entirely convinced their meeting was worth the very real risk of having blown their covers. She decided to play it cool, and asked them what they wanted to drink. It was wine all round. Michelle managed to interpret the menu for them, and confirm it was sardines or sardines; there wasn't a choice. Garvan pulled a face.

'Is that a problem?' she asked with a smile.

'I can't stand sardines,' he owned up.

Michelle called the waiter over, and, in broken Portuguese, asked if there was an alternative to the menu board. The waiter gestured toward his mother, an old lady dressed entirely in black, who was sitting in a wooden chair outside the restaurant and fanning herself against the oppressive heat. Her son seemed welcoming enough and genuinely happy to assist.

'Mama will cook you up an omelette,' Michelle announced.

Garvan thanked her, and found himself, saying, 'I love the hair.'

She was peroxide blonde; she had been a brunette the last time he'd seen her in London.

'Thank you.' She smiled, instinctively touching her shoulder length hair. 'I thought I'd give it a try. I was toying with the idea of having it platinum, but I chickened out, and plumped for this instead.'

They kept the conversation light until lunch was served. The sardines were huge, larger than anything he'd seen back home. Garvan was impressed by the way Spencer and Michelle skilfully removed the flesh from the bones. There was obviously an art to it. Personally, he'd always felt there were too many bones and not enough meat; he'd obviously got it all wrong. Spencer offered him one to try, but he declined. As for Mama's omelette, it was filled with delicious local cheese; in fact, he was so pleased he went over to thank her personally, which went down well with her and her sons.

They were already on their second carafe of wine, before Spencer decided to confront Michelle. He refilled their glasses. 'You better have a bloody good reason for getting us here like this.' His gaze locked hard onto Michelle's face.

She held up the glass, twisting the stem slightly, before taking a sip. 'A German contact of mine mentioned the name Stackler to me.' Michelle looked at them waiting for a reaction. They were giving nothing away.

'What German contact?'

'Gustav von Bertele, he's the.'

Spencer interrupted her. 'I know who he is.'

She blushed slightly.

'Come on, what did he have to say about Stackler?'

'He said that he was a member of the *Einsatzgruppen*, and was here in Portugal on Himmler's orders.' She paused looking at each of them in turn. She suddenly started to feel even more uneasy than she was before, not quite sure if she'd misread the situation; maybe, in the great scheme of things, Stackler wasn't particularly important.

Michelle set her glass back on the table. 'Tell me something,' she said, reaching down for her handbag. 'Am I wasting your time, because if I am, then there's no point in us carrying on.'

'No,' Garvan responded. 'You're not wasting our time.'

She rummaged through the handbag and retrieved a lipstick; she re-applied it. 'I'll be honest with you, Bertele's been pulling his hair out since Stackler turned up in Estoril.'

'Why's that?' Spencer asked feigning ignorance.

'As the Baron's deputy in Portugal, von Bertele has direct responsibility for the day-to-day running of the Abwehr operation in Estoril. Normally, it isn't a bad little number. In fact, most of the time, it's just routine stuff.'

'Does he spend much time in Lisbon?' Garvan asked.

'Not lately. To be honest with you, the Baron prefers keeping him at arm's length.'

'Why?'

'Admiral Canaris is Bertele's Uncle.'

Garvan allowed a smile to cross his face. 'What you're saying is, he doesn't trust his boss's nephew?'

'What do you think?' she smirked, slipping the lipstick back into her handbag. 'From what I understand, Stackler comes with a certain reputation.'

'You could say that,' Spencer said.

'Von Bertele says he's utterly ruthless.'

'Stackler's not only ruthless, he's a bloody psychopath.'

'It hasn't helped, either, his being a close friend of Himmler; it's meant everyone's been watching their backs and treading on eggshells, for fear of upsetting him, in case word gets back to Berlin.'

'I bet they have,' Spencer said. with a strained smile.

'I'll be honest with you, I've no idea why Stackler's here, but seeing you in Estoril with Joyce Leader in tow, well, I put two-and-two together, and couldn't help thinking it probably wasn't entirely unconnected. There had to be something big going on.'

Spencer looked at her thoughtfully; Michelle was on a roll. She gulped back her wine. 'What I'm trying to say is, I can't imagine the Colonel letting you both out of the country at the same time, if it wasn't for something vital.' Michelle was on the point of adding she couldn't quite fathom out why Joyce Leader was with them, but thought better of it. She'd probably said enough already. Besides, they wouldn't have told her why anyway.

Spencer snapped open his lighter to see if it needed more fuel; it was fine, and so he lit a cigarette. 'How did you know we were staying the Plaza Palacio?'

'Doesn't everyone in the Service?'

'But, how did you know my room number?'

'I got chatting to the receptionist, after I saw you in the foyer. I happened to mention to her I'd seen you around and.' She smiled, searching for the right words. 'That I quite liked the look of you.'

He put his hand up, stopping her in midstream. 'I've got the drift.'

Michelle smiled at him uneasily.

'Did you know the Baron returned to Lisbon this morning?' he queried.

Michelle nodded. 'Bertele mentioned it to me. That's another thing,' she carried on. 'With the Baron returning to Lisbon, he's now been saddled with looking after Stackler. Not personally, of course, but he's having to pull out all the stops for him, cater to his every whim, for fear of anything untoward getting back to Berlin.'

'Did he say how long he's expecting Stackler to stay?'

Michelle snapped her handbag shut, and placed it back on the ground beside her chair. 'No more than two days at most, or, at least, that's what he's hoping for. To be honest, I don't think he knows.'

Spencer gave Garvan a sidelong glance, wondering if he'd come to the same conclusion. It was obvious he had. Giscard's cover was blown. Somehow, Stackler had discovered his whereabouts, but how? Spencer's mind went into overdrive. *Where had they gone wrong? What had they missed?* They'd kept a tight ship. The only apparent weak link in the chain was Delgado, but he was inclined to agree with Garvan that Rafael simply had too much to lose by siding with the Nazis, unless they'd managed to get at him in some way.

George Rowlands had already provided armed protection at the flat, and an agent was now permanently stationed at the casino. *But was that enough?* Spencer was still uneasy; he had a bad feeling he was losing control of the situation. He drifted out of his revelry, as Garvan continued questioning Michelle; it was important as he needed to keep up.

'Stackler spent yesterday evening at the casino, drinking with a friend.' He topped up their wine from the carafe. 'Your contacts must know who he is.'

Michelle allowed the merest flicker of a smile to cross her face, but it vanished as quickly as it appeared. 'From what I understand, I don't think Otto Stackler has many friends.'

Garvan sat back in his chair, and placed his hands together. 'But, von Bertele must know who he was drinking with.'

She swept up her glass. 'I'll ask around, but if he was local, I think I might have heard by now.'

'We need to know whether he's in the SS or the Gestapo.'

'He might be Abwehr,' she suggested.

'No, I don't think so,' Spencer said. 'Otherwise, the Baron would have gripped the situation earlier, before Stackler got pissed out of his brain.'

'Do you know if they're staying at the Plaza Palacio?'

'We believe so. I think I saw Stackler's drinking buddy sitting around the hotel pool the other day. Rowlands is checking it out for us.'

Michelle was already beginning to feel way out of her depth, and still wasn't entirely sure how important Stackler was, or even if she'd done the right thing by taking a risk turning up at the hotel. The trouble, was Spencer's deadpan expression was doing little to alleviate her anxiety.

'The other day,' she said, thoughtfully, 'the Baron called Bertele to warn him off about Otto. He told him to be careful, and to watch his back. Von Bertele isn't someone who's easily frightened, but for some reason, Stackler's put the fear of God up him, and it's not just to do with his connection to Himmler.'

Spencer drained his glass, and asked for the bill. 'We'll be in touch shortly,' he said.

Michelle reached out, and placed her hand over his. 'How important is all this?' she asked tentatively.

Spencer paused, and examined her face; he needed to be up front with her. 'Thousands of lives depend on us not screwing up.' He opened his wallet and placed some notes down on the table. 'Just play it carefully, and whatever you do, don't get yourself entangled with Stackler; just keep your distance from him.'

'How am I to make contact with you?'

'Either your normal Double Cross contact at the Embassy, or through George Rowlands' office. Keep contact to a minimum, and don't go taking any unnecessary risks.'

She nodded.

'I don't want you coming near the hotel again, is that understood?'

Michelle sat back in her chair. There was no point questioning anything Spencer did, or said. 'Yes, Major, of course,' she responded flatly.

*Chapter 13*

As they headed out of the Alvor Restaurant, Garvan glanced over his shoulder to see Michelle Rookwood had been joined at the table by a young waiter.

'Do you trust her?' he asked Spencer.

'On a scale of one to five, I'd probably give her a two.

'That low.'

'I know. It's not exactly a glowing endorsement, is it?'

'But, do you think she's lying about Stackler?'

He gave the matter some thought and then shrugged. 'It's difficult to tell,' he said, before adding. 'For all her quirks and conniving, Michelle has certainly buckled down to the job since she's been in Portugal. I don't believe she'd have left the message at the hotel, if she hadn't thought the information wasn't important, but she should have known better by now than to turn up unannounced and risk blowing our covers.'

'Where are we going?'

'I think we ought to drop by the casino again and check on Giscard.'

'Are we going to move him?'

'Yes, it's too risky keeping him there any longer.'

'Have you any idea where?'

'I haven't decided.'

\*

Garvan was about to use his spare set of keys to unlock the rear entrance of the casino, when he noticed it had been forced open; someone had already beaten them to the flat.

'I think we might be too late,' he said.

They ran upstairs to the first floor, and, reaching the central hallway leading to the flat, saw the figure of a man lying in a pool of blood. Garvan turned him over; it was one of Rowlands' agents; he'd been shot twice in the chest. He felt his neck for a pulse, and glanced up at Spencer and shook his head. The execution had been carried out professionally and clinically with a double tap to the chest. A pistol lay beside the body. Garvan checked it out, but it hadn't been fired, and was still fully loaded; he'd obviously been taken by surprise, and hadn't had time to defend himself.

'Come on,' Spencer said sharply. 'Let's take a look inside the flat.'

The lock on the door had been blasted clean off. Spencer shot him a look and gestured for Garvan to follow him. He withdrew his gun from its holster and cautiously nudged the door open. Slowly edging his way into the room, he suddenly became aware an arm was protruding from behind a curtain, and levelling an automatic Colt at him; he could see the arm was trembling uncontrollably. He paused; Garvan was framed in the doorway behind him and instinctively took aim.

'If you're going to kill me,' Spencer said calmly to whoever was pointing the pistol, 'then make it clean, but, either way, you're not going to leave here alive!'

'Just stay away from me!' a voice screamed. It was Claudine; she sounded hysterical.

'Put the gun down!' he said sharply.

He decided to take a calculated risk, and walked over toward the curtain, and gently prised the Colt out of her hand. He then pulled her away from the window.

'Where did you get this bloody thing from?' he asked handing it over to Garvan.

'The dead agent,' she sobbed. 'He left it with us, in case there was a problem, in case anything happened to him.'

'Where's Jean?'

'They've taken him!' Claudine wailed. 'The bastards have taken him!'

Spencer set his pistol down on the sideboard.

'How long ago did they take him?'

'I don't know.' She was trembling uncontrollably. 'Half an hour maybe, it could have been longer!'

Garvan put his arm around her, and gently guided her over to the sofa. Spencer glanced around the room and noticed a phone sitting on the windowsill. He picked up the receiver and began dialling. He needed to contact Frank Lucern's team right away to let them know what had happened. On their arrival in Portugal, he'd been given a dedicated number for the MI6 duty officer in case of emergencies. He waited; it was ringing, and someone picked it up.

'I no longer have control,' he announced cryptically to whoever was listening on the other end of the line. There was a pause. 'Correct,' he added, and glanced at his watch. 'Good, that's fine; so, you'll make all the arrangements for the removal.'

It was short and sweet. Garvan guessed Spencer was referring to the removal of the agent's body from the casino. He then made another call, this time to the Plaza Palacio Hotel, and spoke to George Rowlands; it was another terse conversation, short on words, but conveyed enough for Rowlands to realise Giscard had been snatched by Stackler. He put the receiver down, and perched himself on the arm of the sofa, which allowed him a clear view of the hallway. Then, reaching into his jacket pocket, retrieved his cigarettes and sleek gold lighter. Absent-mindedly, he placed the cigarette between his lips and flicked on the lighter. It fleetingly crossed his mind if Agent Camber, Michelle Rookwood, had invited them to lunch as a diversionary tactic in order to keep them away from the casino. It could have been entirely coincidental, of course, but for the moment, he couldn't exclude the possibility Michelle had turned rogue, and become a triple agent. He blew out a stream of smoke, his gaze locking onto Claudine. The bloody woman was still sobbing in fits and starts.

'Can you try telling us what happened,' he said in an even tone.

She hesitated, not sure where to begin.

'If we're to have a chance of finding him alive,' he continued smoothly, 'you'd better start answering my questions.'

In despair, Claudine held her head between her hands. 'It all happened so quickly. Mr. Rowlands' agent had just left the flat to check the two main entrances were secure. The poor man didn't get very far,' she explained, choking back her tears. 'We heard all this noise, like a scuffle had broken out, and then shooting in the hallway.' She instinctively glanced toward the door. 'They blew the lock clean off! That poor man,' she sniffed. 'He's dead because of us!'

'How many of them were there?'

'There were two.'

'And Giscard,' Spencer demanded. 'What happened to him?'

'He tried to resist and put up a fight, but they were just too strong for him.' She burst into tears again. Garvan handed her a handkerchief, she thanked him and wiped her eyes. 'We scarcely had time to think, let alone to try and defend ourselves.' She blew her nose loudly. 'I thought they were going to kill us.'

Spencer didn't immediately respond; for all he knew, Giscard could already be dead, but he couldn't understand why Otto Stackler would have left Claudine alive. The only explanation was someone had ordered him to spare her life.

'Can you tell me what they looked like?' he asked.

Claudine closed her eyes reliving the moment the men had burst into the flat, and took a sharp intake of breath before answering. 'There was a tall one, blond, I think, yes, blond. He was in charge.'

'How do you know?'

'The smaller man kept looking at him; you know, as if he was following his lead.'

'Did they say anything?'

'No, nothing at all.'

Spencer drew heavily on his cigarette; something was troubling him. Her story wasn't adding up. He glanced around the living room. 'Did they search the flat?' he queried.

She shook her head. 'No, no, they didn't.'

'So, let me get this straight. They didn't speak to either of you, and they didn't bother searching the flat, is that right?'

'Yes,' she replied hesitantly. He looked at Claudine, almost through her. She began to feel uneasy. 'What are you looking at me like that for?' she demanded.

'I don't understand why they didn't search the flat.'

'Why should they?'

'They knew Jean had stolen the blueprint.'

'I'm sorry,' she shrugged. 'I'm only telling you what happened.'

'Think about it.'

Claudine flicked her eyes nervously toward Garvan for reassurance, but his expression remained a closed book.

'They wouldn't have taken your boyfriend without the plans. Do you understand what I'm saying?' Spencer said sharply.

Claudine made to speak but decided to hold back. In truth, she didn't quite know how to respond. As she tried to meet his gaze, there was no denying he unsettled her to the core. Claudine felt intimidated by him, just as she had on their first meeting at the flat when he had so unnerved Giscard as well. There was no anger or passion in his delivery, just an overt stillness about him, and a certain quiet explosive presence. She tried meeting his gaze again, but it wasn't easy; he was still going on about Giscard, and about the blueprint.

'You have to ask yourself, why the hell they didn't turn the place upside down to find the plans. Unless, of course,' he said pointedly, 'someone had already told them the blueprint was in the hands of the Allies.'

He was about to continue when he heard the sound of a chain lock being unbolted and the clanking of keys at the far end corridor; someone was opening the connecting door from the casino. He moved over to the sideboard and picked up his Walther PPK, and gestured to Garvan to keep back and stay where he was. But, as the door creaked open, he visibly relaxed.

'It's only George and Rafael,' he said to Garvan.

Rowlands was out of breath; his faced flushed with the effort of hurrying from the hotel. He allowed himself only a cursory glance at his agent lying in a pool of blood. A flicker of emotion crossed his face as he passed the body. Delgado was right behind him; he pulled up sharp, shocked at the sight of the body, and instinctively crossed himself and said a silent prayer. Rafael had liked the agent, Pete Starling; he'd possessed a ready wit and a dry sense of humour. He'd been unfailingly polite, and had always passed the time of day, and made a point of asking after Rafael's wife or discussing Portuguese history, a subject he had become particularly interested in since his posting to Lisbon. He was a good man, Delgado decided, who hadn't deserved to die, and certainly not like this.

As Rowlands entered the flat, his face registered surprise; it was obvious he hadn't expected to find Claudine alive. He gave a rather wooden smile, and shot Spencer a questioning look. Spencer winked at him; they were on the same wavelength. Claudine should be dead, they both knew that. *Why would Stackler leave a potential witness alive, and why risk her going to the authorities?*

'Have you phoned Frank's office?' he asked Spencer.

'Yes, everything's in hand,' he replied, stubbing out his cigarette.

'What do you want me to do?'

'We need to move Claudine to Lisbon right away.'

Rowlands raised his brows questioningly. 'To a safe house, you mean?'

Spencer shook his head. 'No, to the Embassy.'

Rowlands felt uneasy about the idea; he wasn't sure if it was the right move to make. For a start, they wouldn't have time to forewarn the Ambassador, Sir Ronald Campbell. Rowlands had no wish of getting on the wrong side of him, and, more importantly nor would Frank Lucern. Campbell was a slick diplomat, rich in experience, but entirely dispassionate in his judgement. He surmised having Claudine Gregorie holed up at his Embassy might well prove to be a step too far.

Spencer detected Rowlands' reticence. 'There's no other way,' he reiterated coldly.

Rowlands desperately wanted to counter him, but now wasn't the time or place to argue the point. This was Spencer's call and his alone. Rowlands gut feeling was London would probably end up backing him to the hilt anyway. Even so, he found himself increasingly out on a limb, torn as he was between Lucern's priorities as the Head of the MI6 Station in Lisbon and Spencer's immediate demands. Lucern's main priority was the longer picture and his remit for controlling counterintelligence activities in Portugal. He was constantly treading a fine line, trying desperately not to fall foul of either the local authorities or the Foreign Office. The last thing he needed was for Spencer to rock the boat to such an extent, it might jeopardize MI6's entire Iberian operation.

Spencer realised Rowlands was uncomfortable with the idea of moving Claudine to the Embassy. A smile transformed, and momentarily softened, his face. 'It's my call, and mine alone, George. You're only following orders.'

Rowlands knew he was right, and that no matter how dire the ramifications might be, it was Spencer's neck on the line, and not his. He reluctantly agreed, and volunteered to drive Claudine down to Lisbon. As for the nitty gritty of informing the Ambassador, it would have to wait until he'd spoken with Frank Lucern. No doubt Tar Robertson would also help smooth the way and contact Sir Ronald personally, and explain Spencer not only had the full backing of Whitehall but also of the Prime Minister. The Ambassador would simply have to accept the status quo, and face the music, if the situation in Portugal got out of hand.

'Mr. Starling,' Delgado said anxiously. 'What are we to do with his body?'

Spencer returned the Walter PPK to his holster. 'Mr. Lucern's office will arrange everything for you.'

Rafael looked completely nonplussed and blurted out, if MI6 decided to turn up with a hearse in broad daylight at the casino, how in God's name was he going to explain it away to his staff.

Spencer looked to Rowlands; it was his call. Rowlands explained there wouldn't be a hearse.

Delgado gave him a long questioning stare. 'No hearse?' he asked warily.

'We don't want to go causing a scene, now do we, dear boy?'

The English habit of politeness and understatement was completely lost on him. Rafael took a deep breath and wondered what the hell Rowlands was about to say.

'We'll have the body removed from the casino in a furniture removal lorry.'

'A furniture lorry,' he repeated in disbelief.

Rowlands explained how Starling's body would be taken from the casino in a packing case. No-one, he assured him, would give it a second glance. Delgado wasn't quite sure what to say, wondering if this was standard practice at MI6 for the disposal of bodies. Nor could he understand how Rowlands could be quite so matter-of-fact about his dead colleague, especially someone Rafael knew had been a friend of his.

Sensing his unease, Spencer tried to reassure Delgado, that any visible trace of the murder would be removed from the casino, and everything would be taken care of. Rafael found himself looking at each of them in turn, and finally realised he was a mere novice in their world. They'd answered his questions succinctly, but without a shred of emotion. Maybe this was how they coped with the reality of war by keeping their emotions in check, compartmentalising their feelings. This was business; the job had to be done, and there was simply no room for sentimentality. The only thing he knew, with any degree of certainty, was these British agents scared the life out of him.

Spencer turned his attention back to Claudine, and explained to her he needed to thrash out a few details with his colleagues, before they moved her to Lisbon. The girl looked way too scared to disagree with him. He led the way into the corridor; Garvan closed the door behind them.

'What the devil's going on here?' Rowlands demanded in a lowered voice.

'You tell me,' Spencer said, quietly testing the waters. He could see Rowlands was irritated, it didn't particularly matter to him, but he just needed to know what he was thinking.

'Why the hell would Stackler risk leaving her alive?'

Spencer gave him a cold, hard look. 'Think about it, George,' he said, 'Stackler doesn't act without reason. Claudine's alive for one reason, and one reason only.'

'Christ almighty,' Rowlands groaned. 'You think she's betrayed Giscard!'

'Why else would Stackler have spared her?'

Rowlands didn't have an answer; he was right.

'Himmler ordered Otto to keep her alive.'

Rowlands was thinking aloud now. 'So, we need to touch base with the SOE and Dr. Schwachtgen's network, and re-check Claudine's background to see if we've missed anything.'

'She told Garvan they met in Paris, but he was already working at Peenemunde. You have to bear in mind the only reason Giscard was considered for the project in the first place was because of his friendship with Werner von Braun.'

'I've read the reports.' Rowlands said testily.

'From von Braun's point of view, the only stumbling block to the arrangement was his boss, Walter Dornberger, who'd always resisted employing foreign nationals on the project. We know, for whatever reason, Himmler decided to override Dornberger, and gave his permission for Giscard to work at Peenemunde. So, Giscard's betrayal has become personal to the *Reichsführer*.'

'Maybe she's a plant?'

'There's always the possibility she might be a plant.'

'Is that why you want her moved to the Embassy?' He looked to Spencer, waiting for a response.

Spencer was grateful; grateful Rowlands understood his reasoning. 'With Claudine holed up at the Embassy, she's effectively out of the equation, and more to the point, she'll be unable to make any further contact with the Abwehr.' He asked Garvan to make a thorough search of the flat, to see if he could come up with any incriminating evidence, before turning his attention to Delgado. 'Do you have a switchboard here?'

'Yes, sir.'

'Would you have a record of calls made from the flat?'

Rafael seemed uncertain. 'I'll make some inquiries, but I really wouldn't hold out too much hope.'

'I'd be grateful all the same, thank you.'

*

Claudine wanted to pack some clothes before leaving the flat, but Rowlands gently persuaded her they needed to leave right away; it was too dangerous to delay their departure any longer. 'We'll pack everything up at a later date,' he answered her, 'and get everything to you at the Embassy.'

She seemed a little reluctant at first, but Rowlands had turned on the charm, and she readily agreed.

As Rowlands closed the door to the flat, Spencer said to Garvan, 'You haven't had much to say for yourself, have you?'

'There didn't seem to be any point,' he replied bluntly.

Spencer narrowed his eyes questioningly. 'Come on, I know you better than that. What's on your mind?'

'Do you believe Claudine is our mole?'

'Who knows?'

'Have you ever considered there may be more than one?'

He looked at him quizzically. 'Not lately I haven't.'

'Michele Rookwood,' Garvan ventured. 'Just how reliable do you think she is?'

Spencer lit another cigarette, and gave the matter some thought. 'As I said to you before, she's doing a damn good job reporting on the German espionage system in Estoril and Lisbon.'

'That's not what I asked.'

'I know it isn't.' Spencer drew heavily on his cigarette before responding. 'To be honest with you, I haven't a clue,' he confessed.

'How many people knew Giscard had handed over the blueprint to us?' Garvan held up his hand; he needed to qualify his question. 'I mean, who knew about it here in Portugal?'

Apart from Claudine and the MI6 Lisbon Station, there was also Joyce Leader and Rafael Delgado to take into consideration. Michelle, on the other hand, might have stumbled upon Giscard's importance, but only by default.

'What's your point?' Spencer asked him.

'Are you sure Joyce is completely out of the equation?'

Spencer's expression hardened. 'If she isn't, then we're all up shit creek without a paddle!'

A silence fell between them. Joyce was crucial to their plans, and without her being on side, the entire mission risked imploding. They both knew that.

Garvan made a thorough search of the flat. The bedroom was strewn with unwashed clothes; there was an ashtray overflowing with cigarette butts and an assortment of half empty cups. God knew how long they'd been there, as one or two of them appeared to have a healthy culture of mould multiplying in the dregs. In a chest of drawers, he came across a diary; it was Claudine's. He thumbed through it, and found a couple of telephone numbers; they might be worth checking out at a later date. There were several entries in the diary, but nothing out of the ordinary. She certainly hadn't written in it since her arrival in Portugal.

He wandered back out into the living room and flicked through the books Rowlands had given Giscard to read, before rummaging through the cupboards and drawers. They'd obviously travelled light since leaving Germany, although since their arrival, MI6 had supplied them with new clothes. Even so, there wasn't that much to search through. More to the point, Garvan hadn't expected to find anything of value inside the flat. Whatever else she was, Claudine certainly wasn't a fool.

## Chapter 14

Garvan thanked the waiter for his coffee. Michelle Rookwood was already running late for their appointment; it wasn't as if she hadn't had enough warning. He knew for a fact Rowlands had contacted her first thing that morning to make the arrangements.

Michelle was an intelligent, but temperamental, woman, and, in Garvan's opinion, completely amoral. He did concede, however, since her arrest, she had changed a good deal. She seemed a little more sophisticated, and certainly better dressed than she used to be, nor, was she quite so loud or blousy in appearance. But, despite the changes, she still had more than a few rough edges about her. God only knew how Michelle managed to maintain the German's confidence in her abilities, and successfully inveigle her way into becoming a double agent for Tar Robertson and the Twenty Committee. The whole situation still sat uneasily with him.

Before leaving London, Spencer had shown him reports indicating Michelle had started to develop a rather dangerous tendency to talk openly about her work. Whether she was merely bragging to friends in the local bars and restaurants, he wasn't entirely sure, but from Robertson's point of view, she was starting to appear overconfident, and was getting a little sloppy keeping a grip on security.

Hearing the rattling sound of an old diesel engine, he looked round to see a battered, flat-backed truck piled up with wooden boxes filled with freshly caught sardines. The Alvor's elderly owner appeared in the kitchen doorway, and ambled slowly across the courtyard to inspect the catch with a skilful eye, and bartered a deal with the truck driver for half a dozen crates, before ambling back to the kitchen, leaving her sons to unload the sardines.

As Garvan impatiently re-checked his watch, out of the corner of his eye, he caught sight of Michelle hurrying into the cobbled courtyard. She was out of breath from rushing from the apartment block where she rented a small flat.

'I'm so sorry I'm late,' she apologised, joining him at the table. Beyond that, she didn't offer a reason why she was late. Garvan let it ride for now; there was no point starting off on the wrong foot with her.

'Would you like a coffee?' he offered.

She glanced at her watch. 'It's gone twelve.'

He narrowed his eyes questioningly. 'What difference does that make?'

'Well, if you don't mind, I'd rather have a carafe of wine.'

'A large one, I take it,' he snorted.

'Yes, please.' She smiled.

Garvan attracted the waiter's attention and ordered the wine.

Michelle set her handbag down on the empty chair beside her. 'I thought Spencer was going to be here as well.'

'He was called away,' he replied, finishing off his coffee.

'Was it something important?'

'Presumably, he drove to Lisbon for a meeting with George Rowlands and Lucern.'

Michelle appeared disinterested. 'What's all the fuss about? Why did you want to see me again?'

She searched his face; he was giving nothing away. Even in the 1930s, he'd been an important figure in the police, and had rarely bothered himself with small time crooks. The illegal gambling setup wouldn't usually have registered his interest, had it not been for the fact her boyfriend at the time was, Charlie McClelland. Charlie had viewed their arrest as a rite of passage, an acknowledgment that, in Garvan's mind, he'd made the big time. In his world, it was all about respect, and Garvan was a tough bastard, even harder than many of the thieves he was tasked to track down.

The years hadn't changed him at all; she mused, if anything, since his transfer from West End Central to Scotland Yard, he'd become almost unassailable. He was still the same deadly cold fish, and now, as Spencer's colleague and a member of British Intelligence, he commanded even more respect. After her arrest, Michelle had spent a stretch in Holloway prison. It had taught her a few salutary lessons; firstly, to be more careful with her business partners. In hindsight, it was inevitable, Charlie was always going to be a busted flush, and secondly, she learned never to trust anyone other than herself. She had lived by that maxim ever since, and one way or another had survived pretty well. Admittedly, she had made some horrendous mistakes over the years, not least becoming involved with the Abwehr. At the time, it had seemed like a bit of an adventure, albeit one that had rapidly spiralled out of control.

Michelle shot him a mischievous smile. 'I bet your face was a picture when you joined Robertson's outfit, and found out I was working as a double agent for MI5!'

He smiled in spite of himself. 'To be perfectly honest, Michelle, I thought they'd lost their sodding senses!'

Michelle laughed out loud; she appreciated his honesty.

'The trouble is, I still do.'

'You've always told it as it is; I'll give you that.'

'Do you have anything for us?'

'Yesterday evening, Bertele had a private meeting with the Baron.'

'They must do it all the time.'

'This one was different.'

'Why.'

'They had a blazing row.'

'What was it about?'

She looked suddenly pensive. 'I'm not sure.'

'Why bother telling me, then?'

'Things are pretty strained between them at the moment.'

'You must have some idea.'

She gave a shrug. 'I guess it was about Stackler. Bertele has been pulling his hair out; he's annoyed with the Baron for casting him as Stackler's nursemaid. He's certainly had his work cut out trying to keep him out of trouble. He says the man's a ruddy liability.'

'What kind of trouble?'

'He's overly fond of his drink, and after one too many, that's when it usually starts to kick off.' She let out an earthy cackle of a laugh. 'Mind you, he's not that much better sober. Bertele constantly has to pick up the pieces. Apparently, Stackler severely cut up some prostitute in Lisbon. They had to bribe the pimp and the local police to turn a blind eye. Bertele's concerned. He might not always be quite so lucky cleaning up the mess, and the bugger will end up being arrested.'

The waiter returned with the carafe of wine. Michelle's face lit up immediately. 'Have you finished?' the waiter asked Garvan, and pointed to his empty coffee cup.

'Yes, thanks.'

Michelle smiled flirtatiously at the handsome young man. She'd always had a keen eye for good looking men. It wasn't exactly a weakness, but Garvan hoped she was careful, and a little more guarded than she used to be in London. The waiter set the carafe and two wine glasses down, before clearing the table.

Garvan waited until he was out of earshot. 'I'll give you this you've come a long way, since I arrested you.'

'I suppose I have,' she said, with careful deliberation, not quite sure where he was heading with the conversation.

'I take my hat off to you, luv, full stop. I don't know how the hell you've managed to make it all the way from Holloway nick to sitting here in Estoril. It's quite an impressive achievement,' he replied, pouring them each a glass.

She looked at him doubtfully. 'Are you having me on?

Garvan smiled at her. 'Seriously, I'm impressed. Who'd have thought, seven years ago, when I interviewed you at West End Central, we'd both end up sitting here.' He raised his glass to her. 'And another thing, what's happened to the cockney accent?'

Michelle threw her head back, and began to laugh. 'No, not a bleeding trace is there?' she said, turning on the accent.

'The other day, when we met up for lunch, you could have floored me. I could see it was you, of course, the same Michelle Rookwood of old, but somehow different.'

'What do you reckon, do you think it's paid off?'

'It certainly has. You've managed to completely re-invent yourself.'

Michelle took a sip of the wine, her eyes narrowing curiously at him. It occurred to her, in his own way, he was almost as cool headed and ruthless as Spencer Hall. Overall, they were a deadly combination, and right now, Garvan had started to make her feel decidedly uncomfortable. He was pleasant enough, the compliments were fine, and she felt rather flattered. He'd noticed the change in her, but Michelle knew Garvan well enough to realise there was always a hidden agenda.

He leaned forward, casually resting his elbows on the table. 'But, there's only one problem, as far as I can see.'

'What's that?'

'The trouble is, Michelle, we both know a leopard can't change its spots, not deep down.' His vivid ice blue eyes began to bore right through her.

'I'm not sure what you're getting at,' she countered. 'I've never made any attempt to hide my past, at least not, from the Double Cross team.' Michelle gave a slight shrug. 'Besides, there really wouldn't have been much point. I'd only have delayed the inevitable; they'd have found out eventually, no matter how many lies I told them.'

Garvan picked out a cigarette from a metallic case and offered her one; she declined. Her newly acquired sophistication was just a thin veneer, and the double dealing, manipulative chancer he had arrested before the war was never far from the surface. At the end of the day, Michelle was a survivor, a tough, uncompromising criminal, who had skilfully seen a window of opportunity while trapped in Paris to offer up her services to the Germans. He smiled to himself; only Michelle could then find herself recruited as a double agent. Although she hadn't passed the procedure at Latchmere House with flying colours, she'd still managed to impress her interrogating officer enough to be recommended to the Twenty Committee as a potential agent.

Michelle had always lived her life at full tilt. She certainly wasn't a political animal in any shape or form, far from it, and she didn't give a fig for the rights or wrongs of the war. By nature, she was completely amoral and, therefore, open to the highest bidder. In effect, she would side with whomever offered her the best chance of survival. To Garvan's mind, it made her all the more unpredictable. Before their meeting, Spencer had asked him to fire a warning shot to keep her on her toes. But, for the time being, they still needed her on side. The Germans and, in particular, von Bertele trusted Michelle implicitly, and there was always an outside chance she might be able to provide a steer to Giscard's whereabouts, that was if Stackler hadn't already disposed of him. Since her arrival in Portugal, Michelle had worked hard to ingratiate herself with the Abwehr to such an extent that, without too much difficulty, she had managed to seduce von Bertele. It was a classic honey trap, and he had fallen for it hook, line, and sinker.

It didn't take long for her to down the first glass of wine. Garvan dutifully poured another. Perhaps she hadn't changed that much after all; she'd always loved her drink.

She thanked him before saying, 'Shall we just cut to the chase?'

He allowed a wry smile to cross his face.

Michelle nursed the re-filled glass lightly between her fingers. She knew the reason for their meeting must somehow be connected to Otto Stackler. She certainly couldn't think of another reason Garvan would have risked breaking cover again. She watched his face waiting for a reaction, but she waited in vain.

'I guess, Chief Inspector, we've known each other too long to start playing games. Why don't you tell me what's going on?'

Garvan topped up his own glass.

'It's all to do with Otto Stackler, isn't it?' she carried on.

He held the glass up to his mouth and paused before saying, 'What exactly do you know about him?'

'Not much more than I've already told you.'

He wasn't convinced. Michelle instantly read the mistrust on his face; she needed to say something, something that would keep him off her back. More than anything else, she needed to up her game.

'I think you have to remember there's no love lost between the Gestapo and the Abwehr. Right from the start of their careers, the Baron and von Bertele learned to mistrust the Gestapo, but that's the way things are.'

'But, it's a two-way street.' Garvan countered. 'The mistrust is mutual.'

'You have a point.'

Michelle wasn't exactly telling him anything new; it was common knowledge the various Nazi intelligence factions were in conflict with one another. The leader of the Abwehr,

Admiral Canaris, had long since disapproved of Hitler's methods, and was suspected by the Nazi Party of being disloyal to the *Führer*. Himmler had made several concerted attempts to try and oust Canaris, and take over complete control of the Abwehr himself. So far, Canaris had skilfully managed to outwit him, but it was an on-going power struggle between the two men. Even before Canaris had taken command of the Abwehr in 1935, he was warned about Himmler and Reinhard Heydrich's efforts to gain complete autonomy over German Intelligence. Fortunately, since the death of Heydrich, he'd only had to contend with the *Reichsführer*. But, both men had underestimated Canaris; he was a master of backroom dealings, and knew how to deal with them. But, even while he had tried to maintain a cordial working relationship with the SS and the Gestapo, the antagonism continued with a vengeance.

'What are you trying to tell me?' Garvan continued.

'That the Gestapo and the SS aren't usually willing to share information, at least not with their colleagues in the Abwehr.'

'It's true,' he agreed with her. 'But, you forget, on this occasion, they were involved with Stackler from the moment he stepped off the plane from Berlin. They were ordered to provide him with all the necessary support he needed to complete his mission. We know for a fact, Himmler has been in personal contact with the Baron.' Garvan smiled at her. 'I imagine having Herr Himmler on the other end of the line puts the fear of God into the poor old bugger.'

She returned his smile. 'I daresay it does, but then again, I think he'd have the same effect on most people.'

'What I'm getting at, Michelle, is von Bertele and the Baron have been fully briefed from day one.'

She wouldn't be drawn on the matter. 'That as may be, but Bertele hasn't confided in me.'

'I really don't have the time or the patience for all this bullshit.'

'I don't know what you're on about!' she protested.

'God only knows why von Bertele trusts you; it's more than I *bloody* do,' he shot at her. 'The last time we met you told us Bertele couldn't wait to see the back of Stackler.'

'It's an open secret. Of course he does.'

'Are you expecting me to believe you didn't chance your luck, and ask why he was so bloody desperate to be rid of him?'

Michelle looked at him like a frightened rabbit staring into the headlights of an oncoming car.

'For Christ's sake, Chelle, answer me!' he shouted at her angrily, and crashed a clenched fist onto the table.

Instinctively, she recoiled back in her chair, and nervously licked her lips; no-one else had used her nickname in years. She guessed to Garvan she would always be plain Chelle Rookwood, a petty West End criminal, with an eye for the main chance. She'd lived on her wits for years; it was almost second nature to her, but that wasn't the problem. It was the arrival of Otto Stackler in Estoril which had seriously started to scare her. Up until that point, Michelle had almost become accustomed to living the perilous life of an agent in wartime Portugal, caught between the ever increasing demands of London and the Abwehr.

But, Stackler had changed all that, and, by her own admittance, for the first time, she was feeling totally out of her depth. Ever since their meeting at the Alvor, she'd been constantly looking over her shoulder, fearing she had been spotted having lunch with them, and was under constant surveillance. Michelle had stringently followed the rules, and taken precautions to ensure she hadn't been followed. But, even so, there was always the possibility she might have missed something, or have slipped up somewhere along the line. Whether she had or not, she now found herself in constant fear for her life.

Her eyes slowly began to glisten with tears. Seeing she was about to cry Garvan's expression closed down. There was simply too much at stake to waste time while Michelle had a breakdown.

'For Christ's sake, spare me the tears, Chelle, will you,' he said. 'I know things can't be easy for you right now.'

She sniffed back the tears, desperately trying to regain her composure.

'If it helps any, I don't want to be here anymore than you do,' he said, with a strained smile.

Michelle blinked at him, and half-heartedly returned his smile. 'No, I don't suppose you do.' She heaved a sigh, and shakily reached for her glass; it was empty. They were getting low on wine, so he ordered another carafe. 'This scientist, the Frenchman,' she said hesitantly.

'What about him?'

'Colonel Bertele mentioned something about his having worked on some top secret project.'

Garvan drained the dregs of the old carafe into her glass. 'Go on.'

'I think he said it was in northern Germany,' she added, a crease suddenly furrowing her brow.

'It was.'

'And he's now defected to the Allies.' Michelle looked across the table at him to check she was on the right track.

He shook his head in despair. 'Chelle, why the hell didn't you tell us this before?'

'I didn't know where to turn to,' she confessed. 'When the Baron returned to Lisbon, and left Bertele saddled with Stackler, things were already becoming tricky, but when you two turned up, I knew things must be even worse than I first imagined.'

'Why didn't you tell us?'

She thoughtfully sucked in her lower lip, not quite sure how to respond. 'I'm so sorry,' she said, drawing breath, and reaching for a handkerchief. 'You don't have to tell me. I...I know I've messed up.'

The waiter returned with a fresh carafe of wine; they thanked him. Garvan refreshed their glasses.

'Were you afraid, is that it?'

'When I dropped the note off at the hotel, you have to believe me. I had every intention of telling you everything.'

'What stopped you?'

Michelle looked uneasy, and took another laboured breath. 'It's complicated. Nothing is ever quite what it seems.'

'In some ways, you could say we're both in the same boat; we're both working for the Colonel.'

She looked at him archly, not quite certain what he meant. 'Yes, but we're at opposite ends of the scale.'

'That's not what I meant. It must have been like a baptism of fire, being thrown in at the deep end with the Double Cross.'

Michelle appeared to relax slightly, and managed to raise a smile. 'I was given the stark choice of join or face a firing squad, so here I am.'

'I don't know about you, but I'm still trying to learn the ropes, and still attempting to play catch up with Spencer and Tar Robertson.' He allowed enough time for his words to sink in. 'Right now, you don't have many options open to you, and unless you start meeting me halfway, you'll be closed down.'

'What do you mean, meet you halfway?'

'If the Colonel finds out your holding out on us, what do you think will happen?'

'He'll hang me out to dry.' Michelle looked at him thoughtfully. 'I'd forgotten how good you are at this?' She smiled disarmingly.

He pulled a face. 'What do you mean?'

'You draw people in, you know, make them feel at ease.' She let out a throaty giggle. 'Mind you it's probably just a poo trap to give me enough rope to hang myself.'

'Just tell me what you know.'

'I was scared,' Michelle said honestly. 'The fact Bertele is rattled and out of his depth made me think, and question how vulnerable my own position was. I certainly didn't want to blow my cover and run the risk of crossing Stackler.'

He looked at her quizzically. 'Are you sure that was the only reason?'

Michelle's expression froze. 'Yes, I am.'

There was something else troubling her, of that he was certain. Garvan felt if he pressed her too hard, she'd dig her heels in and clam up on him altogether. She might be running scared, but as a spy, she'd failed to deliver, and time wasn't on her side, Spencer was already on the point of informing London to pull the plug, as she was losing her nerve and ability to operate in the field.

'Tell me, has Bertele mentioned anything else about the Frenchman?'

'He's been tight-lipped, you have to understand he doesn't want to get too heavily involved, that is unless he has to, but I can't say as I blame him.'

'Did you have any luck identifying Stackler's drinking buddy at the casino?'

'Yes, as a matter-of-fact, I've come up trumps. His name is Aldous Meyer.'

'Is he Gestapo or SS?'

'Gestapo, apparently he's an old friend of Stackler's from Berlin.'

'Did they travel together from Germany?'

She shook her head. 'No, Meyer's been in Portugal for about a year now. They met up in Lisbon, and then travelled together to Estoril.' Michelle took a sip of the wine. 'Meyer's been operating around the docks, trying to buy information on trans-Atlantic shipping movements to help their U-boats intercept the Allied convoys.' She stared absent-mindedly into her glass. 'Bertele reckons Meyer's a pretty nasty piece of work as well.'

Garvan raised his glass. 'I guess that probably accounts for his friendship with Stackler, then?'

'I suppose so,' she replied, thoughtfully. 'Bertele said they caused a bit of a scene at the casino.'

'They were certainly pissed out of their brains well before we left!'

Micheele grinned. 'Yes, I got that impression from Bertele as well. He told me the Baron left one of his agents to keep an eye on them, in case there was any trouble.'

'Yes, Spencer and I saw them as we were leaving the bar.'

'But, did you hear what happened when they got back to the Plaza Hotel?'

Garvan confessed he hadn't.

'Stackler smashed up his room.'

'Why the hell did he do that?'

'I don't know, but he smashed all the mirrors in the bathroom and the one on the dressing table. In the morning, Bertele had to calm things down with the manager, who was threatening to call the police and have Stackler thrown out of the hotel. He eventually persuaded the manager to allow him to stay, but it was only on the condition he settled the bill for the damages up front.'

'The intelligence reports suggest he's mentally unbalanced.'

She pulled a face. 'In my opinion, the bloody man should be certified!'

'He's good at what he does.'

'You mean, killing people?'

He had to agree with her. 'The trouble is, with Himmler's backing, no-one dare openly criticise him, let alone try to make a move against him. It's just not going to happen, at least not anytime soon.' He drained his glass. 'By the way,' he said, almost as an afterthought, 'before we left London, Spencer and I were called into to see Tar Robertson.'

Her eyes narrowed curiously.

'He asked us to have a quiet word with you.'

'About what?' she asked, defensively.

'Tar has received reports you've been discussing your work with some of your Portuguese friends.'

Michelle's face coloured immediately. 'As God is my witness,' she pleaded with him, 'I swear to you, I've never mentioned the Double Cross to anyone. Think of it, why would I be that sodding stupid?'

'You're saying the reports are false?'

'Yes, I am!' Michelle said vehemently. 'Where the hell did this stuff come from?'

'George Rowlands filed the reports,' he said matter-of-factly. He could see she was livid.

'You don't believe me, do you?' she cried angrily.

Garvan shrugged indifferently. 'Give me one good reason you think Rowlands would want to lie about you.'

He didn't wait for her to respond; he attracted the waiter's attention and paid the bill. As he closed his wallet, Michelle was still angrily pleading her innocence, but then again, he hadn't expected her to own up.

'Until you can think of a valid reason why Rowlands would file false reports about you, then I've no reason to doubt him. I know you're running scared, but a word of warning, my dear, you're living on borrowed time with London. For your sake, you'd better get a grip, before Robertson decides to have you closed down for good.'

He left the courtyard without another word, leaving Michelle angrily gathering up her handbag, and still defiantly pleading her innocence.

## Chapter 15

Spencer was driven to the British Embassy in Lisbon by one of George Rowlands' staff officers. MI6 had just received feedback from London about the Peenemunde blueprint. It was simply too risky taking the response to Estoril, so there was no alternative other than to meet up in Rowlands' office.

Professor Reginald Jones, or RV as he was known around Whitehall, was a formidable member of the Scientific Intelligence staff at the War Office. Along with his team of fellow engineers and scientists, they'd set about evaluating the missile technology provided by Giscard's plans from the site.

Over the last few months, there had been many disagreements between Jones and his boss, Frederick Lindemann, about the interpretation of the numerous intelligence reports landing on their respective desks. At long last, the two men finally appeared to be singing from the same hymn sheet, and had come to an amicable agreement about the Peenemunde rocket programme. Although Lindemann was Churchill's scientific advisor, Jones enjoyed not only the confidence of the Prime Minister but also the Chief of the Air Staff, Sir Charles Portal.

Rowlands passed Spencer the pink-coloured file stamped Top Secret containing the Professor's notes. 'The Americans flew it over yesterday afternoon,' he explained. 'It makes for a fascinating read.'

'I bet it does.'

'Would you care for some tea?'

'No thanks, George.'

As Spencer started reading the file, Rowlands began to flick through the memo pad on his desk, and every so often, screwed up one of the sheets into a tight ball, and then tossed it into the waste paper bin. For some reason, he seemed distracted, and kept muttering to himself. After a while,

Spencer began to find his mumblings increasingly irritating. He looked up at him once or twice rather pointedly, but Rowlands was completely oblivious and in a world of his own.

'Is anything wrong?' he asked him.

Rowlands rolled his eyes. 'You've no idea the sodding problems you've caused by having *that* bloody woman sent here to the Embassy.'

'What's with the memo pad?'

'I'm trying to write a holding reply to the Ambassador's deputy.' He smiled thinly. 'The trouble is, with these Foreign Office types, you have to watch your Ps and Qs all the time, otherwise they hang you out to dry.'

Spencer sympathised with him.

'Not to mention the day job,' Rowlands grumbled, patting a pile of unread papers in his in-tray.

Spencer looked at him thoughtfully. There was no escaping the fact combing through huge volumes of incoming intelligence was an essential, albeit tedious, part of the job. Spencer flashed him a smile. 'You're talking to the converted.'

'I guess I am, dear boy.'

Spencer didn't doubt the Lisbon posting was demanding. Rowlands was renowned for his effortless skill in cultivating people, whether they were foreign diplomats, local politicians, or just about anyone else he thought might prove useful to MI6. His hard work had borne fruit, and he was highly regarded, not only by his boss, Frank Lucern, but across Whitehall, and more to the point, no-one in the Service had a bad word to say about him.

'That cup of tea,' Spencer said.

'What about it?'

'I've changed my mind.'

'Of course, dear chap, of course,' Rowlands said, getting up from his desk.

Job done, Spencer smiled to himself. At least he now had a couple of minutes alone to concentrate on the report. On the opening page, Jones had described Giscard's blueprint as something of a timely Godsend, as he could now categorically prove his theories regarding the type of weaponry being developed at the site in northern Germany. Spencer guessed his rather barbed comment was aimed specifically at Frederick Lindemann, who had originally doubted Jones' interpretation of the strange cigar-like shapes in the RAF reconnaissance photographs. He made a point of saying how he and his colleagues were keenly aware their sources frequently risked their lives on a daily basis to obtain the information about the emerging rocket programme from behind enemy lines. In fact, several vital strands of intelligence had been received over the last few months from foreign conscripted labourers and concentration camp prisoners working directly on the project. Their bravery, he stated, had led directly to the Government, and their American Allies being alerted to the enormous threat posed by the experimental development work being conducted at Peenemunde.

Two weeks prior to Giscard's plans being received in London, a source embedded in the heart of the German High Command had sent a description of a "winged" rocket, with remote controls capable of being launched by a form of catapult. This intelligence had endorsed the earlier descriptions of the weapons. Spencer recalled reading about the rocket launchers in London. Of the thirty catapults they knew to have been constructed, fifteen were now confirmed by three different sources as being currently serviceable.

The sheer volume of intelligence flooding in had meant it became increasingly difficult for the team to evaluate the contents. The blueprint proved invaluable, and had allowed the team to focus their attention on interpreting the technical data. In Jones' opinion, the only realistic option available to the Allies to counter the growing threat was a recommendation to bomb the rocket site.

He wrote; "*Peenemunde would demand considerable priority over all other places, despite our curiosity to watch the development of the trials. Intelligence would be prepared to take the risk of the work being re-started elsewhere.*" In other words, Jones and his scientific colleagues were all too aware strategic bombing of the site would undoubtedly result in the Germans spreading production to other establishments, and to other countries, to protect the future conduct of the weapons programme.

The Professor described how a recent RAF reconnaissance flight had provided concrete photographic evidence of an increase in the air defences at the site. A Company from the German Air Signals Experimental Regiment had recently moved a Wurzburg radar to Peenemunde as a precaution against possible enemy air attack. He concluded, by confirming it had been agreed at the very highest levels Peenemunde should and would be attacked by Bomber Command on the heaviest possible scale. He added, his colleagues at the War Office were in full support of his decision.

Spencer glanced up from the file, as Rowlands came back with the tea.

'When are they going to bomb the site?'

'Sometime in August, I believe,' Rowlands said languidly.

'I can't help thinking, whatever we throw at the bastards, it'll be no more effective than spitting in the wind.'

Rowlands shrugged. 'You're right, Spence; you know you are. The programme's far too advanced to be halted altogether. My understanding is, they're hoping to delay the manufacture of the rockets for a couple of months, maybe a few more, if we strike lucky.'

'The Nazis must have already earmarked other assembly factories, in case Peenemunde was bombed.'

'Yes, of course, they have other sites. They're not on the same scale or importance as Peenemunde, but I think it's inevitable they'll move more stuff toward northern France. We're currently trying to locate as many as we possibly can, but time is against us.' Rowlands cupped his hands together and rested them down on the desk. 'In the short term, we don't have anything in our armoury to throw back at them. The bottom line is, our scientists need to play catch up with the Germans. They're technically way ahead of us. In the meantime, all we can do is to carry out a series of bombing raids, and hope we can disrupt production and delay their launch.' He sat back in his chair. 'Did you know the latest Government estimates state there could be anything up to two hundred thousand casualties as a result of repeated rocket attacks?'

Spencer puffed out his cheeks, and let out a low whistle. 'Christ, they'll make the Blitz look like a bloody stroll in the park. I take it London's still the main target?'

'Yes, it's still London.'

'How strong are the air defences at Peenemunde?'

'Strong enough,' Rowlands responded. 'The current thinking is for the RAF to conduct a diversionary raid on Berlin to draw away the night fighters.' He picked up his fountain pen and began thoughtfully toying with it between his fingers. 'Unfortunately, there have been heated arguments between Jones and Duncan Sandys about the bombing.'

Duncan Sandys was the Chairman of a War Cabinet Committee, whose specific remit was the defence of Britain against the impending threat posed by the rocket programme. From personal experience, Spencer knew the Professor could be prickly, so wasn't entirely surprised he'd locked horns with Sandys.

'What's the problem?' he asked.

Rowlands explained Jones had envisaged a two-pronged attack on Peenemunde. The first wave of bombers would target the factory workshops; the second would then concentrate on the experimental site itself, the launch pads, and so on.

'What does Sandys want to do?'

'He doesn't only wish to target the development works and installation, but the housing estate where the scientists and engineers live.' He folded his arms, and fell silent for a moment. 'Jones thinks it's a waste of bloody time, and a waste of Bomber Command resources. Killing a few scientists isn't going to impact on the project one bit, it's simply too advanced to make any lasting difference. In his opinion, they'd be better off concentrating on the weaponry itself.'

Spencer considered the matter. 'I think Jones probably has a point. So, who's won the day?'

'Apparently, Sandys has.' He shot Spencer a wry smile. 'Then again, I suppose being married to Churchill's daughter might have carried some weight to his argument.'

Spencer passed the file back across the desk to Rowlands. 'I'm beginning to believe Giscard's whereabouts is almost in danger of becoming something of a side issue.'

'Don't worry your head on that one. Trust me, Jones and his fellow eggheads still need to pick his brains,' he assured him. 'Think about it; Jean has first-hand experience of working at Peenemunde. That alone makes him invaluable.' Rowlands laid his hands on the file and said. 'More to the point he's also a close friend of von Braun.'

'Von Braun, what about him?'

'He's the real driving force behind the entire operation, and the genius who's managed to develop a liquid propellant missile capable of destruction on an entirely unprecedented scale.'

'And your point is?'

'If we manage to get our hands on Giscard, it'll be a coup; an important one, but in the long term, we'll probably never be able to rest on our laurels, without the likes of von Braun being on side as well. He's our ultimate catch, so Giscard may well prove to be a means to an end.'

By all accounts, von Braun wasn't an ardent Nazi. The current thinking was he would probably remain loyal to the Third Reich, right up until the point where his research centre was in danger of coming under direct threat from the Allies. Von Braun's colleagues had found themselves coming increasingly under the command of the SS. In the long term, von Braun probably feared both he, and his fellow scientists, might well end up as some kind of bargaining chip, or that Hitler might take it into his head to order their execution, rather than risk them being captured by the Allies. It was a stark choice.

'Let's face it,' Rowlands continued, 'the chances of finding Jean alive are pretty remote.'

'That's as may be, but if Otto Stackler has murdered him, then why is he still hanging around in Estoril? It doesn't add up; Himmler would have ordered his return to Berlin.'

Rowlands placed his fountain pen lightly between his lips before saying, as an afterthought, 'That reminds me, Giscard's girlfriend, Claudine...'

'What about her?'

'She worries me.'

'Why?'

He pulled a face. 'We're still not sure if she's a plant.'

'We need proof.'

'That's just it; we don't have any.'

Spencer's eyes were cold and watchful. 'I'm not saying she's innocent, by any means, but even if she is guilty, the Nazis wouldn't have taken her into their confidence. I don't think she's any more idea about his whereabouts than we do.'

Rowlands looked doubtful. Spencer wasn't particularly interested in his opinion. 'I take it, as things stand, we still plan on flying her back to London?'

He seemed disconcerted, and took his time to reply. 'It might not be that easy, dear boy. There's been a bit of heated debate going on about her.'

Spencer was nonplussed; it seemed pretty straightforward enough to him. 'What's there to debate?'

'In my view,' Rowlands pronounced, before correcting himself by way of apology. 'How arrogant is that? I mean, *our* view, the MI6 view, is we shouldn't bust a gut to do anything about her. In the great scheme of things, she's not exactly our highest priority. In fact, she's not a priority at all.' He paused, a smile creasing his face. 'Unfortunately, the Foreign Office doesn't want her languishing here at the Embassy any longer than necessary. We can't exactly turn her over to the Germans, *can we*? It would rather complicate matters somewhat.'

'So, when are you flying her back to Bristol?'

'Good God, dear boy, even the Foreign Office blew that idea straight out of the water.'

Spencer shot him a questioning look.

Rowlands felt compelled to explain. 'Ever since she was suspected of betraying her boyfriend, she's tainted goods, as far as MI6 is concerned.'

'However true that is, why waste time-fighting the FO? You know damn well she can't stay here at the Embassy indefinitely.'

A flicker of irritation crossed Rowlands' face; he couldn't help it. 'We're not fighting the FO; we're just saying.' His words began to falter; there wasn't any point arguing the toss with Spencer. 'Besides,' he went on, 'the main reason for not flying her back is that places on the DC3 are in strictly limited supply. You of all people should know that. Priority is always given to agents, POWs, of course, and the usual motley crew of diplomats and businessmen plying their trade. I'll be honest with you, Spencer, Claudine doesn't have a cat in hell's chance of getting on board a flight to England.'

'What do you intend doing with her?'

'We're trying to secure her a slot on a merchant ship, but the devil's in the detail, and we haven't quite managed to thrash it out yet.'

'Well, all I can say is, you better get a move on. No matter what MI6 thinks, or doesn't think, I can't imagine the Ambassador will want Claudine loitering around his Embassy for weeks on end. I still believe we owe it to Giscard to get her on a flight. I'll leave it with you, George, to sort out, but I'd be surprised if Tar would agree to her being shoved on a merchant ship.'

Rowlands bit his tongue. If it weren't for Spencer having decided to move the girl to the Embassy in the first place, they wouldn't be having this conversation. Nor would he be taking the flak from his civil service colleagues at the Embassy.

'I'll see what I can do.'

'Thank you.'

'I won't deny things have been getting a little tricky here lately. The trouble is, you don't want to end up getting on the wrong side of the Ambassador. He's now set his diplomatic minions on us to keep up the pressure.'

Spencer wasn't interested about the in-fighting, and he certainly didn't regret his decision to move Claudine to the Embassy. It wasn't a decision he'd made lightly in the first place. If she had betrayed her boyfriend, at least, she was safely under lock and key at the Embassy and beyond the reach of the Abwehr. He wasn't entirely unsympathetic to Rowlands' situation; in fact, he perfectly understood why he was rattled, and had every right to be annoyed with him. Through no fault of his own, he wasn't only taking flak from the Foreign Office, but also from his boss, Frank Lucern.

After discovering Claudine was being held at his Embassy, the Ambassador, Sir Ronald Campbell, had immediately expressed his concerns to MI6 about having to provide a safe haven for her. If the Germans discovered he had tacitly approved the decision, they would protest to the Portuguese authorities, and cause a minor diplomatic incident. The Portuguese, he'd explained dispassionately to Rowlands, had to appear to remain completely unbiased in their dealings with the Allies and the Nazis. Anything less would jeopardize their own neutrality. If the roles were reversed, and the Germans were harbouring someone the British deemed to be a traitor, he wouldn't hesitate to make a formal complaint. Rowlands had tried to defend his stance by explaining it was thought Claudine might have betrayed Giscard to the Germans. The explanation hadn't washed with Campbell, who had then proceeded to give him a dressing down, and a sharp lesson in the nuances of diplomacy. Whatever the truth might be about Claudine, the Nazis wouldn't fail to make political capital out of the situation; she was still Giscard's erstwhile girlfriend, which was all that mattered.

Whatever Sir Ronald's personal feelings on the issue, he knew full well the situation was to an extent beyond his control. He also knew the views of the Prime Minister's office and had come to realise there was little room to manoeuvre, other than to accept the situation. All he could hope was for Claudine to be removed as soon as possible from the Embassy before her presence became common knowledge.

Spencer made to leave the office. Rowlands instinctively checked the time on the wall clock. 'Are you staying for lunch?'

'Thanks for the invite, but I'd better start making tracks back to Estoril.'

Rowlands picked up the phone and asked for Spencer's car to be ready at the main entrance in five minutes.

'How long are you staying in Lisbon tonight?' Spencer quizzed.

'Only a few more hours, I'll follow you down later this evening.' Rowlands patted the top of his in-tray. 'I just need to tidy this lot up first.'

'Did I mention Garvan's meeting Michelle Rookwood this morning?'

'Then, let's hope she comes up with something worthwhile, for a change,' Rowlands said waspishly. 'If I hear anything in the meantime, I'll contact you at the Plaza.'

Spencer went to open the office door, but hesitated. 'Have you heard anything from the Twenty Committee?'

'Not personally, I believe Frank spoke to Tar on the phone yesterday afternoon. From what I can gather, it was only just to ensure we were giving you our full support.'

'Well, just as long as they're not counting on us finding Giscard in one piece.'

## Chapter 16

Spencer joined Garvan on the terrace of the Plaza Palacio Hotel; he wanted to know about his meeting with Michelle Rookwood. As things stood, the odds of finding Giscard alive were minimal. He was somewhat between a rock and a hard place; Frank Lucern's MI6 team in Lisbon hadn't yet managed to come up with any tangible intelligence. In fact, they'd been met by a wall of silence. Lucern's educated guess was the deadly combination of Himmler's personal involvement, and the psychopathic presence of Stackler, had sent their usual reliable local contacts scurrying for cover. They were now almost entirely reliant upon Robertson's Double Cross agents and Lucern's MI6 operatives working out of Lisbon and Estoril. The only real fly in the ointment, so far, was their increasing concerns about Michelle's suspect reliability.

Robertson had instructed one of his most successful agents, Juan Pujol Garcia, working under the Codename Garbo, who was by chance in Portugal on unrelated business, to put out feelers, and see if anyone knew about Jean's fate, or, at the very least, find someone who was willing to talk about him. One of the main problems for Tar was the Abwehr in Lisbon hadn't made contact with Berlin about Stackler's mission for three days. Whether this was a deliberate decision on the Baron's part, or not, was unclear. As things stood, there was nothing to do, other than to sit tight, and hope some useful intelligence would eventually come to light.

At the Embassy, Claudine had continued to protest her innocence, and that she would never have betrayed Jean to the Germans. Spencer was too experienced, and perhaps far too cynical, to take anything Claudine said at face value; he could only deal with hard facts, and right now, he needed Garvan's opinion, and his copper's detached, analytical mind to help him sort the wheat from the chaff.

As they sat together on the terrace overlooking the gardens, Spencer carefully adjusted his straw Fedora hat to keep the sun from out of his eyes.

'What do you think; is Michelle still holding out on us?' he asked Garvan.

He took his time before answering; his meeting with Michelle had raised a number of issues, and not only about Jean Giscard. As an experienced detective, Garvan had become almost obsessive in playing his hunches close to his chest; having worked with MI5 for the past two years, he was only slowly getting to grips with the idea of actually sharing his thoughts and discussing them openly.

'I think she's probably telling the truth that Bertele didn't tell her they knew Giscard was holed up at the casino.'

'You're probably right,' Spencer conceded.

'However much he trusts her, and he does, there's a "so far," and there's a "too far." The bottom line is, Bertele's got his hands full at the moment, and desperately wants to keep his head below the parapet. Let's face it; as postings go; he could do a lot worse than living out the war here in Portugal.' Garvan glanced around the sun-kissed terrace. 'In fact, I wouldn't mind giving it a go myself.'

'Nor would I,' Spencer laughed. 'What else did she have to say for herself?'

Garvan told him how Stackler had smashed the mirrors in his hotel room.

Spencer shot him a wry smile. 'So, the intelligence reports weren't wrong after all.'

'He's done it before, then?'

'Apparently, there was an incident in Poland. He got himself plastered, just as he did the other night, and ended up smashing a mirror at the military headquarters. They put it down to high spirits, but then again, in the *Einsatzgruppen* it's probably standard behaviour.'

'Michelle did come up with something, the name of the thin, scrawny guy who was drinking with him at the casino.'

Spencer looked suddenly more interested in what he had to say.

'His name is Aldous Meyer, and you were spot on. He is a member of the Gestapo. Meyer's been working in Lisbon for approximately a year, operating around the docks, trying to buy information on trans-Atlantic shipping movements. I guess he probably has a few other strings to his bow as well.'

'What's his connection to Stackler?'

'They're old friends from Berlin.'

'Are they,' Spencer said curiously. 'I'll have to get back to London and have him checked out; they might have something on him.'

There was a slight pause, before Garvan continued, 'I can't pinpoint it exactly, but I still think she's holding out on something.'

'What makes you say that?'

'She's scared witless; that's part of the problem.'

'You mean of Stackler?'

'I think he started the ball rolling.'

'If it's not just about Stackler, then what the hell is she holding out for? We can't afford to pussyfoot around like this, Luke!'

Spencer glanced around the terrace, and attracted the attention of a waiter serving at another table, ordering two large double whiskeys on the rocks.

He rested his right arm on the table, and said to Garvan in a lowered voice, 'Why in God's name didn't you get it out of her?'

Garvan held his gaze; he certainly wasn't about to be coerced into changing his mind in how best to interview Michelle. 'I've already told you,' he replied calmly. 'There wasn't any point; she was too bloody scared. She's just not thinking straight.'

'If she's not up to the job, we'll have to lift her out of Portugal. There's too much at stake for her to start messing us around.'

'I'll sort it.'

'You'll have to. We're running out of time. The last thing we need is for her to crack. Do you think she's likely to?'

Garvan gave a considered reply. 'I think she'll hold up.'

Spencer pulled a face. 'You're not giving me a warm feeling about this, Luke. Are you sure? Otherwise, I'll have to approach Tar, and ask him to reconsider his order about Joyce. I need someone in the Club I can trust; we can't afford this going tits up again.'

'I think she'll be fine.'

'I hope to God she is. Otherwise, we're all in the shite.'

Garvan decided to steer the conversation away from Michelle. 'Have you heard anything from the SOE about Claudine?'

Spencer shook his head. 'Nothing, at least, nothing they can pin on her. So far, she appears to be as clean as a whistle. The French Resistance are also trying to see if they can come up with anything.' He regarded Garvan thoughtfully. 'You've never been convinced about Claudine, have you?'

'I've kept an open mind.' He hesitated for a moment; he had nothing really to go on other than a copper's instinct. 'I might be wrong, but I can't help thinking someone else betrayed Giscard.'

Spencer narrowed his eyes, searching his face. 'You mean another mole, is that what you're saying?'

Garvan drew heavily on his cigarette. 'Yes, I suppose I am.'

Spencer impatiently looked around for the waiter; he was nowhere to be seen. 'Where the hell's he got to?'

He'd hardly spoken, when they were interrupted by the waiter carrying a silver champagne cooler with a freshly opened bottle and three flutes.

Spencer's face registered surprise. 'What's this?'

The waiter pointed toward the balustrade wall surrounding the terrace, with its clear sweeping views of the tree-lined gardens and the sandy beach beyond. 'The lady over there ordered the champagne for your table, sir. I'm sorry, gentleman, would you still care for your whisky?'

'No, thank you. The champagne's fine.'

Joyce raised her hand in greeting, and headed across the terrace toward them with an expensive tan-coloured leather clutch bag tucked firmly under her arm, and matching high-heeled, roped-soled espadrilles, sunglasses, and a figure hugging cream silk dress. For all Joyce's faults, and there were many, her poise and earthy outspoken honesty was at times like a breath of fresh air. She joined them at the table.

Spencer's eyes rested on her for a moment. 'Why the champagne?' he asked her.

'Don't get too excited now, darling, will you,' she said smoothly.

'I wasn't. Have you had any luck?'

She grimaced. 'That all depends on your point of view, but I do have some good news.'

Garvan poured them each a glass of champagne. She thanked him.

'Stackler's definitely still here in Estoril,' she smiled.

Spencer scowled at her, and sighed wearily before saying, 'Come on, is that the best you can do?'

Her gaze was intense, with an undertone of contempt. She didn't rise to the bait. Spencer was a hard-boiled cynic, and loved to provoke her, and the hint of sarcasm in his voice certainly wasn't lost on her.

'I've heard,' she said, raising her glass, and watching the bubbles rise to the surface, 'Stackler is booked onto the next Lufthansa flight out of Lisbon on Monday morning.' Her announcement was met with a wall of silence. She looked at each of them in turn; slightly disappointed they didn't appear to be following her drift. Joyce took a large gulp of the champagne, before setting the glass back down on the table. 'I've discovered the day after Stackler kidnapped Giscard from the casino, there was a scheduled Lufthansa flight to Berlin.' Joyce coolly flicked her tawny blonde hair out of her eyes. 'You have to ask yourself, why Stackler wasn't on board?'

Spencer's gaze locked hard onto Joyce. 'We've been asking ourselves the same question for days. So, you tell us. Why wasn't he on it?'

Before she could provide him with an answer, Garvan interrupted. 'Who told you he's flying back to Berlin on Monday?'

She pursed her lips together, and said in a slow, considered manner, 'It was simple I cut out the middle man.' She meant von Bertele. 'I caught the train first thing this morning up to Lisbon, and had lunch with the Baron.' She took another sip of champagne. 'Actually, it turned out to be rather good timing.'

'How was it good timing?' Garvan asked.

'He hadn't been long off the phone to Bernard Drescher.'

'He's your controller in Berlin.'

'Yes.'

'Was it about Giscard?'

'Yes, it was.' She smiled. 'Stackler has been forced to hang around Estoril far longer than he planned.'

'Why?'

'It seems Himmler had a change of mind about having Giscard assassinated.'

Spencer looked dubious. 'There's got to be a catch.'

'There's always a catch. The *Führer* has finally come around to Himmler's idea that, for the time being, there was more political capital to be gained by keeping him alive, albeit temporarily. They'll film the trial in Berlin, and it'll be an ideal opportunity to make a public example of him, to send a warning, not just to foreign nationals, but to any would-be German dissenters as well. With Hitler's approval, things have moved on a pace, and Oswald Rothaug has been chosen to preside over the trial.'

'Giscard's still alive, then?' Spencer queried.

A slight smiled crossed her lips. 'Yes, yes he is.'

Spencer had heard of Rothaug; he'd become somewhat notorious, not only for his ardent support of the Nazi regime, but for the severity of his dealings with those brought to trial. He was a member of the powerful National Socialist Lawyers League; any German lawyer wanting to be recognised officially by the State had to become a member. Oswald basked in the limelight, and desperately wanted to curry favour with the government. He was always the first to volunteer his services as a judge to preside over any high-profile cases involving enemies of the State. Rothaug was ruthless by nature, and viewed it as a way of furthering his career with Berlin.

Without exception, the court proceedings were always a travesty of justice, and even without any evidence being presented during the trial, the outcome never varied, and a death sentence was always enforced.

Unfortunately, in Jean Giscard's case, the evidence against him was already damning. Spencer couldn't help thinking the Frenchman would have been a whole lot better off if Stackler had put a bullet through him, rather than endure the ignominy and mockery of a public trial. Political prisoners and enemies of the Nazi state were usually sentenced to be hanged, as the regime believed it to be a far more humiliating end than being shot by a firing squad.

'Do you know where they're holding him?'

'That's the problem.'

'Come clean, Jo. You don't bloody know, do you? Spencer said.

'That's about it,' she owned up truthfully.

'We haven't got long to try and track him down.' Spencer picked up his champagne flute. 'For his sake, I hope to God we do.'

Joyce opened her clutch bag and retrieved her ebony cigarette holder. 'There's one other thing.' She had their attention; she smiled tightly. 'It's the name of an agent.'

Garvan passed his lighter across the table toward her. 'Is it one our agents?'

Joyce slowly tapped a cigarette into the holder, before picking up the lighter. 'That's a moot point,' she answered cryptically.

'What's their name?' he asked.

'*Schornsteinfeger*.'

It meant nothing to Garvan, but Spencer pulled a face of disbelief. 'Is that some kind of a joke?' he asked dubiously.

'No, no, it isn't,' she assured him.

'Will someone please tell me what's going on?' Garvan said irritably.

'A *Schornsteinfeger* is a chimney sweep.' Joyce explained, and flicked on the lighter. 'The Baron says they're far and away their best agent operating in Portugal.' She looked at them coolly and smiled. 'Thinking about it, it's quite an inspired choice of name.'

'How in God's name is it inspired?' Garvan queried doubtfully.

She blew out a stream of smoke. 'Back in 1937, Himmler introduced a law, making chimney sweeping compulsory for every household throughout the length and breadth of Germany.'

Garvan still couldn't quite see the connection.

'Think carefully.' She smiled, wafting her holder. 'Love him or loath him, as the Chief of the SS, Himmler has ruthlessly consolidated and exploited his power since the Nazis seized control of Government. He's second only to Hitler, and completely untouchable. He rules through a combination of fear and brutality. In fact, he controls every facet of daily life in the Third Reich.' She drew thoughtfully on the holder. 'The law that came into effect in 1937 was passed under the guise of a fire prevention act.'

Garvan looked at her incredulously. 'What was the problem?'

'On the surface, it appeared harmless enough, but it was a ruse to allow the *Schornsteinfeger* access to every German household, and also the right to call the police and firefighters to break down people's doors, if they didn't allow them access. In effect, the law was nothing more than a means of spying by the back door, but it was spying all the same. It was just another method of controlling the population, and, more importantly, to weed out undesirables. In effect, the *Schornsteinfeger* had become the eyes and ears of Himmler's fascist national police and the SS.'

Spencer raised his champagne glass, and shot her a knowing look. 'Maybe there's a simpler explanation,' he suggested.

Joyce was curious.

'At New Year, isn't there a German tradition that *Schornsteinfeger* trinkets are given out as a sign of good luck?'

'Yes, there is.'

'Perhaps your friend, the Baron, views his latest recruit as a token of good luck.'

Joyce gave him an unflinching look. She had taken offence at the Baron being described as a friend. Spencer knew it wasn't warranted, but he liked to keep Joyce on her toes, and occasionally goad her. He'd once described her to Garvan as possessing the sensuality of Greta Garbo and the eyes of Caligula; he guessed, right now, he hadn't been that far wrong. Her expression was glacial, and the shutters had come down on him. Spencer felt a frisson of self-satisfaction; it was exactly the reaction he'd hoped to provoke.

He was the first to admit Joyce had conviction, courage, and luck. In fact, she had all three in abundance. As the war progressed, Joyce knew she was important to the end game; they'd told her so. That her peculiar talents, were not only suited to the situation but were vital for the Allied fight against Nazi Germany. The Double Cross had no one to match her. Even so, Joyce still hadn't been entirely convinced by their rhetoric.

What she hadn't appreciated was Spencer genuinely admired her bravery and, in their own way, they had much in common. Even when faced with extreme danger, Joyce had never once faltered, or outwardly, lost her cool. She was, in effect, playing a dangerous balancing act between both the Allies and the Abwehr. One false move, or a word out of place, would have resulted in certain death.

Spencer was concerned British Intelligence hadn't picked up on *Schornsteinfeger's* name before now from the wireless transmissions between Lisbon and Berlin. They'd long since broken the German codes, and the breakthrough had subsequently enabled MI5 to keep a comprehensive track of their communications. It crossed his mind fleetingly, perhaps the wily old Baron was playing some kind of tangled counterplot. *Had he perhaps started to have doubts about Joyce's allegiance to the Reich?* On the other hand, Joyce was probably too experienced not to have picked up on the signals, if the Baron had started to doubt her integrity.

'Tell me something,' he said thoughtfully.

'What's that?' she asked.

'Why in God's name hasn't he mentioned *Schornsteinfeger* to you before now?'

Joyce blew out a cloud of grey cigarette smoke. 'I don't know,' she replied honestly. 'His name came up in conversation when he was chatting about Otto Stackler. To be honest with you, he seemed rather pleased with himself it had all worked out so well.'

Spencer looked at her searchingly. 'Meaning what, exactly?'

She pursed her lips, and took another long drag on the ebony holder. 'Well, for a start, he reckons without the help of *Schornsteinfeger,* they'd still be no further forward in finding Jean Giscard's whereabouts. Not only has his agent come up trumps, but with Otto intending to fly back to Berlin on Monday morning, it leaves the Baron to get on with his day job.' Joyce held Spencer's gaze. 'And perhaps, more to the point, he believes his agent hasn't been detected by the Allied Intelligence Services.' She flashed him a slight, but meaningful, smile. 'I guess the old bugger does have a point.'

Spencer couldn't argue with her; she was right. Somehow, the Baron's agent had managed to duck under their radar. His thoughts were in freefall. MI5 had long since suspected there was a mole, but this was far worse than he had initially suspected. So far, they had successfully operated right under their noses, without being detected. *Were they embedded in British Intelligence, or perhaps, a member of the OSS, the American equivalent of MI6 in Lisbon?* Whoever it was had to be well-placed, as only a handful of people had known of Giscard's whereabouts. *Maybe Schornsteinfeger was one of their own double agents who'd turn rogue?* He'd no way of telling. The traitor might not even be based in Portugal at all, but sitting smugly at MI6's HQ in London; and then, there was the casino manager, Rafael Delgado, to take into consideration. *Was he the weak link in the chain?* His expression had hardened, and he slowly became aware Joyce was staring at him. 'Did the Baron have anything else to say for himself?'

There was stillness about her, as she shot him an upward glance. 'Not a great deal, no. The trouble is,' she continued, 'young Claudine Gregorie appears to be entirely innocent of betraying her boyfriend.'

Spencer didn't respond. Joyce was right. He should have trusted Garvan's instincts, and his judgement about Michelle holding out on them; she might have somehow managed to get wind about a rogue agent working for the Baron. He wanted Garvan to set up another meeting with Michelle, as soon as possible, and to throw the name of *Schornsteinfeger* into the conversation to see if it provoked any reaction.

Spencer made to leave the table; he'd barely touched his champagne.

'Where are you off to?' Joyce asked him.

'I need to make some calls.'

Her gaze followed him across the terrace. Garvan topped up her glass.

'You were never convinced about Claudine betraying Giscard, were you?' She smiled at him.

He wouldn't be drawn; there didn't seem any reason for going over old ground, at least not now.

'This agent,' he said to her. 'Why do you reckon we don't know about them? We should have picked something up from the code breakers.'

Joyce savoured the champagne, and gave his question careful consideration, before answering. 'I would imagine they haven't been up and running for that long, but it's only a guess.'

'If they're that important, why hasn't the Baron's team contacted Berlin about them?'

'I suppose he has his reasons.'

'What reasons could he have?'

Joyce looked at him sharply. 'I get the impression the Baron sees *Schornsteinfeger* as his protégé, someone to cultivate and to bring on. In his place, I probably wouldn't have contacted Berlin, either, at least not before they'd proved themselves.'

'And, now, what do you think he'll do?'

'It's a feather in his cap *Schornsteinfeger* has helped them track down Jean Giscard.' Joyce absent-mindedly traced her fingers around the rim of the flute, and glanced across the table at him; it was flirtatious, but he guessed it was no more than a reflex action. 'Just think about it. Stackler is Himmler's man, and the Baron's boss is Admiral Canaris.'

Canaris was a shrewd, brilliant spymaster, and much admired by his British counterparts. His position in the hierarchy of the Reich was complicated; he was an unknown quantity, and his loyalty to Hitler remained suspect. While Canaris had once been highly thought of by Hitler, he'd always been completely mistrusted by Himmler. Despite this, he appeared to have little difficulty outwitting his powerful adversary. There were wheels within wheels, she explained, and the Baron was playing a dangerous game. He'd supported Stackler in Portugal to appease Himmler, but ultimately, his only real allegiance was to Canaris, and to the Fatherland, and not to the criminal folly of Hitler and the Third Reich.

It was common knowledge Canaris was increasingly out of step with Berlin. As early as the invasion of Poland, he'd been completely appalled by the wanton brutality of the SS. It was on record he'd saved the lives of at least seven Jews who were about to be transported to a concentration camp. Canaris had personally complained to Himmler the Gestapo were arresting his agents; it was an outright lie, of course, but a very brave one. His intervention saved their lives, and, to the Admiral's mind, it was all that mattered. The Jews were subsequently handed over by the Gestapo to the Abwehr, and taught a few minor secret codes. It was just a cover, of course, but it had kept them from Himmler's clutches and almost certain death.

'Where does this leave us?' he mused.

'To be honest with you, I'm not entirely sure. It all rather depends on whether Stackler can deliver Giscard safely to Berlin. Until then, I guess the Baron will keep his agent well under wraps. He certainly won't want to publicise his involvement until he knows it's safe to do so.' The merest flicker of a smile crossed her lips. 'Unfortunately, once London manages to intercept his wireless transmissions, to Berlin, it'll be too little, and too late, to make any real difference.'

## Chapter 17

It was Michelle's idea to meet up at a nondescript café nestled along the beach front. Stepping inside, Garvan thought it looked like the Portuguese equivalent of a down market British greasy spoon. It was overwhelmingly dark, with an oppressive, almost claustrophobic feel. The air was filled with an unsavoury combination of stale cigarette smoke, and the aroma of freshly cooked *torrada*, the Portuguese equivalent of toast, mixed with freshly brewed coffee. It caught his breath; it wasn't necessarily a good fusion of smells, or at least not this early in the morning.

Glancing around the café, Garvan again couldn't fault Michelle's choice of venue. As with the Alvor, it appeared to be popular amongst the locals but was scarcely likely to attract anyone from the German community.

There were a handful of customers enjoying their breakfast a mother with two young children, a group of men dressed in overalls, and an elderly couple. Michelle was sitting by herself near the doorway to the kitchen. She was waving at him, trying to attract his attention. On joining her at the table, he noticed a wine bottle in the centre, with a candle perched inside encircled by a congealed lava flow of dried wax. Michelle pushed it to one side to give them more room.

'I've already ordered coffee,' she said, patting a metallic pot. She poured him a cup and topped it up with milk. He took a sip and grimaced; the coffee was unbearably bitter. 'Is there any sugar?

Michelle nudged a small glass bowl toward him. 'Help yourself.'

He heaped up two large spoonfuls and stirred the coffee, then, took another tentative sip. The sugar hadn't helped much; the coffee was still incredibly bitter.

Michelle smiled at him awkwardly. 'What's this all about, Chief Inspector? Why did you want to see me again?'

'Believe me, Chelle, it's certainly wasn't by choice.'

Garvan wrapped his hands around the coffee cup. 'I still feel as if you're not being entirely straight with me.'

Michelle appeared to be genuinely taken aback by the accusation. 'I-I'm sorry,' she stammered, 'what do you mean not being straight?'

He allowed a silence to fall between them. He wanted to keep Michelle on edge; she seemed tense anyway, and he needed to keep it that way. 'We go back a long way, don't we?'

'At least ten years,' she agreed with him.

Michelle's mind began spiralling into overdrive. She'd already confessed, albeit belatedly, she'd known about Giscard's arrival in Estoril, and had also hoped to regain a small measure of credibility by revealing the identity of Stackler's drinking partner, Aldous Meyer. She'd hoped it might be just enough to keep him off her back for a while longer. She should have known better, and had stupidly miscalculated the seriousness of the situation.

George Rowlands' damning report to London hadn't exactly helped either; it had placed her entirely on the back foot. She was playing catch up, not only in the eyes of British Intelligence, but, more importantly, with both Garvan and Spencer. The fact she'd initially held out on them, and was seemingly reluctant to share the information she had on Giscard and Meyer, meant she was effectively living on borrowed time. This wasn't a game. One more slip-up and she'd be thrown to the wolves, and the mercy of Robertson's Twenty Committee.

'Do you remember the first time I interviewed you at West End Central?' he continued smoothly.

Michelle could hardly forget it; had been like a baptism of fire. He'd been tough, uncompromising; he was every inch the hard bastard who'd earned the respect of London's underworld. She'd slowly caved in under the cross-examination, as he steadily, but remorselessly, wore her down with his slick interrogation.

'I've been asking myself something, Chelle.'

'I'm sure you have,' she responded flatly.

'I don't understand why you've been holding out on us.' He allowed his words to sink in. 'I guess it's something about the eyes.'

'What do you mean?'

'They always give the game away when someone's lying to you.'

Michelle chose not to respond. She figured out she'd already dug herself in one hell of a deep hole, and didn't want to make matters any worse.

Garvan picked up his cup. It crossed his mind to give the coffee another try, but decided against it, and set the cup promptly back down on the table. 'Do you know what worries me, Chelle?'

'I have no idea.'

'There're no two ways about it; you're in such a prime position to betray us.'

Her eyes widened questioningly.

'To betray the Double Cross,' he said speaking the words slowly.

The menace in his voice wasn't lost on her. The colour instantly drained from her face. 'Do you honestly believe after all I've been through I'd risk blowing everything? Why the hell would I?' she said defensively.

He held her gaze. 'I'm not sure; you tell me.'

Michelle looked agitated; the ball was very much in her court. She knew he was playing with her. 'I know you probably won't believe me, why should you.' She thoughtfully chewed her lip. 'Although life here in Portugal isn't always exactly a bed of roses, I certainly wouldn't want to return home to England. The weather's lovely; there's no rationing, and no fear of bombing. Whatever else you think of me, I'm not a bloody fool. I know if I mess up again, there's no going back. Robertson will have me closed down.'

A silence fell between them; Garvan was in no rush to break it.

Michelle placed her hands together. 'I know you hate me, Garvan, but you're the only one I trust!' she pleaded with him.

His expression remained unreadable. 'Then, why not start by being completely up front with me?' He watched her face; she didn't have an answer for him, or, at least, one she was willing to share. 'Tell me something,' he said slightly softening his tone. 'Have you heard of an agent called *Schornsteinfeger*?'

It was written all over her face she had. Michelle looked at Garvan warily. 'Yes, yes, I've heard the name.'

'Who told you?'

'Oberst, I mean, Colonel von Bertele.'

He looked through her, rather than at her. 'Then, for Christ's sake, Chelle, why the hell didn't you say something. What's your problem? How long have you known?' he persisted.

Michelle pursed her lips. 'No more than a week,' she said defensively.

He allowed his expression to register surprise. 'Why haven't you contacted London?'

'I wanted to make sure.'

Garvan cut her off. 'Make sure of, what exactly?'

'That *Schornsteinfeger* wasn't just some kind of bluff, a ruse set up by the Germans to deflect attention away from Stackler.'

'Perhaps if you'd pulled your finger out sooner by alerting London there was a potential rogue agent at large, we might not be in the position we are now, and we could have had time to move Giscard out of the casino before Stackler and Meyer managed to get their hands on him. For Christ's sake, have you any idea what you've done?'

Michelle drained her cup; she didn't quite know where to look. Garvan reached into his jacket pocket and retrieved a pack of cigarettes; he placed one between his lips and flicked on his lighter.

'But, why the chimney sweep?'

'I don't have a clue.'

'Didn't you ask why?' he queried.

'Of course, I did. I thought, at first, it was some kind of a joke, and von Bertele was pulling my leg.'

'What did he say?'

Michelle closed her eyes and smiled. 'It was a very one-sided conversation.'

'He didn't tell you why?'

'He plays games with me, Chief Inspector.'

'But, he trusts you.'

'But, only up to a certain point,' she countered. 'Besides, it was the Baron's idea to name them *Schornsteinfeger*.'

'Who is the chimney sweep?' he pressed her.

Michelle looked at him guardedly. 'What makes you think I know?'

'I'm ever the optimist. Are you going to disappoint me?'

She cracked a smile. 'Yes, I am.'

'Surely you have your suspicions?'

Michelle reached down for her handbag and hurriedly re-applied her bright red lipstick. 'Bertele says the chimney sweep's recruitment by the Baron was a real coup for the Abwehr. That the old bugger has pulled off a blinder with an agent who's well placed within the Allied Intelligence agencies.' Her eyes rested on him for a moment. 'I guess Bertele wasn't that far wrong; you obviously believe *Schornsteinfeger* was responsible for betraying Jean Giscard to the Germans.' She snapped the handbag shut, and offered him more coffee. He declined. So, she poured herself another cup.

'For all we know, Chelle, you might be the chimney sweep.'

She rolled her eyes. 'I wondered when that one was coming!'

'You can't be shocked.'

'I guess not.'

'From where I'm sitting, it could explain why you didn't bother contacting London.'

'I suppose it might look that way,' she conceded.

'When are you going to understand, Chelle, this isn't West End Central, and you're no longer some bloody bit part player. You're playing with the big boys now.'

Michelle knew only too well George Rowlands' report about her to the Twenty Committee had severely damaged her reputation.

'I thought I was doing the right thing,' she pleaded. 'After Rowlands reported me to Tar, I knew I was on a hiding to nothing. I had to try and claw my way back into the Committee's good books.

Garvan narrowed his eyes questioningly. 'Why didn't you tell them about the chimney sweep then?'

'I wanted to wait until I had something worthwhile reporting,' she tried explaining.

'Anything is better than nothing,' he suggested.

'I was afraid unless I came up with a name, London would end up thinking it was some cock and bull story I'd conjured up to save my own neck.'

'But, you know how the system works.'

She looked at him sharply, and parted her lips as if to speak but thought better of it.

'For Christ's sake, Chelle, it's not for you to pick and choose what you pass across to MI5. It's up to Tar Robertson and the Twenty Committee to decide what's important or not; you know that.' He inhaled heavily on his cigarette, as if he was in need of a nicotine fix. 'You've been a double agent long enough now to understand you report everything back to London, no matter how seemingly trivial.'

She lowered her face and began to cry. 'I know I've screwed up,' she wept.

'Well, judging by what you've just told me, is it any wonder you're under review?'

She cast him a petulant look with her doleful eyes. 'That's as may be, but it doesn't help any knowing Spencer despises me.'

Garvan flashed a fleeting smile. 'Don't flatter yourself too much, Chelle. I don't think he gives you *that* much thought at all.'

He hadn't meant it unkindly; he was merely telling her the truth.

'I don't understand him at all.'

'If I were you, I wouldn't even bother trying.'

'He frightens the shit out of me!'

'He does that to everyone.'

Garvan mentioned Joyce Leader was of the opinion Giscard was still alive. He knew the two women had locked horns in the past, and there was certainly no love lost between them. Michelle was feisty, with a devastatingly short fuse, but had always been in complete control of her sexuality, which she'd used skilfully to her advantage. She'd never been too overtly sexual; she was far subtler than that, but in an oddly, unemotional fashion. If truth be told, Michelle probably had more in common with Joyce Leader than she cared to admit. There was an openness and willingness about her to learn, and a genuine empathy for people, and if the situation demanded, like Joyce Leader, she was more than capable of selling her soul to the devil.

Garvan couldn't help noticing Michelle appeared to have lost some of her sparkle, but he desperately needed her to start thinking straight, and to regain a measure of her old self-confidence and composure. He needed the dubious qualities which had led her from a life of crime to volunteering her services to the Abwehr, and then, successfully wheedling her way into British Intelligence. She was undoubtedly driven by self-interest, but, in the past, she had proved to be good at espionage. Otherwise, she would never have landed herself a key role in Portugal.

Michelle hurriedly dabbed her eyes with a handkerchief, and then, screwed it up tightly in her fist. She knew this was her last chance to prove her worth. She certainly wouldn't get another opportunity. The Double Cross team wasn't strong on patience, and anyone deemed to be a potential liability was dealt with swiftly.

Michelle also knew it wasn't exactly helping her cause having Joyce Leader working directly alongside Garvan and Spencer. It was only natural they'd end up making comparisons about their ability to produce results through their Abwehr contacts. The two women had only met twice before, and on each occasion, Joyce had struck Michelle as being aloof, and almost glacial, in her demeanour. But, beneath all the outward arrogance and haughtiness, there was no denying she possessed an underlying innate elegance, and a certain charm, which she could seemingly turn on and off at will. Joyce appeared only willing to let people into her life on a superficial level. Michelle wondered if that was why she was so good at what she did. During their last meeting, she recalled Spencer had praised Joyce's astuteness as a spy. She figured out there was probably no greater accolade.

'We're rapidly running out of time,' she heard Garvan saying, 'and so are you, unless you can start turning things around.'

'Honestly, I don't know whether your Frenchman's still alive,' Michelle said curtly. 'But, if Joyce says he is, then I guess it's true. She's excellent at getting information out of people, especially the Baron.' She sniffed derogatively.

It was a barbed comment, but it missed the mark. He guessed she was no doubt implying Joyce was sleeping with him. It didn't matter much either way to MI5, just as long as she came up with the relevant intelligence.

'But, however good she is,' Michelle said archly, 'you must have your doubts about her as well.' She paused, a smile playing around her mouth. 'The Baron's always singing her praises to von Bertele.' Michelle's eyes danced mischievously. 'Is she perhaps your Agent *Schornsteinfeger*?'

He stubbed out his cigarette in a glass ashtray, already filled to the brim with discarded dog ends. 'The bottom line is, no-one's above suspicion, no matter how good they are, you know that!'

She appraised him speculatively. 'As a matter-of-fact, I do have something else for you.'

'Go on.'

'Von Bertele told me Otto Stackler is flying back to Berlin early next week.'

At least, she'd confirmed Joyce's information was correct about his returning to Germany. She poured herself another coffee; it was her third.

'God knows how you can drink that stuff.' Garvan observed, with a grin.

She returned his smile. 'It's an acquired taste, but you get used to it after a while.' She gently set the metal pot back down on the table. 'I don't know whether it's important,' she said hesitantly, 'but Bertele mentioned he was throwing a dinner party on Saturday evening.' She shot him a nervous look. 'From what I understand, he's invited both the Baron and Otto Stackler to the meal.'

'What's on your mind?

'Maybe I'm reading too much into it.'

'Why not let me be the judge of that,' Garvan suggested, and handed her a cigarette, hoping it might help calm her nerves. She thanked him.

'Bertele's holding the dinner party at a club on the outskirts of town.' Michelle placed the cigarette between her lips. Garvan flicked on his lighter for her.

'What's the place called?'

'The Wulf Club.' She pulled on the cigarette and exhaled slowly. 'It's owned by a middle-aged German couple, Meinhard and Agentha Wulf. Their son is a respected officer serving with the $2^{nd}$ SS Panzer Division, the Das Reich. It's all very discreet and run exclusively for the German community here in Estoril and Lisbon.'

Garvan knew the Das Reich was an elite division fielded by the Waffen-SS. The Wulf family's connection might well have helped to account for the club's popularity amongst the German community.

'I believe they've been running the place almost continuously since the beginning of the war.'

'Have you been there before?'

'I've had dinner at the Wulf with Bertele a few times. People tend to come down for the weekend to Estoril, and let their hair down, without having to worry anyone's listening in on their conversations.' She pondered the matter for a moment. 'It just got me wondering.'

'Go on,' he said to her.

'If your Frenchman is still alive, I assume they're planning on taking him back to Berlin?'

She was spot on; Garvan explained how Joyce had heard from the Baron Giscard was to face a show trial by the end of the week.

'Are you sure?' she asked.

'Well, as sure as we can be.'

'The poor sod,' she sighed sympathetically. 'My understanding is Stackler is going to head down to Lisbon directly after the meal is over.'

'Is he?'

'I was just thinking. Presumably, he'll be taking Giscard with him to catch the next available flight to Berlin.'

Michelle had a point, a good one; she might well be on to something. 'I'll run it by Spencer when I get back to the hotel. Do you know if Aldous Meyer is going to be there?'

'Not that I've heard.'

'That's a pity.'

'If it's any help, I could always show you where the club is?' she suggested.

'You may have to. Have you been invited to dinner?'

'Bertele hasn't asked me.'

'That doesn't mean to say he won't.'

'But, I can't guarantee he will.'

'We'll need you to be there,' he said flatly; it wasn't open for discussion.

'I'll try my best.'

He gave her an unflinching, penetrating smile. 'We've already messed things up once. We simply can't afford to make another mistake. We have to get our hands on Giscard, before he boards the plane to Berlin.'

'*Is he really that important?*'

'Do you honestly think we'd be having this conversation if he wasn't?'

Garvan suspected Michelle was on a fishing trip for information. She already damn well knew their presence in Portugal was confirmation enough of Giscard's importance to the Allies. What she didn't know, or was pretending not to know, was precisely why they needed him.

She searched his face questioningly. 'Even if you do manage to rescue him from the Germans, you've still got one hell of a problem on your hands.'

'You mean, Agent *Schornsteinfeger*?'

'Yes, I do.'

Garvan pulled his wallet out to pay for the coffee. Michelle placed her hand over his. 'This one's on me.'

'Why?'

'You hated the bloody stuff.'

He smiled. 'In the end, it doesn't matter who settles the bills, does it?'

Rookwood looked at him blankly.

'Who's paying our wages?'

She suddenly tossed her head back and laughed. In the end, their expenses came from Tar Robertson's budget, and they were both in effect being bankrolled by the Double Cross team and MI5.

'I'll be in touch,' he said, coming to his feet.

'Where's Spencer got to? Is he avoiding me?' she asked.

Garvan couldn't help smiling to himself; he knew Michelle believed Spencer to be her nemesis. For that reason alone, he was rarely far from her thoughts. 'I guess he thought it might be better if I had a word with you. You know what he's like; diplomacy isn't exactly his strong point.'

'How are you going to contact me?' Her voice seemed empty of all feeling.

Up until now, they'd always contacted her via a third party. Michelle had phoned a pre-arranged direct number to either one of Robertson's team or MI6 at the British Embassy. It had been a little convoluted, but was deemed necessary, for security reasons.

'I'll call you at your apartment.'

'But, I think it's bugged.'

'I'd be surprised if it wasn't.'

'Then, you'll have to be careful what you say.'

He smiled at her briefly. 'I'll say your laundry's ready.'

'But, you don't speak Portuguese.'

'And nor do you, at least not very well. I'll put on an accent and speak in English.'

Michele seemed doubtful whether he could pull it off. If he didn't, she might well find herself outed by the Abwehr.

'Don't worry. I'll ask Joyce to give me a few words of Portuguese, just to make it seem kosher.'

'But, where will we meet?'

'Don't worry, I'll let you know.'

## Chapter 18

Spencer was at the wheel of the car, as they turned off the main coastal road in the direction of the Wulf Club. Garvan was beside him in the passenger seat, with Michelle perched on the backseat. She'd finally managed to secure an invite from Colonel von Bertele for the dinner party on Saturday evening. Spencer decided, while they still had time, to drive up to the club and check out the lay of the land. He certainly didn't want to take any chances, and run the risk of allowing Jean Giscard to slip through their fingers again.

Everything was going according to plan, when the road unexpectedly petered out to a narrow track littered with deep potholes. He was forced to slow down to a snail's pace, as it was simply too dangerous to go any faster. But, it wasn't only the potholes causing them problems; there were also a number of small boulders to negotiate. He started to become concerned. If they became grounded over one of them, they'd end up being forced to ask one of the local farmers to help rescue them.

The area was steeply wooded to one side, with a sheer cliff edge to their right. Garvan gingerly peered through the passenger window; they seemed perilously close to the edge. One mistake, and they'd have plummeted down the jagged rock face.

Spencer glanced over his shoulder toward Michelle. 'Are you sure we're on the right road?'

'Of course, I am!'

Garvan instinctively closed his eyes, as Spencer braked hard to avoid a deep crack on the uneven track.

'Bloody hell!' he shouted. 'How much further is this place?'

'Not too far,' she said.

After about a mile, they found themselves on a cobbled road as they passed through a tiny village of neat, whitewashed houses clustered around an ancient roughly hewn stone church. The village was awash with an array of colourful trumpet flower vines nestling against the buildings. Unfortunately, the tiny cobbled streets didn't extend much beyond the village perimeter, and they rapidly found themselves back on the rough dirt road.

'We're almost there,' Michelle announced excitedly. 'It's just up there on the left-hand side.'

As he gripped hold of the dashboard to steady himself, Garvan said drily, 'Well, it can't be on the bleeding right-hand side, can it?'

She nervously peered out of the window and viewed the seemingly sheer drop. 'No, I guess not.' She hurriedly turned her head away; she wasn't particularly good with heights.

'Are you telling me this is the same route the Germans use to get to the Wulf Club?' Spencer queried, as he fought to lower the gears in a bid to get some traction.

'Yes, it's the same road I came in Colonel von Bertele's staff car.'

Spencer found himself having to swerve and slam on the brakes. A local farmer had just rounded a sharp bend up ahead of the. He was in the middle of the track, and, judging by his speed, hadn't been expecting to come across anyone driving in the opposite direction.

Garvan lurched forward, his hands taking the full brunt of the impact on the dashboard. If they'd been driving any faster, he'd have smashed straight through the windscreen. Michelle wasn't quite so lucky and smacked her face on the seat in front.

Spencer looked around. 'Is everyone ok?'

'I'm all right,' she said.

He thrust the car into reverse, and tried to edge his way around the truck. The farmer was shaken up, and still couldn't quite believe they hadn't crashed. He wound down his window, and let rip with a stream of expletives. Spencer just managed to scrape past the truck with barely an inch to spare, but not without giving the farmer a finger sign. It brought with it another salvo of expletives, as they crawled on up the track.

After another quarter of a mile, the dirt track began to open slowly out, the steep slopes on either side gradually gave way to a large expanse of woodland with splashes of colour from the bougainvillea growing along the roadside.

'There it is!' Michelle suddenly shrieked from the backseat.

Garvan almost leapt out of his skin. 'Crikey, Chelle, don't shout like that!'

She placed her hand over her mouth and mumbled an apology.

Spencer pulled the car over and parked up beneath a secluded canopy of trees. 'What's at the back of the club?' he asked.

'There's just a car park. The club doesn't usually open during the week until seven, unless someone's hired it out for lunch or a party, although I think they open for Sunday lunch.'

'It doesn't look that big,' Garvan said, peering through the windscreen.

'It's quite deceptive from this angle.' She suggested they drive on past to get a clearer view of the layout.

Spencer lifted off the handbrake and drove down toward to the rear of the club, and into the large circular car park surrounded on its perimeter by a bank of pine trees.

'What's beyond the trees?' he asked.

'There's a drop.'

'Is it steep?'

Michelle grimaced. 'To be honest with you I can't remember.'

Spencer pulled up and turned off the engine.

'What are you doing?' she asked, warily.

'We might as well take a good look around,' he said, opening the driver's door. He briefly glanced round at her. 'There's an old army saying, time spent in reconnaissance is never wasted.'

Michelle looked at him blankly.

'It's just my army training.'

'That's as may be,' she snorted, 'but if it's all the same to you, I'd much rather stay put.'

'Do as you please,' he said dismissively.

Garvan joined him outside the car.

Spencer nodded toward the club. 'That back door, what do you reckon it is?'

'I guess it's probably the entrance to the kitchen?'

'Could well be,' he replied setting off toward the pine trees surrounding the car park.

Garvan followed him. The wooden fence around the perimeter had seen far better days, and beyond was a steep slope, which appeared to lead down to a narrow cattle track. Garvan tentatively peered over the edge; it looked almost vertical. Although he was by no means afraid of heights, he found himself feeling slightly dizzy.

'Well, it's a ruddy long way down, *that I do know*.'

'Yes, yes, it is,' Spencer replied thoughtfully.

As they gazed toward the track, there was a light, welcoming breeze passing through the bluish-green needles of the pine trees. Spencer slowly turned away from the precipice, his hands thrust deep into his trouser pockets.

'Why don't you get back into the car?' he suggested to Garvan.

He looked at him suspiciously, not quite sure why he was trying to fob him off.

'I'm staying put!' he announced.

Spencer winked at him. 'Follow me, then.' He headed off toward the club.

Michelle, who'd been keeping a wary eye on them from the relative safety of the car, closed her eyes in horror, seeing Spencer try the back door. Finding it open, he checked Garvan was right behind him, before stepping inside. Michelle's heart was in her mouth. Although the club was closed, she assumed the staff would be preparing the evening meal.

'I'll do all the talking,' he whispered to Garvan.

They found themselves in a long dark corridor, with doors leading off to either side. They could hear the sound of someone laughing; it appeared to be coming from an open doorway a little further on. Spencer motioned for Garvan to follow.

'Are you sure?' he mouthed silently to Spencer.

He gave him the thumbs up, and sauntered off down the corridor, as if he owned the place. Garvan shook his head in disbelief, but remained glued to his tail.

Standing four-square on in the open doorway, he announced, '*Guten Morgen.*'

There were three women in the kitchen, and, as one, they looked round to face the door. They were dressed alike in dark blue dresses, with pristine, starched white aprons. Spencer turned on the charm like a tap; his trademark persona of the hard-boiled cynic had vanished. Garvan didn't have a clue what he was saying, but they started to giggle like bashful schoolgirls, which he guessed was probably a good sign.

Spencer pointed toward him, they nodded, and smiled warmly. Garvan smiled back; it seemed the right thing to do, even though he was standing there, feeling a bit like a spare part, not quite sure what to do, other than play along. When one of the women began speaking animatedly to them, Garvan nodded when he thought it appropriate to do so. Much to his surprise, it all appeared to be going rather well. He managed to gather one of them was called Gretchen, but God only knew what Spencer had told her, as she almost seemed to be on the point of curtseying to them.

Gretchen gestured for them to follow her out of the kitchen and along the corridor. Spencer quickly glanced over his shoulder at Garvan and winked.

'You bastard,' he mouthed back.

A faint smile crossed Spencer's face.

Gretchen was still happily chatting, as they trailed after her down the passage. All the while, Spencer smoothly continued the charm offensive; Garvan could only surmise she was probably flattered by the attention. For some reason, she pointed out the male and female toilets on either side of the passage. He couldn't understand why she'd do such a thing, unless Spencer had asked her. Gretchen opened the heavy wooden door at the end of the corridor, which led directly into the Wulf Club's main dining area. She explained to Spencer von Bertele had hired out the entire venue for Saturday evening.

Although the dining room was in semi-darkness, a slow bemused smile started to cross Spencer's face; it was as if they'd been suddenly transported into an upmarket *bierkeller* in the heart of a Bavarian village. There were long wooden tables with benches running the length of the restaurant, a large bar with imported Germans beers, and shelves decorated with ornate Stein beer mugs. The walls were adorned with picturesque Bavarian landscapes, and pride of place behind the bar was given to a large framed photograph of Adolf Hitler.

He guessed on Saturday evening, the guests would be served up traditional *bierkeller* fare of wiener schnitzel and bratwurst, served on a bed of sauerkraut and mashed potato. The Wulf wasn't only a reminder of home for its members, but, perhaps more importantly, a haven, somewhere they could relax and enjoy themselves without the constant fear of being overheard. In effect, it was far beyond the reach of the Allied Intelligence Services, or so they believed.

He took his time taking a look around the club, before cupping Gretchen's hands in his own, and thanking her warmly. She blushed. Garvan had the distinct impression, for some reason, she seemed strangely in awe of him. Lord only knew what he'd told her.

Heading back toward the car, he turned to Spencer. 'What the hell did you say to that poor woman?'

Spencer smiled. 'She thinks I'm Heinrich Himmler's cousin.'

A look of undisguised horror crossed Garvan's face. 'Christ almighty what are you playing at?'

'It worked, didn't it?'

'But, even so...'

'My commanding officer was always telling me, "prior planning and preparation prevents a piss poor performance." '

'Meaning what, exactly?'

'If we're going to have a cat in hell's chance of rescuing Giscard, we needed to recce the club.'

Garvan looked at him.

'I needed to check out the floor plan. If anything starts to kick off, we can't afford to be blindsided.'

Garvan couldn't fault his logic, but wondered if introducing himself as Himmler's cousin might not have been a step too far. Spencer dismissed him out of hand; Gretchen was flattered, if not a little overwhelmed by having such an illustrious visitor.

'So what did you tell her we were doing?'

'That a friend of my cousin, *Sturmbannführer* Stackler is a guest of von Bertele.'

'And she bought it?'

'Why wouldn't she? I told her the *Reichsführer* had asked me to check out the security arrangements.'

By the time they returned to the car, Michelle was leaning against the bonnet, her arms folded defiantly; she was obviously upset with them.

As he opened the driver's door, Spencer said sharply, 'What's the matter with you? You've got a face like a smacked arse.'

'I didn't know you were going inside the club.'

'Nor did I,' he replied, clicking the driver's door shut.

'You'd better get in,' Garvan said bluntly.

She pulled a face at him and hesitated slightly, somewhat reluctantly doing as she was told.

'I was starting to get worried,' Michelle tried explaining from the back seat.

Spencer fumbled in his jacket pocket for the car keys. 'Why?' he grunted.

'I didn't know what the hell was going on. I was scared stiff you might be in trouble.'

Spencer flicked the ignition switch on. He checked out Michelle's reflection in the rear-view mirror; she still had a face like thunder. Garvan climbed into the passenger seat beside him.

'I think we need to have a serious chat, don't we,' Spencer said to her.

'Do we?'

He allowed the engine to idle, and twisted himself round to face her. 'What do you think we're doing here?'

She didn't respond.

'Bertele's already told you. After dinner, Stackler is planning on leaving the club, and driving down to Lisbon.'

'Yes.'

'The intelligence reports indicate Meyer is going to meet up with him, here in the car park. We have to assume he'll be turning up with Jean Giscard to head off down to Lisbon.'

He'd never appeared more incredibly calm or self-assured. It crossed her mind Spencer was probably perverse enough actually to enjoy the danger. The adrenaline rush of living life constantly on the edge, he literally appeared to thrive on it.

'Do you want me to go over the plan again?' he asked.

She took a sharp intake of breath, and repeated almost mechanically, 'At nine-thirty, you want me to make my excuses, and head for the car park.'

Michelle looked at him somewhat pensively, and couldn't help feeling although she'd managed to sweet talk herself into being invited along to dinner, Spencer still didn't entirely trust her, but then again, she mused, why would he?

'All I need you to do is confirm everything's still on schedule with Meyer, and there hasn't been a last minute change of plan.'

Spencer examined her face closely. He knew Garvan believed she was capable of stepping up to the plate on Saturday night, but personally, he wasn't at all convinced she'd pull it off without buckling. If there'd been a choice, he'd much rather have had Joyce Leader positioned inside the Wulf, and not Michelle, but the decision had been taken out of his hands. Tar Robertson refused permission to allow one of his most valued double agents to be exposed to such a high degree of risk. As it was, Tar had been extremely reluctant for Joyce to join them on the mission to Lisbon in the first place. As harsh as it might seem, Michelle was deemed to be expendable whereas Joyce Leader was far too valuable to the Twenty Committee.

Spencer put the car into reverse and headed slowly out of the car park. Garvan glanced over his shoulder and tried to reassure her.

'Spencer won't have a problem entering the Wulf Club on Saturday evening.'

Michelle narrowed her eyes suspiciously. 'Why's that?'

'He's managed to convince the kitchen staff he's Heinrich Himmler's cousin.'

The colour drained from her face, as she began to shake her head in disbelief. Bertele had once described Himmler as the Third Reich's architect of death; even Baron von Gruber had visibly quaked when he discovered Stackler was a close friend of the *Reichsführer*.

*Were they perhaps both as mad as one another?* God, there was no way of telling. From what little Michelle knew, Spencer had always lived his life at full tilt, and was completely unflappable. But, she'd hoped in vain, that somehow, Garvan might have provided a calming influence over him.

But, right now, the only thing she knew with any degree of certainty, was, come Saturday evening, her life would be firmly on the line.

## Chapter 19

There was a knock on the door of Garvan's hotel room. As he opened it, he was surprised to see Rowlands standing there.

'Hello, George, come in. I wasn't expecting to see you until tomorrow morning.'

'No, I guess not.' He smiled at him.

Garvan closed the door. Judging by the drawn expression on Rowlands' face, he asked, 'You look like you've had a bad day.'

'That obvious, is it?'

'In which case, why not relax and have a drink?'

He already knew what the answer would be. Like most of his MI6 colleagues, George was a formidable drinker. Garvan opened a cabinet with an array of spirits. George pointed to a bottle of Ballantine's whisky.

'Do you want it straight or on the rocks?'

'Straight.' Rowlands grinned. 'Real men don't have ice.'

'Do you want a splash of water?'

Rowlands shook his head. 'No, just as it comes, thank you.'

Garvan poured a generous tot and handed it to him.

Rowlands followed him out onto the balcony overlooking the gardens and the sweeping shoreline beyond. The sun was beginning to set, melting seamlessly but swiftly on the horizon into the darkening night sky. Rowlands momentarily found himself enthralled by the sight, and basked in the warm glow illuminating the hotel. The sky was a myriad of colours, red, pink, and purple all mixed together to give the picture of a perfect landscape. He took a deep swig of the Ballantine's and gazed thoughtfully at the sunset, finding it brought a short, albeit fleeting sense of tranquillity, as the fiery colours of the sun sunk swiftly into the glistening sapphire ocean.

'What brings you here, George?'

'I was hoping to see Spencer; do you know where he is?'

'He's running a bit late.'

Rowlands looked at him and asked by how much.

'Only about half an hour or so. He should be here shortly with Joyce Leader. Is anything wrong?'

'No dear boy, in fact, quite the opposite,' he said, slowly swirling his glass. 'I didn't want to take a chance speaking on the phone, scrambled or not, you never know who might be listening in.'

'It comes with the territory.'

Rowlands raised a lame smile.

Hearing Garvan's room door open they both turned round to see who was there. Without waiting on ceremony, Spencer had let himself in with Garvan's spare door key. Joyce followed him into the room and closed the door.

Spencer sauntered casually out onto the balcony to join them. He glanced at Rowlands speculatively. 'Is everything okay?'

'Yes dear boy, everything is under control. The two new cars you wanted for tomorrow night are parked out the back of the hotel.'

'Good,' Spencer said, and held out the palm of his right hand toward him.

Rowlands placed his drink down on the balcony wall, and retrieved the car keys from his trouser pocket, placing them on his upturned palm. Spencer closed his fist tightly, and regarded Rowlands thoughtfully.

Having helped herself to the drinks cabinet Joyce appeared carrying two martinis, one for herself and one for Spencer.

'I'd make myself at home, if I were you,' Garvan said sarcastically.

She flashed a smile and winked at him.

Spencer thanked her for the martini, and asked Rowlands, 'Is there any news about our flight? Are we still on schedule for Monday morning?'

'That's why I decided to drop by to let you know everything's set up and ready to go.'

Joyce interrupted them, 'But, there isn't a scheduled flight to Bristol until Tuesday.'

'Well, there is now,' Spencer said, sipping his martini.

'But, won't the Nazis smell a rat?'

'One of our DC3's developed a technical fault enroute to Lisbon the other day, and was forced to make an emergency landing at Vigo Airport in Spain.'

She looked at him curiously. 'Was it a real or imaginary fault?'

He broke into a smile. 'It was real enough when I ordered it to develop one.'

Garvan breathed an audible sigh a relief. Not the best of flyers, the last thing he needed to hear was their plane was likely to develop some kind of bloody engine trouble on the trip back home.

'What time do you want us to meet up tomorrow evening?' Rowlands asked.

Spencer perched himself down on the balcony wall. 'I want to be gone from here by no later than six. I don't fancy taking any risks on those roads after dark.'

'Where are we going to park up?' Garvan queried.

'I was thinking of the wooded area just up the road from the club. There's enough cover there for us to be concealed from the road, and it also gives us a good vantage point of both the club and the car park.' He paused thoughtfully, before adding, 'The club officially opens at seven, although I understand people start arriving at about half-six onwards.'

Joyce drained her glass. 'I still think you're making a big mistake!'

He turned to face her; Joyce had always been feisty and opinionated, and he guessed it was probably asking too much for her to start changing now.

'Go on, Jo. Why not get it off your chest. What's your problem?'

'While I don't particularly like the woman.'

He cut her off. 'You mean, Michelle Rookwood?'

'Yes,' she responded sharply, unable to disguise her irritation at the interruption. 'It's just, I can't help thinking she could do with a bit of moral support tomorrow evening.'

Spencer narrowed his eyes at her. 'What, from *you*?' he said sarcastically.

Joyce looked affronted. 'As I was saying, I don't like the bloody woman, but she's got a hell of a lot on her plate with Bertele and Gruber, not to mention Otto Stackler!'

'And your point is?' he asked coolly.

He was starting to wind her up; he was doing a good job. Her expression immediately closed down.

'I just think it would have been better all-around if I'd wangled an invite to Bertele's dinner party from the Baron. At least that way, I could have given Michelle some backup inside the club.'

'What do you think is going to happen to her?'

'Having Stackler there is more than enough reason to be worried about her!'

Spencer handed Rowlands his empty glass, and asked if he'd mind getting him a top-up. Rowlands readily agreed. If nothing else, it gave him a chance to pour himself another Ballantine's.

'I know what you're trying to say, Jo, but I thought we'd gone through this once already.'

'But, it's not too late,' she suggested. 'I could still contact von Gruber.'

'My answer is still no,' he responded in a measured tone.

She wasn't so much angry as frustrated. 'But, I don't understand. I could easily have persuaded the Baron to get me an invite. He has a weakness for blondes, even peroxide ones like Michelle.'

'Tell me something I didn't already know. Getting an invite isn't the issue. Tar Robertson has refused point blank for you to go; it's as simple as that. Besides, I need you with me outside in one of the cars.'

Her face was suffused with frustration, and she pressed him again. Spencer admired her courage, but he wasn't about to change his mind, and he certainly wasn't about to counter command Tar's orders, no matter what she said. As it stood, things were already dangerous enough, and there were no guarantees any of them would get out of the mission alive.

'Do you really want to know why he doesn't want you inside the club?'

'Yes, I do.'

'It was difficult enough persuading him to agree your being with me outside the bloody place, let alone attend the dinner party. The bottom line, Jo, is Michelle Rookwood is expendable, and, quite simply, you're not.'

For once in her life, she'd been rendered speechless. During the time of the investigation into the murder of Sarah Davis, Joyce had then been viewed by British Intelligence as being entirely expendable. In fact, if Garvan and Spencer hadn't managed to out another agent as the murderer, she was in no doubt whatsoever, to protect the Double Cross system, MI5 would have liquidated both her and the other agent. Anyone who threatened the spy network was ruthlessly dealt with. The stakes were simply too high for them not to do so.

Of course, things had moved on since then, and she'd known for some considerable time Robertson and the Twenty Committee valued her work, but she still felt more than a frisson of sympathy for Michelle. From personal experience, she knew what it was like to be undervalued, and to be nothing more than a pawn in the shadowy games played out by both the Allies and Axis Intelligence Services.

Rowlands returned to the balcony with fresh drinks all round on a small silver tray, as Spencer continued to go over his plans for Saturday evening.

Joyce still couldn't help thinking they didn't understand what it was like for a woman to have Stackler within touching distance. She'd met many hardened men in her life, including Spencer, but Stackler was an entirely different beast altogether. Thinking about it logically what was it that made him stand out from the crowd. *Was it just the unnervingly dead expression in his eyes, or the indefinable coldness which had made her skin crawl?* In hindsight, it was probably a combination of both. Joyce couldn't help but imagine, before the War, he'd probably been some low life street fighter or local hard man. It was all speculation, of course, but his posting from the SS to the *Einsatzgruppen* spoke volumes, and only served to enforce her very real concerns for Michelle's safety. She knew Spencer would argue neither Bertele or Gruber would allow her to come to any serious harm, which she accepted was entirely true, but even so, Joyce had a nagging suspicion, given the opportunity, Stackler would chance his luck, and try to come on to her.

Before Reinhard Heydrich's assassination in the Prague suburb of Liben in 1942, Otto Stackler's willingness to kill, and his personal reign of terror, coupled with his extremely violent and uncontrollable temper, had made him stand out from his fellow officers. In fact, Otto's paranoid schizophrenia was the ideal vehicle for the *Reichsführer's* plans. His undying allegiance to the Third Reich, and more importantly to the *Führer,* had cynically made him the ideal assassin; someone Himmler had skilfully cultivated, not only to carry out his personal vendettas, but to work on the behalf of the State. The fact he was chosen to track down Jean Giscard was a sign of the esteem in which Himmler now held him.

Joyce suddenly became aware Spencer was calling it a day; he'd had more than enough to drink, and needed to keep a clear head for tomorrow evening. Rowlands somewhat reluctantly, went along with his decision and said his goodbyes, before following Spencer out of the hotel room.

Joyce had barely touched her martini, as Garvan gently ushered her off the balcony. He left the windows open to take full advantage of what little warm breeze there was coming in off the sea. Next week, if they were lucky enough to return home safe and sound, they'd probably be cursing the rain and the cold weather, and Estoril would be nothing more than a distant fond memory.

She turned to him. 'Be honest with me. Did I make a fool of myself in front of Spence?'

'No, no, you didn't,' he assured her. 'Why do you say that?'

'Are you sure?' she pressed him again

He was intrigued; it was completely out of character. She didn't normally suffer from self-doubt, far from it. But, for some inexplicable reason, her ingrained calculating arrogance of old seemed to have faltered. She'd always skilfully manipulated men's feelings, and, in essence, remained something of an enigma to him. However trustworthy Joyce had become in the eyes of the Double Cross, Spencer had always warned him that trust always came with a particular caveat, and a certain question mark over her ultimate reliability.

Garvan wanted to believe in her sincerity, and it was something of an open secret he was attracted to her. But, he knew full well Spencer was right. He needed to retain the upper hand in his dealings with her, and to take a step back. He simply couldn't afford to lose sight of the fact, at the end of the day, Joyce was a double agent and, when it came down to it, a traitor.

'Spencer won't let Michelle down, if that's what you mean?' he found himself saying.

'I hope not.'

The truth was, it didn't matter if Michelle lived or died. Tragically, she was no more than a bit part player. The only thing that mattered to British Intelligence, and their American Allies, was Jean Giscard wouldn't end his days facing a show trial in Berlin. Above all, they needed his knowledge of the Peenemunde rocket programme.

## Chapter 20

As the soft evening sunshine began to fade, they parked up beneath the bank of trees near the Wulf Club. Rowlands was the first to jump out of the lead car, and open the boots of both vehicles. Garvan followed him.

'It's all I could get at short notice,' he said, almost by way of apology.

Garvan peered inside the boot; his expression registered surprise seeing four Sten guns. He couldn't help wondering what else Rowlands would have turned up with, if they'd given him more than a couple of days' notice.

Spencer joined them at the rear of the car. 'Leave them there,' he said sharply.

Rowlands looked at him questioningly. 'We might need them.'

'But, only as a last resort.'

'What do you want us to do now?'

Spencer checked the time on his watch. 'There's nothing we can do, other than staying put until nine-thirty.'

'And then what?'

'Don't worry, George. If things start getting messy, we'll make use of your Sten guns.'

Rowlands didn't respond; he knew his place, and it was very much Spencer's show and his alone. He'd effectively killed the conversation dead. As far as Spencer was concerned, they'd gone through the plan enough times already, and there had been ample opportunity for everyone to question his decisions. At this stage, he didn't need Rowlands to start getting impatient and perhaps a little trigger happy. He let the matter rest. The only doubt in his mind was whether Michelle would be able to carry it through, without giving the game away. He knew she could easily pull it off with Bertele and von Gruber, that wasn't the issue; the only unknown quantity was her ability to hold it together in front of Otto Stackler. In fairness to her, it was a tough call.

They spent the next few hours watching the comings and goings of the Reich's higher echelon; it was literally like a veritable who's who of the great and good of the Nazis regime in Portugal.

By twenty-past-nine, Joyce was starting to get edgy. She had to say something. 'Hadn't you better start making a move?' she suggested to Spencer.

He was in no mood to be rushed, and certainly not by Joyce Leader. 'You know what you're trouble is, Jo, don't you?'

'What's that?'

'You're too impatient.'

She cast him a withering look; it spoke volumes.

'Patience is a virtue,' he shot back at her.

'How in God's name would you know!' she scoffed.

\*

Inside the club, Michelle anxiously glanced at her watch. She'd arrived earlier in the evening, in some style with Colonel von Bertele, in a sleek black Mercedes staff car. A group of grey-uniformed Wehrmacht officers and their sinisterly black-clad SS colleagues were lined up on the steps, awaiting Bertele's arrival. As the driver opened the rear door, and he alighted from the Mercedes, they greeted him as one in a typical Nazi salute with upraised hands and shouts of "Heil Hitler." He returned their mark of respect with the briefest of smiles and a salute; it was no more than his due as the Baron's second-in-command.

Michelle almost had to pinch herself, but she carried it off perfectly. Beneath all the smiles and social chit chat, she couldn't help wondering how his fellow officers really viewed her. She knew there'd been raised eyebrows when their affair first came to light, for she was not only Bertele's mistress but a British national, albeit one supposedly working for the Reich. She knew there was disapproval within the German community about his bedding someone whose country they were at war with. On hearing of their relationship, the Baron had formally ordered him to his office to voice his concerns. Bertele had skilfully defended Michelle by reminding Gruber that, in spite of her nationality, she was a valued Abwehr agent, and had loyally served the Third Reich for many years.

If anyone at the club still harboured any serious doubts about her loyalty, they certainly never allowed it to show. To a man, they were always respectful, and although one or two of them occasionally ventured to flirt with her, they were still very mindful of the fact she was very much Colonel von Bertele's mistress.

She carried their arrival off seamlessly, she was all smiles, and seemed to bask in their overt flattery, but beneath all the smiles lurked a lot of self-doubts as to whether she could pull it off, without starting to rouse their suspicions.

As they were escorted inside the club, flanked by their greeting party of senior Nazi officers. Michelle had casually looped her hand under Bertele's arm. Once inside, Michelle steeled herself for what was to come, as she found herself on a wooden bench sandwiched between Bertele and von Gruber, which, in itself, wasn't a problem, but for the fact she'd been seated directly opposite Otto Stackler.

While neither Gruber nor Bertele had little time for his particular brand of Nazi brutality, it seemed to Michelle as if they were almost entirely oblivious to his predatory approach to women. She began to wonder whether von Bertele, perhaps naively, believed, as his lover, it somehow afforded her protection, and she was strictly off limits. Michelle assumed Stackler probably didn't quite see things that way. In his eyes, she was probably still fair game.

With the drink flowing freely inside the club, it didn't take very long for things to start becoming rowdy. Since the club opened, its owner, Meinhard Wulf, had decided against employing local staff; all his employees were either of Austrian or German extraction. The waitresses were dressed uniformly in traditional Bavarian costume, with a Dirndl, and a low cut white lace blouse to show off their cleavage. Michelle sometimes wondered whether a large bust wasn't a pre-requisite for working there; either way, the girls were certainly popular with all the Wulf's male customers. The waitresses kept up a steady supply of beer served in litre-sized stein mugs, accompanied by large steaming platters of sausage, Schnitzel, and mashed potatoes, served on a hot bed of Sauerkraut.

After about an hour, Meinhard put in an appearance at their table to check whether von Bertele was entirely satisfied with the food and service. He raised his right hand in a stiff Nazi salute. 'Heil Hitler,' he said with gusto. Michelle couldn't help smiling to herself. In many respects, Meinhard was almost like a caricature of the *bierkeller* proprietor, from his felt hat to the fancy waistcoat, to the Stein grasped firmly in his left hand.

Although Michelle's German was by no means fluent, she understood enough to catch the gist of their conversation; Meinhard asked about the food and the quality of the beer. Bertele politely expressed his thanks to the staff for putting on such a successful evening. The Baron joined in the conversation, and let it drop he was thinking about holding his own birthday party at the club. Meinhard appeared dutifully honoured at the prospect. He then pointed toward the Lederhosen-clad Oompa Band setting themselves up in the corner. Michelle wasn't entirely sure what was being said, but Wulf appeared to be asking permission for the band to start playing. Bertele checked with the Baron, who enthusiastically agreed.

From past experience, she knew only too well once the music started, the conversation would become almost non-existent. Her gaze rested on a sign hanging above the bar; it read, *"ACHTUNG! AUFMERKSAMKEIT, KEIN TANZEN AUF DEN TISCHEN."* She believed the loose translation was; "no dancing on the tables." Somehow, she doubted if anyone had ever seriously taken any notice of the warning. Besides, the chances of the owner ever forcibly remonstrating with a bunch of drunken SS officers letting their hair down seemed almost bordering on the suicidal, and Meinhard certainly didn't strike her as a man with a particular death wish.

As the evening wore on, Michelle found it increasingly difficult to keep a tight rein on her nerves. If she messed this one up, London wouldn't only come down on her like a ton of bricks, but they'd pull the plug once and for all. She cast a wary eye around the club. The air was thick with a heady combination of smoke and the pungent smell of beer; it was also stiflingly warm. Von Gruber, in particular, appeared to be suffering from the heat, and repeatedly dabbed at his face with a handkerchief to wipe off the beads of perspiration on his forehead. He was obviously uncomfortable, but still seemed to be enjoying himself, and readily sunk another stein to keep pace with Stackler. Gruber had a renowned capacity for drink, however she'd lost count of how many beers he managed to get through, and even Bertele appeared to be struggling.

Stackler continued to sit across the table in stony silence, nursing his beer; his face looked flushed; it probably wasn't surprising, considering the number of steins he managed to down. He didn't appear as if he was particularly enjoying himself; he seemed rather bored with all the small talk, or maybe he simply had too much on his mind, hoping there were no last minutes hitches with Giscard. Bertele had once told her Stackler was as cold and unrelenting as the Russian winter. In many ways, he was almost the perfect idealised Aryan Nazi, tall, blond, and passably good looking, but what unnerved her was the menacing expression in his eyes. It was unblinking, dead-like; it simply wasn't normal, and made her skin crawl.

So far, at least, everything appeared to be running smoothly. Michelle played it well flirting with the officers, and hanging on their every word. *Why did men always love to talk about themselves?* Fortunately, they never once asked about her, which, under the circumstances, suited Michelle down to a tee.

There were times when they became careless in her company; she'd lull them into a false sense of security, and occasionally, they let slip the odd snippet of intelligence which she would then religiously pass on to London. Robertson had wanted her to cultivate Bertele, and she certainly hadn't let him down. In fact, she'd far exceeded his expectations. Michelle's relationship with von Bertele had proved to be invaluable for the Double Cross. As expected, there was a certain amount of low-grade dross in her intelligence gathering, but more often than not, she managed to come up with high-grade information.

In stark contrast to his deputy, the Baron had never personally rated her worth as a spy. She knew that, but despite Gruber's misgivings, she'd still managed to wheedle her way into Bertele's charmed inner circle of trusted agents dexterously. The fact she'd had to sleep with him had merely been the means to an end. Basically, Michelle slept with anyone she found attractive, and Bertele was an attractive man. Bedding him hadn't exactly been a hardship, far from it, and in the process, he'd broken all the rules by falling in love with her.

Whereas Michelle needed to be physically attracted to someone, she suspected Joyce Leader wasn't particularly interested in the sexual side of things, and the intimacy it entailed. For Joyce, she guessed, it was all about the power and the control over her conquests. She didn't know for certain whether Joyce had slept with the Baron, but the prospect would have tested Michelle's mettle and have been a step too far. She simply couldn't have gone through with it. Fortunately, Michelle knew she wasn't von Gruber's type, and although Spencer had once joked she scrubbed up rather well, she knew her looks were an anathema to Gruber. Her bleached blonde hair, dyed to within an inch of its life, and heavily applied make-up, were too common for von Gruber's liking. In hindsight, it was probably something of a blessing. She could only thank God Robertson hadn't asked her to cultivate the Baron, rather than Bertele.

The trouble was, she actually liked Bertele. Behind the handsome face and greying blond hair, there was a genuinely kind and thoughtful man. She guessed, rightly or wrongly, he had been caught up in a situation way beyond his control; he'd certainly never given her the impression of having any deep-rooted political beliefs. It could always have been a ruse, of course; there was no way of telling.

As the Oompa Band began to play, Michelle braced herself, knowing things would start going rapidly downhill. Fuelled by a lethal combination of beer and schnapps, the officers started to sing along to their favourite marching songs, and with each one, the singing became ever more raucous, as they uniformly crashed their clenched fists on the tables, and stomped their feet on the Wulf's stone floor in time to the music.

One particular song, *Panzerlied,* seemed to whip them up into a full frenzy of nationalistic pride, and as always, they requested it to be played time, and again, throughout the evening. With each rendition, the noise and fervour increased alarmingly.

Sitting in their midst, Michelle couldn't help feeling intimidated, if not a little overwhelmed. There was a certain irony about it all. Here she was, a double agent working for

MI5, surrounded by the great and good of Hitler's regime, singing *Panzerlied*.

Internally, she almost understood their ritualistic, infectious enthusiasm; it was frightening but strangely stirring, all at the same time. Every one of them seemed to be swept along on a tide of emotion. They were amongst their own kind, she told herself, with people they could relax and trust, without fear of been spied upon.

So far, she was managing to keep it together, and appeared to be enjoying herself, smiling broadly, as they belted out their jingoistic songs. When Hitler had finally managed to seize total power in 1933, Goebbels had been appointed the Reich Minister for Propaganda. His mission had been to instil in the German people the concept of the *Führer* as a kind of demi-god like figure, and also their destiny as the rulers of the world. Looking around the Wulf Club, Michelle couldn't help thinking Goebbels had done a pretty good job brainwashing them to the point where they possessed an almost totally blind adulation to the *Führer* and the Third Reich.

Men like Stackler, she assumed, would always have been impressionable and swayed by the rhetoric, and the staged managed theatrical propaganda. What she couldn't quite understand was where educated men, such as von Bertele and the Baron, fitted into the equation and their real feelings about Hitler's regime. Bertele was always guarded in discussing politics, it was a way of life, and criticism of the Reich was strictly forbidden. Hitler's power was absolute, and any attempt at dissension was brutally and swiftly stamped out; there were no exceptions to the rule.

Michelle was only too aware she was very much a bit-part player in their world, entirely expendable, and caught in a deadly battle between Robertson's Double Cross team in London, and Baron von Gruber's Abwehr operation in Portugal.

She checked her watch again; it was twenty-past-nine, only another ten minutes to go before she'd have to make her excuses to leave the table, and meet up with Spencer.

As she downed a shot of schnapps in a single gulp, Stackler leaned across the table toward her. '*Fräulein*, do you have a problem?'

In spite of the menace in his eyes, she managed to hold his gaze and smiled pleading ignorance.

He tapped his watch. 'You keep checking the time, *Fräulein*.'

'Do I?' she said blankly.

'Yes, you do.'

'This noise, Colonel, it's too much for me,' she responded, cupping her hands over her ears.

He looked right through her; it made her feel distinctly uncomfortable, but the moment passed, as the Oompa Band struck up *Panzerlied* one more time. Stackler enthusiastically joined in the singing. *Here we go again*, she thought. It was all so hideous, and yet disturbingly infectious.

## *Chapter 21*

Michelle excused herself from the table; it wasn't quite half-nine, but she wanted to start making a move. As she made to leave, von Bertele affectionately caught hold of her hand.

'*Mein Liebling*, where are you going?'

'I need to powder my nose,' she said, winking at him flirtatiously.

He smiled at her. 'Don't be too long.'

'I promise I'll only be a minute,' she whispered, gently slipping her hand from his grasp.

Inside the lady's toilet, Michelle set her handbag down on the shelf above the sink, and rested her hands on the washbasin, staring thoughtfully at her reflection in the mirror. She needed a few minutes to collect her thoughts, before meeting Spencer. Even in the relative calm of the lady's toilet, the throbbing, pulsating music and sound of raised drunken voices was still almost overwhelming. Closing her eyes in an attempt to calm herself down, she heard the toilet door swing open behind her. Michelle's initial reaction was one of surprise; she knew there were only two other women who had been invited to von Bertele's dinner party, and before making a move, she'd made a point of checking they were still both in the dining room. She opened her eyes half-expecting to see one or other of them, to her horror saw the towering, menacing black-uniformed figure of Otto Stackler standing in the doorway, with a drawn pistol in his right hand.

'Ah, *Fräulein*, I was hoping to find you here,' he said.

Without saying another word, he came at Michelle and shoved her forcefully against the sink, and then whacked her violently with the butt of the gun across her face. She cowered in fear, and raised her arms in a desperate bid to defend herself. Galvanised by fear, before Michelle knew what she was doing, words were leaving her mouth. 'What the hell are you doing here?' she cried out in terror.

As he hit her again, Michelle recoiled under the sheer force of the blows, and cried out in pain, as she fell against the sink, and watched helplessly as her handbag spun across the tiled floor toward one of the cubicles. Her pistol was inside, and she couldn't reach it. She was physically no match for him, but in spite of the disparity between them, it galvanised her into a sense of self-preservation, a sense of survival, that she was going to have to fight for her life.

Michelle became acutely aware of her surroundings, and her heart was pounding in her ears. She was frozen with fear, she tried to open her mouth to scream, but it was impossible. Her mouth had dried, she was unable to utter a sound, in fact, and to her horror, she found herself paralysed, rooted to the spot, and unable to move. She had to scream; it was her only hope of attracting someone's attention. Finally, after what seemed like an eternity, but was probably no more than a few seconds, she found herself able to move again. She tried desperately to remain outwardly calm. The feral instinct, Garvan had once said she possessed, started to kick in with a vengeance. As deranged as Stackler was, she needed to communicate with him on some level; it was her only chance of getting out alive.

'Why?' she pleaded. 'Why are you hurting me?'

'I've been watching you!' he said, and slapped her across the face again.

Michelle reeled under the force of the blow. 'But, what have I done?' she cried.

He didn't answer, and roughly caught hold of her arm and pushed her violently against the wall. There was a combination of alcohol and tobacco on his breath. She instinctively recoiled, and wanted to retch in repulsion.

'I know you want it,' he said, in his heavily accented English. 'I've seen the way you are with the Colonel and the Baron.'

Michelle's mind raced as he pressed the gun beneath her chin. *What was he going to do, rape her, or shoot her, oh God, would she hear the sound of the gunshot before she died, please, no, please don't let me feel any pain,* she thought. Her body stiffened was she going to die.

'How the hell are you going to explain this to them?' she whimpered.

Without a word, Stackler brutally forced Michelle to the floor. He wasn't interested in trying to explain himself to her; he just didn't care what she, or anyone else for that matter, thought about him. She tried desperately to fight him off, but he was simply too strong, too powerful to resist, and all the while, it kept flashing through her mind for him not to hurt her. He placed the revolver in its holster, and clamped his hand over her mouth. Knowing what was about to happen, she froze again. Her whole body went into a kind of numb spasm, almost as if her brain was trying to block out what was going on.

\*

Spencer drew up in the car park behind the club. The military staff cars belonging to the high-ranking officers and diplomats attending the dinner party were uniformly parked up side-by-side. Fortunately, their drivers were still enjoying a meal in the Wulf's kitchen, at von Bertele's expense. *The old boy must have been in a good mood.* Spencer decided. He certainly wasn't renowned for splashing his money around.

There was no sign of Michelle. He checked in his right pocket for his Walther PPK, and in his left, he felt for the silencer. He'd acquired the pistol in Berlin, and it had remained his weapon of choice ever since. The PPK was standard issue to the German forces. In his view, it was far superior to anything either the Americans or the British had in their armoury.

The kitchen door was wide open, so he slipped on the silencer to the PPK. The corridor was empty. Something must have gone very wrong; there was still no sign of Michelle. He walked past the kitchen, and briefly glanced inside; the staff car drivers were seated around an oval table, tucking into their dinner. No-one noticed him, so he carried on along the corridor toward the dining room. The club was still vibrating to the sound of raucous singing and stomping on the clubs stone-flagged floor.

Having reached the end of the corridor, Spencer glanced through the small circular window set in the door; he could see Bertele and von Gruber, but there was no sign of either Michelle or Otto Stackler. As he started to turn away from the door, he heard a noise; he waited, and then he heard it again. It was a woman's voice, pleading, screaming, it was Michelle's. He ran back along the passageway. She screamed again; it seemed to be coming from the lady's toilet.

Spencer pushed the door open, and saw Michelle lying helplessly on the floor with Stackler astride her. He allowed the door to slam shut. Otto looked round at him, almost casually. Michelle's face was frozen in terror.

'Get off her!' Spencer ordered him in German.

Stackler had the temerity to hesitate; that is until he noticed the PPK pointing directly toward him. He looked up into Spencer's face, and knew instinctively here was a man of his own ilk, who'd killed before, and wouldn't hesitate to do so again. Reluctantly, he released his grip on Michelle, and slowly came to his feet.

'Do I know you?' he asked suspiciously.

Spencer fixed him with a hard stare, but didn't respond; he was more concerned about Michelle. 'Are you all right?'

She nodded but couldn't trust herself to speak, and tearfully tried to straighten her dress.

Stackler's eyes were cold and watchful. 'We've met before, haven't we?'

'Yes, at the casino.'

'No, I've met you before,' he said, gesturing in a short, sharp stabbing motion. 'I never forget a face. Berlin! That's it; that's where I know you from.'

A smile registered on Spencer's face. 'Very good *Sturmbannführer*. To be precise, it was the 20<sup>th</sup> of April 1939.'

'Yes, yes, I remember now. It was after the *Führer's* birthday parade.'

'You have an excellent memory.'

'In my business, I need to.'

'I'm sure you do.'

Stackler examined his face closely. 'Are you one of the Baron's men?'

'Does it really matter?'

'It does to me.'

'Then, I'm not.'

Stackler desperately needed to know who he was. Like himself, he was obviously a military man. *If he wasn't a member of the Abwehr, who was he? Was he a member of the Wehrmacht?* No, he dismissed the idea almost immediately.

'Gestapo, SS?' he probed.

'What do you think?' Spencer's voice was low and fierce.

Staring down the barrel of Spencer's Walther PPK, Stackler warily moved his almost hypnotised gaze toward Michelle, and realised he had to play for time. He carefully considered his answer before responding. 'No, you're not Gestapo.'

'What makes you say that?'

'You're military, a soldier, like myself.'

'Then, we're rapidly running out of options, *Sturmbannführer*.'

Spencer felt bemused Stackler believed he was a member of the SS. In the long run, it probably wasn't such a bad thing, as he wasn't quite sure how to react. In fact, he'd managed to unnerve him. Stackler's thoughts went into overdrive. *Had Himmler perhaps instructed this man to keep an eye on him, to oversee his mission, or had he displeased the Reichsführer?* If he had, Stackler knew he was facing certain death, for no-one had crossed Himmler and lived to tell the tale.

He calmly looked Spencer up and down; there was an overt stillness about this man, an aura of a hardened soldier, like himself. If he was going to get out of this alive, he needed to make a move, and to make it fast. There was a sound behind him; he glanced round. It was Michelle retrieving her handbag off the floor. Otto guessed she was probably armed. He had to do something, and desperately reached in his jacket pocket for his pistol, but he wasn't quick enough. In a split second, Spencer fired the PPK in a double tap to Stackler's forehead.

Stackler didn't have time to react; he slumped to the floor, his body contorting in a convulsive spasm.

Michelle instinctively cupped her hands over her mouth. 'Oh, my God,' she gasped. 'What are we going to do now?'

Spencer calmly returned the pistol to its holster, and glanced round the lady's toilet; he spotted a door near the main entrance and went over to try it. It was unlocked, so he looked inside; it was the cleaner's cupboard and was full of mops, buckets, and other paraphernalia.

'Give me a hand,' he said in a low, urgent voice.
'What do you want me to do?'
'Clear out the cupboard.'
'And then what?'

'We'll stuff his body inside. At least, that way, they won't find him straight away, and it'll give us a head start.'

Michelle mutely agreed, after all; Spencer had just saved her life.

As they hurriedly emptied out the cupboard, it kept running through her mind she didn't fancy touching Stackler's body. In fact, she'd never seen a dead body before. She braced herself, hoping upon hope Spencer wouldn't need any help, but judging by the size of the cupboard, she reckoned he'd probably be unable to do it all by himself.

After they'd emptied it out, she waited helplessly as Spencer caught hold of Stackler's arms. His head lolled back, as Spencer dragged his lifeless body across the floor toward the cupboard.

'Give me a hand,' he said.

Her gut instinct was to recoil, but she didn't have a choice. Michelle tentatively caught hold of his feet; her expression spoke volumes, but Spencer wasn't in the mood to pander to her squeamishness. They pushed and shoved until his body was wedged tightly in the cupboard. They then piled the cleaner's mops and buckets on top of him. Spencer found a metal sign on a string; his Portuguese was almost none existent.

He held it up. 'What does this say?'

Michelle pulled a face; she was by no means fluent, but thought it said out of order. Spencer smirked, and hung it around Stackler's neck. He then shut the cupboard.

They had to move fast. There was some blood on the floor, which they wiped up with a mixture of toilet paper and hand towels. They flushed the paper down the toilets, and tossed the towels into the cupboard on top of Stackler's body.

Spencer turned to her. 'You're face doesn't actually look too bad.'

She instinctively felt her cheek. 'Are you sure?'

'It probably won't look too choice in the morning,' he smiled at her.

Michelle checked herself out in the mirror; her left cheek looked flushed but no more than that. She fumbled in her handbag, and shakily re-applied her make-up, in a bid to cover up any sign of the assault.

'What do you want me to do now?'

Michelle met his gaze; it was softer than she remembered, but she knew instinctively Spencer wanted her to return to the dining room. He was right, of course; there was no reason for her not to do so. Stackler's body wouldn't be found until the cleaner started her morning shift. But, she was still frightened, and wasn't quite sure what would happen once his body was found. Not only would her world implode, but so would von Bertele and the Baron's, as well. Berlin would start demanding answers, and she really didn't have any wish to be in the firing line.

'Is the Baron returning to Lisbon this evening?' he asked.

'Yes, he wants Bertele to go with him.'

'How are you getting back to your apartment in Estoril?'

'They're dropping me off.'

'In which case, I'll arrange for Garvan and Rowlands to pick you up later, outside your apartment.'

'And then what?' she said uneasily.

He answered matter-of-factly. 'Trust me. I'll take care of everything.'

Michelle was barely holding herself together. if Spencer hadn't arrived when he had, Stackler would have raped and killed her.

He reached out to Michelle, and briefly wrapped his arms around her. 'I know you've been to hell and back; I'm not going to let you down.'

He released her from his grasp, and pushed open the door to the corridor. She knew he'd meant every word, and it wasn't just an empty gesture on his part. Michelle braced herself, and headed back to the dining room, but paused and mouthed, "thank you," to him.

Spencer stepped outside. Although it was dark, a full moon was bathing the surrounding woodland in a pale, unearthly gleam, and above, the night sky was ablaze with a canopy of twinkling lights. In another time, and another place, he might have taken the time to marvel at the spectacle, but he didn't have the time. His life was an endless spiral of deceit, and a fight for survival. If the Allies stopped fighting, the world, as they knew it, would cease to exist.

He looked round; he heard a voice. It was Rowlands.

'Over there,' Rowland pointed.

Spencer followed his gaze across the car park. 'What am I looking at?

'That grey van parked up near the trees.'

'What about it?'

Rowlands checked over his shoulder to Garvan, as if for support. 'We thought it looked like Aldous Meyer was driving.'

'Is he still inside?'

'Yes.'

There was a tenseness about Spencer, Garvan hadn't seen before. Sensing there was something wrong, he asked, 'Is Michelle okay?'

'That all depends on what you mean by okay.'

Spencer wasn't in the mood for lengthy explanations, but gave them the gist of what had happened inside the club.

'You shot Stackler!' Rowlands said in disbelief.

'I didn't have a choice.'

'Christ almighty. When they find his body, all hell's going to break loose.'

Spencer shot him a look; Rowlands was stating the bleeding obvious, but right now, it wasn't important. 'Stay here,' he said bluntly to them.

They watched in mute silence, as he strolled across the car park, and headed toward the trees, where Meyer was parked up in the van, waiting for Stackler to arrive. He stopped near the perimeter, and casually gazed out across the dark, undulating countryside, and placed a cigarette between his lips, and then patted his trouser and jacket pockets, as if searching for a match or lighter. He made eye contact with Meyer, and calmly approached the van. Meyer wound down the window.

'Do you have a light?' he asked pleasantly.

Without hesitation, he reached forward to the van's console for a cigarette lighter and made to hand it over to him. Spencer leaned forward through the open window, and, taking Meyer completely by surprise, smashed a fist into his face, and with one short, sharp forcible twist broke his neck. Spencer looked up from the van, and gestured to Rowlands and Garvan to join him.

Rowlands tentatively glanced inside the van; Meyer was slumped in the driver's seat. 'Have you knocked him out cold, or what?'

'You could say that.'

'God Almighty,' Rowlands exclaimed. 'Don't tell me, you haven't killed him as well, have you?'

Garvan peered inside the van; it was obvious Meyer was dead.

'We haven't got the time to argue the effing point!' Spencer grunted.

Rowlands shook his head; at heart, he was a desk man. For the most part, the sharp end of wartime espionage had happily passed him by. Hearing that Spencer was being dispatched to Portugal, Frank Lucern had jokingly remarked the body count in the country was likely to increase at an alarming rate. If killing a Gestapo officer, like Meyer, wasn't bad enough, taking out someone of Stackler's standing was a whole different ball game altogether, and was bound to cause a diplomatic incident in Lisbon, resulting in the Portuguese President being placed in a politically sensitive situation caught between the warring factions.

Spencer tossed the van's keys to Rowlands; he caught them. 'Open up the back,' he said sharply.

He unlocked the back doors, and although it was dark, they could just make out the figure of a man bound and gagged lying in a foetal position on the floor. Garvan clambered inside, and instantly recognised Jean Giscard, but, more importantly, he was still alive.

'It's Jean,' he called out.

'Is he alive?' Spencer asked.

'Yes, yes, he is,' he said hurriedly removing the restraints.

Giscard answered for himself, as Rowlands reached inside to give him a helping hand. 'Yes, I'm okay, thank you.'

At least, he appeared to be in one piece, and outwardly, none the worse for his ordeal in captivity. Spencer felt in his jacket, retrieved a pocket torch, and then flashed it toward the woods to signal it was safe for Joyce to join them.

'What do you want us to do now?' Rowlands queried.

'We can't afford for either of them to be found until the morning.'

'How are we going to get rid of Meyer?'

'We'll push the van through the old wooden fence and over the edge.'

'Where does it lead to?'

'There's a steep rocky slope beyond the trees; it's almost sheer. There's nothing but a cattle track below, or, at least, that's what it looked like.'

Joyce pulled into the car park, and drew up beside Meyer's van; she'd hardly turned the engine off when Spencer ordered her to open the passenger door of the van and release the handbrake, as he couldn't quite reach it. Joyce complied, but as she opened the door, she momentarily hesitated seeing Meyer's lifeless body slumped in the driver's seat. There wasn't time to ask what had happened. By now, Spencer was barking out orders. They were to push, while he tried to steer the vehicle by leaning through the open window. They slowly managed to edge the van forward through the dilapidated fence, without too much effort, but as they hit uneven ground toward the precipice, it started to become increasingly difficult to keep the momentum going, and they almost ground to a halt.

Spencer glanced over his shoulder, and noticed Giscard was standing there watching their efforts. 'Are you sure, you're all right?' he shouted at the Frenchman.

'Yes,' he answered, nonplussed.

'Good, then put your back into it, and help push the bloody van!'

Jean mumbled something by way of an apology, and joined them in trying to shove the van through the trees toward the steep rocky incline. It was hard going, and took them almost five minutes, before they finally managed to reach the drop. As the front wheels nudged over the edge, Spencer hurriedly released his grip on the steering wheel. It seemed to hover precariously, swaying, teetering into the dark void below. He joined them at the rear of the van, and with one last ditch effort, they managed to tip the van end-over-end down onto the rocks below, before it came crashing noisily to a halt on the cattle track.

Spencer turned to Joyce. 'Get Jean into one of the cars. I'll be with you in just a minute.'

'Where do you want us to go?' Garvan asked.

'Take the other car with George to Michelle's apartment, and wait outside until she gets home from the club.'

'And then what?'

'Drive her down to the Embassy.'

Rowlands interrupted, 'But, won't von Bertele be spending the night at the apartment with her?'

'No, as soon as they leave the club he's travelling with the Baron to Lisbon.'

'Do we know why?'

'My gut instinct is they want to ensure everything goes smoothly for Stackler's return to Berlin.'

Rowlands pulled a face. 'Well, that's not going to happen anytime soon, is it?'

'That's why Michelle needs to be lifted tonight. We can't leave her alone here in Estoril; it'll be far too dangerous.'

'What do you want MI6 to do with her?'

'Nothing at all,' was his sharp response. 'She'll be returning to London with us on Monday.'

'You'll be lucky to swing it, at such short notice.'

As soon as he'd opened his mouth, Rowlands realised he'd overstepped the mark. Spencer not only had the ear of the great and good in Whitehall but Tar Robertson, it was a deadly combination. The powers that be trusted Tar's judgement implicitly, and if he wanted Michelle on the next DC3 to Bristol, then they'd move heaven and earth to ensure she had a seat. It wasn't up for discussion.

As Rowlands headed off to one of the cars, Garvan turned to Spencer. 'Where are you going now?'

'We're going to meet Frank Lucern.' He smiled breezily. 'I'll see you later.'

'I'm sure you will.'

## Chapter 22

As Spencer swung out of the Wulf Club's car park, he asked Joyce to check the map resting on her lap. She turned on a slim pencil torch and scanned the page, as they drove along the uneven road in pitch darkness.

'We keep on here, until there's a fork in the road.'
'And then, what?'
'Take the left fork.'
'Are you sure?'
She flashed the torch in his face. 'Yes, I'm sure.'
'Just checking.' He smirked.

*

That afternoon before they had set off for the club, Spencer met one of Lucern's agents, Graeme Overington, at the hotel. He'd strolled into the Plaza's foyer, seemingly without a care in the world, a cigarette resting in the corner of his mouth, and a large briefcase stuffed under his arm. Spencer was waiting for him in the lobby.

'You're late!' he'd barked at the young man.

Overington had looked genuinely surprised. 'Am I, sir?'

Spencer guessed he was probably new to the Service with much to learn, and still wet behind the ears. No matter how he tried, Spencer couldn't help taking an instant dislike to the man.

'Frank promised you'd be here by three o'clock.'

He casually consulted his watch; it had just gone five. 'I'm sorry, sir, I would have been here earlier, but we had a few problems to sort out, before I could get away from the office.'

They took the lift to Spencer's room, where Overington had placed the briefcase down on the table, and released the catch. He reached inside and handed over a manila coloured envelope. Inside, was a map containing details of Spencer's proposed rendezvous with Lucern. He placed it down on the table, and opened it out.

'Show me exactly where we're going to meet up.'

'Here,' Overington said stabbing his right index finger on the location circled in red ink.

Spencer leaned over the map to take a closer look. 'Is this the depot?'

'Yes, it supplies aviation fuel to the airports at Portela and Sintra. We've used it a few times for covert operations. There shouldn't be a problem. Frank has set everything up for you.' He reached into the briefcase again, and produced three large bundles of Escudos.

'What's this for?'

'It's a sweetener for the guard at the front gate.' He passed them over to Spencer, and then, retrieved three cardboard boxes containing cigarettes.

'Don't tell me, another sweetener?'

'Yes, they are,' Overington said, closing the briefcase.

'How much money is here?'

'More than enough,' he assured him. 'If I were you I'd try the guard with just the one wad, for starters, and see how it goes from there.'

'What do we say to him when we get there?'

'Just ask for the Boss.'

*Not very original*, Spencer had thought to himself, *but as long as it worked, that's all that mattered.* 'And will Frank be waiting for us?'

'Yes, sir.'

Overington had then headed off, and presumably returned to Lisbon.

\*

On the drive down to the depot, Giscard remained understandably anxious. He seemed a little happier in himself after Joyce assured him Claudine was in safe hands, and hiding out at the British Embassy. 'At least, she was alive,' he'd mumbled from the back seat.

Joyce flicked on the torch light again and consulted the map; they were on the main road now.

'It can't be much further,' she suggested.

'What's that up ahead,' Spencer said, pointing to their right.

Silhouetted against the night sky, were the tell-tale cylindrical shapes of the depot's aviation fuel containers.

'It's got to be the depot. There's nothing else shown on the map on that scale.'

Spencer started to slow the car down.

'Is everything all right?' Giscard asked nervously.

'Yes, don't worry,' Joyce said soothingly.

They were now almost level with the main entrance to the depot. Spencer hesitated. The road was clear, and there was no-one else around. He decided it was safe enough to approach the large metal barrier guarding the entrance. Immediately to their left was a wooden hut, a light on inside. Hearing their engine ticking over, a guard peered through the window, and half-heartedly acknowledged their presence with a cursory wave. As he opened the door and approached the car, Spencer wound down the driver's window.

'*Boa tarde,*' he called out, hoping he'd just said good evening. As Joyce didn't react and give him a sharp warning nudge in the ribs, he guessed he might have pulled it off.

The guard replied in kind and peered into the car; he seemed amiable enough.

'We're here to see the Boss,' Joyce announced in Portuguese.

The man smiled broadly at her. 'Ah, yes, I was expecting you.'

She retrieved a single bundle of the Escudos and a box of the cigarettes, and leaned across Spencer to hand them over to him. He seemed content with just one of each. Had he known there were two more bundles of banknotes, he might not so readily have been prepared to open the barrier. He unbuttoned the jacket of his uniform and carefully stuffed the bundle of notes inside. He then bent down again and gave them directions, before opening the large metal barrier.

As the guard waved them through, Spencer turned to Joyce. 'Did you understand what he was saying?'

'Yes, we need to take the first turn on the left, and it should be the second building along on the right-hand side.'

They pulled up outside a large building not dissimilar in appearance to an aircraft hangar. There was a large dog tethered on a long chain near the entrance, its eyes eerily reflecting in the car's headlights. It stood up, but, for some reason, didn't bark.

Drawing to a stop, Spencer peered through the windscreen. 'Is this it?'

'I think so.'

'Keep the engine running, until I've had a chance to take a look round.'

She reached down for her handbag in the front well of the car and took out a handgun. Spencer opened the driver's door, and withdrew his Walther PPK from its holster. The building looked as if it was in complete darkness. He couldn't understand why Lucern hadn't posted someone to keep an eye out for their arrival. Perhaps the bugger was getting a bit rusty driving a desk in Lisbon; he probably needed to get back out in the field again, and get his hands dirty. He had certainly expected something a little slicker than this.

Spencer tried the main doors; they were locked, so he wandered around the side, and found a small metal door slightly ajar; there was a glimmer of light inside. He nudged it open further, and warily stepped inside to find himself in a vast cavernous space. It was obviously a mechanical workshop, as there were four fuel tankers lined up in various states of disrepair.

Somewhere from within the gloom, he heard a voice; it was Frank Lucern. 'You must have put your foot down. I wasn't expecting you this early.'

Spencer looked up to see him, descending an open metal staircase.

'What the hell are you playing at, you bastard!' he exclaimed, his voice echoing in waves around the workshop.

He burst into laughter. 'It takes one to know one.'

Lucern was as thin as a wand, with a ready smile invariably never far from his face. On first impressions, he appeared deceptively mild-mannered, which had on occasions resulted in his being underestimated by both his colleagues and hostile intelligence agents alike. But, beneath the outward happy-go-lucky persona, lurked a stubborn, steely character whose inherent skills as a spy were second to none.

Lucern had cut his teeth at the beginning of the War as a member of Tar Robertson's team in London. He had remained entirely loyal to him, and was one of his men to the core. Like Spencer, he had been a founding member of the Double Cross system. As the War progressed, Robertson had appeared reluctant to part company with Frank, especially to MI6. It didn't initially sit at all easily with him, or, at least, that's the way he wanted it to appear across Whitehall. To this day, Tar was forever sounding off to anyone who was willing to listen, all his best people were being poached, but the reality was somewhat different. In effect, all his agents had remained good and loyal to him; their first allegiance lay firmly with Tar, and, in fact, acted as plants, and were his way of being able to keep the finger on the pulse of the various rival strands within British Intelligence.

Lucern possessed a slightly unruly shock of thick wavy grey hair and watchful pale grey eyes. Before the War, he'd been minding his own business, working as an aero engineer; word had it, he was quite accomplished in his field. Spencer always assumed that's how he'd first come to the attention of the shadowy men in grey suits. The Intelligence Service required people with a variety of skills. As an ex-aero engineer, his initial work had been to help evaluate technical information stolen from the Nazis. Eventually, he'd fallen into Robertson's hands, and ended up working alongside Spencer. His ability as a field officer in counterintelligence meant his name began to become widely known within the Service and Whitehall generally.

Spencer slowly returned the PPK to its holster, and waited for Frank to make the long walk across the maintenance hangar.

'Do you have Giscard with you?' he asked.

'He's in the car with Joyce Leader.'

'Thank God for that,' he replied, following Spencer outside.

The engine was still running, and the driver's door wide open, just as he'd instructed. On seeing them, Joyce immediately relaxed and reassured Giscard; he was safe, and everything had gone according to plan. Spencer reached inside the vehicle and turned off the engine. Recognising Lucern, the Frenchman appeared a little less anxious. They'd met a couple of times in Lisbon, before the decision had been made to transfer him out of the city, and along the coast to what had appeared to be the relative safety of Estoril. In hindsight, Giscard felt, he might have been better off staying in Lisbon, but the decision had been made at the time with the best of intentions.

Lucern warmly extended his hand in welcome to Giscard. 'It's good to see you again, my friend.'

Since his arrival in Portugal, Lucern had handled the Frenchman's volatility with tact and diplomacy. Giscard liked Lucern, for he had always seemed genuinely concerned and willing to listen. It was all of a piece, really. Perhaps he was doing no more than paying lip service to him, but right now, Jean was just relieved to see a familiar face again.

Lucern led the way into the workshop, and up the steep open metal staircase into an office; he explained it was the manager's, and was theirs for the weekend, until work resumed first thing on Monday morning. As he looked around the place, Spencer couldn't help wondering just how many neatly rolled banknotes Lucern had been forced to part company with in order to the persuade the depot manager to turn a blind eye to their activities over the weekend and allow them free access to the site.

Lucern sat himself down behind the manager's desk. There were a couple of easy chairs in the office, which he invited Joyce and Giscard to use. Lucern pointed to the corner at a rather dirty looking green brocade affair, which turned out to be an antiquated rocking chair, that creaked violently to one side as Spencer sat down.

'Sorry about that. We found it out the back.'

Joyce started to giggle, and the more she tried to stop, the harder it became. Even Giscard raised a smile. Spencer knew only too damn well Lucern had deliberately sat him there, but it had the desired effect of breaking the ice between them.

'Are you hungry?' Lucern asked the Frenchman.

'Yes, yes, I am.'

'Wright!' he shouted. 'Where are you?'

They heard the thud of heavy footsteps; a man appeared in the doorway. He was a large, bear-like figure of at least six-four. Charlie Wright was, like Spencer, an ex-commando seconded to British Intelligence at Lucern's request, on Spencer's personal recommendation. He was known in the commandos as "Nasty Wright," because of his explosive temper and his ability to kill without compassion. It was hard to believe before the War; he'd worked as a freehand sign writer, but "Nasty" had come a long way since then, and was now employed as Lucern's bodyguard. While the Lisbon posting was ostensibly deskbound, it wasn't entirely without risk of alienating certain rogue elements within the Axis intelligence community. Wright's forbidding presence was probably enough of a deterrent in itself to deter any would-be assailant, or so Lucern hoped.

On noticing Spencer, Wright immediately sprang rigidly to attention and saluted, even though he wasn't in uniform. 'Sir!' he barked out.

'How are you, Mr. Wright?'

'Good, sir, very good.'

'Is Mr. Lucern looking after you?'

'Yes, but obviously not as well as you did, sir.'

'I've got a lot to live up to.' Lucern smiled before asking, 'Did you remember to bring the sandwiches?'

Spencer smiled to himself. If he knew anything about Wright, it was he was never likely to have forgotten to bring along something to eat.

'Yes, sir, they're out back.'

'Then bring them in, would you, please.'

Wright nodded to his boss and turned, caught Spencer's eye, and gave him a crafty wink, before disappearing back down the corridor.

'If you don't mind,' Lucern announced to Giscard, 'I've taken the liberty of bringing you a present.' He tugged open the bottom drawer of the desk, and cheerfully presented him with a bottle of Courvoisier brandy.

Giscard smiled broadly. 'You are too kind, *Monsieur*, thank you.'

Lucern opened the bottle and rummaged in the desk for some glasses. 'I know I put them in here somewhere,' he mumbled, before finding them under a pile of the manager's paperwork. Joyce was about to decline the offer of a drink; it wasn't her tipple, but as nothing else was likely to be on offer, she accepted.

Wright duly returned to the office with the sandwiches. Unfortunately, the bread by now was dry and had started to curl, but Giscard seemed not to notice, and even Joyce was prepared to give them a try.

'So, tell me,' Lucern asked Spencer, 'how did it go this evening? What's the damage?'

It was a loaded question. Lucern knew full well any attempt to snatch Giscard from the clutches of Stackler and Meyer wouldn't have been without cost, but he needed to know exactly what had happened, and steeled himself waiting for his response. But, as usual, Spencer completely wrong-footed him, and went off at a tangent. Whether he was avoiding giving him a straight answer or not, he wasn't entirely sure.

'We need to find a seat on Monday's flight for Michelle.'

He certainly hadn't expected his opening gambit to be about Michelle, far from it, and alarms started to ring. 'The plane's already full.'

Lucern knew it was, as he'd only approved the final passenger list, three hours ago. In fact, nobody moved out of Portugal on a British plane without his personal authority. He noticed there was a certain cold detachment about Spencer as he spoke. Lucern had seen it before, and knew he would start to dig his heels in, but Lucern wanted to play for time, and didn't want to be steamrolled into making decisions, without knowing why Michelle being on the plane was non-negotiable.

'I'll have to check the passenger list,' he announced.

Spencer merely stared at him.

'You know I'll have to take someone off the plane.'

'I guess you'll have to,' was the flat response.

Lucern toyed thoughtfully with his pen. 'Do we need to pass this by Colonel Robertson first?'

Spencer cast him a long considering look. 'Why should we?'

'It just crossed my mind; Tar might not be best pleased if we lifted Michelle out of Portugal, without getting the okay from him first. You know how he hates to be blindsided.'

'After all she's been through this evening, Frank, I can't afford to leave her alone in Estoril. For one thing, she's likely to crack, and for another, it'll be too dangerous for her to continue operating.'

'Where is she now?'

'Rowlands and Garvan are driving her to the Embassy tonight.'

Lucern threw his pen down on the desk. 'You really must stop using the British Embassy like some personal hotel for all your waifs and strays, Spencer. You know the Ambassador doesn't like it!'

Spencer smiled almost as if to himself; he wasn't interested in the Ambassador, or anyone else, for that matter.

As Lucern reached into the breast pocket of his jacket and retrieved a small leather bound notebook, Spencer knew he'd rattled him, and things were starting to get serious. He was renowned for making meticulous notes during meetings. Afterward, he would punctiliously follow-up by providing everyone with a carefully typed record of when and where the meeting had taken place, and precisely what had passed between them. He was doing nothing more than covering his own back, of course, but he'd brought it almost to the point of an obsession. His missives would always start in the same manner, "My understanding is we agreed/confirmed the following .... if you disagree I request you contact me immediately." While Spencer understood Lucern's need to keep things on a formal footing, notes or not, realistically, there was more chance of hell freezing over first before he'd ever manage to put one over on him.

Spencer came clean, and described in detail precisely what had happened at the Wulf Club, and how Stackler had unsuccessfully tried to rape Michelle, and, in order to save her life, he'd been forced to shoot him dead. Lucern's face was both a mixture of horror and surprise; his pen hovered lightly over the notebook.

'The body, what did you do with it?'

'We stuffed it in the cleaner's store cupboard.'

'Do they open the Wulf on Sundays?'

'Only for lunch,' Joyce piped up.

Lucern scribbled in his notebook, the nib of his fountain pen making a scratching noise across the page as he wrote. He thoughtfully looked up from his notes toward Spencer; his expression troubled, for Stackler wasn't only a close associate of *Reichsführer* Himmler, but held a Knight's Cross, with Swords "for prodigious valour on the Russian front." The award was a distinct honour, and had catapulted his standing amongst the Nazi elite, and set him apart from his fellow officers in the SS and the *Einsatzgruppen*. He was, therefore, a man to be both admired and feared in equal measure, and to cap it all, Spencer hadn't only shot him dead, but had then stuffed his body in a cleaner's cupboard. The reaction from Berlin would undoubtedly be one of outrage at Stackler's death, but the undignified disposal of his body would only serve to add fuel to the fire. Officially, they'd make political noises through the usual diplomatic channels, but in reality, behind the scenes, they would seek revenge for the shooting.

Spencer assumed Lucern was not only concerned about the ripple effects Stackler's death would have on his day job, but the fact he'd also have to inform the Ambassador and his American counterparts personally. It certainly wasn't going to be an easy ride for him, even less so when he discovered Aldous Meyer had also been disposed of. He'd have to come clean about that as well, and as he did so, a look of unrestrained horror crossed Lucern's troubled face.

'You are kidding me, Spencer, please tell me you are!' But, he could tell Spencer was being deadly serious, and placed his left hand over his eyes in despair. 'Christ almighty, say there isn't anyone else to add to the body count!'

He was unperturbed by Lucern's reaction, and said somewhat provocatively, 'If there is, Frank, you'll be the first to know.'

Lucern was by nature a worrier, and the first to admit he lived continually on his nerves. It irritated him Spencer appeared to breeze through life, seemingly without a care in the world, and was capable of being completely focussed, fearless, and, when demanded, utterly ruthless, and yet, at times, could also turn on the charm and be great company. He was all those things, but Lucern still couldn't quite understand how it was, after killing two prominent members of the Reich's elite, he could still appear to be so incredibly calm and collected.

Lucern reached for his briefcase beneath the desk and retrieved his pipe, a habit he had picked up while working for Tar Robertson. As Head of the MI6 Lisbon Station, he'd proved his worth time and again, as had his methodical approach to the work at hand. At heart, he possessed a much admired deep-rooted core of honour. Although Lucern had been far too professional to express an opinion on his erstwhile colleague, Spencer supposed he probably viewed him as something of a loose cannon. But, in their ever-changing world of ruse and treachery, even Lucern was forced to admit they needed men of Spencer's ability to face down someone as profoundly dangerous as Otto Stackler.

Lucern opened a tin of tobacco and began to fill absentmindedly the briar.

'Should you be smoking here?' Spencer said, with a wry smile.

'Sorry?'

'Are you forgetting we're in the middle of a bloody fuel depot?'

'I'm sure it'll be fine.'

Lucern suddenly became aware of how pale and drawn Giscard was, as he clutched the brandy glass tightly between his hands. He struck a match and sucked on the pipe until the tobacco began to glow in the bowl. He then made a point of closing the notebook.

'Forgive me,' he said, addressing the Frenchman.

Giscard arched his brows questioningly. 'I'm sorry, *Monsieur?*'

'You've met Major Hall before, of course,' Lucern said, gesturing toward Spencer.

'Yes, at the casino in Estoril.'

At the time of their first meeting, the only thing he'd known for certain was Spencer was a member of British Intelligence. Security had dictated he wasn't permitted to know either Spencer or Garvan's names.

Lucern then inclined his head toward Joyce Leader and introduced her. Giscard managed to raise a somewhat nervous smile in her direction. Lucern pursed his lips together, and exhaled a cloud of smoke.

'I'm not quite sure how to describe Joyce to you.'

She looked through him, as if he wasn't there. 'Say what you like,' she answered in a deadly tone.

Lucern noticed there was more than a hint of challenge in her glacial expression. He'd first met her shortly after she started working for MI5 as a double agent. Since then, Joyce's importance as a member of Robertson's system had become pivotal in the Twenty Committees deception plans against the Nazis regime. Lucern was also only too aware even Spencer regarded her very highly.

He noticed Spencer eyeing him speculatively. The look on his face convinced him, he'd probably better draw a line under any further reference to his agent. He flicked open the notebook again, explaining to Jean it would be necessary to make a record of their conversation. Although it was getting late, he needed to know precisely what had happened to him from the moment Stackler and Meyer arrived at the casino and shot dead one of his agents.

'You mean, right now?' Giscard queried.

'Yes,' Lucern replied, as he topped up Giscard's brandy glass. 'I can see you're worn out, and are wondering why the hell it can't wait until the morning.'

Giscard raised his hand. 'There's no need to apologise, *Monsieur*; I know if Major Hall hadn't managed to rescue me this evening…' His words momentarily trailed off, as he took a sharp intake of breath. 'Let's just say, *Sturmbannführer* Stackler took a particular delight in describing the fate awaiting me in Berlin.'

'Did either of them physically attack you?'

'No, not after they snatched me from the casino. I had a few cuts and bruises at the time, but I guess they didn't want me appearing in front of the cameras at my trial, battered and bruised.' A slow self-deprecating smile played around his mouth. 'I suppose there wasn't much point in beating me to a pulp, when they knew I was going to be found guilty, and hanged at the end of the week.'

'I think you'll find he was ordered by Himmler not to lay a finger on you before the trial,' Spencer said.

'Maybe so, Major.'

Giscard recounted how he had been bundled into the back of a van, a grocery van, the same one they'd rescued him from earlier in the car park. He estimated he was probably inside the vehicle for no more than half an hour or so, after being taken from the casino.

'To be honest with you,' he said, almost stumbling over his words, 'I thought I was going to suffocate. They placed a hood over my face and tied my hands behind my back. It was so hot inside the van, I could scarcely breathe.' He took a large gulp of brandy. 'I just kept wondering why they hadn't put a bullet in me, there and then.'

'Do you have any idea where they held you?' Lucern asked.

Giscard shook his head. He recalled being manhandled out of the van, and shoved across an uneven pathway. Inside the building, a house, he decided, was cool, and the floor had echoed to the sound of their feet. He presumed it was either a tiled or stone floor. They were met there by another man, who spoke fluent German; he understood them perfectly, but they were careful not to say too much in front of him.

After a short discussion, he distinctly remembered being dragged up four flights of stairs, the last one being much narrower than the others, as he kept bumping into the walls. He'd then found himself bundled into a room, where the hood was finally removed from his head. At first, Stackler was reluctant to untie his wrists, but had been persuaded by Meyer to release him.

'And this other man,' Lucern asked, 'did you see him again during your stay there?'

'I saw him again that same evening, when he gave me some water to drink. After that, he brought me all my meals, and emptied out my slop bucket.'

'Was there a window in the room?'

'Yes, a small one.'

'Could you see out of it?'

'There wasn't much to see,' Giscard confessed. 'I think it must have been in the attic. There was a single bed and a chair, and that was it. I had to stand on the chair to take a look out of the window. We seemed to be high up on a cliff, overlooking the sea.' He cradled the brandy glass thoughtfully between his hands, and added with an ironic laugh, 'At any other time, I really would have rather admired the view.'

Lucern was busily writing in his notebook but suddenly paused. 'What did this other German look like?'

Giscard shrugged indifferently. 'Tall. As tall as Stackler, maybe,' he hesitated, 'but much broader set, I mean fatter.'

'How old do you think he was?'

'I'm not very good at this, *Monsieur*.'

'You're doing just fine,' Lucern assured him.

'Forties, perhaps a little older, it's hard to say.'

'Did they use a name?'

'Not in front of me. They were very careful.' He took another gulp of the brandy. 'Now that you mention it there was one occasion, they'd just locked the door when I overheard Stackler address my jailer as Meinhard.' Jean caught Lucern and Spencer exchange glances; it was obviously significant. 'Who is he?'

Lucern scribbled the name down in the notebook and underscored it. He then looked up at Giscard. 'The Wulf Club's owner is Meinhard Wulf. And guess what?'

Giscard stared back at him blankly.

'He owns a palatial property with spectacular views overlooking the coast. In fact, it's only a few miles south of the club.' Lucern placed his pen down on top of the notepad and sat back in the chair, fingertips lightly touching together. 'I think we should start calling it a day, don't you?'

Giscard looked palpably relieved he wasn't about to be subjected to any further questioning at least, not for the time being. After his ordeal, he was both physically and mentally exhausted. Lucern called out for Charlie Wright again, who appeared from the neighbouring office.

'We have a camp bed set up for you,' Lucern explained to the Frenchman. 'There's more food and coffee, or brandy, if you'd prefer.'

'And tomorrow,' Giscard asked tentatively, 'are we to stay here?'

'We have the run of the administrative offices until first thing on Monday morning, when the staff report back for work. God willing, you'll be on your way to the airport by then.'

It all seemed so cut and dry, so matter-of-fact, but Giscard was wary. It had all gone drastically wrong once before, and he was somewhat jittery about further glib promises about his safety.

'Will Claudine be on the plane?' he asked.

'Yes, don't worry. She'll be there.'

Giscard hesitated, as if he was on the verge of asking another question, but the moment passed. He'd thought better of it and stood up to leave. He made to follow Wright out of the office, but turned around, and reached his hand out to Spencer.

'I cannot begin to thank you enough for rescuing me this evening, Major,' he said, his eyes glistening with tears as he spoke.

Giscard was simply too exhausted to trust himself to say anything else, without the fear of breaking down completely. Spencer looked slightly embarrassed, as he watched the Frenchmen leave the office. After he'd left, there followed a rather awkward silence between them; it was Lucern who broke it.

'So, come on, Spencer. Why the last-minute changes of plan? What happened?'

'It was your safe house.'

'What about it?'

He frowned, a muscle twitching in his jaw. 'We'd had a whisper it might have been compromised.'

As Lucern steadily held his gaze, alarm bells started to ring again. As Head of Station, he should have been informed immediately if there was thought to be anything amiss. He knew Spencer was in direct contact with London by Morse code. He didn't want to cause a scene right now; it would have been entirely unprofessional, especially in front of Joyce Leader. Perhaps he was simply reading too much into the situation, or maybe there hadn't been time to alert him in Lisbon.

'Compromised,' he repeated, thoughtfully. 'Do you mean by *Schornsteinfeger*?'

Spencer nodded. 'Has everything been arranged?' he asked cryptically.

'Yes, of course, it's all in hand.'

Spencer made to leave the office.

'Where are you going?' Joyce demanded.

'For Christ's sake, Jo, give me a break, I need to have a pee!'

She looked slightly embarrassed, and slumped back in her chair, watching Lucern methodically place his notes back into the briefcase.

'How are we going to get Giscard to the airport?' she asked suddenly.

He glanced up at her. 'We're on Plan B at the moment.'

'That's not what I asked.'

'I know it isn't. Why not try asking Spencer?' he suggested, and snapped the briefcase shut.

Joyce realised, no matter how high her standing was with Robertson and Spencer, Lucern still couldn't bring himself to either like or trust her.

He carefully emptied out the contents of his pipe into an ashtray, before shooting her a penetrating look. 'No doubt I'll see you at the airport on Monday morning.'

With that, he was gone.

Spencer was waiting outside the workshop for Lucern; he had a cigarette on the go. A car pulled up driven by another bodyguard, and by the look of him, he exceeded Charlie Wright in both size and girth. Spencer smiled inwardly; Lucern obviously wasn't taking any chances about his personal security.

Lucern asked the driver to keep the engine running. The dog was still on its chain, but had now decided to wag its tail playfully at them.

'What's his problem,' Spencer said, gesturing toward the dog.

'The manager reckons they're only aggressive when they're let off the leash.'

Spencer lifted an enquiring eyebrow.

'It apparently makes them easier to handle that way.'

Lucern went over, and put his hand out to the dog to take in his scent. Leashed or not, Spencer decided he didn't fancy taking his chances, and kept a healthy distance from the creature.

'How many other guard dogs are there?'

'Half a dozen,' Lucern replied, and decided it was probably safe enough to give it a pat. 'Or, at least, that's how many I've paid to keep chained up over the weekend.' The dog responded to his touch, with another wag of its tail.

'I'm sorry, Frank, but this caper must be costing you a small fortune.'

Lucern looked back at him. 'Just cut the crap. Why wasn't I given heads up about *Schornsteinfeger* compromising one of my safe houses?' There was an unmistakable edge to his voice.

Spencer considered his answer, before replying, 'There simply wasn't enough time to let you know.'

'This so-called whisper it might have been compromised. Where did it come from?'

'Where do you think?'

'Our code breakers, but what have they got to do with it?'

Since Spencer arrived in Lisbon, Lucern had always felt as if he was holding out on him, and had never been quite up front, and now, he finally realised, his initial concerns had been entirely justified. *But, why hadn't he received the same intelligence from Bletchley?* They received information all the time, so there had to be a particular reason the MI6 Station had been left out of the loop.

'They intercepted a message from Lisbon to the Abwehr HQ in Germany,' Spencer explained.

'What did it say?'

'That British Intelligence was planning on preventing Giscard from boarding the plane to Berlin.'

'And they mentioned *Schornsteinfeger*?'

'It was clear they were the source of the information.'

'But, was there explicit mention of the safe house?'

'Not in itself,' Spencer said cagily, 'but under the circumstances, there's no way we could have risked moving him to Lisbon. Besides, there was a possibility *Schornsteinfeger* had verbally confirmed the location of the safe house to the Abwehr.'

'There's something not quite right about all this.' Lucern decided.

Spencer looked at him questioningly.

'If the Baron and Bertele suspected there was a possibility of an intercept by MI6, why didn't they increase security around Giscard?'

Spencer gave the matter some thought, before replying, 'The message to Berlin was relatively short on details; it wasn't that specific.'

'But, even so...'

'If I'd have been in Stackler's shoes, my main concern would have been about the overnight stay in Lisbon, and the drive to the airport on Monday morning.'

There was no easy way of telling Lucern he'd been holding out on him. He wasn't a fool and must have realised, shortly after his arrival, the information he was receiving from both Spencer and London was highly selective.

On a personal level, Spencer liked the man, and in the past, he'd always found him to be a sleek, no-nonsense operator, but since taking over control as Head of Station, Lucern had somehow allowed himself to drift steadily into the eye of the storm, and had lost control of the Lisbon operation.

His selection for the job had been an endorsement of his proven abilities in counterintelligence, so it was all the more surprising over the past year, he had consistently been outmanoeuvred by Baron von Gruber. London had become increasingly concerned, not only about the quality of the intelligence emanating from Lisbon, but also by the increasing number of leaks Bletchley Park was intercepting from Portugal. Frank hadn't gripped the situation, and at the moment, MI6 appeared to be very much on the back foot.

Spencer flicked his cigarette butt onto the ground and stubbed it out under his foot. 'Do we know where Stackler was going to shelter Giscard on Sunday, until they flew back to Berlin?'

The merest hint of a smile crossed Lucern's face. 'They were going to stay at the German Embassy.'

Spencer laughed out loud. 'So, it's not just me, then, is it!'

'No, I guess not.'

'Does that mean the German Ambassador is as jittery as Sir Ronald?'

'Well, officially, he doesn't have an opinion; privately, of course, is quite another matter. Whatever the Third Reich's motives may or may not be, their Ambassador still has to play the diplomatic game.' Lucern briefly glanced up at the canopy of stars above them. 'In their own way, our diplomats walk a tightrope, just as deadly as ours.'

Spencer reached into his jacket pocket, and produced a scrap of paper, handing it to Lucern. 'I'm sorry,' he apologised. 'I was under orders.'

'What orders?'

'That I wasn't to say anything, until we knew for certain.'

'Knew what?'

'Agent *Schornsteinfeger's* identity.'

It was too dark to read the note, so he moved into the glare of the staff cars headlights. He angled the paper and read the name; he then read it again in disbelief.

'Are you sure about this?'

Spencer's expression said it all, he was sure and more importantly so was London.

'Keep the engine running!' Lucern barked at his driver, as he moved out of earshot. 'What the hell's going on, Spencer? Why have I been kept in the dark? I had my suspicions something was going on, but this,' He angrily waved the note at him. 'All I seem to be doing lately is chasing my tail trying to fix things. I had six effing hours to set this lot up for you!'

'I was under orders, Frank; we couldn't take the risk.'

'What risk?'

Spencer pointed to the note containing *Schornsteinfeger's* name. 'Since the beginning of the year, we've known a mole has been operating out of Portugal.'

Lucern's face was suddenly creased in horror. 'And you suspected *me?*'

Spencer gave him a look, and shrugged slightly.

He touched his forehead in despair. 'For Christ's sake, we've been friends long enough.'

Spencer raised his hand to silence him. 'You know how it is, Frank. It's nothing personal. It's work, and it's what we do.'

'It's nothing personal!' Lucern spat back at him furiously.

He began to pace up and down, in a bid to keep his temper in check, and it wasn't helping any Spencer was playing it cool. His expression remained unreadable, as he watched his friend tussling with his emotions, and the perceived shame of having been placed under suspicion of being a traitor.

Lucern suddenly came to a halt, and turned to face him, and said accusingly, 'Why did you really come to Lisbon? Was Giscard just an excuse?'

'Well, only in a manner of speaking.'

'I think you owe me the truth!'

Spencer moved slowly back toward the guard dog; it started to wag its tail again. Lucern followed him.

'Why did you bring Garvan along for the ride? Tar wouldn't normally sanction someone's involvement from outside the Service.'

He appraised Lucern with a shrewd expression on his face. 'Garvan's untainted and out with the system. I needed someone I could trust, and without having to feel constantly the need to watch my back all the time. Since his secondment, he's kept his distance, and yet still managed to retain his integrity as a member of the team. You have to understand, Frank, the Service had some concerns about the quality of the intelligence coming out of Portugal.'

Even in the half-light, he could see Lucern was affronted by the accusation. As Head of Station, it was his show, and ultimately, he'd not only failed to produce consistently high-grade intelligence, but had failed to realise a mole was operating out of Portugal. Spencer might have said the investigation wasn't personal, but from Lucern's point of view, it was more than personal. It was an indictment against his integrity, and he'd failed as the senior MI6 officer-in-command of what was perceived to be a crucial posting.

Spencer felt obliged to explain the reasoning behind his mission. Lucern was already reeling, and with every new piece of information, his world was surely but steadily imploding. There had been umpteen issues, not just with MI6 and MI5's double cross agents, but also with SOE's involvement in transporting escapees through occupied Europe, and across Spain to the Portuguese border. Lucern appeared slightly mollified, but only slightly, that the SOE had also come under scrutiny.

Spencer explained how things had come to a head, once they knew Giscard had defected from the Peenemunde rocket project. Although the Special Operations Executive had successfully extracted him from northern Germany, with the help of an underground network run by Dr. Fernand Schwachtgen, their main concern had been the final transfer between the Spanish and Portuguese borders.

Both London and Washington viewed Giscard as being pivotal to the Allies' fight against the German army's weapon development branch, and the rocket programme in particular. Spencer had been parachuted into northern Germany, and had made contact with an agent called Gorski, who'd been handed a microfilm about the project by Giscard. Although significant in itself, his remit had also included ensuring the Frenchman's escape route via the SOE. There had already been one too many occasions when important escapees had been intercepted trying to cross the Spanish border into Portugal.

Spencer's mission was to attempt to track down the weak link in the chain, the SOE, MI6 or MI5's Double Cross agents. At the time, there had simply been no way of knowing, but a pattern had started to emerge, and London remained convinced the Abwehr were in receipt of high-grade intelligence, which meant only one thing, one of their agents had turned rogue, and was in the pay of the Nazis.

Spencer bided his time, and waited for a response from Lucern; there wasn't one. His expression hardened. 'For Christ's sake, Frank, as Head of Station, you must have questioned why so many different people were being picked off by the Gestapo at the border with Spain?'

'It happens all the time.'

'Does it?'

Lucern eyed him uneasily, and he knew London probably viewed him as a busted flush. His reputation was in tatters, and as things stood, he had little, if any, hope of retaining his position. But, for his own self-respect, he needed to salvage something, and try to redeem himself in the eyes of the Allied Intelligence community.

In the meantime, Spencer was still on a roll. 'But, surely, you must have questioned it, Frank? There were just too many important escapees being selectively picked up at the last minute by the Gestapo and the Abwehr? It wasn't just coincidence; we were either becoming sloppy or someone was giving the game away.'

In self-defence, Lucern tried to explain how he'd raised a number of issues with the MI6 Iberian desk in St. James's about the problem. Spencer listened, but didn't respond. A brief silence fell between the two men.

'As I said, we didn't know where to start. The mole could either have been a member of the SOE, MI6 or even the Double Cross, there was simply no way of knowing. It was like looking for a needle in a haystack. To a certain extent, we were running blind, and totally reliant on the intercepts between the Abwehr and Berlin. It still wasn't an easy nut to crack. We didn't only have to concentrate on the escape routes through occupied territory; there were also some other issues confronting us at the same time.'

Lucern looked at him uneasily, and wondered what the hell was coming next.

'The messages we received from the code breakers indicated the Abwehr, von Gruber, and Bertele, in particular, had a pretty good idea about the Allies' future plans in the Mediterranean.' Spencer took his time by taking another drag on his cigarette. 'And then, of course, there was the issue with the *Evening Standard.* It was just all starting to add up.'

The hint of sarcasm in his voice wasn't lost on Lucern. Shortly before Lesley Howard's plane was shot down flying back to Britain, a series of well-informed articles appeared in the *Evening Standard,* detailing the intelligence operation in Portugal. Churchill had personally ordered an internal investigation into the potentially damaging leaks. One of Lucern's desk officers subsequently discovered the newspaper's local correspondents were passing typed copies of their well-informed editorials in letter form, via a particular KLM crew member, on one of the regular BOAC flights operating between Lisbon and Bristol. A warning was subsequently issued to both the British and Dutch crews operating the flights security in the UK would be stepped up on both arrival and departure.

The *Standard's* articles had immediately ceased to appear in the British Press. Although the cynic in Spencer thought it probably had more to do with the crews fearing they were about to lose their lucrative trade bringing illicit booze and cigarettes back to Britain, than any great sense of morality or doing the right thing. But, the fact remained, the *Evening Standard's* journalists were well-informed, and were either bribing or receiving secret intelligence from one or more British agents. While Spencer could understand Lucern's anger at being left out of the loop and being placed under suspicion, as the Head of Station, he had to accept overall responsibility for the serious lapses in security, which had happened on his watch.

Although personally innocent of any wrongdoing, he'd somehow allowed himself to take his eye off the ball. Lucern's career was very much in the balance, and he knew it.

'We have to let London know what's happened,' he said to Spencer.

'It won't be necessary.'

Lucern looked at him uneasily. 'But, we have to.'

He cut him dead. 'It's taken care of.'

Lucern hesitated, but knew there was little point in taking the matter any further. He no longer had control.

Spencer watched him drive off in his staff car toward the depot's main gates, before opening the boot of his vehicle. He reached inside and pulled out a wooden box. Then, he retraced his steps to the workshop manager's office. He closed the door, turned the key, and locked himself securely inside. The box contained a so-called "straight key." He preferred the U.S. model, known as the J-38, to send Morse code messages direct to MI5 HQ. Time was of the essence, and Morse was the easier and faster option, but also the most secure. He lit another cigarette, and withdrew a notebook containing the codes from his jacket pocket. It was getting late, but hopefully, Tar Robertson was probably still burning the midnight oil in the office. He wasn't wrong.

*Chapter 23*

Tar Robertson had just returned to his office at MI5 HQ in St. James's Street after a long, protracted meeting with the Prime Minister and the Director of Naval Intelligence in the Cabinet War Rooms, a deep subterranean bunker situated beneath the streets of Whitehall. Churchill was, by nature, a night owl, with a prodigious ability to work throughout the night with little, if any, sleep. Tar had considered getting his driver to take him back home, but it had already gone two o'clock by the time he eventually emerged from the meeting, and the cot bed he'd had set up in his office seemed the easier option.

He slumped wearily into a high-backed swivel chair behind his desk, and almost immediately began to doze off. The meeting with the Prime Minister had gone rather well, or so he'd hoped. There hadn't been too many problems, other than the usual glitches and possible poo traps raised by Churchill's razor sharp questions. Robertson had presented him a report with the specific caveat, "*PM FOR YOUR EYES ONLY.*" Churchill had asked to be brought up to date about the current situation regarding Jean Giscard. It probably wouldn't make for a pleasant read, Robertson decided, as he'd handed over the document. Churchill had thanked him, and set it aside for his bedtime reading.

There was a knock on the office door; it was Captain John Eldridge, the night duty officer.

'Sorry to disturb you, sir.'

Robertson blearily opened his eyes. 'I hope it's important. What is it?'

'A coded message has just come in from Portugal.'

'Who's it from?'

'Major Hall.'

Robertson sat upright; the Double Cross team were under strict instructions not to decode any messages received from Spencer. Instead, they were to be passed directly to Robertson, and no-one else was authorised to handle them.

'Thank you, that'll be all for now,' he said curtly, as Eldridge handed over the message on a piece of folded foolscap paper.

'Yes, sir.'

Eldridge left the office, and closed the heavy oak panelled office door.

Tar swivelled round in his chair to a large brown metal cupboard behind his desk, and twirled the tumbler lock carefully five times to the right, then to the left four, and so on, decreasing the number of turns each time, until it clicked open and released the combination. He reached inside, and retrieved a small hardbound book with "His Majesty's Government" stamped on the cover above a Royal Crown. Inside, was a set of codes devised by the code breakers at Bletchley Park, specifically for the mission to Portugal.

Robertson hesitated, as he caught sight of his not-so-secret stash of whisky on the second shelf of the cupboard. There was a moment's indecision, but he decided against having a dram, as he'd already sunk several brandies at the War Rooms, and he needed to keep a relatively clear head to decipher Spencer's message.

He sat back down and opened the cipher book, unfolding the paper handed to him by Eldridge. The message took a while to decode, not that it was particularly long, far from it, in fact, Spencer wasn't into long preambles. His messages, like the man, were both precise and to the point. Robertson just wanted to ensure he didn't make any mistakes. As he scribbled it out in long hand from the seemingly random and unintelligible code, a message started to emerge. Robertson sat back and read it through.

*"GISCARD SAFE. STACKLER AND MEYER DEAD. AWAIT PERMISSION TO RETURN ON BOAC FLIGHT 788*

*AT 09.30 GMT WITH SCHORNSTEINFEGER AND AGENT CAMBER."*

Robertson re-read the message, and hurriedly wrote a reply. All it said was *"PERMISSION GRANTED."* He picked up the phone on his desk, and asked Eldridge to step into the office.

Eldridge appeared. 'Yes, sir.'

He handed over the response. 'Have this sent off to Major Hall immediately.'

The young man glanced down at the note, it didn't mean anything, of course, but it did seem very short.

'Get a move on,' Robertson said sharply.

'Sorry, sir, right away.'

As Eldridge closed the door, it ran through Tar's mind he would have to update the bloody report he'd just handed to Churchill. It was going to be a long night.

\*

After leaving the Wulf Club, Garvan and Rowlands drove over to Michelle's apartment on the outskirts of Estoril. It was gone midnight, and there was still no sign of her. They were starting to get concerned, in case something had happened after they left, when a large black Mercedes drew up outside the apartment building. To their relief, Michelle emerged from the chauffeur driven car, followed closely by von Bertele. He was well lubricated, judging by the look of it. He caught hold of her hand, whispered something in her ear, and then wrapped his arms around her.

Rowlands had a cigarette on the go. 'Dear God, why don't they get a room,' he drawled.

Garvan shot him a sharp look. 'What the hell's she supposed to do? Just go easy on her, will you.'

Bertele had left the rear door open, leaving the Baron on the back seat behind the driver. It wasn't long before von

Gruber lost his patience, and shouted at his colleague to get a move on. Bertele glanced over his shoulder, and reluctantly loosened his grip on Michelle.

'I'll give you a call in the morning,' he promised, and got back into the Mercedes.

The military driver put the car sharply into reverse, and did a three-point turn before driving back down the street. Rowlands and Garvan ducked out of sight as they drove past. Michelle was standing forlornly outside the entrance to the apartment block, watching the staff car until it disappeared out of sight, before fumbling in her coat pocket for a door key. She looked vulnerable, and not quite sure what to do with herself.

When it was safe, Garvan wound down the window, and called out to her. 'Chelle, over here. Come on, get in,' he beckoned.

Even in the gloom of the street lights, he could see a palpable sense of relief on her face. Michelle ran the short distance along the pavement to the car, and opened the rear door. Garvan pressed on the starter, and eased off the brake.

'Are you all right?' he asked.

'I guess so,' came her somewhat tremulous reply.

Rowlands twisted round in his seat, and saw she was crying, the tears smudging her heavily applied mascara. 'Here take this,' he said, passing her his cigarette.

She thanked him, and leaned forward to accept it. He immediately lit another for himself.

'Where's Spencer?' she asked, with undisguised concern etched in her voice.

'With Joyce Leader,' Garvan told her, turning left onto the main coastal road.

'Did everything go okay? Did Aldous Meyer turn up with Jean Giscard?'

'Meyer's dead,' Rowlands said bluntly.

'Christ, what happened?'

'Major Hall killed him.' Rowlands chuckled, and looked briefly back over his shoulder at her. 'Not bad going, bagging two senior Nazi officers within an hour of one another, is it?'

Michelle closed her eyes, half in disbelief, and half in dread. 'Oh, my God,' she murmured, almost as if to herself. 'But, is Giscard safe?'

'Yes, he's with Spencer.' Rowlands said.

'When did they start to realise Stackler was missing?' Garvan asked.

'It took them a while,' she whispered. 'By the time I returned from the lady's,' Michelle's words faltered, as she tried to regain her composure, and closed her eyes again. But, every time she did so, she kept getting flashbacks of lying helplessly on the floor, with Stackler on top of her and unable to fight him off. She puffed nervously on the cigarette Rowlands had given her. She started again, hesitantly at first. 'By the time I returned from the lady's,' she repeated, 'von Bertele was propping up the bar with a bunch of cronies. The Baron had taken himself off to another table.' She thoughtfully chewed on her lower lip. 'The singing had started to die down, so Meinhard suggested the band take a break, while they had the chance.'

As the musicians started to drift out of the dining room, Michelle decided on joining Bertele at the bar; there was quite a crush around him. With the food having been served, people had started to mingle and swap places at the tables. Initially, no-one noticed Stackler had failed to return, until the Baron suddenly realised it was getting late, and decided to have a quiet word with Bertele. But, by now, Bertele was half-cut, and didn't seem to be particularly interested in Stackler's whereabouts, so Gruber then ordered Meinhard to take a look around, and see if there was any sign of either him, or Meyer.

'Didn't they think it strange he'd left without saying anything?' Garvan queried.

She pulled a face. 'No, not really. It wasn't the first time he'd upped sticks and left a meal, without saying a word to anyone. He wasn't interested in social niceties, so they just assumed he'd had enough, and taken himself off to meet Meyer. You've got to remember, he rarely bothered to confide in either of them; they were there to support him, not the other way around.' She took a long drag on the cigarette. 'He was totally fanatical in his allegiance to the Reich, and, like his friend Himmler, held a deep-rooted mistrust of the Abwehr. He always treated the Baron and Bertele with utter contempt, and he certainly never held back in letting them know his feelings.' Michelle glanced out of the car. 'Where are we going?' she asked distractedly.

'To the British Embassy,' Garvan said

'Why are we going to the Embassy?'

'It was Spencer's call. When they find the bodies, things will really start to kick off.'

She puffed out her cheeks. 'I thought things had already kicked off.'

Rowlands swivelled round in his seat to face her. 'You really won't want to be in Estoril after tomorrow.'

There was more than a hint of panic in her voice, when she answered. 'But ,won't it make matters worse?'

'How will it?'

'But, won't it look suspicious I've fled without saying a word?'

'Think about it,' Rowlands said patiently. 'When news of their deaths reaches Berlin, especially Stackler's, the blame game will begin here with a vengeance, and heads will start to roll, and I don't just mean in the Abwehr. Their locally employed agents will also come into the firing line. They'll go through everything, and everyone, with a fine-tooth comb.' Rowlands could see he still hadn't entirely convinced her.

'Berlin will temporarily lock everything down, until they can discover the truth. You do understand, Michelle, the Baron and von Bertele won't only be fighting to save their professional lives, but a recall to Berlin.' He allowed time for his words to sink in. 'You do realise what being recalled would mean, don't you?'

Rowlands caught the look on her face; yes, she obviously did know a formal recall would certainly result in their being put to death. Michelle also read between the lines; Rowlands was trying to tell her, regardless of his personal feelings toward her, von Bertele would no longer be in a position to offer his protection.

'How long am I going to stay at the Embassy?' she asked no-one in particular.

'We're flying back to England on the same flight as Giscard,' Garvan told her.

'I'm to return home?' She sounded surprised.

'We've told you, Michelle; it's too dangerous for you to remain here any longer. Besides, I'd have thought you'd be relieved to be going home.'

Michelle pursed her lips thoughtfully. A nagging doubt began to cross her mind. *If she was to be repatriated to London and, in effect, closed down, was it perhaps a sign of failure? Could she no longer be trusted as a double agent?* Michelle fell into an uneasy silence for the remainder of the journey, until Garvan parked up in the Embassy compound.

He opened the door for her. 'George will take care of you, and show you up to your room.'

Michelle smiled in thanks, her eyes suddenly welling up with tears. 'Did Spencer tell you what happened at the club?'

'Yes, he told me about Stackler,' he said gently.

'I just wondered, that's all,' she whispered.

'We'll arrange for you to be driven down to the airport on Monday morning. In the meantime, you'll be safe here.'

'Where will you be?' she asked, uneasily.

'That doesn't matter,' he said cutting the conversation dead.

As Michelle watched him drive back out of the compound, she found Rowlands was smiling at her.

'Come on, let's be getting you to bed.'

Michelle wasn't sleepy, far from it. But, at least the Embassy had provided her with a temporary haven far away from the ensuing fallout.

## *Chapter 24*

After dropping Rowlands and Michelle off at the British Embassy, Garvan returned to the Plaza Palacio Hotel in Estoril. He stayed the night, and in the morning, packed all their suitcases, and then settled the bill. Lucern's people were going to arrange for the luggage to be collected from the hotel, and then transported to the airport on Monday morning. Joyce's excess baggage was to be shipped back separately at a later date, and MI6 would invoice her accordingly for the excess costs.

Garvan phoned ahead to let Spencer know he was about to leave the Plaza. By the time he arrived at the fuel depot, Spencer was waiting for him at the entrance. The guard opened the barrier, and waved him through.

Spencer raised his hand in greeting, and jumped in the car beside him. 'Is everything okay?' he asked. 'How was Michelle?'

'Tearful,' Garvan said, following his directions to the workshop.

'Were there any problems?'

'No, it went like clockwork.'

As they pulled up outside the workshop, Spencer said to him, 'Don't mind the guard dog; Lucern reckons it's a pussy cat, unless it's let off the leash.'

Garvan got out of the car, and cast a wary eye at the creature. 'It looks like a cross between a wolfhound and a ruddy donkey with fangs.'

'I know, but try telling that to Jo. She's been out every five minutes, feeding the bloody thing.'

As they headed inside, Garvan said, 'So, come on, what happened to Plan A?'

He mentioned the safe house might have been compromised. It told on his face; he was reluctant to elaborate any further, and Garvan said as much.

Spencer smiled. 'What you don't know, you can't tell.'

He eyed him with trepidation. 'Why not just try giving me a straight answer for once.'

'I will, if I can.'

'Okay. If this thing goes belly up, is there a Plan C?'

'What do you think?'

'That's a no, then?'

'You're right. There's no Plan C.'

Inside the workshop, Garvan took a long hard look at the massive fuel tanker trucks lined up, side-by-side.

'We have a bit of a problem,' Spencer said.

'We always have a ruddy problem.'

He ignored the jibe. 'The tanker driver has refused to take the truck down to the airport.'

'You surprise me,' Garvan said sarcastically.

'Yes. We tried to grease his palm with some extra dosh, but he still wouldn't budge.'

'Why was that?'

'For some reason, the poor bugger got it into his head he might end up being ambushed on the way.'

'The poor sod didn't fancy getting himself shot up. I can't say as I blame him; I don't fancy it much, either.'

'It's only a minor blip,' Spencer said cheerfully, as he climbed into the driver's cab of a tanker. 'He's more than happy to take over, once you've reached the airport and get you through security. Just relax. Lucern's people will take care of all the arrangements.'

Garvan gave him a glassy stare. 'Are you being serious?'

'I'm sorry about what?'

'Do you really want *me* to drive Giscard to Portela Airport?'

'Is there a problem?'

'What do you reckon my chances are of getting this ruddy thing to the airport in one piece,' Garvan said, patting the side of the cab.

Gripping hold of the large steering wheel, Spencer glanced down at him. 'I don't know what you're so worried about. You've driven trucks before; I know you have.'

'Jesus wept,' Garvan grunted. 'Only once before, and that was, what, eight or nine years ago now.'

He knew Spencer was referring to a bank robbery in Pimlico. At the time, it had been a high-profile heist, and had made the headlines in all the National newspapers. There'd been an insider tip-off, which had resulted in the Flying Squad lying in wait for the gang. The plan went like clockwork. They arrested the entire gang. The only fly in the ointment, as far as Garvan had been concerned, was after the forensic team had finished their work at the crime scene, his Guv'nor had ordered him to remove the security lorry, containing the banknotes, to a secure police compound in Hammersmith. The drive down to the compound hadn't exactly passed without incident. Driving a car was one thing, but handling an enormous bloody lorry was a different matter altogether.

'I'm sorry, but this won't work,' he said. 'I'll not only end up killing myself, but your precious bloody scientist to boot.'

'What makes you say that?'

'I ended up taking the ruddy gate out at the police compound, and nearly finished off the Duty Sergeant.'

'Well, you can get in some practice today at the depot.'

'There's got to be someone else you could ask, surely.'

'Like who?'

'What about Charlie Wright?'

Spencer roared with laughter. 'Charlie's great with an automatic, but I wouldn't trust him with a frigging tanker full of aviation fuel.'

Garvan supposed it was a compliment, of sorts. 'Even if I do manage to steer this thing all the way to the airport, without killing anybody, aren't you forgetting something?'

'What's that?'

'Well, for a start, I don't speak Portuguese, and I certainly don't look like a local.'

Spencer agreed with him. 'It's not a problem. As I said, you'll pick up the driver near to the airport, and he'll do all the talking.'

'How near?'

'Just before you reach the main delivery gate, there's a disused warehouse called the Porto; he'll link up with you near there.'

He looked up at Spencer in the cab. 'How have you managed to get a free run of this place for the weekend?'

'How do you think?'

He gave him a thin smile. 'How much did it cost?'

'Frank's still counting.'

Garvan guessed as much, and added thoughtfully, 'This tanker driver of yours…'

'He's not exactly mine.'

'Well, whatever, but this plan of yours.'

'What about it?'

'If we manage to get through security, what do we do then?'

'Take the tanker over to the plane. Park up, and when the driver's refuelling the Dakota, one of the crew will get you safely on board.'

To Garvan's mind, it all seemed just a tad too easy. When they had landed at Lisbon Airport, he distinctly remembered each of the Axis and Allied planes had been allotted an armed guard. Spencer breezily brushed his concerns aside, and assured him the KLM crew had been thoroughly briefed by MI5; everything was in hand, and they'd take care of the guard.

Garvan stared at him sceptically; he had a way with words, and a way of making everything sound so plausible. Most of the time, common sense dictated Garvan should have pleaded he was only on secondment from Scotland Yard, and was not a fully paid up, gun-toting field agent. But, he didn't, and Garvan sensed Spencer had his measure, and knew, after his customary preamble, he'd eventually rise to the challenge.

'Spencer. Spencer, there's a call for you.'

They both turned round to see Joyce standing at the top of the metal staircase to the manager's office.

'Who is it?'

'Frank Lucern. He says it's urgent.'

Spencer took the call. 'Is there a problem?'

Lucern's filled his ear. 'No, relax. I just thought you ought to know, Gruber and Bertele are returning to Estoril today. In fact, they should have arrived by now.'

'Is that *it*?'

There was a slight pause; it sounded as if Lucern was sucking on his pipe. 'Word has it, they've discovered both bodies.'

'Are you sure?'

'Well, let's put it this way. All hell's broken loose, and the communication lines between Lisbon and Berlin are starting to become red hot.'

'I'd be surprised if they didn't.'

'The Reich's Ambassador has already demanded a personal interview with President Salazar.'

'What's that all about?'

There was another moment's silence, as Lucern sucked on his pipe again. 'Our people reckon he's going to lodge a formal complaint against the underhand activities of the Allied intelligence agencies. Under the circumstances, with the death of two senior officers, and one of them a close friend of *Reichsführer* Himmler, it's the very least he could do.'

'And how has Sir Ronald Campbell taken the news?'

Lucern sighed wearily. 'Not well. He's having lunch tomorrow with the American Ambassador to discuss the situation. They intend concocting some response or other to make sure their singing from the same hymn sheet. No doubt it'll be the usual diplomatic gobbledygook, you know, lots of words without actually saying anything of substance. The Allies will no doubt express their outrage at the accusations, and strenuously refute any wrongdoing or involvement in the deaths of either Stackler or Meyer. Then, they'll continue going around in ever decreasing circles, until the next real or perceived crisis raises its head.' There was yet another pause down the line, as he continued to puff on the briar. 'Is there anything else you'd like me to do?'

'Not that I can think of.'

'Then, I'll see you at the airport.'

'All being well, yes, you will,' Spencer said pensively, replacing the receiver on the cradle.

\*

As they drove out of the depot at first light on Monday morning, Garvan and Giscard were dressed in matching blue overalls, with the fuel depot's distinctive logo of an oil derek embroidered in gold thread. Garvan started the engine, and engaged the gear, before releasing the handbrake. There was a very different feel to handling an entirely laden fuel tanker than on his practice run around the depot the previous day. He did manage to get through the gates, without stalling, which he felt was something of an achievement in itself. Turning left onto the main road, Garvan checked his wing mirror, to make sure Spencer and Joyce Leader's black saloon had dropped in behind them. The plan being they would provide an escort for the journey down to Portela Airport.

'It's okay,' he assured Giscard. 'They're right behind us.'

The Frenchmen nodded. He seemed twitchy, and it wasn't helping Garvan's peace of mind any; he was nursing a Sten gun across his lap. In case they ran into any trouble, Spencer had taken the precaution of placing two guns inside the driver's cab. But, rather than store them behind their seats, Giscard insisted on keeping one close to hand. He certainly wasn't going to take any chances of being taken by the Germans again, at least not alive.

'Have you ever fired one of those bloody things before?' Garvan asked.

'No,' he replied flatly. 'But, Major Hall showed me how it's done.'

'Just remember, matey, we're sitting in a ruddy tanker, loaded to the gunnels with aviation fuel. One stray bullet from that thing, and we're going to be blown to kingdom come!'

Giscard looked at him with an expression of utter contempt. Garvan knew he was stating the obvious, but thought it had to be said all the same. After all the man had been through over the last few weeks, Garvan knew he'd rather die in a blaze of glory than risk being taken to face trial in Berlin. While he sympathised and imagined, in his shoes, he'd probably have felt the same way, the prospect of having a suicidal Frenchman sitting beside him in a lorry full of fuel wasn't necessarily a great combination. And, no matter how many times Spencer tried to reassure him, the German intelligence service was probably in too much disarray to mount any serious attempt to retrieve Giscard from their clutches, he couldn't help thinking a rescue attempt might well be the only possible way to try and deflect Hitler's retribution.

For the first few miles, the traffic was relatively light, and to Garvan's relief, he was only once forced to judder to a halt at a set of traffic lights. Although it wasn't exactly textbook smooth, he stopped all the same, and successfully avoided rear-ending the car in front of him. Glancing in the wing mirror, he could see Spencer chuckling at his somewhat clumsy attempt to bring the tanker to a halt.

As the lights turned to green, he silently mouthed to himself, 'Don't let the ruddy clutch slip, don't let it slip.'

He moved off slowly, the engine straining, as he fought to engage the large gear stick. The palms of his hands were damp, and not just through the increasingly sultry heat but anxiety. The winding coastal road was extremely narrow in places, and at times, he found himself almost on the point of holding his breath, in case they met any on-coming traffic.

As the road slowly began to open out, an Opel saloon overtook and sped past them. The vehicle was carrying local number plates, so he thought nothing of it, at first, until he noticed Spencer was flashing his headlights, and indicating for him to pull over.

'Major Hall wants us to stop.'

Giscard's grip instinctively tightened around the Sten. 'What's wrong?' he said, leaning out of the cab window.

Garvan started to brake and manoeuvre the tanker into the side of the road, before shooting the Frenchman an anxious look.

'Will you do me a favour, and keep your bloody finger off that trigger?'

Giscard glanced at him, but had no intention whatsoever of loosening his grip on the Sten. After coming to a stop, Garvan made to get out of the cab.

'Stay where you are!' Spencer shouted, as he ran toward them. 'I need to drive on.'

'Why?'

'The car that overtook us was carrying von Bertele, and what looked like a couple of Gestapo officers. We'll have to check it out.'

Before Garvan had time to answer, Spencer was on his way back to the car, and sped off, leaving them undefended.

'Just sit back,' he said firmly to Giscard.

Giscard didn't respond. He had a feeling the Germans weren't going to give him up that lightly, especially after the deaths of two prominent, highly regarded officers. It crossed his mind if they'd been in occupied Europe, their deaths would have resulted in revenge attacks against the civil population. All the local men, women, and children would have been rounded up by now and shot out of hand. Neutral Portugal, of course, afforded a degree of protection. The locals would be left unmolested. But, the fact remained he was a marked man, and in the eyes of the Nazis, a traitor who had not only jeopardized the Peenemunde rocket programme, but in effect, had also potentially threatened the final outcome of the War, by revealing their secrets to the Allies.

Garvan checked the road signage; there was still another fifteen kilometres to the airport. He thought of putting his foot down, but common sense dictated he didn't want to chance his luck. Besides, there were still a number of steep inclines to negotiate, and with an entirely laden tanker, they'd be reduced to a slow crawl, anyway.

\*

Spencer followed Bertele's car for some distance, before losing sight of it along a meandering stretch of road, where there were several turn-offs to either side. After a while, he decided to call it a day; his top priority was to protect Jean Giscard, so he turned the vehicle around, and drove back on himself to link up with the fuel tanker. They'd only driven a couple of kilometres, when they suddenly came across Bertele's car, drawn up at the side of the road on a rocky verge banked by fir trees. Somewhere along the line, they must have made a U-turn down one the of the side roads, and returned to lie in wait for the tanker. One of the Gestapo officers was leaning nonchalantly against the side of the Opel, smoking a cigarette. Standing at a little distance from the car, under the relative shade of the trees, was Bertele and the second Gestapo officer.

'That's him!' Joyce said pointing.

'I know,' Spencer responded. 'We've got to do something.'

She looked at him uneasily.

'We can't risk the tanker getting this far up the road. They'll blast the bloody thing to kingdom come, taking Garvan and Giscard with it.'

Joyce instinctively reached for the Sten guns wedged between their seats. They were almost level now with the Opel.

'When I give the word, make a break for it, and go behind the rocks over there.'

Joyce glanced anxiously out of the window; she was frightened, but a sense of self-preservation rapidly kicked in. It wasn't as if she'd been given a choice; there wasn't one. They were literally going to have to fight for their lives.

'Where will you be?'

'I'll head for the trees on the opposite side of the road, but you'll have to give me some cover.'

'Christ, Spence, what are you going to do?' she asked in growing alarm.

He unexpectedly flattened the accelerator to the floor; the engine revved up, and as they speeded past the staff car, Spencer suddenly did a handbrake turn, and slewed the vehicle violently across the road in a screech of burning tyres and dust. The Gestapo officer, who'd been leaning against the car having a smoke, swung round and immediately drew his pistol.

'*Raus, Raus!*' he yelled at his companions.

Von Bertele and the other officer ran to the Opel, and reached inside for their *Schmeisser* sub-machine guns. Spencer and Joyce flung open the doors, and dived for cover on either side of the road, before letting loose with the Stens. Bertele crouched down behind the staff car, and began returning fire. Almost immediately, the Germans found themselves pinned down; their only option was to try and make a dash for the trees. Whoever was attacking them, they were certainly professionals, spraying them with an almost constant blanket of gun-fire.

As Bertele tentatively leaned out from behind the car to fire off his *Schmeisser*, he could scarcely believe his eyes; it was Joyce Leader, of all people, firing back at him. Bertele slumped back behind the Opel; the bitch had completely blind-sided them. He couldn't understand why they hadn't picked up the fact she was a double agent. Something had gone very wrong with their intelligence system; he could only guess at the extent of the damage she had managed to inflict. But, *just how long had she been working for the Allies?*

The plan to snatch Giscard from the tanker, or take him out by blowing up the lorry had been the Baron's bright idea. Bertele had complained it was far too risky, but he was having none of it. To appease Berlin, the Baron needed results. Agent *Schornsteinfeger* had come up trumps again, with a tip off detailing the intended route to Portela Airport. It was simply too good an opportunity to pass up. If they pulled it off, then they might just manage to salvage their reputations in the eye of the *Führer*.

Since the deaths of Stackler and Meyer, Gruber had been bombarded by a series of calls from Hitler's chancellery demanding action, and also from Himmler, ordering retribution for the loss of two esteemed Nazi officers. Failure wasn't an option. The consequences of allowing British Intelligence to rescue Giscard from under their noses would undoubtedly result in their being formally recalled to Berlin for a personal meeting. This would not only be with the *Führer* but also with *Reichsführer* Himmler, to explain their actions, or lack of them, in protecting Stackler and helping to deliver safely Giscard to face trial on charges of treason against the Third Reich.

Bertele aimed his *Schmeisser* toward Joyce and fired; if he was going to die, he wanted to make damn sure he took her down with him. The rounds ricocheted off the rocks; she ducked down for cover, as Spencer tried to attract their fire. Bertele then saw him gesture to her. This British agent knew what he was doing, and guessed he was probably going to try and move closer to them under the cover of the trees. It crossed Bertele's mind whether to make a dash across the road, in an attempt to head him off, but Joyce was no mean shot, and would have picked him off easily. Bertele erred on the side of caution and decided, for now, at least, he had little choice. other than to stay put where he was.

Joyce continued to keep up a relentless stream of gunfire, and managed to wound one of the Gestapo officers. He fell awkwardly against the Opel and dropped to the ground, before dragging himself behind the car, while still managing to keep a tight grip on his sub-machine gun.

'Are you all right?' Bertele called to him.

'Yes,' he said, bleeding heavily from a shoulder wound.

Joyce was about to open fire again, when she heard the rumbling sound of a heavy diesel engine; it had to be the tanker; one stray bullet would send them into oblivion. She glanced anxiously over her shoulder, as the tanker came to a grinding halt around the bend.

\*

Before Garvan turned the corner, Giscard had already shouted at him, 'What's that noise?'

'What noise?'

He couldn't hear anything over the noisy groan of the trucks engine.

'Listen, listen!' he pleaded agitatedly.

He did listen, and above the sound of the straining engine, he heard the unmistakable repetitive *rat-a-tat* of machine gun fire. By now, he'd already started to turn the corner, and was forced to put his foot to the floor to slam on the brakes. The movement of the fuel inside the tanker made it difficult to keep a straight line. The lorry jerked forward, and came to a violent halt, rocking the cab with the force of the momentum.

He could see Spencer's black saloon slewed across the road, the car doors wide open. He then became aware of Joyce Leader crouching behind a rock, desperately trying to take cover at the side of the road. She looked away from the tanker, and carried on firing her Sten toward Bertele's staff car. The Germans were still putting up a ceaseless barrage of return fire, with their powerful *Schmeisser* submachine guns. He took a quick look around, but couldn't see any sign of Spencer.

*That's it,* Garvan thought to himself, *we're sitting ducks we need to get out, and get out fast.* Without hesitating, he reached behind the driver's seat, and grabbed hold of a Sten gun, jumping down from the cab. By the time he hit the ground, to his horror, he saw Giscard was already running suicidally from the truck, like a man possessed, spraying the gun wildly, and hitting everything in sight, trees, bushes, and even the road. Joyce turned around in alarm, and flattened herself down behind a boulder.

Having decided they were at greater risk of being killed by Giscard than the Germans, Garvan took matters into his own hands, and rugby-tackled him to the ground. As they landed with a jarring crash, all bloodied and grazed, he shouted, 'Take cover, you effing little idiot. You'll get us all killed!'

After a moment's hesitation, Joyce got to her feet again, and started firing off another salvo.

'If you don't crawl over toward those bloody trees, there I swear to God, I'll shoot you myself!' Garvan spat at him.

Giscard realised he wasn't joking, and reluctantly crawled across the road toward the trees, dragging his Sten gun at his side under a constant hail of machine gun fire. Garvan followed him, and once they'd made it to cover, he looked anxiously back across the road toward Joyce; she nodded at him, and so he started to open fire. Several rounds pierced the German's car. Someone was shooting from behind the vehicle; he couldn't see who it was, but von Bertele had somehow managed to crawl a short distance away from the Opel, and was now taking cover behind a tree.

As he let loose with the Sten, Garvan wondered where the hell Spencer was. There was still no sign of him anywhere. He hadn't thought to check if he was dead in the car. As he let loose with the Sten, he noticed movement in the trees up ahead, and then saw the dark shape of a figure; there was no mistaking it was Spencer. Thank God, he was still alive, and then, it suddenly dawned on him. He'd left Joyce to fight it bravely out alone, as he made his way through the steeply banked woodland to get closer to von Bertele's staff car.

Garvan thought he was holding something in his hand; it looked like a grenade. They continued to keep the Germans busy, too busy for them to notice Spencer had fleetingly stepped out from behind a tree, pulled the pin off the grenade, and lobbed it toward the Opel. In the ensuing commotion, von Bertele caught movement out of the corner of his eye. He swung round, and watched helplessly, as the grenade rolled inexorably beneath the rear axle of the car.

Spencer dived for cover, as von Bertele called out a warning to his fellow officers, but, they had too little time to react. Within a split second, the grenade exploded taking the petrol tank up in a fierce blazing fireball. The windows blew out, and the car lifted off the ground with the force of the ear-splitting explosion, shards of jagged metal shot out in every direction. Von Bertele and the Gestapo officers were hurled bodily into the air, in a weird kind of surreal slow motion. A strange, eerie silence followed the blast.

Spencer calmly emerged from the trees, with his Sten gun cautiously aimed at the Germans, who had been blown some distance from their vehicle. He systematically approached each of them in turn, before swiftly moving back down the road.

'Dead, all dead,' he called out to them.

Garvan helped Giscard back to his feet.

Spencer coolly checked his watch. 'Right, let's get going.'

Garvan hurried back to the tanker, and waited until Giscard was safely inside the cab, before pressing the starter button. Fortunately, the heavy diesel engine caught at once. As he drew level with Spencer's bullet-riddled black saloon, he marvelled, in spite of all the damage to the bodywork, the windscreen had somehow managed to survive intact. He pulled up, and waited to see if they needed any help, but after some persuasion, Spencer managed to nurse the engine back into life, and once again, fell in behind the fuel tanker.

As they drove past the bodies of von Bertele and the two Gestapo officers lying in the road, Giscard glanced out of the cab, without any particular expression on his face. He still couldn't be persuaded to part with the Sten gun, at least not, until Portela Airport finally came into sight. Even then, only when Garvan ordered him to place it behind their seats.

\*

Following the tanker down toward the airport, Spencer turned to Joyce. 'Is the radio telephone still in one piece?'

She glanced down at the console. 'It seems to be okay.'

'We need to contact Lucern.'

'Do you think we're in range?'

'We should be by now; we're not that far off from the airport.'

She lifted the receiver and waited, nothing seemed to be happening, and then, there was a click, they were connected to the MI6 operations room. The call had been picked up by the duty officer.

'Three down,' was all she said.

There was a pause, as the call was handed over to Lucern. 'Three?' he repeated.

'Yes, three.'

'Are they ours?'

'No.'

There was a protracted silence. 'Anyone we know?'

'2IC.'

Lucern visibly blanched, 2IC was the codename for von Bertele, and was short for his position as the Baron's second-in-command.

'And the others?'

'Gorillas.'

"Gorillas" was the MI6 nick-name for Gestapo officers; the body count was certainly growing. 'Is the convoy safe?'

'It's en-route.'

Spencer glanced across at her. 'Ask him if we're meeting Rowlands at the airport.'

She asked the question.

'Affirmative, I'll also be there.'

'Tell him,' Spencer said, 'We'll leave the car at the Porto warehouse.'

Joyce returned the receiver to the console. 'Where's the Porto warehouse?'

'Near the main delivery entrance of the airport. Before the War, it was used for storing export goods, but since 1940, it's fallen into disuse.'

Glancing out of the passenger window, she noticed a road sign for Portela Airport. Inwardly, Joyce breathed a sigh of relief. Although not given to displays of emotion, it had been a close shave, and they'd been lucky to escape with their lives. Joyce clasped her hands tightly on her lap in an attempt to stop him seeing she was shaking. As she puffed out her cheeks, she suddenly became aware of Spencer looking at her.

'Keep your eyes on the road. We might have an accident,' she joked.

There was a half-smile on his face. 'Do you know you shot like a professional back there?'

'Did I?' she answered dully. 'Then, I guess you'll have to thank my father for that.'

'Why?'

'As a youngster, he taught me how to shoot.' She coolly returned his gaze. 'You weren't too bad yourself.'

He looked through her, rather than at her, and said distantly, 'But, it's what I'm paid to do.'

'Well, whatever.' She sighed. 'But, at least, there's one thing we *don't* have to worry about.'

'It makes a change. What's that?'

'We killed von Bertele, before he had a chance to out me as a double agent.'

Spencer smiled. 'Do you know, I think that's what probably gave me the edge?'

She looked at him searchingly not quite sure what he meant.

'He seemed so hell bent on killing you he completely lost sight of me.'

Joyce threw back her head and laughed; he was probably right.

As they reached the road running past Portela Airport, Spencer flashed on his headlights, and indicated they were going to start pulling back. Up ahead, Garvan noticed a car parked by the side of the road. Standing in front of it was the large, unmistakable figure of Charlie Wright, Lucern's bodyguard. On seeing them, he raised his hand in greeting, and stepped back onto the pavement. Garvan pulled into the kerb alongside him.

'Sir,' Wright said. 'Is everything okay?'

'It's been a bit touch and go, but at least we've made it in one piece.'

Wright opened the passenger door of the car, and a man in his mid to late forties climbed out, wearing dungarees with the fuel depot's distinctive logo of an oil derek embroidered with gold thread. Garvan visibly relaxed; thank God, it was the tanker driver. Wright introduced him; his name was Osvaldo. There was a brief exchange between them in a mixture of Garvan's almost non-existent Portuguese, and the driver's broken English.

Garvan shuffled across the seat toward Giscard. 'I'm sorry,' he apologised. 'I'm afraid it's a bit of a tight fit.'

'Don't worry, *Monsieur*, we're nearly there.'

\*

Spencer turned off the main road, and drew up in the disused grounds of the old Porto warehouse; it hadn't come a moment too soon. The increasing volume of traffic around the airport meant their bullet-riddled car was becoming something of a liability, and was starting to attract a good deal of attention.

'Will the car be all right here?' Joyce asked, closing the passenger door. 'Do we leave the radio and the guns where they are?'

'It's Lucern's problem, not ours; they'll either collect it, or torch the ruddy thing. Either way, it can't be traced back to MI6. The car's registered to a local German importer down at the docks in Lisbon.'

He reached inside, retrieved a navy-blue blazer from the backseat, and eased it on. 'How do I look?'

Joyce wrinkled her nose. 'If you button it up, you might just about manage to cover the blood stains on your shirt.' She then instinctively, glanced down at herself. 'I wish I could say the same thing!'

'It's not too bad.' he said, helping dust down her navy-coloured dress. 'It's not too bad.' He took a step back. 'You'll pass muster.'

'Are we going straight to the terminal?'

'No, I just want to check they make it through airport security.'

As they turned right out of the dilapidated front gates of the warehouse, they could see the fuel tanker drawn up at the delivery gates. The Portuguese driver appeared to be handing over the delivery documentation to a police officer at the checkpoint.

*

Inside the cab, Garvan held his nerve, as the police officer carefully checked through the officially stamped paperwork. He was mumbling incoherently, almost as if to himself, before heading back to the control post.

'Is anything wrong?' Garvan asked Osvaldo.

He appeared not to understand.

'Is everything okay,' he said slowly.

The driver smiled at him, and gave the thumbs up sign. 'Yes, okay.'

Garvan glanced at Giscard and gave him a nudge. 'When he comes back out, will you promise to do something?'

The Frenchman looked at Garvan blankly. 'What do you want me to do?'

'I don't want you making eye contact with him.'

Giscard looked at him with narrow-eyed suspicion and asked sharply, 'I'm sorry what do you mean?'

'Because coppers the world over have a sixth sense when something's not quite right, and at the moment, it's written all over your ruddy face. You're on edge, and he's going to pick up on it.'

Jean looked at him searchingly, before answering flatly, 'Whatever, you say.'

It was an anxious wait for the guard's return from the control post. He didn't fancy him having a last-minute panic attack, and making a sudden bolt for it.

'Are you all right?' he said to him quietly.

Giscard nodded but couldn't trust himself to speak; his gaze unseeingly transfixed on the open doorway of the control post. His heart was pounding as the Portuguese police officer finally re-emerged clutching their documentation and a clipboard. He handed the delivery note back to the driver. They spoke briefly to one another, before he ordered the gates to be opened and waved them through.

'Thank Christ for that,' Garvan said, heaving a weary sigh of relief.

As the tanker edged its way slowly through the heavy metal gates, they were met by another uniformed policeman, who jumped onto a motorbike. He indicated for them to follow him across the airport's apron toward the main hub, where neat rows of Axis planes emblazoned with swastikas on their wings were lined up side-by-side with their Allied counterparts. As Garvan remembered on their arrival, each of the aircraft had been detailed with an armed police guard.

Pulling up alongside the sleek BOAC Dakota, Garvan's heart was in his mouth. The KLM crew was dressed in their smart, pristine uniforms. They were gathered around the plane, laughing and joking with the armed guard. It all seemed very relaxed and routine, and by the look of it, they had obviously met him before. The motorcyclist waved at the tanker's driver, and peeled off back across the airport's apron.

They drew to a halt beside the plane; Osvaldo jumped down from the cab. He gestured toward Garvan to follow him, but held up the palm of his hand, and said to Giscard, '*Não.*'

'Just stay where you are, until it's safe for you to board the plane.' Garvan's voice was low, and strained.

Giscard nervously peered through the cab window, watching Osvaldo connect up the tanker to the Dakota. Garvan made out to help him as best he could, before being approached by a member of the crew.

'We've been expecting you, sir. I'm Alex Jansen, the co-pilot. If you'd like to collect your friend from the cab, I'll help get you on board.'

He was young, this Dutchman, blond, blue-eyed, and very tall. More to the point, he looked scarcely old enough to be the co-pilot of a ruddy great thing like a Dakota. Garvan thanked him, and duly returned to the plane with Giscard. Jansen quickly checked the armed guard was still in deep conversation with his colleagues, before leading them toward an assortment of suitcases, and carefully stacked container boxes waiting to be loaded into the hold. Garvan looked at Jansen questioningly. He smiled in response, and said in his near perfect English.

'Our loadmaster is waiting for you inside. You'll be able to get out of your overalls, and freshen up, before we take off.'

As they climbed the steps, he called out after them, 'We'll be opening the champagne shortly.'

Garvan looked down at him. To hell with the champagne. All he wanted right now was to make certain there were no last-minute hitches.

## Chapter 25

George Rowlands was standing in the terminal building with Michelle Rookwood. He lit a cigarette, and glanced up at the black and white art nouveau style clock above the main entrance. It crossed his mind Spencer and Joyce were cutting things a little fine. The plane was due to leave in ten minutes. But, then again, he assumed the Dutch crew would try their damnedest to delay take off for as long as possible, without arousing the suspicion of the Portuguese flight controllers.'

Sucking heavily on his cigarette, he finally caught sight of Spencer holding the swing door open for Joyce. He smiled in welcome, and went over to greet them.

'I was starting to get worried about you,' he announced. 'I've got your suitcases from the Plaza Hotel with me.' Rowlands couldn't help noticing, beneath Spencer's blazer, his shirt was badly stained. Nor was Joyce quite her usual immaculate self.

'Is that blood on your shirt?' he queried.

'It's not mine,' Spencer said flatly.

'My God, what's happened?' Rowlands exclaimed. 'Where's Giscard and Garvan? Are they all right; did they make it to the airport?'

'Yes, they did,' answered Lucern.

Hearing the familiar tones of his boss, Rowlands sprung round. His expression registered surprise, seeing his boss standing beside Charlie Wright. Spencer dropped the car keys into Lucern's upturned palms.

'I'm sorry,' Spencer apologised. 'It's in a pretty bad state.'

Lucern gave him a half-smile. 'How bad is it?'

'Let's put it this way. You won't be driving it to church on Sunday morning.'

Lucern's grip closed around the keys. He smiled. 'In which case, then, I can have a lie-in.'

Spencer still felt another apology was in order. 'I really am very sorry about the body count Frank, if there'd been any other way…'

He put his hand up to silence him, and without a flicker of emotion, responded, 'Apologies accepted.'

Spencer couldn't help noticing Michelle was sporting a rather painful-looking black eye. 'Are you all right?'

'You mean, apart from this?' She said, pointing at her eye. 'I've a few cuts and bruises, but that's about all.'

Judging by the traumatised expression etched on her face, he could only assume while the physical wounds might heal, the attack would probably leave her mentally scarred for years to come. Spencer couldn't help but feel desperately sorry for her. He suggested she should start making her way through passport control with Joyce.

The unexpected slight edge to his voice alerted Joyce something was wrong. She parted her lips, as if to speak, but the look on his face made her realise his decision wasn't up for discussion. Joyce exchanged a meaningful glance to Michelle, before taking her to the passport desk.

Rowlands extended his hand toward Spencer, and said with genuine warmth, 'Let's not leave it too long before we meet up again.'

Spencer shook his hand. His grip tightening so hard, Rowlands winced in pain.

'For Christ's sake, Spence, what's wrong?'

He released his grip almost immediately, but the cold, dead-eyed threat on Spencer's face was unnerving. 'You have a choice,' he said huskily.

'What choice?'

'We can play it, one of two ways, Rowlands.'

Rowland's looked completely nonplussed. 'My dear boy, what are you talking about?'

'Frank has a travel clearance signed and sealed for today's flight to Bristol.'

'What's that to do with me?'

'I am addressing Agent *Schornsteinfeger*.'

'I'm sorry?'

'*You* are *Schornsteinfeger*, aren't you?'

The colour visibly melted away from Rowlands' face. 'Good grief man, you can't be serious!

'Can't I?'

'You're making a terrible mistake, Spence.'

'I really think it's you, George, who's made a terrible mistake.

'What are you on about?'

Lucern raised his hand sharply, to silence him. 'I'd hoped to keep you at arm's length from today's show. But, God only knows how you managed to get wind of it.' Lucern's voice was low and strained. 'That was clever of you, George, very clever. The trouble is, in many ways, I do actually rather admire your resourcefulness as a spy. But, the one thing you must never become is arrogant, or over-confident. You were starting to become a little slapdash, George; you began to make mistakes, careless ones, and now...' He hesitated, a thin smile on his lips. 'How did you find out about the change of plan to move Giscard to the airport?'

Rowlands shrugged dismissively. 'It wasn't that difficult.'

'How did you find out about the fuel depot?'

'A few months ago, your secretary changed the combination to your personal safe.'

Lucern's eyes narrowed questioningly.

'You asked her to write the numbers down disguised in the form of a shopping bill, and she left it out on your desk for you to collect in the afternoon. I just happened to be chatting with her when she was writing it out. I asked her what she was doing, and in all innocence, she told me. I glanced over her shoulder, and made a mental note of the numbers.' A rather smug smile crossed Rowlands' face. 'So, that's how I found out Frank; I now had free access to your safe. When no-one was around, I'd have a little rummage to see what I could find.'

Lucern stared through him. *So, that's how the bastard had managed to betray not only Giscard, but the escapees crossing the Spanish border into Portugal.* He'd also wreaked havoc amongst the SOE, many of whom had died in the process because of his duplicity. When he finally spoke, it was in a controlled, rather clipped, manner. 'If I were you, George, rather than stay here, I'd catch the plane, and take the consequences with Colonel Robertson in London.'

'I think what Frank's trying to say,' Spencer mused. 'Is that if you stay here, MI6 will throw you to the wolves, and by the time his contacts have informed your Nazis spymasters you've been playing a double bluff against them, you'll be floating down the Tagus River by the end of the week.'

Lucern handed Rowlands his passport and travel papers. He made to speak, but what was the point. Given the choice, he'd much rather face the consequences of his duplicity in London, than be shot or knifed to death down some shadowy dark alleyway at the hands of the Gestapo.

Lucern's expression remained utterly impassive, as he looked at his agent; only his eyes gave any hint of the anger and disgust he felt toward him.

'Well, George, what's it to be?' Spencer pressed.

There was no trace of embarrassment, as he faced him. 'My dear boy, I'll take my chances in London.'

'I thought you might.' He then shook hands with Lucern, and said his goodbyes, before following Rowlands across the concourse toward passport control.

\*

Having changed out of their dungarees in the loading bay and into the lightweight suits thoughtfully provided by MI6, they were escorted on-board, where Giscard and Claudine had a somewhat tearful reunion, which was much to the annoyance of a stiff-upper-lipped businessman seated in the row behind them. He kept tutting loudly, as he tried in vain to concentrate on reading a document, and at one point, asked the steward if it was possible to move seats. He was politely, but firmly refused, and told all the seats had been allocated specifically by the British Embassy.

Garvan anxiously peered through the window; they were already running late, and there was still no sign of Spencer boarding the plane.

'What's taking him so long?' he called across the aisle to Joyce Leader.

She shrugged indifferently. 'I haven't a clue.'

'What was he doing in there?'

'He was talking to Lucern and Rowlands.' Joyce attracted the attention of the steward, and flashed him a broad flirtatious smile. 'Can I ask you a small favour?'

'Certainly, madam,' he said, resting his arm on the seat in front of her.

'I know it's not usually allowed...' she said in a whisper.

He leaned a tad closer, and returned her smile. 'What do you want?' he replied, lowering his voice.

'I'd really love a gin and tonic right now, but go easy on the tonic would you, sweetie.'

The steward seemed smitten; her charm offensive had the desired effect. He winked at her, and mumbled something about he wouldn't normally do it, but as it was her, he'd make an exception. She flashed him another flirtatious smile, and then looked across the aisle to Garvan.

'I'm sorry,' she apologised. 'I should have asked for one for you as well.'

'It doesn't matter,' he said, and took another peek through the window.

Much to his relief, he saw Spencer climbing the steps to the plane, accompanied by George Rowlands. Garvan looked puzzled; something must have happened.

The pilot was waiting for them at the top of the steps; he seemed to know Spencer. They shook hands, and briefly chatted to one another. Spencer then made his way slowly down the aisle, and made a point of stopping to talk with Jean Giscard and Claudine, before taking the time to have a few words with Michelle Rookwood.

'Did Joyce tell you what happened today?' he asked her.

She nodded, her eyes glistening with tears. 'Yes, she told me von Bertele's dead.'

He gently placed his hand on her shoulder, gave her a squeeze, and then, carried on walking down the aisle, leaving Michelle silently weeping with her thoughts for the man she had grown to like and respect. In many ways, she had played von Bertele like a fiddle. She'd certainly honed in on his weaknesses, and his love of women, and had successfully seduced him. They'd become lovers, and as a result, she had successfully fed London high-grade intelligence, but somewhere along the line, Michelle's feelings had started to blur. Von Bertele had certainly been critical of the Nazi regime, and was in many ways a victim of circumstance, but above all, he was kind, and had loved her deeply, and in her own way, Michelle had also loved him. She knew there hadn't been a choice, and he had to die, but she still felt his loss keenly, and a part of her mourned for him, for the man who wasn't just an Abwehr agent, but a generous, caring lover.

As Spencer neared the rear of the plane, he turned round to Rowlands. 'Sit there!' he said sharply, and pointed to where Joyce was sitting.

She looked up, her face registering surprise. She was seated in the aisle seat, and reluctantly moved across to the window, with her freshly delivered gin and tonic. Rowlands' face was devoid of all expression, as he sat down beside her. Spencer then took his own seat beside Garvan.

'Why's George coming back with us?' he demanded.

'MI5 would like have a little word with him.'

Garvan looked at him thoughtfully. 'Reading between the lines, what's that supposed to mean?'

Spencer looked faintly amused. 'You've been working with us for too long; that's your trouble.'

'What's going on?'

'George, bless him, is our mole.'

A look of disbelief crossed Garvan's face. 'You mean *Schornsteinfeger*?'

'Yes, one and the same.'

'Surely to God there's been some mistake; it can't be George!' he said incredulously.

'The only mistake is, we didn't pick up on him earlier.'

Garvan looked across the aisle towards Rowlands. If he'd overheard their conversation, he was certainly giving nothing away.

As the Dakota's engines noisily sprang into life, Garvan automatically gripped the arms of his seat, thinking the only thing that could possibly spoil their mission now was some trigger-happy *Messerschmitt* pilot flying over the Bay of Biscay.

*Chapter 26*

Rowlands glanced around the elegant room. For all intents and purposes, it was a rather swish living room, all antique furniture, beautiful pale green silk curtains, and an array of expensive gilt-framed paintings adorned the walls. Robertson had chosen the location, an MI5 safe house in Mount Street, in the heart of Mayfair.

As the door closed behind him, Rowlands guessed there had to be a hidden microphone somewhere. He was damned sure Robertson would have wanted the interview recorded. His eyes glided around the room. There might be a clue, once he knew where they wanted him to sit. In the end, George decided it probably didn't much matter where they'd put the bloody thing, but he was certainly more nervous than he was willing to let on. Outwardly, he appeared to be his usual urbane self, elegant, dressed in a well-cut pinstripe suit from his favourite tailor in Savile Row, with a white shirt, a pale blue silk tie, and matching handkerchief spilling out from the top pocket of the jacket. Under his arm, he carried a thin blue folder, which he occasionally tapped almost to reassure himself it was still there.

Rowlands mentally started to brace himself for the onslaught. He was left, he felt, deliberately entirely on his own for a quarter of an hour. It was standard practice to keep the guilty party on edge. Counterintelligence, after all, was about psychological tactics, mind games, and retaining the upper hand. He passed the time inspecting the paintings on the walls, but without ever really seeing them. More than anything, he wanted the interview to be over and done with.

He heard the door click open. He swung round, and saw Tar Robertson, smart as always, dressed in a khaki jacket, with the tartan trousers of the Seaforth Highlanders, and an empty pipe clutched loosely in his left hand. He was followed into the room by Spencer Hall, wearing full uniform as well. Garvan was the last to enter, and closed the door behind them.

Rowlands felt an almost vain frisson of disappointment; Garvan wasn't decked out in uniform. He wasn't entirely sure if he'd ever seen a Scotland Yard officer in full parade dress before. Admittedly, his suit was of a rather good cut. Although he admired the tailoring, it was perhaps not quite of Savile Row quality.

He had known Robertson since his recruitment to the intelligence service. Their paths had crossed on many occasions, although they had never actually worked together. Tar always seemed to be a rather remote, austere figure, and was perhaps privately disparaging about his recruitment to the Service. Rowlands had never really understood Robertson's set up and the Twenty Committee's importance, and the bigger picture of the Double Cross system. Robertson ran an exceptionally tight ship, and more importantly, as a member of MI5, had deliberately held MI6 and Rowlands at arm's length. The historical animosity and distrust between the sister organisations had in some ways increased, rather than lessened, since the outbreak of the War.

Robertson moved over to an ornate, walnut veneer cabinet, and produced drinks for each of them. He knew Rowlands was a formidable drinker, and wouldn't refuse the offer of an extremely large gin and tonic.

'Gentleman,' he announced smoothly, 'shall we be seated.'

He gestured toward a circular table in the centre of the room, with four clawed-footed dining chairs strategically spaced around it. As they took up their seats, Rowlands nervously adjusted his tie, and casually glanced up at the chandelier above their heads. So, *that's where the bloody microphone was*, he thought to himself. He then waited nervously, as Robertson took his time filling his pipe with tobacco. There was a pretence of politeness, which somehow made it all the more difficult. Tar wasn't in any particular hurry to start proceedings.

Rowlands placed the blue folder down in front of him, and glanced nervously around the table, first to Spencer with his arms folded. He hadn't taken his eyes from Rowlands since the moment he'd sat down. He assumed Spencer probably viewed the interview process as an unnecessary layer of red tape, and a complete waste of his time. Why bother going through the legal niceties, when everyone knew Rowlands was as guilty as hell of being a traitor.

Rowlands' gaze drifted to Garvan; now, he was a difficult one to read, the renowned Chief Inspector from Scotland Yard. He didn't give too much away, but always gave the impression of storing up mental notes whenever he engaged in conversation with anyone. Rowlands watched, as he placed a briefcase on the table, a heavy brown leather affair with a crown and "GR" oriented just above the lock printed on it in large gold lettering. He opened it, and retrieved a small notebook with lined paper, and then, placed the briefcase back down on the floor at his feet, suddenly aware of Rowlands' interest in what he was doing.

'I learned to do shorthand at night school years ago,' he said, retrieving a pen from the inside pocket of his jacket. 'It's been a Godsend for things like this; it just makes life so much easier.'

Rowlands passed him a rather awkward smile. He surmised Robertson was probably worried the microphone concealed in the chandelier might not capture a clear enough recording of the interview, so wanted the notes as a back-up.

He studied Robertson, as he placed the pipe between his lips, and took a test draw to check the air was flowing freely. He then struck a match and lit his pipe; the room quickly began to fill with smoke.

'What's that?' Tar asked, pointing at the blue folder.

'A signed confession,' Rowlands responded, nudging the file across the table toward him.

Tar eyed the folder, thoughtfully puffed on his briar, and after some consideration, reached forward and opened it. Inside, he found half a dozen typed pages. He quickly scanned the first page; his expression remained impassive. He then slowly looked up at Rowlands.

'I was hoping you'd come clean, of course, not only for the sake of the Service, but your own as well.' He closed the folder and methodically began to drum his fingers on the cover. After a while, it started to irritate Rowlands, as Tar guessed it would. 'Did you hope by providing us with a sanitised version of events, you'd somehow avoid facing an interrogation?' Tar held his gaze; his voice was cold. 'If you did, then you completely misjudged the situation.'

Rowlands' expression appeared remote and withdrawn. He didn't make any attempt to respond; instead, he reached into his jacket, and retrieved a slender silver cigarette box.

'Do you mind if I smoke?'

'I could scarcely object, could I,' he said, puffing on his pipe.

Tar watched Rowlands taking his time opening the silver box and deftly tapping the end of the cigarette on the table, before slipping it casually between his lips.

'You haven't answered my question,' Tar said evenly.

Rowlands lit the cigarette.

'I was hoping,' Tar continued, 'it might make things a little easier all around, if you just came clean.'

Rowlands drew on his freshly lit cigarette, becoming increasingly aware Spencer's dead-eyed gaze still hadn't wavered from him. He knew, at some point the interrogation would develop into a three-pronged attack. Tar's slick, deceptively languid manner disguised the iron fist in a velvet glove. Spencer, on the other hand, was an open book, ruthless, aggressive, but with an astute head on his shoulders. Garvan again was an entirely different kettle of fish; he never gave much away, but he did come with a reputation for demolishing hardened criminals.

As Rowlands looked slowly around the table at his would-be interrogators, a thought suddenly crossing his mind. He didn't have a cat in hell's chance of swinging it, and perhaps, the best he could hope for, was avoiding being hanged at Wandsworth Prison. In the great scheme of things, he might prefer the option of taking his own life. As things stood, the Head of MI6 had pointedly refused a face-to-face meeting, and had effectively thrown him to the mercy of Robertson and his MI5 brethren.

Rowlands suddenly became aware Robertson was talking to him.

'Do you know what I think, George?'

'No, sir, I do not.'

'I think you're an utter shit, but a clever one, I'll give you that.'

Rowlands stared at him in a state of barely concealed panic; he could feel his face starting to redden. Tar nudged the blue folder back across the table toward him; he wasn't interested in it. He wanted a verbal confession from him, and to get a feel for the extent of his duplicity. At the moment, he could only hazard a guess as to how many people had been betrayed by his treachery and double dealing.

'This business,' Tar said. 'Has caused a panic of seismic proportions around Whitehall.'

Rowlands met his gaze with openness; he seemed not in the least bit fazed.

'When Churchill discovered one of our own MI6 agents was in the pay of the Abwehr, he hit the roof, and to be perfectly honest with you, he would have personally had you shot on the spot. I have to say, George, he still feels very much the same way.' Tar took his time and chewed thoughtfully on his pipe before continuing. 'You duped us all into believing you were one of us.'

Garvan glanced up from his notebook. 'In fact, you've played a blinder, George.'

Rowlands sat back in his chair and fixed his gaze firmly on Garvan. 'You have to understand something, Chief Inspector; MI6 is a club and we always look after our own.'

'Isn't that part of the problem?' Spencer exploded. 'Too much effing nepotism in the Service?'

It was a barbed comment, and one that wasn't entirely lost on Tar Robertson, either. His recruitment to the Service had been via the Old Boy network in his case via a family friend, who just happened to be Sir Vernon Kell, the then Head of MI5. Traditionally, MI5 had recruited from the military, the police, and, in fact, anyone with the right profile and qualifications for the job in hand. Members of its sister organisation, MI6, were mainly drawn from the rarefied world of Oxbridge academia, and were, in many respects, an entirely closed shop.

Spencer looked to Rowlands and asked pointedly, 'Why in God's name did you want to join the Service?'

He met his gaze, without a flicker of emotion. 'I know you probably won't believe me, but I wanted to do my bit.' He paused, before adding, 'To be perfectly honest, it sounded rather exciting.'

Robertson cut in. 'You might believe MI6 look after their own, George, and I know they do, and very well, but loyalty to the Service is everything.'

'I know that,' he said stiffly.

'But, aren't you forgetting something.'

Rowlands looked at him speculatively.

'The Double Cross isn't a part of your cosy club, as you call it, and Churchill won't tolerate traitors to function at any level within the Service. The stakes are far too high to take unnecessary risks, and we certainly can't afford to carry passengers. It says something that even your own boss, General Menzies, will have nothing more to do with you. So, club or not, I think you're rather deluding yourself into thinking they'll provide you with some sort of safety net.' Robertson blew out a cloud of swirling grey smoke. 'You're a very efficient field officer,' he conceded, 'or should I say, *were,*' he corrected himself. 'In the early days, you made all the right contacts, the people who you thought might prove useful in your future career.' His face creased into a smile. 'And you certainly made a point of befriending Spencer, did you not?'

It seemed churlish to disagree with him.

'You admired his professionalism, but more importantly, you feared it.'

Rowlands' gaze glided toward Spencer; he gave him a long, dispassionate stare. Even after he had become a double agent, in his strange convoluted world, he'd still valued Spencer's advice and support, and his intuitive gift for the counterintelligence game of smoke and mirrors.

'Yes,' he found himself saying, 'it's true, I feared his professionalism. I knew when Spencer arrived in Lisbon, I'd have to be on my guard and watch my back.'

'Didn't you worry he'd get wind of your double dealing?'

A flicker of either amusement or arrogance crossed his face; Garvan couldn't quite decide which it was.

'Lucern rarely bothered me,' he explained stiffly. 'I know he was once on your team, Colonel, but he's too trusting.'

'I think that you've underestimated Lucern,' Robertson cut in.

Rowlands raised his brows, his expression dismissive. It was obvious he disagreed with Tar's opinion of his erstwhile protégé. It seemed futile trying to point out

Lucern's failings as a spy, so he let it rest. If you're going to argue, you might as well do so from a point of strength, and at the moment, he wasn't exactly in a position to make any derogatory remarks about his boss, at least, none that would be taken on board, least of all by Robertson.

Garvan suddenly pointed his pen thoughtfully toward Rowlands. 'Before Jean Giscard was moved to the casino in Estoril, word has it you manufactured the intelligence about his being under threat at the safe house in Lisbon. Is that true?'

Rowlands sucked in his lower lip, and appeared discomforted by the question.

Garvan made as if to write down his answer; he waited a moment, before looking back up at him. 'Well, George, did you manufacture the intelligence?'

'Yes, Chief Inspector, I did.' There was almost a sneer in his voice, but it merely masked his uneasiness.

'And whose idea was it to transfer Jean and his girlfriend, Claudine Gregorie, to the casino?'

'It was mine, and mine alone.'

'But, you obviously ran it by Lucern first, before having him moved?'

'Of course, I did.'

'How did you manage to persuade him?'

He gave a slight shrug. 'It wasn't that difficult,' he said condescendingly. 'We'd used the casino as a bolt hole before. It was a good cover, and the manager, Rafael Delgado, was already well known to us, and has been on the payroll for a few years now. He's a reliable source, and is ideally placed at the casino, with an endless supply of high profile customers on both sides of the political fence. We targeted him shortly after the outbreak of the War; we pay him well, and he's given us many valuable tip-offs during that time.'

Garvan stopped writing, and as he did so, it randomly crossed Rowlands' mind he really ought to have learned shorthand himself. It really would have been a Godsend during his time with the Service.

It was Spencer who piped up next. 'Let me get this straight then, George, did *you* move Giscard to the casino?'

'Yes, I did.'

'When did you inform Baron von Gruber of his whereabouts?'

'He knew that I'd sealed the deal to have him moved to Estoril, it was then just a matter of confirming timings.'

'Does it play on your mind?'

'Does what "play on my mind?"'

'That you're responsible for the death of Pete Starling.'

There was a look of genuine horror on Rowlands' face; he seemed affronted at the accusation he had somehow sanctioned the murder of his own field agent. 'Are you implying I ordered him to be killed!' he said incredulously. 'Are you being serious?'

'I'm deadly serious, George. You've already admitted telling the Baron of Giscard's whereabouts.'

Rowlands returned his gaze but didn't respond.

'Are you honestly expecting me to believe you can't see the connection between Starling's death and your treachery?'

'I never expected they'd shoot him, if that's what you mean.'

'Then, you're a bigger bloody fool than I thought you were!' Spencer said scathingly. 'You knew full well Stackler was acting on Himmler's orders to snatch Giscard from British Intelligence. I also know for a fact you personally detailed Starling to guard him that day. You'd have to be deaf, dumb, and blind not to realise you were practically signing his death warrant. You knew Stackler's profile; he was never going to take any prisoners, Starling was in his way, and he killed him; it was as simple as that.'

Rowlands again vehemently protested the accusation. 'It wasn't like that at all!'

Garvan placed his pen down on the table, and sensing Spencer was struggling to keep a lid on his frustration cut in. 'Tell me what it was like, then?'

'Things were starting to get hairy. Gruber and Bertele were coming under enormous pressure from Berlin to start getting results.'

'How did that affect you?'

For the first time, Rowlands appeared slightly flustered, as he tried to exonerate himself from any wrong doing in Starling's murder at the casino.

Robertson languidly removed the pipe from his mouth, and said in a quiet, studied manner, 'You had him killed, seemingly without either remorse or regret. But, what I simply fail to understand is, Pete Starling was more than just a friend to you. You're the godfather to his young son, Hugo, and from all I understand, you were two-faced enough to provide his widow, Ann, a shoulder to cry on.' He placed the pipe between his lips and added sourly, 'That to my mind takes for a particular brand of callousness. As I said to you earlier, George, you really are an utter little shit!'

Rowlands' silence was, in itself, an admission of his guilt.

Garvan had been right. Spencer was struggling to keep a lid on things. Something snapped, and he exploded angrily.

'What made you do it? What the hell turned you? Your name was being mooted for promotion as a Head of Station; very few people are given that opportunity.' He clenched his cigarette lighter so tightly, his knuckles began to turn white. 'I'll give you this, George, you were once a very polished operator.' He released the lighter from his grasp. 'For Christ's sake, just tell me what went wrong?'

The pain of betrayal was etched on Rowlands' face, and Spencer's unexpected praise for his abilities as a spy had only served to make his discomfiture and guilt all the more damning. Ultimately, self-preservation had overridden his deep sense of loyalty to British Intelligence, which was very real and heartfelt. Their mutual trust and friendship had fractured beyond repair.

He was deeply ashamed and said stiltedly, 'I know I've let the Service down.'

'Not just the Service, George, you have let yourself down as well. What happened?' Spencer pressed him.

He stammered his response. 'I-I should have seen it coming, but I didn't.'

'Didn't see what?'

'A honey trap, or, at least, I think it was,' he said rather vaguely.

'What happened?'

Rowlands stubbed out his cigarette and immediately lit another. 'Well,' he said, flicking on his lighter, 'I guess you know how things are.'

Garvan looked across the table at him. 'I'm not a bloody mind reader, George. What are you on about?'

Rowlands took a deep breath. 'The Baron discovered that I was in...in,' he hesitated slightly, '...a relationship with a young Portuguese boy, Alvaro Dimas.' He looked at each of them in turn, waiting for some reaction, but they were far too professional to give anything away, and he continued to tell them what had happened. 'Alvaro's father is a minor official at the local tax office. We met at a bar in Lisbon.' He drew heavily on his newly lit cigarette. 'We'd been together for a couple of weeks. It was certainly no longer than that, when an envelope was posted through the door of my flat.'

Garvan guessed what was coming, but asked all the same. 'And inside, I take it, there were some intimate photographs of you?'

'Yes.'

'Was there a note delivered with the photos?'

'No, not initially. They left me to stew for a while.' A slow ironic smile crossed his face. 'It's standard practice, of course, to leave the victim in limbo and slowly pile up the pressure.'

'And Alvaro,' Garvan asked, 'I take it you told him about the photographs?'

'Yes, yes, I had to,' he said, as Robertson poured another round of drinks, while continuing to listen intently on their conversation.

'What did he have to say for himself?'

Rowlands shrugged and shook his head. 'No more than I expected. He pleaded ignorance.' He blew out a swirl of cigarette smoke. 'I dropped him immediately, and broke off all further contact, but I guess it was too little, too late; the damage was already done.'

'Where were the photographs taken?' Garvan queried.

'All rather sordid, really. It was in a hotel in Lisbon.'

'And who made the booking?'

'Alvaro did.'

As Robertson handed Rowlands his gin and tonic, he rolled his eyes in despair. 'That was rather amateurish of you, dear boy, wasn't it?'

Rowlands thanked him for the drink, and took a large gulp; he couldn't exactly deny the accusation.

Tar resumed his seat. 'I'm surprised you, of all people, walked into their sordid little trap with your eyes tight shut; I would have thought you'd have seen it coming a mile off.' Tar thoughtfully tapped his pipe out into a cut-glass ashtray, before refilling the bowl with fresh tobacco. 'The first rule of espionage, George, as you know well, is to trust no-one; it has to be earned.'

Rowlands watched as Tar carefully packed the tobacco in his pipe. In truth, he feared him, for his subtle interrogation methods and undoubted talent for getting people to talk. They called him the Gentleman Spymaster within the Service; he was discreet and fiercely loyal, but at the same time, ruthless in his handling of those who threatened the Double Cross system and Britain's wider intelligence battle against Nazi Germany. He was widely regarded by his peers as one of MI5's greatest assets. The smooth charm hid someone who was, ultimately, just as deadly as Spencer Hall ever was, and, in some ways, even deadlier.

Tar engaged his eyes, a slight smile hovering on his lips. 'What I don't understand is how someone of your experience and skill missed the warning signs.' He continued to pack the tobacco neatly into the bowl of his pipe. 'You know how the game's played.' Robertson withdrew a matchbox, and looked across the table at him. 'In your time with the Service, how many people have you had placed under surveillance?'

He couldn't give him a number.

'But, when we do, what are we looking for?'

Rowlands said nothing.

'We target the ones with a chink in their armour, some weakness or other, some angle we can use against them.'

Rowlands became almost mesmerised, as Tar placed the pipe to his mouth, and took a test draw to see if he'd packed the tobacco too tight. It was fine, so he struck a match, and let it burn for a few seconds to get the sulphur off. He then gently drew on the pipe, and moved the match in a circular movement over the surface of the tobacco until it was evenly lit.

'Let's face it, George, you've always been so careful, so meticulous. Why was this one so different?'

Rowlands briefly closed his eyes. 'To be perfectly honest with you, I'm not sure. I suppose, looking back on it, I was flattered, flattered someone as young and good looking as Alvaro found me attractive.' He took another large gulp of the gin and tonic. 'I made a fool of myself, and I guess Gruber was surprised at my gullibility and how quickly I fell into his trap,' he confessed with unexpected honesty.

'Presumably, the Baron started to crank things up with the photographs?' Spencer asked.

'Yes, I received a letter with the second batch. It didn't say too much, but enough. There was an implicit threat copies of the photos would be sent to Frank Lucern and the Ambassador.' He started to roll the glass thoughtfully between his hands. 'They also threatened to send copies to my mother.' As he spoke about her, Rowlands' eyes burned red with tears. 'I mean,' he sobbed, his words trailing off, 'can you imagine.'

'It's the name of the game,' Tar said flatly. 'You were Gruber's prize catch. He probably couldn't quite believe his luck he managed to snare you.'

Rowlands wouldn't be drawn, but knew he was right.

'He cultivated you,' Tar continued smoothly. 'I guess his next move was to make direct contact. As far as he was concerned, it was a fait accompli; you were no more than putty in his hands. You must have realised by this time, you were under surveillance, spied upon day and night.'

'Of course, I did.'

'But, even so, he didn't want to rush things.'

Rowlands didn't disagree with him.

'Let me guess,' Robertson smiled enigmatically. 'Did he suggest meeting up for dinner or a drink? Somewhere discreet of course, and you were to make sure you weren't followed?'

The expression on Rowlands' face told him he was right.

'And so,' he continued, 'with each subsequent meeting, Gruber slowly, but surely, reeled you in a little bit further each time, then blackmailed you to the point where self-preservation overtook both your loyalty to your friends and the Service.'

Although, at times, Rowlands had been viewed as an awkward and somewhat uncompromising character, the Service had still held him in high regard. His renowned charm had made him popular throughout the ranks of British Intelligence. News of his betrayal had sent palpable shock waves throughout their ranks. There was still even now an element of disbelief that someone of Rowlands' standing could have betrayed the Service, and become a double agent.

'I know,' Rowlands confirmed to them. 'I've not only let down myself but the Service as well.'

Robertson wasn't overly interested in what he had to say and cut to the chase. 'I'm curious,' he said. 'Why did von Gruber decide to call you *Schornsteinfeger?*'

Rowlands' expression crumpled, almost by way of apology. 'It was all about being a clean sweep; it was a play on words, really.'

Tar looked totally bemused, 'My dear boy, you've completely lost me.'

'As you said earlier, he regarded me as a prime catch; I was Bertele's opposite number, Lucern's second-in-command, just as he was to the Baron.' He absent-mindedly tapped his cigarette flicking the ash into a brass ashtray. 'Over dinner, Gruber announced rather pompously he wanted me to "*reinen Tisch machen*."'

'Meaning what exactly?'

'I was highly placed, and he wanted me to make a clean sweep through MI6, to sweep up the intelligence.' Rowlands shot Tar a wary look. 'In Germany *Schornsteinfeger's* are seen as a sign of good luck, a symbol of good fortune.'

An uneasy silence fell between them. It was Garvan who ended it. 'I want to know about the report you passed to London about Michelle Rookwood.'

'Fire away, Chief Inspector. What about it?'

Garvan took his time looking back through his notes. Rowlands couldn't quite decide whether he was deliberately taking his time, or genuinely couldn't find the right entry. He eventually stopped at a particular page, and ran his index finger along several lines of neatly written shorthand.

'You've admitted manufacturing the intelligence about there being a threat against Giscard when he was initially staying at the safe house in Lisbon, did you not?' Garvan waited for a response, while tapping the tip of his pen repetitively on the notepad.

'Yes, I did,' he said tautly.

'Then, I was just wondering whether you'd also concocted the story Michelle was starting to become a liability.'

Rowlands found the repetitive tapping of the pen irritating, but he surmised it was probably meant to. 'What possible reason would I have to make it up? As far as I was concerned, she wasn't particularly important to MI6.'

'Not to you, maybe, but she produced consistently high-grade intelligence for the Double Cross.'

'Precisely. Michelle was one of your agent's, and not mine, which is why I didn't have any real interest in her activities. She didn't report directly to me, and for the most part, as far as I could see, she kept her head down. But, she was, so to speak, still operating on MI6's patch. I became increasingly concerned by the intelligence landing on my desk; she was getting a little too slapdash, and a little too overconfident.' He took another gulp of the gin. 'In my opinion, she was becoming a risk, so that's why I raised the report to alert MI5 of what was happening.'

There was a half-smile on Garvan's face; he surmised Rowlands probably couldn't see the hypocrisy of what he was saying. He glanced down at his notes again. 'Are you sure you didn't have another motive raising the report about Michelle?'

Annoyance crept into Rowlands' expression. 'I haven't the foggiest idea what you're on about!' he said sharply.

'Michelle was very well connected. She was Colonel von Bertele's lover, his mistress, and she enjoyed his protection. Weren't you just a little worried, that at some point, he might let slip that you were *Schornsteinfeger?*'

'The thought never crossed my mind. Why would he reveal my identity? It wouldn't have been in anyone's interest, least of all his.'

'But, you see, George, Bertele trusted her, and after one too many drinks, he had a tendency to confide the odd nugget of intelligence to her. The beauty of it was, when he did manage to sober up in the morning, nine times out of ten he couldn't remember what he'd told her. You must have known that.'

He wouldn't be drawn.

'Have I missed something?'

'I'm sorry, Chief Inspector, I'm not following you.'

'The one person, who was in a prime position to out you, was Michelle Rookwood. It must have played on your mind any moment, she might have discovered *Schornsteinfeger's* identity.

He looked thoughtfully at Garvan. 'It was a calculated risk.'

'But, I don't understand why you didn't just kill her and cancel out the risk altogether. To my mind, it doesn't add up.'

Rowlands coolly met his gaze. 'Let's just say, I kept her alive as a kind of insurance policy.'

'What do you mean by an insurance policy?'

'If things started to go belly up, I'd have deflected the flack by naming Michelle as our rogue agent.'

'You mean that she was *Schornsteinfeger?*'

'I'd already sown a seed of doubt in your minds by filing the report about her. From there on in, it really wouldn't have been that difficult to convince you she'd turned rogue. She was, after all, Bertele's mistress; he looked after her well and massaged her ego, and let's face it, why wouldn't a little slapper, like Michelle, not have had her head turned by all the attention? You'd have accepted she'd crossed the line, and become too embedded with him.'

Robertson leaned on the table and clasped his hands tightly together. 'I could be entirely wrong, George,' he said reflectively. 'But, I still have a nagging suspicion you simply don't understand the amount of damage you've inflicted on the Service.'

'I understand perfectly, sir,' he responded woodenly.

'You see, I'm trying to think it all through,' Robertson said, touching his forehead thoughtfully. 'You knew just how important Jean Giscard was, and yet, you still allowed personal interest to override the interests of not only the Service but the future plans of the Allied fight against Nazi Germany. I know for a fact, you've seen umpteen documents about the rocket programme at Peenemunde, and that Hitler's *Vergeltungswaffen*, his vengeance weapons, are likely to result in the deaths of thousands of innocent people back home. Despite all this, you still chose to jump ship and accept their blood money.'

'I've never been paid!' he snapped defensively.

'It's all of a piece, George. Money or not, at the end of the day, you made a fustian pact, and more to the point, you knew precisely what you were doing, and that's what I don't entirely understand. By default, your treachery set off an uncontrollable chain reaction of events, resulting in the deaths of not only one of your own agents, but then Stackler, Meyer, and finally, Colonel von Bertele.'

Tar slowly leaned back in his chair, his pipe hanging out of the corner of his mouth. His coolly appraising gaze started to make Rowlands feel even more uncomfortable than he was before.

'For every decision we make, there's a consequence, a price to be paid,' he continued, 'and in your case, the price has been high, way too high. After the death of Stackler, Hitler personally ordered Jean Giscard's family to be rounded up, and sent to a concentration camp. Up until that point, he'd only ever wanted retribution against Giscard himself. Up until then, the Resistance had managed to provide them with a safety net. Unfortunately, that is no longer the case, and many members of the Maquis have also paid a high price. And that brings me to another matter.'

Rowlands had a look of resignation on his face. 'I'm sure it does.'

'Whose bright idea was it to spare Claudine Gregorie's life at the casino?'

'If you must know, it was mine.'

'Why was that?'

'Isn't it obvious?'

'Maybe,' Tar smiled thinly, 'but I'd like you to tell me, all the same.'

'You mean, for the record?' Rowlands said, pointedly glancing toward the chandelier above their heads.

Robertson didn't miss a beat. 'Precisely, but don't mumble too much, George, otherwise the microphone might not be able to pick everything up.'

'Touché, Colonel,' Rowlands said.

'Why did you spare Claudine's life?'

'To keep you off the scent. I knew if Stackler left her alive, the spotlight would automatically shift onto Claudine. After all, why would he risk leaving a potential witness alive? From your point of view, there was only one logical explanation; she was in the pay of German intelligence.'

'How did you manage to get them on side? It can't have been easy.'

'No, it wasn't. Initially, the Baron had difficulty persuading Stackler to play along with the plan; in the end, it was Himmler who sanctioned the idea.'

'You do move in exalted circles, don't *you*?'

The heavy sarcasm in Robertson's voice wasn't lost on him. 'Whatever,' Rowlands shrugged, 'but it had the desired effect of deflecting Spencer's investigation, and allowing me a little more slack. That's all I wanted.'

Tar puffed on his pipe, emitting a cloud of swirling smoke. Rowlands looked drawn, but he hadn't finished with him yet.

'Tell me something,' he said. 'Did either the Baron or Bertele approach anyone else? Did you suggest people they might be interested in?

'No, it never came up.' Rowlands reached for his gin and tonic. 'Am I allowed to ask a question?'

'Go ahead,' Tar said.

'How the hell did you find out I was *Schornsteinfeger?*'

Robertson looked to Spencer, and was content to leave it to him to explain.

Spencer gladly launched into the tale of how they unravelled his betrayal. London had become aware of various security issues with the SOE transporting escapees through occupied Europe. It also became increasingly apparent too many high-profile escapees had been picked off, and a pattern had started to emerge. There seemed to be a particular problem across the Spanish border into Portugal. But, at the same time, other issues had started to emerge, not least with the quality of the intelligence coming out of MI6 in Lisbon. Fearing Giscard's safety crossing the border into Portugal might already be comprised, Spencer was ordered to meet up with an agent, Aleksander Gorski, who'd been passed a microfilm by Giscard, containing vital information about the

Peenemunde project. If all else failed, he was tasked with getting Gorski safely back to London.

'But, the fact remained,' Spencer continued, 'there were grave concerns about the activities of MI6 in Portugal. Bletchley Park had intercepted transmissions indicating there appeared to be a mole operating out of Lisbon, and in particular, the MI6 Station, and therefore, by default, everyone had come under suspicion.'

'What, even Frank?' Rowlands queried, with a slight smile.

'Yes, even Frank.'

It seemed to amuse him no end; his boss had also been placed in the frame. Spencer held his gaze, and he stopped smiling. There was something about his fixed hard-eyed stare that made him do so.

'It was the main reason I wanted Garvan on board; he was out with the system, and completely untainted.'

'You surprise me,' Rowlands mused. 'The Chief Inspector seems as if he's very much part of the family.'

'Only up to a point. Since his secondment, he's taken a conscious decision to keep a healthy distance from the intelligence community, and the internal politics of the Service.' Spencer drained his gin and tonic. 'More than anything, I needed someone I could trust, and who wouldn't put a knife in my back at the first available opportunity.'

The pointed side swipe at his friend, and ex-colleague, was damning. Rowlands avoided his gaze, and said to no one in particular, 'Where do we go from here?'

It was Robertson who responded. 'You'll be taken into custody and held at a safe house for the time being.' He paused, then glanced around the room, and said condescendingly, 'Not here, of course, dear boy. It's far too grand for the likes of you.'

'May I ask where?'

'You'll find out soon enough.'

'Am I to be charged?'

'You mean with treason?'

'Yes.'

Robertson wafted his pipe. 'The trouble is, George, no matter how much the Prime Minister might personally want to have you lined up against a wall and shot, his advisors have made him see reason, that it might be somewhat less embarrassing to His Majesty's Government if we observed certain legal niceties.' Tar emptied out the bowl of his pipe, and watched the last burning embers slowly turn to ash. 'You know how things stand, of course?'

'Yes, sir.'

'We'll pass a formal record of our interview to your boss, General Menzies, and also to Downing Street. It'll then be entirely in the hands of the Cabinet to decide whether formal charges will be brought against you.'

Robertson inspected the bowl to make sure it was completely empty, and was cool enough to place back in his jacket pocket. 'Are there any more questions?' he asked sharply.

'I've got something to trade,' he announced, 'Information.'

'For Christ's sake, I know what a trade is, George.'

'I thought you might be interested.'

Spencer took his time lighting a cigarette. 'Maybe it's probably a little too late in the day to start making deals.'

'Well, I guess that all rather depends on what I have for you, doesn't it?'

'If you're simply playing for time, then you can forget it.'

'Will you hear me out, or not?'

Spencer seemed indifferent; he was giving nothing away. 'I suppose we've nothing to lose by hearing you out.'

Garvan, who'd closed his notebook thinking they were done and dusted, opened it up again.

Rowlands seemed suitably satisfied he had their undivided attention. 'About a month ago, I overheard a rather interesting conversation between the Baron and a Gestapo officer.'

Spencer wondered whether he was bluffing. 'Or did they want you to overhear them?' he suggested.

Rowlands ignored him and carried on, 'Gruber had set up a meeting at a café near the docks in Lisbon. I'd taken the usual precautions.'

Spencer's eyes narrowed questioningly.

'You know, to make sure I hadn't been followed. I was already running late, so I knew he was probably getting a little pissed off with me. With Stackler breathing down his neck, demanding action, and Berlin piling on the pressure as well, he was getting twitchy about Giscard.'

'What was the meeting about?'

'That I'd managed to persuade Lucern into moving Giscard down to the casino in Estoril. As you can imagine, it was a pretty important meeting, he was waiting to hear if I'd managed to pull it off.'

Rowlands paused, and looked across the table at Spencer, as he took a long, slow drag on his cigarette.

'Don't stop, George, I was just starting to get interested.'

He'd always known Spencer to be an arrogant bastard, and right now, he was indeed living up to his reputation. There was a stillness about him that he'd always found slightly unnerving. The thought crossed his mind he'd probably killed Stackler, without even drawing breath. Rowlands momentarily lost his thread.

'You were running late for your meeting,' Spencer reminded him.

He regained his train of thought, and continued, slowly at first, 'Yes – the meeting was held in a small room above the café. When I reached the landing, I heard voices, one was the Baron's and the other I didn't recognise at all.'

'What did you do?'

'I couldn't make my mind up whether to butt in or wait outside.'

'So, you waited outside?'

Rowlands nodded. 'It was only when I saw him again in Estoril, I realised the Gestapo officer was Aldous Meyer.'

'What were they talking about?'

'About someone they'd tried to recruit. Apparently, they weren't playing ball. Meyer mentioned a colleague of his had recently discovered they were already working for the Soviet NKVD.'

'It's all fascinating, George, but what's this to do with us?' Spencer demanded.

By now, Rowlands' rather smug expression had returned. 'The Baron was naturally disappointed they hadn't managed to bag them, and saw it as something of a lost opportunity. He hadn't quite given up all hope of ensnaring them, that is, unless they were an ideological recruit to the Soviet cause, a hardcore communist, so until he knew for sure, he suggested to Meyer it might be worth another punt at them.'

Since Hitler's attack on the Soviet Union in 1940, Britain and the USSR had become Allies; it was an alliance driven by necessity. Some intelligence passed between the two countries, but dissemination was on a severely restricted basis, neither party being quite able to trust the other. The prospect of a mole interrogating incoming telegrams and papers, from both Britain and America, which might be of interest to the NKVD, would have been especially valuable to Stalin and the Kremlin.

Garvan started to tap his pen on the table to gain Rowlands' attention. 'To be of any use to the Soviets, this mole would have to be operating either out of MI6 or the British Embassy, am I correct?'

The tight smile on his face was answer enough.

'I don't suppose you heard a name?' Garvan pressed him.

'I'm sorry, Chief Inspector, no, no, I didn't.'

He was lying, of course; Garvan knew that. 'Tell me something.'

Rowlands looked at him waiting expectantly.

'Are you hoping by co-operating with us, we'll recommend you're given immunity from prosecution?'

'That's maybe how Scotland Yard works, Chief Inspector, but it's not our way,' he said condescendingly.

While Garvan's expression remained blank, it was running through his mind Rowlands really was an arrogant little shit, but a clever one all the same.

'Why not tell me how it works?'

He looked first at Spencer, and then to Robertson, before answering. 'We've reached something of a stalemate.'

'Have we?'

'There won't be a trial, even a closed one, especially if there's the chance of an NKVD agent operating out of the British Embassy. They'll leave the door open, in case I eventually come up with a name.'

'I thought you hadn't heard a name?'

He smiled enigmatically, 'No, not at the café, I didn't.'

'You *do* have a name?'

'I know a codename.'

'What is it?'

'Toniolo.'

At least it was something to go on, but he was obviously still holding out on them.

Robertson suddenly rose to his feet, indicating the interview was over. He moved over to the fireplace, pressed a small circular brass button set into the wall, and waited. The door opened. Garvan glanced round, and did a double take seeing his old friend and colleague from Scotland Yard, Harry Mackenzie. Their last case together had been investigating the murder of Robertson's desk officer, Sarah Davis.

'Harry,' he called out to him. 'What the hell are you doing here?'

Mackenzie broke into a broad smile. 'I've been transferred to Special Branch.'

'Why didn't you tell me?'

'Sorry, Guv'nor, but you've been a bit hard to get hold of lately.'

Robertson butted in. 'Then, you haven't heard the good news.'

'What news?'

Robertson looked to Mackenzie and smiled. 'Your friend here has been promoted, Inspector.'

'Good Lord,' Garvan exclaimed. 'Congratulations, I have a nasty feeling if I don't get myself back to the Yard anytime soon, you'll end up being *my* Guv'nor.'

Mackenzie chuckled. 'I wish!'

'He's only been working in Special Branch for about six weeks,' Tar explained. 'But, I just thought you'd both welcome the opportunity of working together again.'

Garvan smiled; it was a typically thoughtful gesture on his part. Robertson cared deeply for everyone in his tightly knit team, and perhaps, more importantly, knew Mackenzie was someone in whom he could trust. No doubt he'd also pulled more than a few strings at Scotland Yard to ensure not only his posting to Special Branch, but his assignment to oversee Rowlands' security detail.

Robertson asked Mackenzie, 'Would you please take Mr. Rowlands to the new location.'

'Yes, sir.'

Rowlands stood up; there was an awkward moment, as he didn't quite know what to do or say. They'd finished with him, and he'd effectively been dismissed, but all the same, he tried in vain to engage their gaze once more.

'Are you ready, Mr. Rowlands?' Harry said politely from the doorway.

'Yes, yes, I am.'

'One last thing, George,' Robertson called after him.

Rowlands stopped, and turned around.

'I forgot to mention. I thought you'd be interested to know your friend, Baron von Gruber, has been recalled to Berlin.' A faint smile played on Robertson's face. 'I have a feeling his days as a member of the Abwehr are somewhat numbered. In fact, after his meeting with *Reichsführer* Himmler, he'll be lucky to escape with his life.'

Rowlands expression didn't falter, and without answering, turned to leave. As Harry closed the door on them, Garvan asked. 'What happens now? Is he telling the truth about this Soviet connection?'

Robertson remained beside the fireplace and stood ramrod straight, with his hands clasped firmly behind his back. 'His claims will have to be investigated, of course.'

'But, is he playing fast and loose with us? Is he lying about this Toniolo working for the Soviets?'

Tar considered his response, before answering thoughtfully, 'My gut feeling is he's selective with the truth,' he came back to him, 'I think, in all probability, there is an agent called Toniolo. Whether they are working for the Soviets or the Abwehr is open to conjecture.'

'What are we going to do about Rowlands?'

'It's not our decision to make; our hands are tied. His fate rests solely in the hands of the Government; we must do whatever they wish.'

'But, you must have some idea how it's going to pan out?'

'You have to understand, Luke, even the prospect of a closed trial would end up jeopardising National Security.'

'What you're saying is, we're going to allow Rowlands to walk free?'

'I would imagine he'll end up being detained at His Majesty's pleasure at one of our Internment Camps for German spies.'

After all they had been through in Portugal, he was horrified Rowlands was, in effect, to be given immunity from prosecution. Perhaps Rowlands had been right all along; that their world was some cosy club that protected its own.'

'And after the War,' Robertson continued, 'I expect George will return to the West End, and resume his successful career as a theatrical agent, and live out the rest of his life, as if nothing untoward has happened.'

Garvan couldn't disguise his anger; it was written all over his face.

Robertson felt obliged to add, 'That's the way things are, I'm afraid, and however much we might wish otherwise, the Government will never entertain compromising National Security for the sake of punishing traitors, like Rowlands; it's just not going to happen.' Robertson casually glanced down at his watch. 'I'm very sorry, gentlemen, but I need to start making tracks. I have to report back to No 10 about our interview this morning. I'll see you around two at the office.'

As the door closed behind him, Garvan started to gather up his notebook and the folder containing Rowlands' signed confession. Spencer thoughtfully wandered over to the window.

'Have you heard the latest joke doing the rounds about Tar?' he said.

Garvan confessed he hadn't.

'There are only two things he answers to in life – God and Winston Churchill.'

Garvan laughed and closed his briefcase. Spencer moved the net curtain aside to watch Rowlands being escorted by Inspector Mackenzie to a waiting car. The trouble was, like everything else Rowlands had ever said and done, the story about his meeting with the Baron at the café could have been a concoction of truth, half-truths, and downright lies. The prospect of a mole working for the Soviets, with access to top-secret material about British and American plans, would send shockwaves around Whitehall. Washington would demand immediate action to liquidate the source, and Colonel Robertson and his agents would once again come under increasing pressure to implement their demands. The cycle of deceit would, once again, force them into a deadly spiral of treachery.

'Are you coming?' he heard Garvan saying, and swung away from the window to face him. Garvan tapped his watch. 'The Red Lion's open. Do you fancy having a pint?'

Spencer visibly relaxed and followed him over to the door, taking one last brief glance back into the room, before closing the door.

*If you liked this book you may also wish to read the first in the series by the same author:-*

### Codename Nicolette

A really absorbing story which screams out to be made into a BBC produced series or British produced film ( to catch the atmosphere of the like of Tinker, Tailor). The author gives the real feel of how we were " up against it" and that the strategies of the intelligence services, when needed most, played a critical part. It looks as though DCI Garvan is in the position to provide further adventures into the doings of the cloak and dagger brigade and I look forward to reading them.

### *Dead Man Walking - A Spy Amongst Us*

Awesome spy novel! This was a great trip into the world of British espionage in World War II. I loved how much detail and historical references the author included in the storyline re: Winston Churchill's Britain. The plot and dialogue were top-notch – characteristic of other genre authors like John Le Carre and Ian Fleming (of course, this tale is much more believable than Bond). This book really kept the Kindle pages turning until the end. Great spy thriller!

### *The Downing Street Plot – An agent's Revenge*

I read 'Dead Man Walking' and really enjoyed it, so I was excited to check out Oliver's latest spy thriller. Just like 'DMW' I found this one to be well-researched and well-written. Excellent character development – I particularly liked Oliver's "Virginia Dudley" – who's based on the real-life spy Virginia Hall. I love how he weaves truth with fiction to create a dramatic, intriguing, page-turning thriller. Oliver fills this tale with such detail I felt as if I was right there with Hall (Spencer), Dudley, Stein, Taylor, Bradshaw… Excellent read. If you're a spy thriller fan, you'll love this book. I did. 5 stars.

### *Duty & Betrayal – SS Brotherhood and the NASA connection*

The time is during the 60's. Spencer Hall of MI5 and Jack Stein, of the CIA, are top agents and summoned to defend their countries' most important secrets, nonetheless one of them is concealing something to do with vengeance. As they pursue their even-handedness for previous crimes, ex-Nazis, infiltrators are more disheveled. A gorgeous, double agent, Joyce Leader's life is in danger when she is brought into the commotion and conspiracy. Those wanting to settle matters of World War II are also dealing with those who do not have their best interest in mind. The story takes place in London throughout the cold-war. Toby Oliver has interwoven a tale based on a time period that has great descriptive scenes and will bring you right into the midst of his intriguing plot. Get ready for a page turner.

Made in United States
North Haven, CT
15 April 2022